CALL OF THE DRAGONBONDED

Book of Fire

The Dragonbonded Return Series

Call of the Dragonbonded
Order of the Dragonbonded
Army of the Dragonbonded
Omen of the Dragonbonded

Coming Soon

THE NEW CRONOAN CHRONICLES Series

Chronicles of Nartesis Shazarack: Father of Necromancy
Chronicles of Alicia Farclave

THE FIRST DRAGONBONDED Series

Visit **www.thedragonbonded.com** to get the latest information on these books and other works by JD Hart, to subscribe to the author's newsletter, or to contact the author.

CALL OF THE DRAGONBONDED

Book of Fire

Book 1: The Dragonbonded Return

JD Hart

Dragonbonded
Press

First Printing: May 2018

9 8 7 6 5 4 3 2 1

ISBN: 978-1-949101-00-3

All Artwork by J.D. Hart
Cover Design by Rebeca Covers
Dividers: Created by Kamimiart - Freepik.com

Acknowledgments

This work, along with the entire Dragonbonded Return series, would not be possible without the support, encouragement, and suggestions of many people who have participated in making this work what it is. First, appreciation goes to my awesome editor, Maya Myers.

Also, special thanks go out to the members of our small, local writers group: Matt Myers, Andrea Reimers, and Amy Kuney, and to the many reviewers for providing valuable feedback on this work, including Pablo Corea, Carol Klingler, Bill Loggins, Carol Raedy, Suzanne Hart, Loren Zenker, Craig Schiller, Karyn Williamson-Corea, and Vicki Watchorn.

Contents

Biographer's Note

As some are aware, there are many varied—and to my mind quite inaccurate—accounts of those who lived during the Second and Third Ages of the New Cronoan era. This is especially true concerning the lives put to words in the chronicles that follow. But my mission is neither to inflate nor exalt the myths behind those names. Those who have come before me, bards and poets brazen enough to perpetrate such fables for personal gain, have done so already with regrettable success.

No, the daunting task that stretches before me, one I vigorously embrace with heart and mind, will be abhorrent to some. For this reason, I hereby give the reader fair warning—for my goal in the words that follow is to lay justice to the inexorable truths about these people, as well as others who played a role in bringing about the final transformation. As a historian, I assert my right to correct the inaccuracies of those before. And as a scholar, I do so swear to the authenticity of these chronicles, pieced together from years of painstaking research. It is now with good conscience that I lay pen and ink to parchment.

And as to whether these tales are believable? This I leave for the reader to decide.

- J.D. Hart

Part I

From the Void that was everything and nothing, the Cosmos unfolded and oneness was given form. And in the unfolding, the Astral plane was created, and the Astral Beings became aware of their oneness with the Cosmos. Again, the Cosmos unfolded and the Psychic planes were born. And many Beings became self-conscious and lamented at their loss of being one. Again, the Cosmos unfolded, creating the Mental planes, where many were driven and wailed at the limitations of the minds they had been given. And again, the Cosmos unfolded. And the planet Gaia, amid all the other planets and stars, was spun into the elemental rift that split the planes asunder and held them firmly apart. And into this Physical plane many were driven and given bodies so that they could feel, and still they cried at their loss until their prior selves had been forgotten. And the Psychic Beings beheld in envy what they could not possess. Thus it was in the beginning.

—The Modei Book of Fire (First Book)

Memorial to Tatem Creeg

Conner Stonefield kicked the granite base of the fountain, his patience quickly waning. Dust from long hours in the dry fields rose in a chalky haze and was carried by the bustling swarm of shoppers about him. Few paid the sixteen-year-old much heed as they haggled with local farmers in brightly painted carts over their midsummer produce, metal and leather works, jewelry, clothing, and sundry crafts. Musicians, jugglers, and other performers, with their bonds aloft and afoot, strolled about merrily, hoping to please the patrons enough to receive a few spare coins. Children played and wove through the crowd unabashed, adding a mix of chaos to the otherwise Harmonic afternoon and forcing the merchants to remain vigilant of small hands near their wares.

If there was only one certainty in life, it was that Conner could count on his best friend to leave him hanging. Already, the shadow of the iron weathervane atop the Creeg's Point town hall darkened the bright pool at Conner's feet. Town folk with arms full of goods and heads full of plans for the evening darted up the broad cobblestone streets. Conner tipped his wide-brimmed hat to Anders Whiterock as the farmer shuffled past, the rattle of his empty cart masking the heavy footfalls approaching from behind.

Without warning, a thick, muscled arm wheeled at Conner's head. He ducked and threw a hard jab back, and was rewarded with a gratifying, though unexpected, grunt from his would-be assailant.

"Hey!" Pauli Cloverdale took a pained step back, dirty hands rubbing at his thick stomach. The solid punch had surprised them both.

Conner rose nimbly with a smile, his agile, slender form dwarfed by his brawny friend. "Glad you found your way to finishing your chores. I was beginning to think you'd forgotten where we were to meet."

Pauli squinted up at the statue towering behind Conner. "How could I forget? I've never understood what you find so fascinating about that atrocity. You'd think they could've found a better place to stick that hideous figure than in the middle of town."

Pushing back dark, wavy hair over his trim shoulders, Conner followed Pauli's gaze to the larger-than-life effigy of Tatem Creeg, paragon of the Paladins Order. Of course, Conner had never met a Paladin. The lives and affairs of Eastlanders seldom drew the attention of those from any of the six orders. Once a town elder said the Paladins' dress had changed little in the millennium since Creeg lived. But it was the enigma of Creeg's likeness that held Conner's hazel gaze and spirited his fancy beyond their closed community. Creeg's benevolent, solemn stare seemed an odd contrast to the shaven head, long surcoat draped over full armor, and longsword held expertly in his bronze hand. But whatever words had been engraved on the statue's granite epitaph had been lost to weather and time. "The legend of Tatem Creeg is a curious tale," Conner mused.

Pauli snickered at the other boy's naivety. "The fables of Creeg rank up there with my grandma's tales of Assassins and Necromancers. For sure, a man would have to be half-touched to believe such fantasies. I'd bet my next meal Creeg was some nobleman who won an ancient queen's favor and was granted the town's name in reward. And a coin can buy a bard's bad fable. Nobles work like that, you know." He gave the statue a second glance, beaming at some idea fancying a visit between his ears. "How much do you think that bronze is worth, anyway?"

"Not a tenth the price you'd pay in flayed skin for taking the thought one step further," Conner admonished with a scowl.

Ego bruised and attention fading, Pauli changed the topic. "I'm glad you're wearing dark clothes."

Conner's eyes narrowed. It was always best to take three measures of caution for each measure of Pauli—and there was a lot of Pauli to measure! Guardedly, Conner asked, "Why is that?"

Still rubbing his forgotten stomach, Pauli winked with his usual mischievous grin. "We need to cross Noman's Field in the next hour."

Conner had seen that look too often to let it go unchallenged. "Okay, Pauli, what's up?" A hint of suspicion hung on his words.

Pauli's smile broadened and his eyes sparkled like the surface of the fountain's pool behind him. Through perfect teeth too small for his brawny face, Pauli replied, "I'll tell you on the way."

Far Afield

"**M**y stomach hurts," Pauli puffed, breaking the long silence halfway across Noman's Field.

"Good. Better your stomach than my neck." The boys had been wrestling almost since they could walk, but Conner had not enjoyed Pauli's continued attempts at the sport since they were twelve, when Pauli had put on three stones of weight to Conner's one. Four years was a long time to be outmatched in size and mass. But complaining never helped, so Conner was resigned to match Pauli's friendly challenges with agility and speed. It felt good when the field was leveled.

"So when are you going to tell me where we're heading?"

It took a moment for Pauli to gather enough air to answer. "Owen heard it from his cousin's best friend, a farmer, who overheard another farmer talking—"

Conner groaned loud enough to interrupt Pauli. "Owen?" he barked incredulously. "Since when did you start believing anything that swindling thief said? The last time you listened to him, you lost your dad's best hunting knife. Or did you forget?"

Sweat gleamed from Pauli's forehead in Hemera's late afternoon light. "Of course not." He attempted his best sorrowful pout. Pauli had complained for days about the punishment his father had given him; how cold it had been sleeping in the barn until every last tool, piece of farm gear, and leather strap had been cleaned, polished, and stowed. "Dad reminds me every time I forget to put the plow harness away."

Conner's deerskin shoes slipped rhythmically over the short grass in his natural stride, lulling him into a relaxed state. He could have easily outpaced his friend, but he held back. Not everything needed to be a contest. Besides, he wanted to get the conversation back on the path. "What news did you get from Owen?"

Instantly, Pauli's smile was back, all pains of stomach and churning tree trunks for legs forgotten. "He said there's a legion of Queen's Defenders on Brighom Road, heading for the Borderlands. I thought we could take a peek."

Lifelong best friends, Pauli and Conner had crawled and leaped their way into every kind of trouble. Conner knew well that nothing excited Pauli more than the thought of someday being in the queen's service, fighting for the Harmonic cause along the Borderlands. But Queen's Defenders were no ordinary militia. They were unquestionably the best-equipped and best-skilled fighting force the Harmonic Realms could muster, made up of the fighting guilds and trained by those in the six orders. News of such a military force on its way through this nearly forgotten corner of the Realm, even from such an unreliable source as Owen, was too much for the large soldier-at-heart to let go to seed. Conner smiled despite his annoyance at his gullible friend.

Pauli labored with quick, winded breaths. "Greston Woods offers the best opportunity to get a close look without being spotted." Conner waited through a long pause. "I've heard of people who disappeared when they got too close to Queen's Defenders."

Conner snorted his disbelief. According to rumors, Defenders could be especially secretive about their movements and numbers. In regions near the Borderlands, where spies were thick as crows on a freshly sown field, it was commonly believed that Defenders could be a jittery lot, as willing to kill someone they thought a spy as eat breakfast in the morning. The common tale was obviously used to keep the movement of the queen's forces a secret. The Borderlands a mere day's hard ride to the east, spies were a certainty. How better to quell wagging tongues than by spreading such fables?

"Scoff if you want, but there's no need to take any risks," Pauli said.

The thought of them doing anything not involving risk set Conner into a guffaw. Pauli, for once, caught the source of Conner's amusement, and was immediately infected. It was another mile before they recovered.

Eastlander Spies

Conner settled back, finding a more comfortable position on the high branch near the side of Brighom Road. It had taken half an hour to find a tree with adequate foliage to hide Pauli's large frame. That had been nearly an hour ago. Conner's muscles still ached from the exertion of pulling his big friend onto the thick branch. He scanned for life in the treetops overhead to fight off boredom. Hemera was sinking below the tree line, casting long shadows across the summer green carpet of Greston Woods. It would be dark soon. "How long are we going to wait?"

"Not long now for sure," Pauli stated for the third time.

Conner stared maliciously at Pauli. His friend's eyes, glistening with unblinking anticipation, returned to the rutted road below. Conner started to comment about how much cooler it was here than in town when Pauli gestured to the west with his stubby nose. "There," he whispered.

Conner rolled to his stomach and surveyed the narrow, shady road in the direction Pauli pointed. For the first time, he noted the patchy summer grass that split the double dirt trenches worn deep by heavy merchant wagons and farming carts traveling to Linkenton Point. An encroaching line of trees partially obscured the winding road. He was about to punch Pauli's shoulder for distracting him when movement caught his eye. At the far bend, a gray fox crouched, its tail twitching nervously, black nose testing the air. It trotted closer, but after a dozen quick steps, stopped to scan the road ahead. It repeated this sequence, darting from one trench to the other as it proceeded up the path.

As the fox drew near, two riders came into view. One was a tall woman with salt-and-pepper hair that draped loosely over her shoulders, riding a well-built dapple-gray. The finely polished surface of her breastplate reflected Hemera's rays. She held the red-plumed helmet of a high-ranking member of the Warriors Order under the chainmail sleeve of her left arm while gripping thick reins in her gauntleted right. Hawkish eyes darted often to her gray fox bond ahead. Horse and rider moved effortlessly.

The other rider, a man, was shorter, stockier in frame, comfortably straddling a dark bay sporting no saddle, bridle, or reins. His sky-blue robes rippled with each prancing step of his horse bond, with their mysterious gold symbols glimmering in the breaking light. Older than his Warrior companion, the Sorcerer's gray hair was pulled back in a ponytail, accentuating a protruding snout on a thin, frowning face. Chainmail trousers were pulled over polished black leather boots. A gnarled wooden battlestaff balanced easily across the horse's withers.

Behind the two ordermen rode a procession of Queen's Defenders. Four abreast, these fighters wore dull steel armor under loosely fitted surcoats that dangled past their hips. Upon each chest was the queen's emblem of a bright red griffin, rearing on lion's legs, wings spread wide on a field as blue as the Sorcerer's robes. Mirroring the Warrior before them, each cuffed a steel helmet and wore a lavish assortment of deadly battle weapons about the saddle. Around them, a myriad of creatures hopped, ran, and flew with the sound of a strong wind through autumn trees. Several squirrels scampered past the boys, intent on keeping ahead of their human bonds.

By the time the Warrior and Sorcerer rode past, Conner had counted a full company of eighty mounted Defenders, followed by two companies of marching Defenders dressed to match their mounted comrades.

"The Harmonic spirits as my witness, Colonel, I do not think the left hand knows what the right is doing," the Sorcerer chided, though the Warrior did not show much interest in listening. "How can

General Grimwaldt expect to repel an Anarchic force with ours spread out along the eastern Borderlands?" The elder orderman did not wait for his companion's response, but his voice was swallowed by the sounds of those marching after.

Behind the infantry came another company of foot Defenders. These wore a simple chainmail shirt and leggings over tight-fitting forest green clothes. More loosely organized than their comrades, these Defenders stepped in comfortable strides, thick longbows and overstuffed quivers of arrows slung across their backs. And about them, as with the companies before, came a parade of bonds.

At the rear of the long procession came a lone rider concealed beneath a dark-green hooded Ranger's cape. A falcon bond perched on a leather gauntlet covering the rider's forearm nervously scanned the trees. As the rider neared, the falcon jerked its head in the boys' direction and ruffled its feathers. The Ranger's hood turned, a long, thin staff appearing in the rider's other hand. The glowing rays of Hemera low in the west caught the smooth, feminine features of the Ranger's upturned face. Deep, piercing eyes stared straight into Conner's, and a slight smile crossed her lips.

For some time, Master Ranger Annabelle Loris had been studying the backs of the Archers marching in front of her. She had surmised that these recruits were not ready to withstand, much less repel, the Anarchic assault General Grimwaldt was expecting any day. A forced march two days out of Cravenrock Keep, and they were already showing signs of wear. And they were another day from Striker's Keep, where they would be assigned to defend the eastern Borderlands. Sadly, none were Ranger material, but at least they were strong enough to pull the Grenetian longbows they sported. One could only work with the resources provided.

This line of thinking inevitably brought her attention to Colonel Mooregain. Her eyes shifted to the back of the master Warrior riding proudly at the front of the battalion, her brightly polished armor the perfect target for an Anarchist's arrow. At least this Warrior was decidedly more intelligent than the previous commander, who now occupied a ceremonial plot of dirt near Striker's Keep. A distant relative to the royal family, this one had been trained well in the arts of elemental combat. She was competent in ground tactics and knew how to wield her weapons. She even showed some leadership qualities. But she lacked experience, and that inevitably got good people killed. Annabelle smirked, her face hidden beneath her hood. Count on the Warriors Order to rely on live combat to be their members' primary form of training.

An intense alarm from Annabelle's bond jolted her inattentive mind to the unusual shapes in a tree not far from the road. *Safety is won with hand and arrow when the head forsakes all plans,* her old preceptor would say. Annabelle reached for her wood staff. But something about the two forms gave her pause. Spies would not have survived long being so blatantly careless. The fact the two in Eastlander clothing had escaped every battalion member's eyes did not bode well, a situation she would be sure to remedy. If she had to further this band of misfits' inadequate training, at least she would have some fun. That brought a welcome smile to her dreary assignment. She shoved her staff back into its holster and rode on.

Conner held his breath until the Ranger had disappeared amid the trees to the east, then rolled onto his back. The sky was starting to darken. Judging by Hemera's position, if he started home right away, he would only be half an hour late. That meant another long lecture about the importance of responsibility, but at least he would be alive to hear it. He tried to stand, but his muscles shook with unspent fear and he nearly tumbled from the tree.

"I believe that had to be the most incredible sight I've ever seen." Pauli's eyes were still glued to the east, where the last of the battalion had vanished into the deep shadows. "And we didn't even have to pay ringside carnival price!"

No longer able to resist the urge, Conner slugged Pauli's shoulder, then shook the numbness from his knuckles; Pauli's eyes didn't even waver from the road. Next time he'd bring a mallet. "We nearly paid with our lives, Pauli! Hiding in this tree had to be the most ridiculous idea you've had since you convinced me to help you steal Farmer Windtree's blackberries." After hesitating, he added, "And you've had your share of foolish ideas."

Pauli's eyes widened. "How was I supposed to know they were rashberries?"

Conner bit his lip, not wanting to pick at old scabs. The two had spent a fortnight covered in rashes after gorging on berries Pauli was convinced were edible. Not allowing his comrade to distract him from his point, Conner continued. "I thought for sure the Ranger was going to shoot us out of this tree. Wouldn't that be a fine sight, our bodies dragged home looking like human porcupines." He began sliding down the branch, adding, "If they ever found our bodies."

Pauli blinked, the realization of what could have happened seeping into his dense skull. "You don't really think she would have killed us? I thought you said that was all a fable." He watched Conner skip nimbly down the branches, then leap the final few paces to the ground. "Nice, Conner," he added with a hint of envy.

Conner peered up at his immobile friend. He would not let Pauli smooth talk his way back into his graces that easily. "Why do I let you drag me into these adventures?" He sighed, considering the terrain he had to cover. "I suggest you get yourself home quick as a spit. Your dad is no doubt looking for an excuse to skin you after the last time you got home late." Conner turned to start the long run home, then paused. Glancing back to be sure Pauli didn't miss his words, he called out, "And yes, if the Ranger had truly thought us spies, we wouldn't be having this conversation."

The Guildsman's Apprentice

Conner slipped nimbly over the short stone wall of the Stonefield cottage. Thanks to the rusty hinges on the wrought-iron gate, taking the normal route was a sure way his parents would know he was just arriving. The welcoming glow of soft candlelight and the smell of burning oak drifted through the kitchen window. He ascended the slated front entrance, evading the two steps that needed repair, and crept into the light of the lamp near the wooden front door.

Just as he reached for the handle, a raccoon waddled into view, looking quite pleased, which was nothing new for the creature. Dark eyes sparkled gleefully and she chortled as she patted her paws together. A moment later, the door swung open.

"Thanks, Notorius." Conner sighed at the raccoon.

A balding middle-aged man wearing shabby farm clothes and a solemn look stepped back into the hall to usher his wayward son in from the dark. "Don't be upset with Notorius. Unlike me, she's happy to see you."

Conner forded the entryway, glancing nervously at his father. Notorius scampered through the portal on Conner's heels. Even though Anton Stonefield was a full hand shorter than his son, it was clear where Conner got his lean frame. Long years in the fields had given him sinewy arms and calloused hands. Time under Hemera had aged him beyond his years.

Wondrous smells of hot stew, fresh-baked bread, and sharp spices assailed Conner's senses. Before he could say a word, his stomach moaned. Between morning chores and the afternoon with Pauli, he had forgotten to eat since breakfast.

His father caught the signals and jabbed Conner's midsection with a finger. "I'll tell your mother to put an extra ladle of stew in your bowl. Supper will get cold, so wash up. We'll talk later."

Conner nodded and trudged up the narrow steps to the upper level. Turning into the washroom, he poured water from a decorative ceramic pitcher into a large tin bowl and turned the water dark with grit and dirt from the day's work. He opened his eyes to find a chipmunk inspecting him. Lifting its tiny paws wide in the air, it chirped.

"Mom doesn't need your assistance, Ignatius."

Seeming to understand the remark, Ignatius spun about and flicked his tail so Conner knew who had the final word. Then he hopped from the counter and disappeared down the stairs.

Once certain he would meet his mother's approval, Conner tossed the brown water through a window and headed down toward the delicious smells. Even though the kitchen was large, it was far from roomy. An iron wood-burning stove, cooking counters, and a long, plain-cut table and chairs consumed nearly all of the space. Pots, skillets, and cooking utensils of every size and shape adorned the wood-panel walls. Conner's parents and two younger sisters sat around the table scrutinizing him.

His mother's eyes narrowed, with Ignatius near her elbow watching smugly. In any normal situation, he thought Oshan Stonefield's eyes kind, a calm deep-blue sea on a face with a pale complexion that would have been beautiful with a gentler lifestyle. His sisters—Miyra, fourteen, and Sayra, twelve—could have passed as twins. Both had their mother's eyes and golden hair, a stark contrast to the narrowness of face they had inherited from their father. They often wore the same clothes and expression, which currently was the self-righteous *You're late and are you in trouble!*

He cautiously slipped into the vacant chair, eyeing the bowl of thick stew and bread roll before him, a king's feast for a starving boy. The family linked hands around the table. Sayra flashed Conner a quick smile she knew her inattentive sister would not approve of and squeezed his hand to let him know she was glad he was safe. As always, the family gave thanks to the Cosmos for the bounty of food before them, their safekeeping, and all the gifts of life, bonds, family, and community.

Dinnertime was the one opportunity the Stonefields had to stay connected. Questions were seldom needed to prod conversation, which often flowed without direction or purpose. By the time the last bits of food were scraped from their bowls, each had shared the significant events of the day and the important plans for the next. Miyra and Sayra were in school. Neither found their studies particularly challenging. But at the moment, their adolescent awkwardness demanded their parents' attention. Conner recalled sharing similar troubles as his parents recited the same wise guidance that had helped him through his challenges; that is, when he was smart enough to listen.

Through all of this, Notorius sat by the kitchen entryway, chattering while consuming a boiled egg and portions of meat she washed ceremoniously in a bowl beside her plate. Ignatius sat on the table, packing his cheeks full with the remaining seeds amid his dinner's shells.

Without verbal cue, everyone carried out their assigned chores of clearing and cleaning the remnants of the night's meal. By the time all the bowls had been washed, and nearly all the pots hung in their assigned places, important conversations had reached their fruition. Only then did Conner's mother usher his sisters upstairs to prepare for sleep and the next day's schooling, giving his father a well-orchestrated moment to speak with Conner.

While Conner dried the remaining pots, his father sat at the kitchen table, absently rubbing Notorius's ears. "Don't forget you are to go to Karlana Landcraft's home the morning after Erebus's full for guidance on bonding. She does it as a service to the community, and surely won't like it if you don't arrive on time. She's very particular about that, you know. She has always considered you special, but that won't help if you're late."

This was not the conversation Conner had expected. Like everyone in the Harmonic Realms, he had spent most of his adolescence in anticipation of what would happen sometime in his seventeenth year. When would he receive the Calling? What kind of bond would he get? How would they relate? Was he ready to take care of a bond? His father knew of Conner's eagerness, and that Conner would not forget something so significant. Impatient to get to the real lecture, he took the plow horse by the reins to get the furrow dug. "I'm sorry about this afternoon. After I finished my chores, I went into town to meet up with Pauli. The next thing I knew . . ." His arms waved about, unable to find words to make their adventure palatable to his father.

Anton let out a sudden, quick titter at Conner's gawky gestures, then cut it short at the thought that Oshan might overhear. He leaned forward to speak softly. "Conner, anytime you tell me you're meeting up with Pauli, I resign myself to the fact that trouble is going to happen. Separate, you boys are good. But mixed together, you are green bales of hay on a summer day." He winked. This was his father's way to say he did not want to know anything more about what had happened. "I'm glad you two are safe."

Notorius, content with food and attention, hopped down and waddled back to the social room. Anton continued. "When you reach the age of Calling, Conner, you are an adult, in the eyes of Realm law and in mine." He nodded his approval, then stood. Looking up with pride, he placed his hand firmly on Conner's shoulder. "I have given you everything you need to meet your destiny, whatever that may be. I can teach you nothing more, and no punishment I could exact will change the path the Cosmos guides you on. You are a man now."

Conner could have listed a dozen directions this conversation might have taken, but this one was not even in the same county as any of them. Speechless, he did the only thing he felt compelled to do. He reached out and hugged his father close. For the first time since he was little, he felt his father's strong arms around him.

It was several moments before they became aware of Oshan standing at the kitchen entrance, regarding them with pride, fisted hands on hips. They released each other awkwardly.

She swiftly masked her smile with a stern look. "When you two are done with your father-son moment, maybe we can discuss the matter of Conner's entrance into the Apothecaries Guild."

Conner gawked at his father with bulbous eyes. For years, his parents had worked to set aside the funds necessary for him to achieve his lifelong dream—to be accepted as an apprentice to a master Apothecary. His mother had learned to weave baskets from dried cornstalks from the corn Anton harvested each fall. Twice a fortnight, she sold her baskets at the town marketplace. After each trip, they saved half the coins for this goal.

Anton beamed. "This morning, I met with Master Apothecary Merich Cleaverbrook. A fortnight ago, his apprentice Jess Tandoor successfully advanced to the rank of student, so Master Cleaverbrook is without a pupil. When he met you last year, he was quite impressed with all you knew about plants, and believes you have the smarts to be a good guildsman. He has agreed to take you on as his next apprentice."

Conner was dumbfounded. A freeman becoming a guildsman was extremely rare and a significant jump in social status. He knew of only three in all of Creeg's Point history who had won the honor of acceptance into a non-fighting guild. Of no lesser significance was the fact that with this new status came money. An Apothecary guildsman, Conner could work in a town or city guildshop, make a comfortable living, and still give back to his parents what they had provided.

More moved than before, he grabbed his surprised mother with a long arm and hugged her tight. She did not even try to protest.

Ignatius, perched at the end of the table with pouches bursting with seeds, lifted his tiny paws wide in the air and squeaked.

High Law

Princess Veressa of Griffinrock sat grimacing, only slightly aware of her ring-adorned hands straightening and pulling restlessly at her blue silk dress. It was tight and loose in all the wrong places in a way she would never get used to. Was it really so difficult to design royal clothing to fit more like hunting clothes? She was certain that Gareth Nantree, the imbecile her mother referred to as the Royal Chamberlain, had commanded those of the Tailors Guild to design this monstrosity purely for her discomfort. Nothing pleased the man more than to know Veressa was in distress.

But it was the hardness of the intricately carved chair that held most of her brooding thoughts, or rather the tension in her back and numbness in her seat. The idea of axing the horrific chair into pieces and burning it for kindling brought a welcome smile. She nearly giggled wondering whether she could wait for the first winter snows to have the splintered wood warming Graystone's banquet hall.

The cold, hollow sound of closing doors echoed through the queen's lavish reception hall. Someone was calling her name.

"Veressa!" the queen repeated, whispering and yelling simultaneously. Only after Veressa dropped her hands from her dress and looked up did her mother continue. "You could show some semblance of respect and at least *act* like you are interested in learning how to deal with affairs of state."

Veressa regarded her mother. Izadora, the queen of Griffinrock, exuded a regal presence Veressa was certain she would never attain. From the precisely placed hands in her lap to the slightly lifted head and dark, piercing eyes, Izadora's posture on the royal throne stated without question she was in complete command of the Realm. Her long, dark hair fell in unbroken waves across bare shoulders, accentuating a face of radiant complexion. The royal crown of Griffinrock, bulky and round, rested perfectly on her head. A warm, caring smile completed her regal face, despite the discomfort maintaining such a majestic pose—and the anger she felt at the moment toward her daughter. She always spoke with a voice as commanding as her appearance. And she used that voice to full advantage.

"How can you expect to rule these people as their sovereign matriarch if you are not prepared to govern them wisely? There are reasons for the old ways, Veressa. A queen's wisdom comes from observing her mother, as I learned from mine, and she from hers. It does not come from the back of a horse searching for tracks to the evening meal or for clues on some dangerous quest."

Despite the queen's rebuke, Veressa felt admiration for her mother. She nodded, not wanting to inflame the situation further, which disarmed the queen completely.

Izadora sighed softly and gestured toward the door from which two lords involved in a disagreement over the ownership of a horse had departed. "Despite the occasional bickering, they are a good people. They have endured centuries of hardship. Of the three Harmonic Realms, Griffinrock is responsible for the largest portion of the Borderlands. We must continue to remain vigilant against the evil that would destroy all we possess. These people deserve a matriarch they can believe in, someone they can turn to with confidence for steadfast guidance in times of need. As their queen, it is my responsibility to ensure you are prepared to assume that task."

The queen waited for the words to settle into Veressa's heart, then gave the girl a moment to prepare for what would hurt the most.

Sensing the queen's apprehension, her northern goshawk bond bobbed his head nervously. The queen rose, gently smoothing Tyresus's feathers and soothing the goshawk's desires to be in the open skies. "I feel obligated to remind you of what you already know. You are at the age of bonding, Veressa. Your thoughts of adventures are a distraction. The sooner you clear your head of such fantasies, the happier you will be when you assume the reins you were born to hold."

Veressa inhaled her mother's painful words. She let each syllable etch its way across her heart, feeling the gulf between what she was and what her mother wanted her to be. "Yes, mother. You are right, of course. I will try harder."

Veressa forced a smile, attempting without success to convince her mother she would be happy. She willed herself to glance about the hall, noting the cold emptiness of the gold-and-white-marble floor. She studied the intricate wall patterns and the large colored rug in front of the throne where, in a few moments, those with the next High Law grievance would stand faithfully awaiting Izadora's decision. Two guardsmen stood at wooden attention before polished mahogany doors. Were they there to keep others out or keep her in?

Karlana Landcraft

For three days, Conner floated on clouds. Master Cleaverbrook was to leave soon for Kallzwall Castle to acquire some necessary supplies; Conner would begin his training once the master returned and Conner bonded. Cleaverbrook promised to visit the Stonefields again to reassess the situation in early fall. Until then, Conner's parents convinced him it was best to keep his plans for the future a family secret.

But as Conner walked south along the road into town with Pauli, he found it difficult to keep the truth from his best friend. The two shared everything. And Pauli was particularly sullen this morning, which was never a good sign. It was not until they entered Creeg's Woods, the thick, pristine forest of walnut, maple, and evergreens forming a natural buffer between the small town and the world beyond, that Conner broke the long silence. "You got in trouble the other night?"

"You could say. Dad will have me doing double shift in the fields for a fortnight." Pauli never shifted his dejected gaze from the road beneath his large feet, but a sly smile crossed his lips. "Of course Dad didn't bother to tell Tobi I was being punished. So I convinced Tobi that I was doing him a favor taking his chores for a while. I got him to agree to return the favor later this summer."

It was just like Pauli to find blood in a turnip. Not that it was difficult to draw blood from his younger brother Tobi. Gullibility was clearly a trait that ran thick in Pauli's family.

Before long, the deep green canopy of trees above and gentle carpet of summer grass beneath faded away. Neither waited for more than a breath before taking to the Creeg's Point cobblestones, marching south toward the town square where Tatem Creeg's statue stood. Along the way, store owners on either side bustled about the densely packed buildings, shouting their good mornings to friends and early shoppers as they prepared for the day, their shops bursting with assorted wares of necessity and some of mere pleasure.

Near the square, the two boys steered clear of the marketplace busy with merchants in their colored wagons. They turned west, Hemera casting long shadows before them; the sounds of merchants arguing over the best spots around Creeg's statue receded behind. At street's end, the boys came to a stop and stepped into Karlana Landcraft's home.

Most had a problem calling Karlana's place a home, since only the eastern side was walled, and that wall was simply part of the adjacent building. Thick woods to the west and north did afford some privacy for the living space. The tightly slatted hardwood floor was littered with wooden benches, tables, and chairs of every shape and size. No two pieces of furniture could have possibly come from the same woodworker. And over, under, and around this furniture scurried, crawled, hopped, fluttered, and slithered a menagerie of every creature Conner could name, and a few he could not. Several were in cages and containers—the most dangerous ones, he hoped, though eyeing the brightly striped snake slithering over his shoe, he was not so certain.

Pauli leaned close. "See? I told you she's bonkers," he whispered, waving at the scene with vindication.

At a table near the back sat two girls the boys' age, their expressions of distress slowly transforming into ones of relief in having friends with whom they could commiserate. Pattria Morelace offered Conner one of her infectious smiles that never seemed to fade, while Moni Treelore contrasted Pattria's smile with a perpetual frown, especially long at the moment. With the flair of youthful bravado, the boys strolled in, sidestepping any creatures they thought might bite or kick.

Before Conner could ask if the girls had seen Karlana, a thin, middle-aged woman jumped from behind a cabinet near the stairs, brandishing a red book. "Found it!" Animals scattered in every direction at her abrupt proclamation. Immune to the chaos rippling through the room, Karlana Landcraft eyed the new arrivals. "Well! Conner and Pauli! I was about to give up on you two. I should have expected you to be together. But amazingly, you are both on time." Smiling, she combed long fingers through frizzled hair, then waved ceremoniously at two chairs across from Pattria and Moni.

Each checked the seats for anything living before committing their backsides.

Karlana did not wait. Flourishing her forgotten book, she leaped into a lecture she had clearly given many times. "Welcome to you all! It's so nice to know you are interested in learning about your wonderful adventure ahead.

"I have heard all the fables about bonding and bonds, so I want to make sure that you understand everything you need to prepare for the Calling you will receive sometime in the next year. So if you have any questions, feel free to stop me."

Without pause, she promenaded about the room, touching every animal she came near. "Let's start with a brief history that will answer some questions you may have." Karlana stepped behind Pauli and he reminded Conner what he thought of history with an exaggerated roll of his eyes. Karlana slapped Pauli's shoulder with her book. He winced in response.

"In the age before our forefathers arrived in these lands, it is said Cronoans had no bonds. In that time, our ancestors were reckless, selfish people, with no regard or care for other creatures, even to the very brink of destroying their homeland." She lifted a mouse sitting on a table nearby, closely examining a paw wrapped in cloth. Squeaking to it softly, she set it down. "It is for this reason, so it is written, the Cosmos brought a great calamity upon them. Many perished. Those who survived sailed south across the Antaric Sea to start again here in the land of the Modei. But the Cosmos was not done, for the One knew Cronoans would need help reestablishing their connection with the natural world. That is why, according to legend, every person, without exception, is given the gift of a bond.

"It is not known when the species and gender of a bond is determined. Some believe this happens before the human's life begins, others argue it happens at birth, and yet others say it is decided at the time of the Calling. But when this happens is not as important as the effect such beliefs have on how we prepare for this wondrous event.

"And this brings me to one common mistake about bonds that we will dispel right now. Unlike what some of you have been told by your parents to keep you in line, bonds are a gift." Karlana gave Pauli an especially stern look that made him blush. "They are not a punishment for any unlawful, immoral, or unkind acts you have done or will do in the future. I know of no one whose life was filled with suffering or remorse due to their bonding."

Moni's sigh of relief made Conner chuckle, earning him flagrant stares from both girls.

Karlana stopped to give a seed to a large, brightly colored bird perched on a wooden bar. The bird skillfully rolled the seed in its long curved beak. Satisfied with the offering, it bobbed at Karlana several times. This seemed to delight the woman.

"The animal bond is, in reality, a surrogate for the Physical plane to the human. To be more precise, bonds fulfill an inner part of the human psyche needed to maintain an understanding of his or her place in, and link to, the Physical. This is one of three Cosmic laws about bonding.

"This brings me to the second common misunderstanding about bonds. If you see a serf slaving hard in the fields bonded to a lowly mouse or sparrow, you might think the lowest of creatures go to the lowest of people. And if you see a nobleman bonded to a wolf or fox, you might think the more intelligent animals are given to those of higher social ranks. But you would have the logic backward." Karlana padded Pauli's head as if forgiving him for some error in thought.

"If bonds are what we need to stay connected to the Physical plane, then it seems clear the peasant, who toils in the fields planting and harvesting does not need the strength of a wolf or fox bond to be reminded. The wolf is better served bonding with those who are not so grounded in the Physical."

Karlana paused again as a fawn pushed its nose into a pocket of her bright green robe. Behind the fine rows of white dots speckling its rump, its short tail twitched, greedily eating whatever treasure it had discovered. Karlana giggled, stroking its forehead. The fawn's ears jerked nervously, but it refused to back away.

It was several minutes before Karlana remembered she had pupils. "By the stars, where was I?" She reached up to scratch her head, surprised she was holding a book. "Oh, it will come to me in a moment," she said, sounding more hopeful than realistic. "Does anyone have a question?" She smiled warmly at the group.

Pattria spoke tentatively. "I am not sure I understand how I will communicate with my bond. Could you explain it better than my parents did?"

Karlana patted Pattria on the head as she had the fawn. "Why of course, child."

Astonished at being treated so, Pattria glared at Conner, her cheeks reddening.

"You and your bond will not converse as we do. You will communicate on a more subtle level. Your connection is a Mental link between two Physical beings. Each of you will sense the feelings of the other. At first, this will be disconcerting for you both, even a bit disorienting. However, over time, you will learn to discern your feelings from those of your bond.

"Nor can you convey thoughts through the link with your bond. You may get a feeling that your bond is suffering or hurt, but you won't be able to identify the thoughts or feel the pain that is the source of your bond's distress. All of this, as I said before, is to help us stay connected with the Physical plane." Karlana absently stroked the scaly back of a large gray lizard stretched across the table next to her.

"Karlana, could you describe the Yearning?" Conner interjected.

Karlana examined Conner closely, her smile fading. "Yes, Conner, good question. I think I should tell you a little about the Yearning." She cleared her throat. "If your bond is far away, the Mental connection you share weakens. Yearning is the feeling you get when the two of you are separated." Her eyes lost focus as she continued; her voice became hauntingly vacant. "This feeling is like a loss, or maybe a hole or gap in you, something missing or sucked from your memory." She placed the tip of her forefinger to a point behind her ear, rubbing the spot gently, then continued with a look of concentration. "You can't quite put your mind to it. It eludes you somehow, but you feel the loss, the Yearning always there."

Karlana stood motionless, her students once more forgotten. Amid the long, uncomfortable silence, tension grew. Then just as quickly, the calm was broken. "Bonding requires physical contact with the animal. And your one bond is for life, so the lifespan of a bond is the same as humans. If the human dies unexpectedly, the bond will often return to the wild to live its remaining days. But not all go back." She gestured at the large bird she had fed earlier. "Ingress here is a macaw."

At the sound of her name, Ingress let out a piercing squawk, ruffling a colorful plume of bright blue feathers on her crown. Karlana cooed lovingly at the bird. "She was the bond to a close friend of mine who died in an accident several years ago. She chose to stay with me." She gestured at the menagerie about her. "Several of these were bonds of those who lived in this area."

Noting the shrinking shadows of objects in the street, Karlana exclaimed, "By the fire of Hemera! Where has the morning gone? I am sure your parents do not want me standing in the way of chores you have yet to complete today." Again, Karlana rested her hand on Pauli's shoulder. Pauli shrank at her touch, making his large, imposing frame melt into his chair.

"So let me mention one more important rule. Your bond has its own will. It is not a servant or slave. Do not think for a moment your bond has been given to you to do your selfish or foolish bidding. You cannot command it to do what it does not will itself to do." She paused one more time, signaling to her pupils that they could rise, but giving each a stern look. "Do not let me hear you are attempting to train your bond like a pet, or you will wish you had never tried. Now, get out so that I can carry on with my other duties."

They rose and she clasped her hands together, the book again forgotten, then slightly tilted her head as if admiring just completed artwork. "All of you will do fine if you remember what we have discussed."

As Conner stepped past Karlana, eyeing the large lizard on the table, he felt the woman's hand on his chest. He stared questioningly at her.

She searched his eyes for a moment with her perpetually warm smile. "Yes, Conner, you especially will do well with your bond. The important thing to remember is that there are no exceptions to the Cosmic Laws. Do not fight your connection." She let her hand slip away.

Conner smiled back, always appreciative of her words of encouragement and guidance, and thanked her once again. Departing, he could not shake the feeling that her eyes were still upon him.

By the time Conner stepped into the street, Pattria and Moni were halfway to the marketplace, with Pauli nearly walking on their heels, as if farm chores were much more exciting than staying one moment longer around Karlana. Near the town center, Conner caught up with

Pauli, who squinted under the bright rays of Hemera and glanced back toward Karlana's home. "As sure as I walk on Gaia, that woman is disturbing," Pauli remarked.

While Conner found great amusement in seeing such a big man so completely unhinged by someone as frail and unimposing as Karlana, he thought it best to find a new field to sow. "Are we on for tonight?"

"Sure!" Pauli's eyes sparkled, Karlana forgotten. "I was surprised Dad gave me permission to be out, but I wasn't about to debate. I think he knew someone needed to be there to keep you out of trouble." He winked at Conner and elbowed him hard in the ribs. "I'll come by right after supper."

After trading their good-byes, Conner wove his way through the bustling marketplace and found his mother bartering with several shoppers who had stopped to admire her baskets. After the last basket had sold, the two walked home, discussing the afternoon chores. All the while, Ignatius rode nimbly on his mother's shoulder, squeaking defiantly at anyone who got too close for his comfort.

The Palaver Room

That evening, Conner leaned against the short stone wall forming the boundary to the Stonefield property. Pauli was late as usual, but Conner did not care. His pleasantly stuffed stomach almost made up for all the aches acquired from working extra hours to complete his chores before dusk. Erebus hung large in the eastern horizon in a sky littered with twinkling points of light. The air was cool for the first time in a fortnight. For the moment, he was content enjoying the tranquil night sounds.

Talking about the Calling at Karlana Landcraft's home that morning had left Conner restless. Sometime in the next year, he would bond with an animal that would in some way alter his view on life and possibly change his course in it. There was not a time Notorius and Ignatius had not been around, so he could not imagine life without them. The two were, in every way imaginable, extensions of his parents. And though both could be quite frustrating in their own ways, they were as much a part of the family as his sisters.

The heavy crunch of leather-soled shoes brought Conner from his deep reflections. He glanced north as Pauli materialized at the fringe of his home's pale porch light wearing his best freeman clothes and his usual toothy grin.

Conner hitched his stride to Pauli's flank and they proceeded through Creeg's Woods. The sounds of crickets and barred owls made for a perfect evening to converse. By the time they reached town, Conner had extracted every detail of the few slightly interesting events of Pauli's afternoon. The town crier had lit the lamps lining the street, while a few exhausted merchants attempted to usher the last unflagging shoppers and their bonds from their stores.

Near the town square where Tatem Creeg's likeness stood silent in the dark, the boys turned their attention to the building on their left. Two large, white columns supported an imposing marquee featuring the outline of a prancing horse pulling a cart, while the balconies for the six floors overhead vanished into the night sky: Estora's Tavern and Inn. Two wide, hardwood doors held panes of colored crystal in the shape of frothing mugs, exaggerating the bright lights and lively movements of those within.

The two stepped through the portal and were immediately assaulted with the sights, sounds, and smells of the tavern. Several dozen tables crowded the room, filled with patrons and bonds busy eating, drinking, laughing, and arguing over recent local events. Several servers with brightly colored dresses and exhausted smiles wove through the crowded room, trying to keep up with demands while steering clear of roaming hands.

Conner and Pauli slipped through the noisy tavern, offering a nod to the plump bald man to their right. Estora's husband, Minch Elflander, returned a haggard nod as he deftly placed several filled pewter mugs from each fist onto a waiting tray. The boys forgotten, Minch grabbed three more empty mugs placed on the bar by an impatient server and turned again to the dark oak barrel of Narwalen ale at his back.

The two continued through the middle section of the inn, sounds from the raucous tavern receding behind. To their left, the inn's receptionist sat nearly hidden behind a tall, dark counter, staring inattentively at a book. To their right, a narrow wooden stair with painted iron rails spiraled to the six floors above where those leasing rooms would find their quarters.

While the two had walked with resolute certainty through both tavern and inn, their determination faltered when they arrived at a door near the back. They had never been in the Palaver Room, heightening its mystery and lore. Unlike the rest of the structure, the ancient oak-planked wall looming before them was completely void of decorations or hangings, except for the thick double doors beneath an archway containing an unusual stained glass window.

It was the seemingly random pattern of colored glass that gave the Palaver Room its enigmatic reputation for the arcane. The flickering glow of a fire within the room lit the glass, casting a distorted bowl-shaped image across the white ceiling over Conner's head. His vision was taken by the radiant images coming to life in the reflected light. Warriors and Barbarians brandishing longswords battled while around them fallen comrades lay twisted and dying beneath the horses' hooves. In the background, a keep wavered like a flag on a shifting hillside. And above the scene danced the blood red words, *Let the light within illuminate that which is cast out.*

The scene depicted Striker's Battle, a pitched conflict of four hundred years before, more than a hundred years after the Anarchic War ended. Colonel Striker and half a score of ordermen leading two hundred Queen's Defenders had ridden out from their newly built keep near the Borderlands to confront an invading army of over one thousand Anarchists commanded by two score Barbarians, Warlocks, and Black Knights. Every Warrior and Defender died that day, and the Anarchists claimed the keep. But the enemy forces had been so severely depleted by Striker's assault that the keep was taken back by Harmonic forces the next fortnight. It had never been lost again. The keep had been renamed Striker's Keep in honor of those fallen.

"Well? Are you two going in or do you plan to stand there until you grow roots?" boomed Estora Elflander from behind. She smiled warmly at them, a copper pitcher in her hand. The owner of the inn was a big woman, though her size was not in height. Her thin blond hair hung without a hint of curl, making her round face with small eyes and large lips seem even rounder. It was commonly rumored the woman had worked every day of her life, even, it was said, the afternoon she had given birth to her daughter, Niora, twenty years before. From her current disheveled appearance, Conner doubted she had taken a break all day. Though many thought her brazen, he knew the woman had a heart exceeding her frame. But her smile faded into a frown when the two made no move to either go in or get out of her way.

"Oh, now really! I don't have all day to wait for you two." She parted them easily with her thick arm, crossing the few remaining steps to the door they had been reluctant to take. She twisted the brass knob hard and pushed the doors wide. Without pause, she crossed to the fireplace, a red fox trotting close in tow, to pour a dark brown liquid from the pitcher into a large copper pot hanging near the fire. The boys took advantage of her entrance and trailed her through the doorway. The strong aroma of hot ciderbrew, a local concoction of lightly fermented apples, pears, and mulling spices, filled the smoky room.

The Palaver Room was the only part of Creeg's Point that had survived the fires that nearly destroyed the town close to the end of the Anarchic War. It was a dark, rustic room ten paces across and ten deep, made of thick, mature oak. Wide beams of tightly pressed dark planks formed the flooring that did not creak even under Estora's imposing weight. The fireplace, made from boulders of different shapes and sizes, spanned the entire back wall of the room. Embedded into the wall, a thick beam that matched the floor served as the fireplace's mantel. A hearty fire crackled and popped in the large half-circular firebox, but Estora was not satisfied and heaped on another split log.

The other walls were made from the same hard oak as the floor. Adorning every section from floorboard to ceiling hung portraits, murals, tapestries, and plaques of people with names Conner did not know. About the room sat a dozen people Conner and Pauli's age, studying them.

"Who enters without being noticed first?" A gruff-looking boy jumped from his seat, pressing up close to Conner. "Why have you come?" Judston demanded with a brooding scowl. Shy of a year older than Conner, the boy had always enjoyed bullying him.

All the others who had a moment before been sitting relaxed slowly rose to their feet.

Conner stiffened, too confused to answer.

Undaunted by the threat, Pauli stepped around Conner to get face-to-face with Judston. "We're here for the pre-bonders meeting, but if this is fight night, then you can still count me in!"

To Conner's surprise, this shattered the tense moment. Everyone broke out in laughter and crowded even closer, welcoming the two into the group with shakes and back slaps. After a few minutes, Conner edged his way to Pattria, who stood apart. "Where's Moni?"

"She couldn't come. Something to do with helping her dad prepare his shop for tomorrow's sale. She'll have to wait until the next meeting to be inducted."

After a few minutes, Judston closed the doors and called the group back to order. The title of dean of the pre-bonders was assigned to the oldest of those who had attended Karlana Landcraft's school but had not yet received the Calling. Though it was generally reserved for secretive town council meetings, Estora allowed the pre-bonders to use the Palaver Room for their social gathering once every fortnight and talk privately about their future as bonded adults in the community. After refilling their mugs with fresh, hot ciderbrew, everyone took their seats. Conner quickly took the chair beside Pattria.

Several of the older members started teasing the three new initiates about attending Karlana's school. This was all Pauli needed to start in about the events of the morning. When Conner interjected how Karlana seemed to know what he was thinking, everyone in the room nodded their agreement.

"Yeah, that can be quite spooky," someone commented.

But the statement did not pacify Pauli, who declared, "Karlana is more than spooky. I'm telling you, as sure as plants grow in dirt, the woman is crazy!"

Estora, who had entered to check on the copper pot, rounded full on Pauli, a pudgy forefinger wagging in his face as she scolded. "Pauli, as always, you do not know what you are talking about!" Several chuckled at her back. Estora moved to the firebox so she could take them all in with a stern look, fists planted on wide hips for emphasis. "A fool sees only the sickness that grips a man without seeing the man who grips the sickness." She waited to let them consider the words. A few glanced down with newfound embarrassment while Pauli wrestled with the meaning. "Since you are all pre-bonders, I will go easy on you this time." The entire room went deathly silent.

Since Estora had their attention, she continued. "Let me tell you a story. Once, there was a young, free-spirited orphan girl who showed exceptional promise in sorcery. In fact, she was so exceptional she was adopted by a Lady Sorceress, who took responsibility to school the girl properly. At the age of fourteen, she was accepted into the Sorcerers Order, younger than anyone ever before, even among those of privileged birth. It is said that by the age of bonding she had advanced to the rank of magus. And three years hence became magi adept, a rank less than half of all those in the order apparently achieve by midlife.

"Now, this woman had taken an eagle for a bond, but no ordinary eagle. The bird possessed an intelligence unseen in other animals. As she advanced her skills in sorcery, her preceptors began to observe her fighting style changing into a form heretofore unknown—a style possessing certain qualities of an eagle. Indeed, by the age of twenty-five, she was so powerful she could best most Sorcerers in practice.

"The Lady Sorceress was very proud of her adopted daughter's accomplishments. So when the Sorcerers Order's Council of Lords began speaking of making the young woman their Advocate for the Realm, the sole person their order would put forth as the next monarch's Champion of the Realm, the Lady Sorceress heartily agreed. But while the young woman possessed all the necessary qualities to compete against the other orders' advocates on the Field of Contest, she had none of the medals of honor or valor needed for advocacy. So the order's lords requested that she be assigned to Striker's Keep to complete the necessary requirements.

"For three fortnights, she saw little combat. Then one evening, she was assigned to lead a small patrol of Queen's Defenders inside the Borderlands to investigate some suspicious activity. When the patrol did not report back the next morning, the keep's colonel dispatched two full companies. They found the patrol, their bodies littering a hill, butchered to a man. And over the hill to the east, they found an entire battalion of Anarchists, two hundred strong, also dead to a man. But the Anarchists had not just been killed. Many had been dismembered, others disemboweled. Yet others were found with limbs and heads ripped from their bodies. In the midst of this gruesome carnage, they found the Sorceress's eagle, dead from a dozen arrows. Though they examined each bloody corpse and sent scouts in every direction, they were unable to find the young sorceress.

"Several days later, a farmer east of here was bringing crops to market when he came upon a young woman wandering alone on the road, near to death from exhaustion, her cloak drenched in blood, though she had few cuts on her. He brought her straightaway to town, where Etrum Benhaven labored three long days to restore her health, and though her body was healing, her mind was slipping away.

"News of the Borderlands battle reached town, as it inevitably does with so many lost, so it wasn't hard to put the events together. So the town council sent a message to the Sorcerers citadel near Loren Canyon. The Lady Sorceress arrived with her entourage to find her adopted daughter in an unfortunate state of mind. Nothing more could be done, so the Lady Sorceress purchased the last unfinished building in town. The town council agreed to take care of the young woman."

In the silence following, Conner spoke the name on everyone's mind: "Karlana Landcraft."

Estora regarded him sadly. "That is her name now, yes." She studied each face with a broad glance about. "There is enough awareness left in Karlana that she insists on repaying what was done for her, in the only ways she can. She heals bonds when they are sick, takes care of animals in distress, assists in schooling, and prepares those who soon will receive the gift she so gravely misses.

"I was told no one knows why Karlana bonded with such a powerful animal. But I overheard one magus here with the Lady Sorceress say it was because she was schooled in the elemental arts too early. I don't pretend to know the ways of the orders. But I do know this, and it is something to heed well in your life. If your bond dies before you, may the Harmonics forbid, you will spend many years in Yearning. And for the simpleminded, or when the bonding is strong like it was with Karlana, Yearning can surely become maddening."

Conner glanced up at the words etched into the stained glass above the door. He considered how a little knowledge could change his perspective on life.

No one seemed interested in breaking the silence, forgotten mugs of cooling ciderbrew in their hands, so Estora started toward the door. "I think I'd better make sure my tavern is still there." She pulled the doors closed behind her without looking back.

Alton, a short stocky boy sitting next to Pauli, clenched his fists. "That wouldn't have happened if it weren't for the Anarchists. For five hundred years, they have attacked the good people of Griffinrock and the other Harmonic Realms beyond. They refuse to abide by the agreements signed at the end of the Anarchic War. They aren't going to leave us alone until they are destroyed." A few nodded agreement, giving him the courage to continue. "I, for one, am going to join the Queen's Defenders once I have bonded. And if I'm not good enough for the fighting guilds, then I'm going into the militia. Either way, I'll die before I let Anarchists walk the Eastlands again."

Pauli's eyes lit up at the mention of the Queen's Defenders, and he immediately hitched his plow to the back of Alton's comment. He went right into how he and Conner had encountered a battalion of Queen's Defenders in Greston Woods a few days before. Having captured everyone's attention, he began embellishing the story so much Conner began to wonder if he was talking about a different escapade.

Near the end of Pauli's tale, Conner became aware that the raucous din from the tavern had died away. No longer fascinated by Pauli's wild fable, he moved cautiously to the door. Others noticed the unusual silence as well. By the time Conner reached the doors, everyone was crowded close behind with puzzled looks, attempting to peer over his tall shoulders—all except for Pauli, who stared blankly in mid-sentence at the backs of his once-attentive audience.

Conner pulled the doors wide. The stillness that met the group was palpable. Everyone in the tavern sat at their tables, captivated by a young woman standing between the inn's stairs and the tavern's ale bar beyond.

It was said the voice of Niora Elflander, Estora's daughter, could make the most ardent of merchants pause, even while haggling over an especially profitable deal. Niora held a dulcimer, which she began to strum while her meadowlark bond, perched on the spiral railing behind, bobbed and pranced about. Those around Conner held their breath in anticipation. Someone pressed from behind. He turned to find Pattria smiling up at him. He stepped to the side and she slipped past, her narrow shoulders pressing against his chest.

From Niora's dulcimer came the opening strains of "The Dreamer Sails and the Sailor Dreams," an ancient Grenetian ballad sung along the Realm's sea towns. As she sang, her meadowlark bond interjected melodic overtones in precise timing.

CALL OF THE DRAGONBONDED

In the days when I was young
Many songs of love I'd sung
But the words never seemed to rhyme;
The meaning always wrong,
And the verses seldom long,
For it seems that only dreams could keep time.

Won't you give me just one smile?
Yes, laugh with me a while,
For the songs of my past now seem sad.
Through the many endless years
I have cried a million tears
As I roamed for the home I never had.

Setting sail upon the sea
I wanted only to be free
From the songs as a youth I had known.
Carried by the changing tide
I crossed the oceans wide
Searching for a distant shore to call my own.

Then on a bright, clear morn
A new song in me was born
For that day I sailed into view
Of a land I'd only known
Where the seeds of dreams are grown;
Never clear, never near, till I met you.

Won't you sing for me your song
For my journey has been long
But I'm sure that my course has been true.
Will you take me by the hand,
And write our names into the sand?
For it seems I've found my dreams here with you.

It was nearly a minute before the enchantment broke, but when it did, the tavern erupted into loud applause. Niora curtsied with flushed cheeks, and immediately, a crowd of admirers lavished the singer with praise so she would be sure to sing again soon.

The evening waned and chores waited at first light, so those around Conner began saying their good nights. Through all of this, Pattria stared up at Conner expectantly. All had departed—except for Pauli and Alton, holding an ardent discussion on the numerous strengths of the Queen's Defenders—so Pattria hooked her arm into Conner's. "Walk me home?"

As they stepped past Niora, Conner paused. "What a lovely song, Niora."

Niora flashed Conner a warm smile. "Thank you, Conner. I am glad you liked it."

He opened his mouth to offer more admiration, but a hard tug on his arm sent him two steps nearer the doors, Pattria gripping his elbow all the tighter. They exited with haste before she slowed to a more comfortable pace.

"You really are quite incorrigible," Pattria said with false irritation.

This of course, as she knew it would, only broadened his smile. He scanned the sky and pointed at Erebus nearing its zenith. "At least you know what you're getting into."

Pattria grunted disapprovingly, though she put little emotion behind it. In a small, private community as old as Creeg's Point, it was vital to keep kinships strong. The future of the very community had to be considered from a greater vantage point when making decisions affecting others. So marriages were planned through rational discussions among parents. The Stonefields and Morelaces had long since agreed to Conner and Pattria's betrothal.

They walked the remaining hundred paces in silence, neither willing to break the tranquility. Conner ached to tell her of his acceptance into the Apothecaries Guild. But he might as well inform the town crier as say one word to Pattria. After the two reached the

Morelace home, Conner waited until Pattria was inside, climbing the narrow stairs to the brightly lit rooms above her father's grocery, before turning back toward the inn.

He found Pauli impatiently waiting outside Estora's, and the two started north with Erebus lighting the dark road before them. Once out of town, talk about the evening became banter, and soon they were playing a game they had invented years before called Name Your Bond. In this game, one declared what kind of bond the other would get based on their behavior that day.

Conner considered how Pauli had behaved that morning leaving Karlana's home. He cringed and squeaked, "Mouse."

This got him a scathing look. Pauli responded, "Sheep."

Conner glared back. Pauli was not far from the mark. He could be timid when confronted with conflict. The image of Pauli pressing his barrel chest into Judston's came to him. Like so many times before, Pauli had come to Conner's defense. Conner couldn't resist the reminder. "Badger."

Pauli grunted at Conner's futile attempt to rebuke his aggressiveness. Pauli knew his guardian tendencies infuriated Conner, but coming to his friend's rescue was as innate as eating. Clasping his palms together, Pauli pressed the outside of his left hand to his right cheek. Then, looking skyward, he fluttered his eyes and sighed sweetly, "Turtle dove."

The reference to Conner's affection for Pattria was just the excuse Conner had been waiting for. He leaped upon Pauli's back and battered the bigger boy with a series of pelts sure to leave him completely unharmed.

Untethered

The warbling chatter of a nightingale singing merrily in a pine outside the bedchamber pierced Conner's ears long before he dared open his eyes. Tan chiffon curtains in the window fluttered in the warm breeze. Hemera's light, having made its morning path across his bed, warmed his legs beneath the light sheets. By this time on most days, the eastern plot would have been hoed and watered. But this morning, more than a week after his first pre-bonders' meeting, was his chance to sleep late. And he was ready to take full advantage of it—until the tantalizing aroma of fresh-baked rolls and eggs frying in butter convinced him otherwise.

Unable to take his stomach's protests any longer, he stretched away the night's stiffness and dressed. A quick detour to the washroom brought the gentle sounds of his father humming "Darling, I Love You, But What's For Dinner" through the open window as he worked a hoe through the dirt behind the house. Letting his large nose lead the way, Conner stumbled downstairs to the kitchen where he found a steaming plate of food waiting on the table.

Conner used to wonder how his cunning mother always knew precisely when to have his breakfast ready. He fantasized she was a mysterious Mystic with powers of clairvoyance. But sixteen years in the Stonefield home had been long enough to acquire an understanding of her secrets. Conner pinched off a corner of a steaming roll. Ignatius, Oshan's personal spy, bounded across the table and greedily removed the crumb from between his fingers. The chipmunk shoved the crumb into his pouch, then joyfully squeaked his appreciation.

The Calling came on to Conner without warning.

It began as a strange sensation flowing through him, as if someone were pouring cold water down his back on a hot summer's day. He bolted upright, his spine arching forward. Every muscle in his body quivered uncontrollably to the point of convulsing.

"Do be careful, Conner, and don't burn your mouth," Oshan cautioned as she scrubbed the iron stove. "The rolls are fresh from the oven."

Several moments passed before Conner could breathe. His muscles quivered. His nerves vibrated as tremors oscillated up and down his body. And beneath these tremors was a wrenching pull at his mind, as if he were being drawn toward the intense heat of a raging, distant fire. Whenever he focused on the tugging, his attention turned to the northwest. The sensation was so powerful and clear, he was certain that if he were blindfolded and spun in a circle until dizzy, he could still point to that fire.

He rose, unable to think of anything meaningful to say. The resonating sensations consumed all his attention, making rational thought elusive. He shuffled out onto the front porch. Fresh air peeled away some of the queasiness, though the tension was still there. As if for the first time, Conner noticed the tall oaks and pines growing sparsely between the house and road, swaying and creaking in the warm breeze. A few dozen blackbirds winged swiftly overhead in a bright blue sky holding but a few fluffy, white clouds. Yet despite this heightened awareness of his surroundings, Conner's thoughts never wavered from the northwestern horizon.

Oshan appeared at his back. "Conner, what . . .?" But with one glance, her expression softened. She gently patted his shoulder. "I will get your father to pack your things. You'll want to leave straightaway."

The next hour was a blur. Conner alternated through a series of peaks and valleys, first hot then cold, from raw intensity to numbness.

He only partially recalled his mother coaxing him back inside to eat his plate of eggs. His father was there, speaking to him about the supplies he would need, then was gone. His mother appeared again, smiling as always, reassuring him that the feeling would soon pass. Later, he felt something small and soft on his forearm. He looked down. Concern darkened Notorius's otherwise mischievous face as the raccoon lightly patted Conner's arm, chattering something important Conner should know. At last, Conner's smile satisfied the raccoon enough that she stopped her incessant pacing along the stone wall.

Conner leaned forward, his arms locked, head bowed to fight back his overwhelming sense of urgency. Focusing his attention on his surroundings helped clear away the fog. And though he felt edgy, the physical world was starting to shift back into focus. Soon, he was feeling his normal self—except for the constant distraction of the raging bonfire in the distance.

The next time the front door opened, his parents appeared with arms full of supplies. His father carried the deerskin pack he had made for Conner's bonding trek. Anton clasped his hand on his son's shoulder. "It's good to see you back. I packed you one extra set of clothing. There's enough food and water there to last a week. I hope that will be enough." He stepped back with a smile, hand slipping hesitantly from Conner's shoulder.

His mother stepped closer and pressed a small leather purse into his palm. "Take this in case of an emergency."

Conner pulled at the leather strings woven around the purse's lip and counted forty coins inside. He started to refuse the offer, but Oshan was prepared for such a response. She placed her steady hands around his, giving him a stern look. The coins were not open for discussion.

Conner hesitated. There was something different about his parents. Since Cronoans first set foot on this land, the Calling had signified the coming of age. The trek to find one's bond was the journey of self-discovery each must take to better understand the

Cosmos and his or her place in it, a necessary rite of passage into adulthood. It was celebrated for the anticipation of what was about to be gained, not mourned for what was being lost.

He needed them to believe he was ready, that he would return to shoulder his responsibilities as a guildsman's apprentice. He squeezed his mother's hand, then pushed the bulging purse into his pocket.

Shouldering the heavy pack, he started toward the stone wall, leaving his parents standing arm in arm on the porch. Every beginning starts with an ending. One must be ready to let go of the old before the new can be embraced. It was one of Karlana's fondest sayings. Whatever waited, Conner had spent his life in preparation for this moment. He stepped through the iron gate, ignoring its objecting groan. Then, with a light step and the burning fire's relentless tug, he started north along the road.

Part II

Just as a Being's life is but a phase in one's existence, so too is life a series of many births. Lives, birthdays, sunrises, even heartbeats mark beginnings along a timeline of different scales. One's lack of mindfulness does not make this simple truth less compelling. It only marks the Being's loss in not seeing the Cosmic opportunities waiting with the next breath.

—The Modei Book of Fire (First Book)

Cravenrock

Conner had always heard Cravenrock to be a big, dirty, bustling city, but as he stood atop a hill to the southeast, he considered that maybe all of that had been drastically understated. His imagination of the sheer size of the city did nothing to prepare him for what he beheld. Linkenton Point was the largest community he had visited. But Cravenrock made that town look like a village. And most disconcerting of all was that he could not recall ever hearing anything good about this place.

Situated in the rugged northern region of the Narwalen Plains, Cravenrock was the hub of life for three types of people. The first, and by far the greatest in number, were the transients. These included a boundless variety of adventurers, mountainmen, trappers, miners, drifters, gypsies, and explorers who visited the city to trade their goods and stories for food, supplies, and, on occasion, a good time. Transients stayed in the city until they tired of the crowds—not because the city was crowded, which it was, but because inevitably crowds made communities, communities made Realms, Realms made laws, and laws were too confining. Most discovered quickly that overstaying their welcome resulted in being imprisoned . . . or worse. The second were the settlers, mostly merchants and traders, who made their living, directly and indirectly, off the transients, though few willingly admitted to this. And the third were those stuck in limbo somewhere between the transients and valued members of the community—namely charlatans, cutthroats, thieves, and marauders. Yet, while this type kept a considerable number of city folk employed as guardsmen, the criminals were not what most transients and settlers had on their minds when it came to safety. Most were concerned that the northern Borderlands ran east to west seventy miles north of the city.

Cravenrock had thrived for six hundred years because of a number of defenses against Anarchist attack. First, the massive Dragon's Back Mountain Range ran from the northeast to the southwest between the city and the Borderlands, forming a natural barrier for the entire region. Next were four hills surrounding the city, creating an impediment to attacking forces. Watchtowers rose high atop every hill, manned by city guardsmen who scanned the plains for potential threats. Then, there was the dark stone wall ten paces high surrounding the city. And if an invading force were successful in fording the massive mountain range with their war machines, braving a long charge up the hills under a hail of arrows, and scaling the city walls, it would still have to contend with Cravenrock Keep.

The keep was a tall, single tower constructed against the eastern city walls. Built by masters of the Masons Guild shortly after the city wall was completed, the keep had walls similar to those of the city. Griffinrock maintained a full garrison of forces in the keep, including a strong contingent of ordermen, mostly Warriors, and Queen's Defenders who patrolled the northeast plains, providing safe passage for travelers through the region.

Conner turned and scanned the wide dirt road winding down the sloping hill behind him and across the plains to the southeast. It beckoned him to return. Two days out and already he missed the comforts of home.

But the subtle, relentless tugging at his mind brought him back. His eyes darted to the northwest, and to the formidable dark city sprawled before him. The heat was already building, and the early morning shadow of the southeast watchtower offered little relief. Conner had tarried long enough. He would purchase a few supplies in the city and maybe get a decent meal before moving on. He dug deep to find the courage to take his first step along the last mile to Cravenrock's southern gate.

As Conner walked, a line of heavy covered wagons, each pulled by a team of four horses, appeared through massive gates along the southern wall. The lead wagon came to a split in the road then rolled west, ambling away along the only other route out of the valley. By the time Conner reached the city gates, the wagons had disappeared over the ridge that split the western watchtowers, along with a small company of Queen's Defenders.

Dust from the wagons hung in the air as Conner walked through the gates. Several city guardsmen stood at ease with their bonds inside the entrance, out of Hemera's heat. A dozen more strolled along the top of the wall, occasionally glancing through embrasures at those passing below. None seemed interested in him, nor anyone else for that matter, so he stepped into the cool shadow of the gate. A sudden rush of excitement flowed through him as he gazed at his first city.

Conner dawdled near an open dirt courtyard extending fifty paces to the north of the gates and nearly half that distance east and west. Except for a few city folk, their bonds, and an occasional patch of hardy grass, the courtyard was barren, so Conner assumed the space had been designed as a staging area to organize large fighting forces before taking to the plains for battle. On the other side of the courtyard was a well, where Conner found a bucket of fresh water. After splashing water over his neck, he surveyed the busy city farther to the north.

Tall, old buildings leaned precariously into narrow cobblestone streets filled with frowning people jostling in every direction. At one time, the buildings had been painted white to reflect the heat like those in Linkenton Point, but here the worn paint had flaked away, exposing the dirty clay bricks beneath. All the roofs were poorly thatched in dried brown straw bundled tight with hemp. Many of the cobblestones were loose or worn with gaps, making walking difficult. Two deep depressions ran along each street, worn from centuries of heavy wagons squeezing between the buildings. Since all the streets looked the same, Conner chose the narrow one directly ahead. After a brief pause, he lurched forward in search of supplies.

Shortly, Conner entered into an open cobblestone courtyard with a thriving marketplace similar to the one in Creeg's Point. He moved nimbly about the carts until he came upon a stocky fellow with thinning blond hair that reminded him of Pauli's dad. The merchant seemed too busy to answer questions about the city, so Conner settled with purchasing several bread rolls, strips of dried beef, and hard-boiled eggs. Cradling his prizes, he moved on past the busy market until he came to a short brick wall. In the shade of a great oak, Conner sat on the wall and ate his food ravenously, watching the merchants barter their wares.

Marcantos's Code

Long before Hemera rose, Grandmaster Warrior Marcantos Evinfaire was pacing the halls and corridors high in Cravenrock's keep. He had awakened especially testy that morning. And breakfast had made him all the more irritable. Whenever Marcantos questioned his long-time preceptor, Grandmaster Blake Friarwood, as to why he had brought him to this Cosmos-forsaken armpit of the Harmonic Realms, Blake would reward him with dismissive grunts and cryptic comments such as, "We shall see." Well, it had been more than a week, and his patience was wearing thin.

Piercing hazel eyes gazed at the large mass near his bed. Though unsettled thoughts had kept sleep away, his bond slept happily in the warm bedchamber. Nothing fazed the beast when it came to sleep.

Unable to stand the anxious tension, Marcantos went into the keep's ward to practice a long series of Warrior forms called Fangs. "*Ponther energi epithodigos*," he began by incanting the spell that would guide his blades in the forms' intricate patterns of attack. In his mid-thirties, his sleek body glided through the forms, crisscrossing the empty ward in soft shoes and trousers, his upper body bare.

He liked the simplicity of this set of forms—the fluid shift from symmetric to asymmetric movements and back again as he drew upon the Water elemental, circular motion changing from thrusts to retreats as he directed the Air elemental. The forms forced him to focus on the basics—footwork, balance, breathing, relaxation. His twin blades whirled rhythmically. He had refused to learn Fangs using the normal, duller practice blades, so he bore several deep scars as reminders of his momentary mental lapses.

He finished the dozen forms just as the sky began to brighten. Using the new light, he inspected his arms for cuts, gratified to find none. He swiftly climbed the stairs from the ward to the keep's eastern parapet, where Hemera was breaking through a few thin clouds along the horizon. Here, everything was basic, simple like Fangs, when the rest of his life was filled with senseless politics and the petty dealings of others. This was where he felt closest to his Harmonic existence— Hemera's rise, the sounds of birds taking to the skies for their morning feast, life in an ever-flowing balance about him. The fireball rose a brilliant red, turning orange, then yellow. He closed his watery eyes, feeling Hemera's rays warm his face.

Later that morning, Marcantos stared down from a west balcony of the keep's tower, scraps of his forgotten morning meal on a table next to him. His dark hair, pulled back in typical Warrior style, was still damp from his ritual workout.

Heat boiled from the ward of Cravenrock Keep, making cheerful souls edgy, the optimistic depressed, and the disciplined inattentive to their work. The shadow of the eastern wall slowly descended the western wall, Hemera heating the keep's dark stone to the temperature of an armorer's forge. Guardsmen pacing the parapet shimmered in the dusty air. Occasionally, they paused to wipe sweat from brows, the scene playing out below a welcome distraction.

There, as on every morning for five hundred years, master Warriors instructed their apprentices in their order's basic fighting style, as well as the other skills they would have to master before they could advance in rank and be entrusted with the wisdom of how to combine Air and Water, the elemental forces of the Warriors Order. Men had long since stripped to their waists; women down to tight, light colored tops so their shoulders and stomachs could breathe.

It was this age-old ritual that chafed Marcantos to near the point of exploding. Since arriving in Cravenrock, he had watched these masters coddle their lowly apprentices. And each morning, he fumed as the pupils learned nothing about real combat.

One particular master instructing an apprentice on how to wield a mace drew his attention. The apprentice moved like she carried a sword, not a heavy, blunt weapon. Her footing was wrong, making her swings weak and inaccurate. With a bashing weapon like a mace, she should twist more with her hips, her shoulders following through to give the weapon more force on impact not needed with a cutting weapon. The apprentice's attacking thrusts were so far off, the instructor hardly needed to move to avoid being hit, yet he did nothing to correct her.

Marcantos knew his unsettling anger at the master Warriors in the ward was misplaced. His experience and mastery of combat should have kept him above such irritation. But what started as a pebble of annoyance cascaded into a landslide of rage. A violent torrent of energy coursed through him until he could no longer deny the emotions whipping at him, struggling to control him. It was time those below understood what it meant to be of the Warriors Order.

He left the balcony and exited his bedchamber. The large mass of brown fur next to his bed, unscathed by its bond's irritability, never stirred. Marcantos skipped gracefully down the single set of steps, passed through the southern end of the keep's main entrance hall, and proceeded into the dusty ward. Crossing to the northern side, he rummaged through the weapons rack until he found five particularly pathetic practice swords.

By that time, everyone in the ward was aware of Marcantos's arrival. Practice dwindled until they gawked curiously at the grandmaster's presence. Returning to the center of the ward, he turned the worst of the five swords pommel up and drove the point into the ground. Marking off ten paces to the east, he drove another sword into the ground. He then proceeded in a circle around the first sword, stopping to the north, west, and south, repeating the same action.

Returning to the center of the makeshift circle, he signaled the four master Warriors to step forward. They reacted without hesitation, confusion painting their sweat-streaked faces. Once they drew near, he stated softly, "I want you to go to a sword and draw it. When ready, I want you to try to kill me."

Uncertainty belayed the confidence the four masters had exuded moments before with their apprentices.

"Do it now," he commanded.

Clear that Marcantos would offer nothing further, the four took positions near the swords.

"Oh, I forgot to mention," Marcantos interjected. "If I sense you are not seriously attempting to kill me, or if you pull your attacks, I will gut you like a fish." He smiled pleasantly at each one.

Murmurs echoed across the ward. Guards stopped to gawk from the parapets above.

To those looking on, Marcantos's actions surely seemed risky. But without their personal weapons to focus the elemental forces of Water and Air, they would be forced to fight using melee skills alone. Besides, since his arrival, he had been observing the masters' fighting styles. The tactical advantage was his.

In front of Marcantos was a Warrior he called Huffy—a big man who preferred intimidation over finesse. He was hotheaded, his actions dictated by emotion. Huffy would strike first, fast and hard.

To his left was Doughty, a strong, dexterous man of average frame. This one reminded him of himself. Doughty had picked the most advantageous position, with Hemera at his back. Unafraid to take risks, he fought with a precision that spoke of many hours of practice. This, of course, would be his downfall.

To Marcantos's right, in the tactically worst position, was Anxious, a thin fellow with eyes that never settled. The man would not know how to take advantage of a situation even if it were served to him with a flourish on a silver platter. Anxious was impetuous. He fought like a man cornered, even when on the attack.

And behind Marcantos was Foxy. His play on words for this master Warrior delighted him. The only woman master at the keep, she was lithe and pretty in the face, pure poetry in practice. On the field, what Foxy lacked in precision of weapon skill, she compensated for with the genius of a skilled and aggressive tactician.

Marcantos squared his chest at Huffy, knees bent. He rested his hand on the pommel of the sword, its blade biting the dirt. The anticipation of battle drove his anger away. His heartbeat slowed; his mind emptied. His consciousness ascended into the Mental plane, where he, like all those of the Harmonic orders, accessed Harmonic Sight. In his mind's eye, the Mental forms of his four opponents flared and wavered about him, shuddering with anticipation.

In an instant, Huffy traveled the ten paces between them, bringing his sword overhead for a single killing stroke. At the precise moment that Huffy committed, Marcantos stepped to his left, pulling his sword's pommel with him, the point still in the dirt. The edge of Huffy's blade whizzed past Marcantos's right shoulder. Sparks flew from the hard contact with his blade under the cross guard, the other man's blade carrying through to the ground. Marcantos stepped back to his right and planted his boot on top of Huffy's steel, immobilizing the big man's sword.

Marcantos sensed Anxious cautiously moving in from his right, while Doughty skirted toward Foxy. Huffy attempted unsuccessfully to pry his sword from beneath Marcantos's boot. Marcantos took a moment to smile at Huffy before snapping his left foot into the astonished expression on his face. *One.*

This was the distraction Anxious had waited for. He charged in aggressively. Huffy's prone body forgotten, Marcantos slid his fist to the sword's grip, thumb near the pommel. Anxious thrust hard. Marcantos lowered his leg, pulling his blade from the dirt. His sword protectively positioned between him and the Warrior's steel, he deflected the point of Anxious's blade outward. He noted Anxious's poor thrust, one any master would not have made for a kill. His eyes flashed, the remaining two forms shifting behind.

Snapping his sword upward, Marcantos twisted his wrist, pulling the pommel over his head. The action forced his blade out and up, sliding along Anxious's extended blade before the man could pull back. Anxious's arm went wide. Marcantos let his sword's momentum carry through, spinning to face his two remaining opponents. The hard twist of his hips caused a chain reaction up his spine and shoulders, through his right arm held high to his left, and into his wrist. His sword slashed downward in a pendulum motion left to right. Judging the precise length of his sword from its balance, the tip of his blade etched a thin red line from shoulder to elbow along Anxious's left arm. Anxious cried out and staggered back. *Two.*

Marcantos's sword continued its motion, picking up speed. It arced downward in front of him, then up to his right, intersecting Doughty's backswing that came in short. The contact was at his sword's center of balance, so Doughty took the full shock. The report echoed across the ward.

Compact eddies of energy exploded across Marcantos's mind and he stepped nimbly toward Doughty with a double-loop sword spin, one loop circling his left side, followed by a loop on his right, then back again. The poorly balanced sword forced Marcantos to keep the spinning action tight. Still, the whirling blade drove Doughty back on his heels.

Marcantos sensed Foxy shifting toward him from behind. He extended his arm back with the next whirling loop. The greater arc slowed his rhythm, but the resounding contact of his blade on Foxy's sword had kept his spine from being severed. Having seen Foxy's attack, Doughty reversed his backward motion, expecting Marcantos's attention to be diverted. The rash move would have been effective against a less-skilled combatant. But Marcantos never slowed his footwork. He completed his loop and stepped to Doughty's right, his spinning arc deflecting Doughty's blade out wide.

Foxy had recovered from her failed strike, but she could no longer assist Doughty. Doughty's sword arm extended, Marcantos spun to face Foxy, while driving his sword into a new arc over his head. He drove the pommel down on Doughty's right hand like a smithy's hammer. Doughty shuffled out of view with a pained groan. *Three.*

Marcantos advanced on Foxy, deftly whirling the crude sword in his hand. Foxy took a ready stance for his attack, legs wide and balanced. The edge of Marcantos's mouth twitched. Something different in Foxy's Mental form forced him to pause. Rather than holding his sword in attack position, he stepped toward her with his blade wide, completely open to her. He could sense eddies of Mental energy shifting about him, and through their haunting motion, she too hesitated. He stepped closer, open to her attack, forcing her to choose. Still, she waited.

Let us dance, he thought, his mind moving with churning funnels of life force. They trembled as he weighed each option, altered shape with each decision, transformed with each step. Hypnotized, he moved into one of the eddies, letting it envelop his mind. He rejoiced in the painful exhilaration of its sudden power. The roar of a great thunderstorm raged about him. The energy of the vortex whipped him about, tearing at him, pulsing through him, tugging wildly. He felt his body surge forward, as if under its own volition, but he had no other sensation, no context for what played out in the Physical plane. A thought nagged at him from the far horizon of the pattern of life around him, like someone waving to draw his attention, reminding him of who he was. No, of who he had been. But he was dancing in the eddy, and it danced in him.

Abruptly, the roar and exhilaration were gone, replaced with an agonizing stillness. His first reaction was one of loss. He hungered to experience those sensations again. He fought against awareness of his body, his breathing. But something soft and damp was pressed against him, something moving with a rhythm not his, drawing him back to the Physical plane. He opened his eyes, straight into Foxy's. She was looking at him with . . . fear? excitement? He realized he was pressed against her, her panting the rhythm he had sensed. He had never felt so alive.

He stepped away, forcing his eyes from hers. Foxy was pressed against the ward's north wall. She no longer held a sword. Looking down in shock, he found her sword in his other hand. How had it gotten there? His cheeks burned, gutting him of the anger that had gripped him before. Yet he was quenched, content. He stepped back again, nearly stumbling, then scanned the blank faces of those about silent and staring, measuring him.

He shook away his confusion. It had to be the incessant heat or lack of sleep. Returning to the center of the ward, he drove the two swords into the ground, blades crossing in the middle, noting their resemblance for the symbol for comradeship in the Warriors Order. Cosmic providence? Marcantos studied each Warrior in turn, then announced for all to hear. "Train every day like it will be your last, for someday it will be. Until then, challenge your comrades to seek new strengths, new courage, new levels of endurance that cannot be discovered alone. The person standing next to you may be the one you need to save your life."

With that, he walked from the ward, every eye upon him.

A Tenuous Affair

More eyes were on Marcantos than just those in the ward. In an upper balcony of the keep, two men silently observed the affair unfold below, measuring and assessing from a vantage point that allowed them to see the Harmonic patterns. The older man, General Mikel Grimwaldt, wore the uniform of a grandmaster of the Warriors Order. He had a rugged, round face, wrinkled from many years on the Narwalen Plains near the Borderlands, his white hair cut short. The many medals on his round chest, testimony to his status in the three Realms and his order, were not required to command the respect from those around him, especially from the Warrior at his side.

As Marcantos disappeared into the keep, the general regarded the man next to him. Colonel Dreston Palastar was a stocky man of similar height, but his heft came not from muscle as with Grimwaldt; and Palastar was as soft between the ears as he was in his gut. In every conceivable way, he was an imbecile. Even worse, the man carried himself with such snobbery that the general considered him nothing more than a pompous ass.

It was this deeply undesirable quality that had landed the colonel in his current assignment as Commander of the Cravenrock Keep forces. In the three months previous as Commander of the Kallzwall Castle guard, he had so infuriated the queen's sister, Duchess Mariette of Narwales, she nearly demanded his head on a platter. Only through the quick actions of a few high-ranking members of the Warriors Order, including Grimwaldt, had Palastar's miserable life been saved.

But Grimwaldt's actions had nothing to do with wanting Palastar to keep his head. Grimwaldt would have happily severed the lump on the man's neck from his distended body. No, he had acted to prevent the Warriors Order from taking a further fall in status within Narwales, the largest fiefdom in the Griffinrock Realm. It would have taken years for the order to recover from such a calamity. Unfortunately, the only position available for the colonel was commanding the Cravenrock forces. All that paled in comparison to Grimwaldt having to suffer the colonel's presence long enough to give the man a few basic instructions.

"I see what you mean, General," Palastar stated smugly. "He has exceptional qualities and shows great potential. How long did he take to beat my four master instructors? Thirty seconds?" He hesitated, but when the general did not reply, he pressed on. "It is clear why he is the advocate for the Warriors Order. I can't imagine anyone in all the orders capable of matching his prowess. It seems a certainty he will become Veressa's Champion of the Realm." He grinned smugly at the general, expecting full agreement. When what he had suggested struck his slow wit, the colonel nervously amended, "Let it be the Cosmos's will that day is many years away."

Grimwaldt waited while Palastar's smile wilted under his intense stare. He considered rebuking the colonel for referring to the keep's master Warriors as his own. Of course, Palastar was correct in his assessment, but Grimwaldt made it a point not to agree with a man whose ego exceeded his generous size.

The general retreated to his makeshift personal reception quarters, moving like a Warrior who had fought countless battles and killed an untold number of Anarchists. The portly colonel trailed on his heels. There, Grimwaldt picked through wilted grapes on an ancient stand, then dropped them back on the plate. Artesia, sensing his growing irritation, eyed the general from her perch. The general regarded his bond with narrow, dark eyes and thick brows set over a nose broken many times. He comforted the red-tailed hawk with a gentle stroke. "You are to give Marcantos whatever he asks for,

Colonel. Do you understand?" He stared intensely. It was not a question.

"Why, of course, General," came the meek reply. Palastar bowed respectfully, a nervous smile painting his face.

Grimwaldt hesitated, not sure how to entrust the next instruction in a way that would not send up warning flares. "I have another instruction for you, Colonel, before I leave this afternoon for Loren Canyon—one that is of the utmost importance to our order's high lords." He turned nimbly, given his bulk, to study Palastar, not wanting any misunderstandings.

"Of course you can count on me, General." Palastar stated with complete seriousness. Palastar owed his life to Grimwaldt; he could deny him little.

"I want you to keep an eye on Marcantos's preceptor, Grandmaster Friarwood, without his knowing. You are to report to me what you observe. And above all, no one else is to be involved in this affair."

Palastar crinkled his stubby nose in puzzlement. "Of course, General, but is there something specific I should be watching for?"

Grimwaldt considered this course of action. Something about Friarwood bothered him. His prior probes into how Marcantos's preceptor had entered the Warriors Order had yielded nothing unusual. Still, his concerns remained. While Friarwood had proven to be an exceptional melee fighter and outstanding preceptor, he had not demonstrated the skills a grandmaster should possess. This was highly irregular for someone who had risen so quickly through the ranks.

But Grimwaldt had to be cautious. A Warrior's blade cuts both ways. The hopes of all the order were riding on Marcantos's success. A Warrior Champion would raise their order out of its wretched standing with the Griffinrock crown. Casting suspicious shadows on their advocate's mentor could be dangerous for everyone involved. Of the three mentors Marcantos had through the years, the young Warrior had developed a particularly fond attachment to Friarwood.

Sure, the colonel possessed absolutely no abilities for handling espionage. But Grimwaldt needed information about Friarwood, and he was short on options. "I want you to report to me, and me alone, anything you find . . . unusual about Friarwood's behavior or his training of Marcantos." He would leave it at that and sift through any information the colonel sent his way.

Palastar nodded his understanding.

Grimwaldt waved a thick, muscled hand absently. "You may go." Without returning Palastar's salute, Grimwaldt walked to the balcony, his hawk bond Artesia on his arm.

The colonel might have been slow, but he was correct in one thing: Marcantos had shown exceptional qualities from a very young age. A noble's son, he had been groomed to assume great responsibility in one of the orders. By all recorded accounts, his extraordinary fighting skills, combined with a commanding voice and leadership abilities, had not been seen in an orderman in several hundred years. Since the moment of his bonding, Marcantos had been trained to master all forms of Warrior combat as well as handle affairs of state. As a young officer awarded several commands, he had been victorious in multiple Borderland disputes and decorated many times, including once by Queen Izadora herself. He had everything he needed to become the next Champion of the Realm. A Warrior in such a position would elevate the Warriors Order to its rightful place above the other five orders.

Grimwaldt peered out at the ward below, noting several masters being attended by those of the Physicians Guild. What should he make of this? Was he the only one concerned with the young man's recent shift in behavior? Was the general becoming an old fool, or were the hopes of his order misplaced in this young man? Maybe Marcantos was just exhibiting stress from the responsibility that had been heaped upon his shoulders. Grimwaldt had been given great responsibility at an early age, but not the weight of the entire order. Would he have responded differently under similar conditions?

The general was so deep in thought that he was hardly aware Artesia had taken flight to the northwest, dipping low over the Narwalen Plains. But he could not deny her thrill of the hunt. The trip to Loren Canyon would be fast and hard, but it would be good to be on the road again. He found solace on the open range, where troublesome affairs of state were replaced by life's simple fortunes. Eager to be on his way, he began packing his few possessions.

By providence, Blake Friarwood happened to catch Marcantos sprinting down the stairs to the ward. His pupil's purposeful step distracted him enough from his other business that he elected to watch the combat from a shaded and private northern balcony of the keep's tower. Friarwood reflected on Marcantos's actions. Loosely cut black robes fluttered in the light breeze while he pressed his back to the dark tower stone.

In several dozen heartbeats, his young pupil had taken down four master Warriors. This was the cue he had been waiting for. Friarwood glowed with pride, not only for his personal protégé, but for his own brilliance. To think he had been ready to give up on his unconventional training strategy.

With a lively step, Friarwood crossed the tower hall to his quarters. Carnia squawked her greeting with wings wide, unsure what to make of her bond's rare feelings of elation. He lightly stroked the peregrine falcon's back to soothe her capricious spirit. Certain of Marcantos's potential, he began planning how to rearrange his assignments in Cravenrock. He would need to devote more energy preparing Marcantos for a future he could not even begin to appreciate.

Bandit's Opportunity

From the corner of a nearby building, a boy known only as Bandit surveyed the marketplace for his next score. He rubbed the side of his round nose with a hand that left behind even more dirt, then pushed back the long, oily hair that hung over his thin face. The market was a buffet of luscious entrees, though the food being sold never entered his thoughts. Despite his many choices, he knew that only the right selection would reap the best rewards. A well-dressed townsman strolled through the crowd eyeing the counters, no doubt for items he could resell to turn a profit in his own shop. But Bandit dismissed him right away. Stealing from town folk got the city guardsmen in a huff, and besides, he had picked from two earlier that morning. His attention instead went to more plentiful delicacies. Most transients carried all the money they possessed, and few were stupid enough to complain to the city guard if they were robbed.

A nagging thought forced his eyes to backtrack to a young transient leaning against the wall near the edge of the marketplace. Bandit surmised he was a freeman farmer, probably an Eastlander. From his dusty appearance and the way he was devouring his food, the farmer had been traveling for several days. And judging by the way he was taking in the market and buildings around him, he had just arrived that morning. Bandit praised his Lady of Good Fortune.

Cautiously, he slipped to the north end of the wall. After checking for guardsmen, he moved lithely along the back side of the wall until he was behind the farmer. Bandit squatted and pressed his back to the wall. He checked his surroundings; the trees before him obscured his presence from anyone happening to pass along the street, and a narrow passage between two nearby buildings would serve nicely as an escape route if needed.

Bandit turned to face the wall. The farmer was finishing his meal, so he had to work swiftly. A glance was all he needed to find the leather strings on the farmer's purse. Skillful fingers glided over the wall. A flick of his fingers and the simple knot fell away. Lightly gripping the loose strings between his fingers, he gave the cords a delicate test.

It was easy to be mesmerized by Cravenrock's noisy marketplace. So easy, in fact, that Conner failed to catch the deft fingers on his purse strings. But he was not so enthralled that he missed the gentle tug. His right hand shot back, his fingers clamped around a thin wrist. He dropped what remained of his roll, twisted hard, and yanked upward, hoping to unbalance the thief before he could abscond with purse in hand. Conner was surprised when the wrist came so easily to his tug that he lifted the lightweight body attached to it over the brick wall. Gravity did the rest. Conner torqued the arm hard, pinning the thief to the ground with his foot on the thin shoulder.

In this position, Conner got a good look at the pickpocket. The boy was no more than eleven or twelve. Stringy black hair nearly covered a face caked with dirt, while filthy brown strips of rags for clothing hung from his thin body. Conner glared angrily to keep the snake from squirming away, though in reality, he felt nothing but pity.

"Please don't be killin' me, kind sir!" the boy yelped at Conner, his free hand coming up to protect him from punches Conner might start throwing at any moment.

Conner blinked in surprise. "I'm not going to kill you. Why would I kill you over a few coins?" He hesitated, noticing several people were taking notice.

This response did not seem to satisfy the boy with a wild, frightened stare. Apparently, the boy was not used to getting caught. He stated even louder, "Oh, please sir! I promise I won't be beggin' you again for a coin!" He waved his dirt-streaked arm more vigorously, becoming more distraught by the moment.

Conner eyed the boy suspiciously. A dozen people had stopped to watch, several women aghast with fingers to their lips. This was not going well. Conner decided it better to reason with the young thief. He bent lower, pressing his foot on the boy's shoulder, and whispered, "I know what you are about. I don't want any trouble, but I don't appreciate having my purse lifted."

The boy screamed out in false pain. "Please, sir! There really is no need to be hurtin' a poor beggar boy." Sobbing, he continued louder than before. "I promise not to be botherin' yourself for anything ever again. Just please don't be hurtin' me anymore!"

Having determined the encounter was not worth the trouble, Conner released the boy's wrist. He was about to tell the boy to go away when several pairs of thick black boots stepped into view. He slowly traced up the leather trousers and chain-mail shirts to the burly, frowning faces of three guardsmen. Like those at the city gate, these carried swords in black leather scabbards at their waists. He involuntarily stepped back, removing his foot from the boy.

The guard in front, the eldest and by far the meanest looking of the lot, scrutinized Conner closely from brow to boot with a haughty sneer. Then, turning his eyes to the boy at his feet, he shouted with a touch of annoyance mingled in his thick Narwalen accent. "Here! What be goin' on?"

Before Conner could respond, the boy waved his hands as if warding Conner away. "I only asked him for a coin, sir! He didn't have to be roughin' me up so over somethin' like that!" he sobbed.

The guardsman gave the transient an angry look. "Is that so?"

It was time for Conner to correct the misunderstanding. "That's a lie. This boy was trying to lift my purse!" Conner snatched his purse from his pocket and held it out, the untied string his evidence to the thwarted crime. He was about to continue his argument when he noted the guardsmen were more intrigued with the bulge of the purse than the condition of the leather strap. The one on the right leaned forward and visibly licked his lips. Conner whipped his hand behind his back, tightly clenching his purse, and took a more cautious stance before the three.

This was the distraction the scrawny little thief needed. In a blink of an eye, the boy was over the brick wall, dashing for a narrow street between two large, old buildings that listed dangerously. The guardsmen did not move or even seem to notice, their eyes boring holes through Conner's stomach to the purse at the small of his back.

Uneasiness growing, Conner stepped back against the wall. "Aren't you going to chase down the purse snatcher?"

The guardsman in front grimaced. "Right now, I be wonderin' what an Eastlander is doin' in Cravenrock. What is your business here?"

This had all the makings of a situation gone wrong—having spent so much time around Pauli, Conner knew what one looked like. "I am passing through, sir. I am here to buy a few supplies for my trek." Trying not to look suspicious, Conner started scanning the streets and buildings behind. *Luck favors those prepared for the future,* his father was fond of saying.

The guardsman examined the wall and ground around Conner's feet with curiosity. "It seems you not be movin' too quickly. Where be your supplies?"

The guards' behavior was not what Conner expected. Even if he was an Eastlander, he was a citizen of the Realm, free to enter the city for food and to enjoy the day without getting accosted by thieves or guardsmen. "I arrived shortly ago, and was completing my meal when that little thief tried to snatch my purse." Annoyed, he jerked a thumb in the direction the boy had disappeared, hoping to remind the guardsmen that someone else had been involved in this story. It did not have the desired effect.

The front guardsman shifted his weight. From his expression, he did not like Conner's tone. "Maybe you be tellin' the truth, and maybe not. But we do not be likin' people sashayin' in and mistreatin' our citizens."

The situation was souring like warm milk on a summer afternoon. A different approach was needed, so Conner pasted on the friendliest smile he could muster given the circumstances. "Look. I think you are absolutely right, sir. Maybe I will get the supplies I need and keep on moving." He leaned forward, ready to find the closest grocer and be on his way.

The front guardsman was not swayed by Conner's attempt to resolve the situation honorably. "All that is well and good, boy, but you'll be needin' to be payin' for the disturbance first."

Conner bit back his irritation. "I didn't do anything wrong. And I surely am not going to pay for a misconduct I did not commit."

No longer in control of his anger, the guardsman's face twitched and contorted. "Then it seems we will have to arrest you for assaulting a citizen of Cravenrock." Through gritted teeth, he jerked his head toward Conner with a sneer. "Take him!"

The two guardsmen stepped forward, but before they could grab him, Conner spun about and leaped over the wall. His logic seemed simple and sound. If the narrow street had been a good escape route for the thief, then maybe it would be for him as well. And so he ran.

Shouts from the guardsmen behind coached his legs faster.

Judging from Hemera's position, Conner was sprinting east. The end of the street opened into a wider north-south cobblestone street. Several guardsmen appeared to the south, shouting. They too took up the chase. Options limited, Conner ran north. After a few minutes, he darted east down another narrow street, but this one dead-ended into the back of several crumbling buildings. A brightly painted door opened to his pull, so he ran through the building and into the street on the opposite side.

After that, the chase became a blur, Conner reacting to the shouts of the city guardsmen around him. Evident that the guard's strategy was not working, their plan shifted to one of routing and cutting him off. More and more guardsmen joined in the hunt. Soon, Conner lost all sense of direction weaving madly between the tall buildings hugging narrow streets. He was about to give up hope of ever getting out of the city when he reached the end of a narrow alley opening into the most crowded cobblestone street Conner had ever seen.

Bandit squatted low on top of a tall building east of the marketplace. The city guard had seen his face. And he had nearly been caught. At this point, it looked like a sound beating was more likely than lesser punishments. He started to leave, but his eyes darted to the farmer and city guardsmen below. If he was going to get beaten, at least he would be vindicated with the pleasure of watching the farmer get carted away.

It did not surprise him when the farmer jumped the wall and sprinted his way. What did surprise him was how fast the farmer ran. Against his better judgment, Bandit tailed him from the building tops, watching the show play out below. But as the farmer, unfamiliar with the city, continued to thwart the city guard's lame attempts to snare him, Bandit's interest in him grew. He was either lucky or skilled, and in the thieving business, it was always good to know how to recognize the difference.

Conner stepped into the street, mingling with the lively crowd. The cobblestones teemed with small, brightly colored wooden huts with shutters pulled up and latched to reveal spacious windows on three sides. Every possible type of merchandise hung from these windows, arrayed in no recognizable pattern or order. Gaudy jewelry in one, animal pelts in the next, glassworks after that. From inside each hut, animated merchants busily haggled with the tight throng of people, with their bonds, pushing and weaving their way through the street. To Conner's left stood more tall buildings separated by narrow alleys; to his right, the dark city wall ascended into the cloudless sky. Unable to see another choice, he dove into the flowing stream of human and animal bodies.

Many shoppers carried small bonds tucked in pouches or on their shoulders. A middle-aged woman next to Conner had devised a makeshift wrap of gray cloth slung diagonally, shoulder to hip. Occasionally, a wood mouse poked its furry head from the sling, sniffing the air with its pointed nose while long whiskers and large round ears twitched nervously.

Pangs of homesickness knotted Conner's stomach.

Bandit watched the farmer step out into the Keep's Market. From his vantage point, it was not difficult to see the two thick lines of approaching guardsmen pushing through the crowd, one from the north, the other from the south. The farmer was being squeezed into their trap. After the line of guardsmen coming from the south passed, Bandit used windowsills and doorframes to slip down the side of the building, then dropped the few remaining paces to the street below for a closer look at the pending action. Having spent his entire brief life in the streets of Cravenrock, he knew how to stay hidden, even right under the noses of the city guard.

Conner's confidence was starting to return when the flow of the crowd slowed. A quick glance ahead told everything. A long line of city guardsmen pushed its way in his direction, examining those in the marketplace as they filtered past. His first instinct was to continue on in hopes that the guardsmen did not have a good enough description to pick him out of the multitude. But surrounded by the shoppers' cleaner, more colorful clothing, he was resigned to accept that would not work. He started weaving to his left to take one of the narrow alleys, but guardsmen had barricaded every street. Conner glanced over his shoulder; another line of city guardsmen was closing in from behind.

Opportunity comes only to those with an open mind, his schoolteacher was keen on saying. If he was ever going to get out of this, he would have to think clearly. He moved to his right to get a closer look at the city wall, an insanely desperate idea coming to him.

Seeking Balance

Long after Marcantos had returned to his chambers, he remained unable to shake the feelings of anger he had felt that morning in the ward. He closed his eyes, calming his mind, and was reminded of words he had been taught many years ago by a dear preceptor and sage: *If you are to help others find the courage to accept their responsibility, speak of the thrill of achievement rather than the fear of failure.*

It was then that the realization of what had been nagging at him surfaced. Somewhere along the way, he had lost connection with his foundation in the basics of his art. He had become lost on a shifting mindscape. His footing had slipped. And it came to him how to get it back.

Once Marcantos had worked through all the details, he left his chambers and attacked the stairs three at a time.

Colonel Palastar rubbed at his eyes to make sure he was not daydreaming. Much different from the cooler nights in Kallzwall Castle, it was hard to find sleep in this insufferable heat. He exhaled a longing breath, Marcantos waiting stoically before him for an answer to his request. Palastar's first thought was that Friarwood was somehow behind this appeal. But knowing what he did of Friarwood, he dismissed that idea immediately. No, Marcantos's preceptor would erupt like a volcano when he found out. What was Marcantos up to? Despite Palastar's suspicious nature, nothing came to him, though he would lay claim there was more to Marcantos's petition than the man had mentioned.

Grimwaldt's instructions that morning had been quite clear. Even if Palastar could infer Marcantos's motives, he would not deny the request. He ran a hand slowly down his face, wiping sweat away, then shrugged. Looking up from his desk, he responded, "As you wish, Marcantos. It would be hard to refuse your assistance given the keep's current state of affairs."

Marcantos bowed, a formality not required by someone of nobility, even to one of superior rank. "Thank you, Colonel." He spun on his heels and walked briskly from the office.

Brow furrowed, Palastar rubbed his wolf bond's head as it rested on his thigh. He searched eyes reflecting his own concern, then smiled reassuringly. "It's all right, Garren. We'll keep two pairs of eyes on that one to see what he's about."

A Simple Explanation

Conner noted a place nearby where the wall jutted outward then angled back in. The two lines of guards were nearing, so he worked swiftly. He stepped to the wall near the jut. Reaching both hands over his head, he slid the tips of his fingers along the narrow spacing between two large blocks of the stone wall. He dug his fingertips into the crevice, ignoring the pain. Looking down, he ran the inside of his right shoe along another opening at his knees. He tested his grip, then pressed his chest to the wall and pulled himself up. He released one hand and reached up, feeling his way to the next spacing. Once that grip was secure, he moved his other hand, repeating the action with his feet. He tried to let all his fears go, to focus just on finding the next spacing. Shouts erupted below, demands evolving into threats, then into insults.

An eternity later, Conner reached the top of the city wall. Gripping the lip with both hands, he frantically worked his tired legs to find enough purchase to compensate for arms no longer able to sustain his weight. Finally, he hooked his right leg over the ledge and clambered on top of the wall. His lungs labored for air; his muscles quivered. Pain coursed through every limb.

At last, he peered down. More than twenty guardsmen stood directly beneath, shouting and shaking their fists at him. Behind them, several hundred people stared blankly up. All of this, mixed with the colored huts and old, listing buildings farther on made the scene nothing short of outlandish. No clue what to do next, he laughed at them all.

The excitement rose in Bandit as the north line of guardsmen came into view, but still no farmer. Had he somehow slipped the trap? The guardsmen were nearly toe-to-toe with those from the south when an elderly merchant in one of the colorful market stalls shouted something and pointed up to his right. Following the man's finger, with mouth agape, Bandit goggled at the farmer scaling the city wall. Not only had he never seen anyone do that before, he did not even know it was possible. He stood amid the forest of faces gazing at the incredible spectacle.

Feeling cocky for having just bested the entire city guard, for good measure Conner gave them all a bumptious salute—that unfortunately threw him off balance. To avoid tumbling back into the angry hornets' nest he had worked so hard to get away from, he jerked backward. But his exhausted muscles failed him, and in a flurry of awkward spasms, he rolled past the back ledge of the wall.

The Eastland farmer disappeared over the wall and Bandit shook his head in new appreciation for the young man. He personally would have rather faced an enraged mob of guardsmen here than what waited on the other side of *that* wall. The thief laughed at the farmer's spunk.

Bandit turned to leave, but the vise-like grip of gauntleted hands held him in place. He gazed up into the familiar face of the brawny guardsman he had encountered in the market, his surly grimace replaced with a smile that did nothing to improve the guard's looks.

Conner braced himself for the consequences of his reckless action. He could only hope he would be healthy and conscious enough to slip away from the city before the guardsmen took up the chase once more. So the cushioning of his impact by a large, furry object caught him completely by surprise. Of course, this did not compare to the surprise of the animal upon whose back Conner had so rudely landed. Before he could move, the massive beast bolted, flipping him hard to the ground. Conner lifted his head and gazed at the backside of a very large bear.

Of course, he had heard enough stories about brown bears to be concerned. The fact that they preferred plants and berries did not preclude them eating mammals, especially ones who dropped in uninvited. And if breadth was any indication, this bear had dined on many a fatty food besides nuts. Cautiously, Conner backed away on hands and knees, hoping the bear saw his movement as amicable. He did not have to wait for a reaction. With amazing agility, the bear spun about. Its huge maw inches from Conner's face, the bear roared. Tongue, teeth, and tonsils filled Conner's view. Hot breath rushed across his face. Any caution remaining in him rapidly dissolved into complete and utter fear.

Sweat sparkled off the bodies in the late daylight. The array of Warriors aligned in front of Marcantos had not even been afforded time to pin their long hair back, so matted strands clung to their necks and stung their eyes. A hushed crowd of spectators pressed close, filling the cramped spaces in the keep's ward where afternoon shade provided relief. The only creature truly content in the broiling heat was Marcantos's bond, sunning himself against the western wall, snorting and twitching as he dreamed of chasing elk through a mountain pass.

To his left, Marcantos regarded Huffy, who gazed back with antipathy through bruised, swollen eyes, his broken nose bandaged to his face. He gauged the condition of the other Warriors in formation; each was beyond exhaustion, intent faces flush from the training. He nodded in satisfaction.

"Again!" he called out, assuming the low fighting stance, his thighs parallel to the ground, feet flat, arms wide with palms up. The formation of Warriors mirrored him; a few in the back grunted, legs quivering.

Marcantos closed his eyes and shifted his weight, extending his right leg to the side. Change begins with the stripping away of the heavy burdens and clutter of a complicated life. Sadly, these are the things people cling to most desperately, and yet they have no redeeming value in one's improvement, his old sage would say. The moments wore on in the heat; the only sounds were those of labored breath and pained groans. He shifted his weight to his left.

A crescendo of shouts near the keep's entrance grew steadily, finally breaking his concentration. Before Marcantos could bark his irritation, his bond let out a deafening roar. Surprise and anger coursed through their link. Instinctively, he spun about, drawing his sword in defense of his bond. Next to Copious squatted a lad in freeman clothes. Marcantos stepped forward, the boy turning about to run. But the sharp tip of Marcantos's sword put that thought to rest.

Conner stiffened, his eyes focused on the sword pressed against his chest. Still, he could not help but admire the weapon's masterful workmanship, from the dark, intricately woven patterns and symbols running the length of the polished blade to the inset insignia of the Warriors Order beneath the cross guard to the tightly woven leather grip and gold-inlaid pommel. It did not take a fighter to note that the muscled arm holding the sword belonged to someone quite skilled. Stripped to his waist, a gleam of sweat covered the well-toned and lithe body.

Conner's gaze continued to the face of the sword owner, a man he judged to be thirty. Shoulder-length brown hair hung damp about his face. He wore a friendly smile that did not go to his eyes. And he stood quite at ease, regarding Conner as if considering whether to purchase a choice dinner steak.

The swordsman ran his point up Conner's chest. Placing it under his chin, he pressed upward. Conner rose cautiously in response.

Adrenaline pulsed hard through his veins, blood pounded in his ears. His muscles shook as much from panic as from his climb. A practiced swordsman in front, an angry bear behind, and a hostile mob of city guardsmen over the wall, this was shaping up to be an adventure worthy of even Pauli's praise. *You can't always change your circumstances, but you can change how you see them,* his mother would say. But at that particular moment, every angle of the situation looked hopeless.

Marcantos studied the source of his bond's irritation, guiding the boy up on his feet to get a better look. "Well, Copious, what catch did you drag home today?"

The bear growled irritably through a wide-mouthed yawn.

The boy appeared to be sincerely frightened, eyes frozen on Marcantos's weapon. No doubt, the realization he had stepped into a pit of vipers was getting through.

Palastar really did need to improve the security in the keep! "Sergeant at Arms!" Marcantos called in irritation. "Who let this . . . *Eastlander*," he spat, "into the keep?"

A tall soldier at the entrance cleared his throat. "Apologies, my lord, but he did not come this way."

"Then how . . ." Marcantos scanned up the wall, measuring the distance. He could not recall ever hearing that Eastland farmers could climb walls barehanded. Such feats were reserved for certain ordermen. Another altercation broke out at the entrance, where a rugged sergeant of the city guard was foolishly attempting to force his way past the keep soldiers. "What do you want, Sergeant?" Marcantos asked loud enough to be heard over the argument.

The sergeant sneered and pushed past the two keep soldiers blocking his way. Poking a stubby finger in the direction of the Eastlander, he responded with the kind of Narwalen accent Marcantos found abrasive. "'im, mi'lord! He 'as been eludin' us for near on most of the day. I am just glad my lord didn't run 'im through yet, though he definitely 'as it comin' to 'im."

Marcantos knew the wretched man. A nasty fellow, he abused everyone below in rank or status, and groveled at the feet of those above. He was the kind of person that made the Warrior's stomach knot. After inspecting the Eastlander again, he spoke so all could hear. "So, what are you? A murderer? A thief?"

The city guardsman clarified, "Sire, he attacked a young lad in the marketplace, then resisted arrest."

Marcantos shouted back, "I wasn't talking to you, Sergeant!" The guardsman truly was insufferable. Eyes locked on the boy, he demanded, "Well? What? Speak!"

The boy swallowed hard, a hundred pairs of eyes upon him. "I am . . . was passing through to the north, sir, and came into the city to acquire some supplies when the young boy he referred to attempted to pickpocket me."

It was the look of fire in the boy's eyes that most held Marcantos's attention. "And here I always thought Cravenrock pickpockets were good at their practice." Laughter erupted around the ward walls, but the boy did not reply. At least the boy had sense to know when to speak. So, an Eastlander boy entered the city, successfully prevented a Cravenrock thief from pickpocketing him, got away from the city guards, eluded them for hours, then climbed over a wall ten paces high using just his hands and feet. Well, if the boy was an Anarchic spy, he was a good one. The simplest explanations were most often correct. Still, Marcantos could not hand the boy over to the city guard without being certain. The local marshal would administer punishment for breaking Common Law, a simple slap on the wrists before letting him go. But if he was a spy, High Law of the Realm would have jurisdiction over him. Then Reina, the baroness of Cravenrock and cousin to the queen, would be forced to administer punishment. That made him smile. It would at least bring some excitement into his days of doldrums.

Marcantos stepped back. Turning his blade down, he tossed the sword toward the boy. "Catch," he commanded, and observed the boy's response. The boy's hand shot out, easily finding the grip; but he remained motionless, uncertain what to do next. After a dozen heartbeats, Marcantos said to the boy, as if it were obvious, "I want you to attack me."

The boy scanned the ward nervously.

A few Warriors shifted behind him, making the boy wary. "I believe I am already in enough trouble, sir. You should take this back." He held the sword out to Marcantos.

"Humor me, Eastlander. You won't get into any more trouble than you are in already. In fact, I'll make you a promise. If you can make me yield with that sword, I will make sure the city guardsmen do not arrest you. You have my word." He failed to mention that if a farm boy could best him with a sword, he would be arrested by the keep's commander as a spy.

"What weapon will you use, sir?" the boy asked with apprehension.

"No weapon. I will fight as I am." Marcantos raised his bare arms, showing he carried no weapons. He let the boy weigh each of his very few options. "Do we have a deal?"

The Eastlander shifted to the side to move clear of Copious, who sat on his haunches rubbing sleep from his face, the boy's offense forgotten. The boy lifted the blade carefully between them. Committed, he said, "I don't seem to have much of a choice."

Marcantos smiled back. "We seldom do."

The Warrior did not move, intently focused on how the boy carried himself with sword in hand. Any Anarchist spy would at least be trained in basic fighting styles, if not advanced ones. Their training left telltale signs impossible to mask, even if the spy believed he knew how. By the time the boy moved, Marcantos was ready.

The sword flashed forward in an awkward thrust. Marcantos noted with slight interest that the boy's feet were too close together to stop his forward momentum. And the edges of the blade were poorly positioned—vertically instead of horizontally—making him vulnerable to a counterattack. The sword shuddered as it neared his chest.

Marcantos twisted to his left, sidestepping the sword point. Slipping forward, his chest toward the outstretched blade, he ran his right forearm up the side. In one fluid motion, Marcantos slapped his right hand down on the upturned cross guard and pulled hard, bringing the boy off balance. Moving parallel with the blade, he brought his left arm up, driving his elbow into the boy's forehead. The force snapped the boy's head back; his body followed. Simultaneously, Marcantos twisted the cross guard toward him, wrenching the sword easily from the boy's hand. The grip of the precisely balanced sword slid effortlessly into Marcantos's right hand, point down and away, as the boy tumbled to the ground amid a rising cloud of dust. The Eastlander lay prone, legs splayed wide, attempting to shake the fog from his head.

Marcantos sheathed his sword. Certain the boy was not a spy, he waved the sergeant forward to take him.

The burly sergeant flashed a yellow, toothy grin, then lurched forward with several more city guardsmen to greedily collect their prize.

Marcantos stopped in front of the Warriors. They had clearly lost both their formation and their mental focus for more training, so he dismissed them with a wave. He would pick up again tomorrow, possibly moving on to the next set of forms.

Foxy stepped forward to let the guardsmen pass, clumsily lugging their half-conscious prisoner back to the keep's entrance. Marcantos took in her form, the trim sleekness of her body, tightness of muscle, her catlike step.

She moved in close, measuring him as if unsure how to judge his actions. "You take unnecessary risks, and for what? To determine whether a farm boy is a spy?"

He filed away for later consideration her failure to recognize his superior rank and status. He would also find time to ask her why she had hesitated in her attack during their fight earlier that day. For now, he said, "Do not search for complex motives where there are none. Where is the adventure without risk? Besides, no truth worth uncovering was ever found without taking chances." Scanning the ward, he found Copious rubbing his back against the wall near the entrance to the ward. He walked away, sensing Foxy's eyes upon him.

The Bloodied Messenger

Friarwood brooded in the dark, secluded corner of the keep's hall near the entrance to the ward while the afternoon's events played out. He did not like crowds, and Marcantos was already gathering quite a collection of onlookers. That was no real surprise. Marcantos was not just a high-ranking member of the Warriors Order. He was not even just one of the few grandmaster Warriors under forty. He was, without question, the most skilled Warrior in over three hundred years. And it would be years before he reached his full potential.

Friarwood sneered at those who had come to gawk at the Warrior extraordinaire. What had attracted most of these cretins on a moment's notice was not his mastery of the sword. Those who gawked were too stupid to recognize the beauty of true art in motion. No. It was that Marcantos would surely be Griffinrock's next Champion of the Realm. As word spread that someone of his stature was in Cravenrock Keep's ward teaching basic forms to those of the Warriors Order, it was bound to attract the curiosity of every fool who had a morning hour to waste and could bully their way into the keep.

An hour ago Friarwood had been numb. Now he was incensed. Nothing was entertaining about this business. He was forced to stand there sulking in the dark while the young man frittered away his hours with his new . . . pets! It was enough to make his body ache.

For the fourth time that day, leaving no details unconsidered, he replayed how Marcantos had come to his quarters speaking of his agreement with Colonel Palastar to train all the keep's Warriors for the next fortnight. Friarwood's suspicions kept hanging on the part about Marcantos being honor-bound by his earlier actions in the ward, rendering two masters incapable of performing their duties. In Friarwood's eyes, they deserved what they got, if not more.

A fortnight! He shook with rage.

Friarwood tapped his left forefinger to pursed lips in irritation. What had he missed? The glow of a black onyx stone with spiraling bands of deep blue inset on his large gold ring cast shifting shadows in the dark corner of the wall. He must extract something more useful from the young man to help understand his motives, his reasoning. He needed that understanding, because if he did not glean the logic, he would have to surmise the young man was starting to crumble under the duress of his training. And he did not want to consider that, not when they were so close to achieving his objectives.

Nor would Friarwood accept that being distracted by his other responsibilities might have jeopardized his primary assignment. The council of his true order would not appreciate that. He could juggle more than one knife. He clenched his hand tight, the sneer returning. He was so close! Watching Marcantos discover his prowess in using Anarchic Sight had been thrilling. The most challenging aspect, though also the most rewarding in a twisted way, had been training the great Warrior so that even he was unaware of what he was learning.

The dispersing crowd shook Friarwood from his worries. Fighting back a gnawing impatience, he moved to the entrance only to have a large city guardsman step on his foot while ineffectively directing two more through the portal. A dirty, semiconscious boy dangled between them.

"Here!" the guardsman rounded on whoever had gotten in his way. Recognition flooded the guard's face and he immediately went into the bootlicking act typical of the city guard. "Extreme apologies, mi'lord Friarwood. I did not be seein' you there in the entrance. We do be tryin' to remove this spirited fellow from your graces, though, so please be forgivin' us for any troubles." He flashed a pathetic, cringing grin.

Friarwood stepped to the side and waved them through. "Just get on with it." He watched their comical antics with detached interest. They were all so inept.

Marcantos's pace stuttered as his eyes locked with Friarwood's. The dark-clothed mentor silently shadowed Marcantos into the solace of the keep entry, then on up the stairwell. Copious ambled along behind, looking content to be in the cooler tower. Entering Friarwood's quarters, Marcantos could no longer take his preceptor's quiet nipping at his heels. "I know what you're going to say, Blake, but I have made up my mind."

Friarwood scanned the room, then turned his glare on his student. Of all of the qualities the younger man possessed, stubbornness was at the front of the line. But he had no intention of occupying these substandard living quarters longer than necessary. The room offered none of the luxuries Friarwood had come to appreciate since rising through the Warriors Order ranks. "Maybe you don't fully appreciate how tenuous our current position is," he said in a forced quiet voice.

Marcantos rounded on him. "And what is *our* position, Blake? As I see it, *my* position, my responsibility, is to be fully prepared for the honor of my Realm and my order to assume the reins as the next queen's champion"—he threw his arms up in the air—"whenever that unfortunate moment arrives, Harmonics protect our queen. Every thought, decision, and deed I make is toward that goal. I thought you would see it that way, or at least not fight me over it."

Friarwood patiently patted the air in front of him to soothe the younger man's emotional state. "I do not question your goal, Marcantos. What I question is your strategy for achieving it."

Disarmed, the younger Warrior sighed.

Friarwood took the advantage, considering how best to direct his pupil's thinking. Creating the right mental condition in another was like making a potion, though it had been a long time since he had done that. Having the right ingredients was of no use if you did not know the right proportions and mix them in the proper sequence.

He continued. "This is not a matter of my not trusting your just cause." Friarwood rolled his eyes skyward for dramatic effect. "Astral Beings help me, I do believe in your cause." Another precisely timed pause would help before a gentle reminder of his seniority, at least in age, to keep Marcantos in doubt before he ran off making any more rash promises. "But what you do speaks of an inexperience I would expect from someone your age."

"My actions in the ward are not as rash as you, or anyone else for that matter, might perceive, Blake," Marcantos replied in his own defense. "Everything has been weighed and measured." He spoke as a man trying to convince himself.

Friarwood gripped Marcantos by the shoulders. "If I am going to be your preceptor, you must trust me, Marcantos. You must rely on my wisdom as a swordsman." He emphasized this last part while resting his hand on his pupil's shoulder, a touch of pleading in his voice, laced with just enough respect to balance the inherent threat.

He continued more deliberately, giving his pupil a chance to consider his words. "If you do assume the reins as the next queen's champion, and I see no reason why you won't, don't you want to be the best champion possible? Is it not noble to ensure that you offer Veressa and our Harmonic blessed Realm your full potential to guarantee the queen's security?"

Marcantos responded. "That was the reason for my decision, Blake. But I feel off center, like the ground is shifting under my feet." His voice had a haunting uncertainty as Marcantos considered the new sensations.

Friarwood's artificial smile shifted to one of true delight. This was the piece of the puzzle he had been searching for. He patted Marcantos's arm lightly. "What you feel is normal, Marcantos. That is why it is so critical to listen to my instructions. You are at an important juncture in your training. You must proceed unhindered by superfluous distractions." Facing his student directly, he took a serious posture while gripping both of the younger man's shoulders. "The Mental vision you experienced this morning is but a small taste of what is possible. But you must cultivate it, nurture it. You must learn to control it; otherwise, it will control you. Do you understand?"

Marcantos nodded submissively. "Of course, Blake. You are right, as always."

Friarwood caught a slight movement at the corner of his eye. He glanced to the doorway of his quarters. Something about the shadows in the hall was off. Turning his back to Marcantos, he lightly waved his fingers. *"Ora eftos anakaprosopo,"* he whispered, casting a simple Earth spell, something no true Warrior could do or detect. Just past the door was the shallow breathing of a large man. His brow furrowed. "Good," he said to Marcantos through clenched teeth. "Then we will make do with what we have to work with. Since you have assumed the duties over the keep's Warrior apprentices, it is only proper you continue. But we must set a few limits; otherwise, we won't have time to advance your skills. Are we in agreement?"

Marcantos hesitated, then diverted his eyes from Friarwood's intense examination. "Of course," he agreed with complete lack of conviction.

Palastar slipped from the doorway and retreated upstairs to his office, then sat at his desk for several minutes, drumming out stress with pudgy fingers. Sensing Palastar's tension, Garren nudged his other hand with a nose dry from midday heat.

Palastar rubbed the wolf's furry ears absently. He was not cut out for life this close to the Borderlands. He wished he had been properly instructed in the techniques of espionage. The idea of spies, intrigue, and secrets of the Realm made him queasy. He needed an easier job more central to the Realm.

After some mental exertion, he decided to send a message to the general straightaway, while events were fresh in his mind, even though Grimwaldt had only left that morning. Removing a small parchment from a drawer, he dipped his favorite ostrich-feather quill into the small bottle of ink. His message should be terse since others would read it before the general arrived. Carefully, tongue pressed against his lip to steady his hand, he wrote in flowery lettering:

> General G., be aware, your concerns in the matter mentioned seem well justified. I will continue as instructed. —Colonel P.

Once certain the message contained no grammatical errors, he slipped the tightly rolled parchment inside a hollow metal band. He licked his lips nervously and, with some effort, proceeded up the long stairs to the top level in the tower, Garren at his side. There, a guard standing behind the stairs snapped to attention. Palastar jumped, nearly dropping the metal band down the stairwell.

"Colonel," the guard said formally, eyes straight ahead.

Palastar hesitated, wondering if the guard had noticed his jump. Then stepping to the door on the right, he acknowledged the guard so as not to raise any suspicions. "Good work, soldier. I want to check the condition of the room here. Please make sure I am not disturbed."

The guard nodded stoically.

Palastar waited, expecting a verbal reply, but when none came, he cautiously opened the door. The small room he entered was hot. He tried to ignore the intense, pungent odor as he closed the door behind, taking one last nervous look at the guard. Garren waited in the hall.

Except for a number of wooden cages on tables around the walls, the room was void of furnishings. A bucket of grain and one of water sat behind the door. Pieces of the same straw lining the bottoms of the cages littered the stone floor. In each cage were three to ten pigeons of various colors. Some nested in the thick straw while others paced about. In front of the cage doors were signs with names of various places in the three Realms.

Palastar stepped to the cage marked *Loren Canyon*. After observing the birds for a moment, he decided not to rely on any pigeon nesting contently. He reached in and snatched one near the door. Once the metal band was secured on the protesting pigeon's leg, he stepped to the narrow window facing south and pushed the pigeon through the small gap.

Friarwood marked the minutes while he and his pupil discussed limits on Marcantos's instructional time. In the end, they agreed that Marcantos's lessons would be conducted privately an hour after Hemera's rise. This would ensure Friarwood the opportunity to work with Marcantos alone.

After Friarwood ushered Marcantos from his study with a groggy Copious lumbering behind, he stepped to Carnia's perch. The peregrine falcon, her feathers ruffled, hopped lightly on his arm. He moved to the balcony.

Heat from the dark city wall made the vast plains shimmer. Friarwood waited. After a few minutes, a pigeon appeared from a narrow window farther up the keep's tower, winging south. He lightly petted Carnia. "It seems you will eat well this afternoon." He stretched his arm out and his bond took flight. The warm updrafts lifted her swiftly as she darted south, her meal in sight. Friarwood continued to wait anxiously on the hot terrace. It was not long before his eyes opened wide, his body tensing, letting the exalted rush of emotions from the falcon's kill flood through him.

Shortly, Carnia flew back through the balcony and fluttered gracefully to her perch, the bloody carcass of a pigeon in her talons. Friarwood stroked his bird as he gently plucked the lifeless form from her grasp. He removed the metal band from the dangling leg, then tossed the remains to the grassy plains below.

Carnia screeched her frustration, but Friarwood was busy now. He opened the parchment, scowling at the flowery cursive before crushing the note in his bloody fist. As if dealing with Marcantos's rash behavior was not enough, he would have to add one more item to the list of assorted tasks that had brought him to Cravenrock under the guise of Marcantos's training. Yet another knife to juggle, even if only briefly.

No matter. Such was the way of those whose never-ending task was to sow chaos and discord. He would continue with what he did best: adapt to a changing situation. He pondered ways he might turn this new development to his advantage as he carefully lit the parchment with tinder he had removed from a box. The right push, an adjustment here, a nudge there, Friarwood could still achieve all his objectives. Dark smoke curled up as the paper turned to ash. It would require more attentive nurturing, more hands-on direction, and the assistance of the able assistant he had procured. There were always risks, but new seeds could be brought to bear good fruit.

Part III

Life's meaning is found in the relationships developed over the course of time. Bonds are but one way to guide a Being toward a deeper understanding and expression of self. Family, friends, even strangers—each relationship is like a mirror into the soul. If one wants to truly see their essence, they need merely examine the relationships they cultivate.

—The Modei Book of Air (Second Book)

A Pact in the Dark

The stockade had been deathly quiet for several hours when the gloomy occupant heard the muffled voices outside the cell. The hall fell silent, and the cell's occupant let out a discouraged sigh. But jingling keys and the metallic click of the door's lock renewed his interest.

The wooden door swung wide in response to a booted kick, and a tall, thin man sailed through the dark portal, arms flailing in a futile attempt to control his descent to the stone floor. Even as the man let out an audible grunt from the impact, he was on his feet and running for the entrance. The door slammed shut, casting the cell into a blur of muted grays. "You should have paid for the disturbance!" A deep voice snarled from outside as the lock clicked back in place.

After the new arrival made several frantic attempts to pull the door open with his fingers, he stepped back and kicked it hard with another grunt. For several minutes he stared at the impassive door, then jumped as if stung. He patted down his sides and, after not finding what he was looking for, rummaged through the straw where he had been thrown. Shortly, the man dropped hard to the floor. Stuffing head in hands, he groaned yet again.

There was something familiar about the new occupant. Plans formed and the gloomy prisoner stirred from the shadows of the corner.

Defeat had taken Conner. How could everything go so wrong so quickly? All the emotional ups and downs of attempting to escape from a punishment for a crime he did not commit, and for what? To be stripped of all possessions and coin, then beaten by guardsmen bent on taking out their anger and indignation upon his ribs. He lightly touched the goose egg on his forehead, compliments of the master swordsman. *Okay, Mom, where is the good in this?* He turned his focus on his dank surroundings to fight off the growing sense of hopelessness.

The stockade was an old brick building butted against the north side of the keep's wall. The repulsive stench was enough to reason why it had been constructed far from any city traffic. The guards had marched him past a large metal door on rollers where two more stood watch. One wide dirt hallway ran through the middle of the building. A vaulted ceiling extended nearly to the slanted thatched roof eight paces above. Along each side of the hall was a series of doors. It was through one of these that Conner had been so unceremoniously tossed.

With the weak light coming through the narrow slats in the poorly maintained roof far above, Conner surveyed his new residence. The room was square and large, with a gap between the side walls and the ceiling higher up. The door, which had no latch or pull, was made of tightly pressed hardwood boards held together with several strips of unfinished steel. Whoever had constructed the building had chosen to use the keep's northern dark wall as the back of the cells; the remaining walls had been constructed from the same brick used throughout the city. The thatched roof ran diagonally downward from the keep's wall, covering the entire stockade. A thick layer of damp straw, the source of the stockade's smell, covered a mortared stone floor. In the front corner of the cell hung two buckets, one leaking water. The overall impression of the building was that it had been haphazardly converted from an old barn, likely once used to stable horses belonging to the keep's soldiers.

From the back of the cell came the sound of rustling straw. Conner jumped, crouching low. The sodden straw fell away and he recognized the stirring form. "You!" he snarled, and lurched forward to throttle the source of his consternation.

Bandit threw his arms up to shield himself from the approaching angry farmer. "Please, don't be hurtin' me, sir. I know it was my fault you be in this, but you can't be faultin' me for doing my job."

The Eastlander pulled up short, fists taut. "Did anyone ever tell you that you have a pathetic job?"

Bandit contemplated his short past. "A few, but since no one do be offerin' me something better, I don't be seein' I have much choice in the matter."

That defused the Eastlander's anger. "It seems many of us are short on choices," he stated with a sigh, as if reciting something he had heard recently. "What is your name?"

The boy lowered his arms. "People do be callin' me Bandit, sir." He peered at the Eastlander over knobby knees pulled tight to his chest.

The Eastlander squatted, unwilling to sit in the stink rising from the wet straw. "Don't call me sir. My name is Conner."

"As you will."

"Bandit." Conner considered the name. "I guess that explains a lot. Just how did you end up with this job of yours?"

Bandit grew unsettled. It was the first time anyone had asked him anything about his past. He studied the Eastlander, but he could detect no obscure meaning to Conner's question. In spite of his nature, he told the truth.

At the age of six, hidden behind a wooden crate at the end of a dirty Cravenrock street, Bandit had watched his parents die at the hands of a gang for their few coins. After surviving on his own for several months, a transient woman trapper found him and, feeling some semblance of pity, fostered the boy. After a year of failed attempts, the trapper was resigned to the fact that the boy was a habitual thief. If the boy was going to steal, the trapper reasoned, then he needed to be good enough to stay out of prison. So the trapper trained the boy in a skill she had learned early in her life—the fine art of pickpocketing. The boy had exceptional talent and was a quick study. After his second year, it was clear the boy had learned everything the trapper could teach him. So she took the boy to Pirate, the leader of the Cravenrock Thieves Guild, who agreed to take care of him, giving him the name he used. Without a word, the trapper had walked away. Bandit never saw her again.

Bandit had not thought of the trapper in the three years since, but as he relayed his brief story, one of the trapper's lessons came to him. *If you want to bag a quality pelt, boy, there are four essential steps you must always follow. First you have to have the right bait to attract the right animal; otherwise you will needlessly waste an animal's life and your time. Second, you have to take the time to hide the trap well. An animal won't take the bait if it sees the trap, no matter how good the bait may be. Third, you must be patient. You never want to scare away your prize before it has sprung the trap, or it will surely get away. And lastly, and this is important, boy, having the animal in the trap does no good if you can't get it out without damaging the pelt.*

It was this lesson, Bandit realized, that would not only get him out of the stockade, but would get him back into Pirate's good graces, the Cosmos willing. Tossing Conner in the cell with him was as good as tossing in the key to the door.

Bandit started probing into where Conner was from and how he had learned to climb walls, but these provided nothing valuable for Bandit's plan. But when he asked Conner why he was in Cravenrock . . .

"I am on my trek. As I said to that city guardsman, I am just passing through." Conner hesitated, turning to gaze at, or through, the wall to the northwest. He snatched up a fistful of wet straw and threw it violently at the door. "I can't stay here. I need to go." His voice was anxious and lost.

Here was the bait Bandit had been looking for. He had heard being prevented from finishing the Calling could be a powerful fear. He shifted nervously. "Don't be expectin' to be out of here soon if you be thinkin' of walkin' through that door. The city magistrate is a busy woman these days with all the transients passing through of late. Besides, she is sure to be wantin' you to be stewin' in this cell a while. I wouldn't be surprised if it be one or two fortnights before she be callin' you in for a ruling." He let Conner deliberate on this overstretched truth, then continued. "Then again, I suppose since you lost your coin, you don't be havin' much reason to be in a hurry to leave."

Conner stiffened, eyes hard on Bandit. The boy braced for a tirade of blame. Instead, Conner said, "The magistrate won't let those guardsmen keep my coins. She'll make them give my money back." As soon as he spoke, he realized how foolish the words made him. There had not been much energy behind them anyway. "She will, won't she? She'll make them give them back?"

Bandit let his silence speak what Conner knew to be true. But to be sure, he followed up. "I suspect most of the coin be already spent on Narwalen ale to be fillin' their bloated bellies while we do be sittin' here rottin'." He tossed a particularly bad-smelling clump of straw to the corner of the cell. He had the bait; now, to set the trap. "No matter. Unless you know another way out, you'll probably be hung shortly after you're called in anyway," he lied.

Conner glared at him skeptically. "They wouldn't hang me even if I had done all the things they say. Once I explain my story to the magistrate, she'll have no reason to hold me longer. I have done nothing wrong."

Bandit realized he had pushed Conner too far, but pulling back would make him more suspicious. Besides, he had always heard Eastlanders were a bit dimwitted when it came to Realm law. He had no choice but to set the trap here. "Ahh. Yes, you're right. I'm sure the magistrate will be lettin' you go. Causin' a citywide manhunt for the mornin', disruptin' the town's busiest market, breakin' into a keep of the Realm, and disturbin' ordermen and the Queen's Defenders doesn't sound like any reason to be holdin' you. Never mind the entire city council, along with the magistrate, will likely be called in to be explainin' to the countess why their guardsmen were so inept at catchin' you. I'm sure they'll be quite understandin' of your story."

Conner blew a sigh through pursed lips, then sank into the straw, stench and rot forgotten.

Bandit regarded Conner's dejected look. He wanted to be open with the Eastlander, but could not take a chance that he might not willingly go along with his plan. Getting back to his life hinged on Conner's assistance. Besides, the trap was set. It was best to be patient and see if the Eastlander took the bait. The two sat quietly through the remainder of the day.

At what had to be near dusk, Bandit heard a cart rattle to a stop outside the cell. A small hinged slot above the buckets popped open, letting a speck of lamplight into the darkened room. Inquisitive, Conner watched, though Bandit had a good idea what came next. A large tin ladle appeared through the slot, and a thick, gray porridge was gracelessly dumped into the bucket. A moment passed before a guardsman's eye peered through.

After scrutinizing the two, the guardsman let out a laugh near to the edge of madness. Apparently satisfied with what he saw, he whispered, "Oh, but I do be hearin' you have got the whole city guard up in a ruckus this afternoon, boy. I do believe the treats you got today won't be comparin' much to what's to happen to you soon." The slot slammed shut as quick as it had opened, plunging the room once again into darkness. The cart rattled away with the guardsman's dissolving laugh.

"Okay, what do you suggest we do?" Conner asked.

The Mistress of Good Fortune was with Bandit after all. The trap was about to spring. He replied with disinterest, "What 'we' are you referring to?"

Conner jerked at the question. "I thought you had an idea how to get out of here."

Bandit waited a moment before he lied. "I am not the one who do be needin' to get out of here. In a few days, they'll be releasin' me, though I really think I prefer it here." He took in the room admiringly, adding a toothy smile for dramatic effect, though he doubted Conner could see him. "They do be feedin' me better here, and I don't be gettin' rained on. Besides, when I do be gettin' out, I'll probably be beat for getting caught. Why would I want to be in a hurry to be leavin'?"

"I can't stay here for a fortnight, Bandit. I have to get out. Now, do you have a way or not?" Conner was growing desperate.

"It's possible, but I would have to be goin' with you. Since I am in no hurry, what do I be gettin' out of it?"

"What do you want?" Conner was quick to ask.

Bandit paused, feigning contemplation of something to negotiate. "I do be thinkin' it possible, Conner, we can both be gettin' what we do be wantin' out of this."

"Go on then. I'm listening." Conner leaned forward, not wanting to miss anything important.

"As I see it, you be needin' some coin to purchase your supplies and be on your way." Bandit could sense Conner nodding. "I will agree to help you get back on your trek if you be doin' somethin' for me that will get me back into the Thieves Guild without gettin' beat."

Conner rocked back. "What would I have to do?" he asked suspiciously.

Bandit leaned closer, his voice soft. "You do be havin' exceptional abilities, Conner. You would make a great thief. By now, everyone in the guild has heard of you climbin' the keep's wall and keepin' the entire city guard at bay. The guildmaster would jump at the chance to be enlistin' someone with your talent. I will be helpin' you if you go back with me to the guild. That way, I can be tellin' the guildmaster I let myself get captured so I could convince you to join."

Conner was doubtful about this. "I have never stolen anything in my life, and I don't think I am ready to start."

"You just be needin' to take enough jobs to put coins in your pocket and be on the road again, and surely in half the time you be spendin' rottin' in this stockade. Not to mention the city don't be payin' you to sit here." Bandit could hear the trap snap closed. Conner moved like a man caught in the trawls of the trap's bite. "So, what do you be sayin'?"

"I say I don't have much of a choice." Conner stretched the stiffness out of his exhausted muscles. "This trek so far has been nothing but choosing from one option," Bandit heard him mumble.

Bandit fought off pangs of guilt—a rather unfamiliar emotion. It was time to skin this animal; he had a pelt to sell. "Good. I suggest you be gettin' some dinner down. You'll be needin' your strength later tonight."

An Assassin's Night

The dark form, who sometimes called himself Lacerus, waited motionless on a northern mid-level balcony of Cravenrock Keep's tower. Erebus was but a waxing sliver in the western sky, so the man was certain any passing eyes would not notice him there. Black robes, with their dark Modeic symbols, wavered in the light breeze through the tower hall, cooling the dark stone and bringing its sleeping occupants fleeting relief from the summer heat. The Night Vision spell he had cast illuminated the Narwalen Plains below in an eerie impression of shifting, vibrant grays and greens. Farther on, the outline of the Dragon's Back Mountains formed the jagged horizon of the night sky. It was, by all accounts, the perfect evening for the work at hand.

It had been too long since Lacerus had taken up a quarry, so the anticipation was intoxicating. He took several deep breaths to slow his pounding heart. Some bonds could sense the emotional rush of a pending kill. And he could not afford to be thwarted, not tonight. Once settled, the form made a few slight hand gestures and whispered an ancient incantation. *"Aerora eftos fotivaros."* His hands and feet tingled in response.

One last check for any guards along the keep's wall and the black form placed his palms to the tower's stone, climbing the wall with the agility of a spider. He proceeded first vertically over the balcony entrance, then diagonally upward to the tower's western face. His eyes fixed on a large balcony above, he moved with singular purpose.

Slowing at the balcony railing, the Assassin sniffed the air for any spells of protection.

In a single fluid motion, the form glided nimbly over the railing and landed with the lightness of a leaf. He waited to be certain he had not been discovered. A shadow's shadow, he floated through the balcony entrance and drifted through the bedchamber, eyes glowing from his vision spell. The room was sparse. To the left was a cabinet, straight ahead a desk, devoid of material except for a white ostrich-quill pen and a small bottle of ink. A single person lay in the large bed to his right.

Drifting closer, he examined the body as it emitted light snores. He removed a small vial from his breast pocket then broke the seal, letting its contents mix. One ingredient was a rather mild sedative powder made by grinding the dried leaf from a marbleblade. The other was a tasteless, inert liquid extracted from gin root. Combined in the proper proportions known only by those of the Necromancers Order, the two items created a deadly, though painless, poison. The potency of the poison lasted only a few minutes, making the source of the victim's death impossible to trace. Working quickly, the black form held the vial over the sleeping body's lips. Two drops, the vial's entire contents, fell into the large man's mouth.

The Assassin watched the poison take effect with curious fascination. He could sense the slowing heart rate and slight cooling in the cheeks. But he could not tarry; the man's bond would wake when it sensed its human's reclamation. Reluctantly, he pulled away from the seductive drama. The dark form who sometimes called himself Lacerus slipped over the balcony and evanesced into the night as Garren awoke next to Palastar's bed and howled a mournful cry.

Escape

Despite Bandit's growing frustration, Conner had the young boy go through the escape plan a third time, searching for any flaws in the plan's logic. He had to believe it was fully thought-out to have the steely confidence he needed to pull it off. But truth be told, his lack of confidence had nothing to do with his abilities or the plan. There was no real challenge in the tasks Bandit described. He simply did not trust Bandit. Something about the boy ate at him, but he was helpless to pinpoint what it was. Conner did have a second option. Knowing the plan, he could leave the boy in the cell and be on his way, never to look back. But in his heart, he knew he could not.

Yes, he blamed Bandit for having put him into this situation, but Conner had made a promise. Now it was a matter of Eastlander honor. Besides, the thought of the trapper leaving Bandit with thieves tore at Conner's compassion. It would never come to that, no matter the cost. He would carry through on his part of the bargain, even if Bandit might not do the same.

Bandit slipped close. "It's time," he whispered.

Conner inhaled deep and stretched, grimacing at the bruising on his ribs. He had tried eating some of the porridge, but between its foul smell and the nervous stomach knots he had developed while they discussed their escape, he could not get the slop past his nose. He would try this tired and hungry. But one thing was certain—if he failed, he would not have enough energy to attempt the escape again until the next night. He had but this one opportunity.

He stepped to the back of the cell and ran his fingers up the keep's wall to find the narrow spacing between the stones, as he had done that morning. He tested his grip. Raw fingertips throbbed, stabs of pain shot up his hands, arms, and shoulders. As before, he cleared away all anxiety, retreating to a place away from the physical world and his body's pain.

He focused on how impressed he was with Bandit, more streetwise than any twelve-year-old he had ever known. That, of course, concerned Conner, but since he could not plan for betrayal, he would deal with such events as they came. He thought about how he missed Pattria's reassuring smile. He could have used it now. He thought of Pauli, who would enjoy nothing more than to hear Conner relate his tale, entertained by his misadventures. All this sharpened his nerve. He would return home, if for no better reason than to see the astonished looks on all their faces.

His eyes level with the top of the cell wall to his left, Conner cautiously reached over. Immediately, he knew he had made a mistake. His other hand would not take the added weight. In desperation, he twisted and lunged. His left palm struck first, but cramping fingers refused to respond, and his hand clawed past the lip. Still, his body jolted to a stop, his numb right hand all that held him in place. Shaking the cramps from his left hand, he reached up and gripped the edge, then clambered atop the wall.

Bandit's impatience grew with each agonizing moment. Alone in the darkness, he could not help but wonder if Conner had left him there. Given that he was using the Eastlander, he deserved it. He did not realize how distressed he was until the knotted end of his rope belt struck his shoulder. Near to tears of joy, he reached up with shaky hands.

Conner hung silently, hand and calf hooked over the lip of the wall. He had suggested using Bandit's belt to get the younger boy up the wall. But as he hung there awkwardly, the rope wrapped securely around his wrist, he was starting to reconsider. If he had miscalculated the length, Bandit would not find the other end in the dark.

A slight tug on the belt put Conner's worries to rest. But relief turned to alarm when he was forced to take Bandit's full weight. Legs, arms, and back ached as Bandit climbed. Bricks bit into Conner's calf and palm.

Suddenly, Bandit stopped, dangling from Conner's back.

Conner's first thought was that they had been discovered, but when he heard nothing but snores from the other cells, he risked asking, "What is it?"

"Uh, Conner, I have a problem," came a soft whisper.

Conner's muscles shook violently. "What?"

"My pants do be hangin' about my ankles."

Conner stifled a groan. "Will you get up here? We'll deal with that later."

Bandit started to climb again, then paused. "That's easy for you to say. You're not the one losing his pants."

Half an eternity later, Conner lay sprawled across the top of the brick wall, legs dangling loosely over the sides, while Bandit looped his recovered belt around his waist. He was grateful Bandit had not lost his pants. He was not sure he could stand to look at the boy's bony hips. He was thankful for one thing. If Bandit had weighed one stone more, they would have tumbled back into the cell before they cleared the wall.

Without a word, Bandit stepped lightly atop the side wall in the direction of the stockade's hallway.

Quietly as possible, Conner rose, shadowing Bandit's silhouette on shaky legs to the wall above their cell door, then followed Bandit across one of the large roofing crossbeams. Once on the other side, the slanting thatched roof forced them first to bend, then crouch, and finally, to crawl along the brick wall separating two cells on the stockade's northern run.

This was where Bandit took charge. A lifelong resident of Cravenrock, he knew the guardsmen assigned to watch the stockade at night. Conner waited. Once the route was clear, Bandit slid forward under the loose thatching. Conner followed close behind and reached the edge in time to watch Bandit drop five paces to the ground. They would have only a few moments before the next passing of the guard, so he moved with urgency. He wriggled between wall and thatching, ignoring the sharp straw scraping his legs and back, then dropped next to his escort.

Bandit immediately gripped his shirt and yanked him down, raising his hand as a signal to wait. There was enough light from nearby buildings that Conner could make out moving forms in the distance, but he could not tell if they were guardsmen or city folk. He would have to trust Bandit on this, so he waited. After several stressful heartbeats, Bandit released him. Squatting low, he moved northward away from the stockade. Conner mimicked the boy. Moments later, they were at the dark edge of a nearby building. The boy flashed him a gratifying smile, then turned and strutted calmly northward up a narrow alley. Conner had no choice but to follow close behind.

Thieves Guild

Conner woke with a start, Bandit's dirty face shoved up close to his. His stomach grumbled, and Bandit poked it. "I told you to eat some porridge. Maybe next time you'll listen to me." Bandit suddenly reminded him of Pauli; Conner groaned.

Conner's second groan came as memories he would have preferred to forget flooded back. After Conner and Bandit had escaped the stockade, they had spent what remained of the night on top of a tall building with a slanted slate roof still warm from Hemera's rays. He rolled to his side and surveyed his surroundings, then let out a third more audible groan as he contemplated his current predicament.

This won him a scathing look from Bandit. "Maybe you should try again. I'm sure the city guard will be hearin' you soon."

Conner half ignored the boy, stifling yet another groan when he tried to move a body that had given up on him. He stretched his arms and legs to bring them back to life while Bandit instructed him on a litany of things he hoped would keep him from finding his way back into the stockade while the boy went to the Thieves Guild. Before Conner was fully awake, Bandit disappeared over the edge of the roof.

Every muscle ached from the previous day's abuse, worsened by pangs from an empty stomach. Deciding a walk could not hurt, he moved stiffly about the city, staying mostly on rooftops, all while watching the streets below. It did not take long to realize the city guard was desperate to catch him again, and quickly.

Pirate waited in the pitch-black room, knee and hand pressed to the cold stone floor. He could hear his master's fingers drumming on the large desk as he considered the information Pirate had delivered. He kept his eyes on the floor; Night Vision was forbidden by Thieves Guild rules while in the presence of a member of the Assassins Order, those who oversaw the guild's activities.

To Pirate's frustration, word of an Eastland farmer scaling the keep's wall the morning before, as well as the boy's escape from the city stockade that night, had made its way to Lacerus before Pirate could arrive with the news. His master did not like being left uninformed on matters affecting what he oversaw, so the Assassin had many ears to the ground. Long, deep scars the length of Pirate's back were his reminder of the last time he had failed Lacerus, a mistake he would not repeat. Chipper, Pirate's ferret bond, trembled in his loose shirt, reflecting his growing angst.

At last, Lacerus broke the silence. "Well, if the boy wanted to get our attention, I can't think of a better way to do so, can you?"

"No, master," Pirate replied to the floor. He had given Lacerus every scrap of information he had about the Eastlander, most of which had come from Bandit. He had enough faith in his own interrogation methods to know the boy had left nothing important out. But it was becoming clear that even his master did not possess enough information to discern what was happening. Nothing more could be offered, so he waited. His master would know best how to deal with the situation.

"It is good you brought this news to me," Lacerus added.

The double-edged statement had just a taste of honey. Nevertheless, Pirate tensed. It was also laced with a reminder of the severe admonishment Pirate had received for not being the first to tell Lacerus about the Eastlander's unexpected appearance in Cravenrock. Pirate's informants had been too slow to feed him the information, a failing Pirate would rectify that night.

"Very well, my whelpling," Lacerus stated without affection. "Bring the Eastlander into your pack if it so delights your guildsmen, but keep a tight leash on him. Give him a few assignments and watch him closely to discover what he is about. If he shows signs of being anything other than what he appears, kill him immediately."

"Yes, master." Pirate started to rise.

"And Pirate," Lacerus continued, forcing Pirate back to his knee.

"Yes, master?"

Lacerus's voice took on an air of foreboding. "Do not fail to keep me informed on this matter."

"As you command, master," Pirate responded through gritted teeth. Yes, the situation would be remedied that night.

Lacerus ran the tip of his ringed forefinger across pursed lips, eyes glowing under his black hood. Pirate had a good gut for thieving, but he sorely lacked a leader's intuition. The Thieves Guild needed a brilliant guildmaster if it was to move forward without his constant supervision. He was becoming frustrated with the guild's stagnation under Pirate's limited foresight, but his ongoing quest for a replacement had produced no one worthy of consideration—that is, until now.

Few could have climbed the city wall without a spell known only by those of the Assassins and Rangers Orders. And though the city stockade was not designed to hold anyone with the proper training, it had taken the boy only a few hours to escape. Yet there was no reason to believe the boy was a young Assassin usurper. Assassins were known for their incessant backstabbing to acquire more power, but they were honor-bound to respect territorial rights, even within the Harmonic Realms. This was Lacerus's territory. Besides, he had watched the Eastlander's encounter with Marcantos. The lad did not have a lick of fighting talent in his thin bones. That left only two viable options.

If this Eastlander was someone attempting to infiltrate the Thieves Guild, then, like the Assassin's saying went, *Keep those you don't know close, and your enemies will reveal themselves.* He at least trusted Pirate's competence enough to take care of the problem if that was the case. But if the boy was as he appeared, then he could be a real gem. Such a boy, with the proper guidance, could be a benefit to his guild. And if the boy was as smart as he was talented, he could someday replace Pirate.

All this, of course, was pure speculation until more was known. Patience was one of Lacerus's qualities. With Colonel Palastar's timely demise the previous night, Lacerus would continue to adjust to the changing situation. That was the chaotic way. New fruit was always a possibility.

Just past dusk, while moving half-consciously through an alley separating two tall buildings, Conner was startled when Bandit appeared from a shadow looking like a makeshift scarecrow after a windstorm.

"I told you to stay above street level," the boy berated him, then waved it off as if all was forgiven.

Bandit ignored Conner's questioning about what had happened to him, so Conner was resigned to follow his young cohort's lead. Bandit led Conner to a particularly rundown building in the northwest section of the city, where two rugged, middle-aged men in gray cloaks and hoods pushed a black cloth over his head. Then, with Bandit at his side talking incessantly about the Thieves Guild, the men led him through a maze of underground tunnels. The tunnels were cooler and smelled better than most of the alleys he had passed through earlier that day, though the musty, stale air reminded him of Barrick Morelace's ancient wine cellar. The memory only served to remind him of Pattria, so he pushed the depressing thoughts away before homesickness set in.

After a quick glance up the alley, Pirate slid deftly down a thick iron pole behind a pile of smelly rubbish. He was behind schedule, so he moved swiftly. His grip tightened, sliding to a halt just above a vat of acid. This was the first of several well-placed traps he would negotiate before arriving at the guild camp twenty paces below the city. Having traversed the route many times, he was hardly conscious of stepping from the railing to his left; leaving the railing to the right would have been fatal.

Pirate soon entered a massive octagonal chamber, once the burial tomb for the early settlers of Cravenrock. An ornately chiseled stone sarcophagus occupied the center of the once-grand crypt long forgotten by those who lived out their wretched lives above. Ransacked skeletal remains littered a hundred dugouts along the walls of the chamber, the rotted remnants of once-fancy silk clothes ornamenting their graying bones. Torches hung on opposite sides of the chamber provided light adequate for the conclave he had called.

He stepped to the head of the sarcophagus, taking his position of leadership before the circle of gray-robed guildsmen, motionless amid the decay. Behind him, hundreds of skulls belonging to less influential city dwellers had been meticulously stacked along the wall, giving him an illusory ominous appearance in the flickering light.

Pirate scanned the room, only half aware of Chipper slipping from his shirt and darting from the chamber in search of a tasty meal. He uttered the ritualistic words: "Has the Scribe of the Guild sealed the room for the conclave?"

"All are present. All is as it should be," a tall, thin form with a deep feminine voice replied, stepping to Pirate's right.

"Then let the guild be illuminated," Pirate commanded.

Robed figures on either side of the chamber pulled the two wood torches from the wall. Simultaneously, they dropped them into buckets of water at their feet. The sounds and smell of hissing steam filled the chamber pitched into total darkness. In unison, the cloaked forms incanted the Night Vision spell, *"Ora energi anakafanos."* Glowing eyes, a residual effect of the spell, appeared under the long hoods around their leader. Pirate pushed his hood back; the others mirrored him.

Pirate proceeded with the evening's business, dispatched with the efficiency expected from a group that preferred thieving over talking and planning. Information about the movements of several expensive items was discussed. Tasks were assigned to follow up on leads. Someone complained that payoffs to the city guard were getting too expensive, but no one suggested how to deal with the problem.

When all was done, the chamber fell silent. Pirate tapped the top of the hollow sarcophagus with a wooden mallet. "I call the guild's attention to discuss the acceptance of a new recruit into the guild. By now, you are aware of the young Eastlander who climbed the city wall. This young man is here tonight for us to consider his acceptance. What say the guild?"

As expected, Hook spoke first, with his usual angry tone. "Must I speak of what should be obvious to everyone here? This Eastlander is currently wanted by the city magistrate for escaping the stockade. Nearly every city and keep guardsman knows his face. Furthermore, the entire city guard is in a fury looking for him, making our work all the harder. It is clear the boy is either stupid or prone to rash behavior. We already feel the squeeze from the city guards' grip. I say it is unwise to allow him into our guild." Hook's scowl took in the faces around him.

Lightfoot was quick to respond. "As I hear it, this Eastlander went toe-to-toe with Marcantos Evinfaire in a fight, albeit a very short one." He allowed the chuckling to die down before continuing with a hardy smile. "And the entire city guard couldn't catch him. I mark that as smart, not stupid. Besides, even if we *were* frightened of the city guard, having them frantically scouring the city for this boy means there are lots of things left unprotected." The broad smile filled his thin face, enthusiasm building as he asked, "How many of you can scale the city wall with your bare hands?" The chamber remained silent. "Yes, well, I happened to be in the market when it happened, and to be honest, I wouldn't have believed it possible if I hadn't seen it with my own eyes. Anyone who can do that has my vote."

After a moment of silence, Longfingers, a lanky, long-haired woman on Pirate's left, added, "No one outside this room will know he was accepted into the guild, so I don't see any risk in giving the boy a chance. I say aye."

With that, Pirate put the Eastlander's acceptance to the vote. With only Hook dissenting, Pirate brought the voting to conclusion. "Let the Scribe of the Guild make the mark that the vote has been counted. The boy has been accepted as an apprentice. May the gracious Mistress of Good Fortune smile on all we do." He pulled his hood forward to conceal his face, then turned to Hench, a husky man near the door. "Let the apprentice be seen by all so he may be revealed."

A strong hand on Conner's shoulder pulled him to a stop, and the cloth was unceremoniously yanked from his head. His eyes adjusted to the dim light and he noted he was standing in the middle of an underground antechamber with several entrances. A collection of stone busts stared at him from nooks in every wall, bearing names Conner could not make out in the chamber's lighting. Dust and cobwebs covered every surface. The only furnishings were several rotten tables and chairs along the far wall, where Bandit, Conner, and the two rugged men waited in silence. Motion from under one table drew his attention where a ferret chewed on the bloody remains of a rat. The morbid scene made his cramping stomach lurch, so he glanced away to fight off the desire to heave.

Bandit smiled at Conner, unaffected by the gruesome sight. "Just be rememberin' what I be tellin' you and everything will be fine,"

Bandit whispered reassuringly, though Bandit seemed more nervous than Conner.

While he waited, Conner went over everything Bandit had told him about the Thieves Guild, relieved to find something to distract him from the ferret's gruesome noises. The guild was a secretive organization of thieves spanning the known world. As with other guilds, each region had its own group, led by a guildmaster. Pirate was the nickname of the Cravenrock clan's guildmaster. Each guild member was also given a nickname in case someone was captured and tortured by the city guard. Apprentices were voted into the guild by its members during a conclave, then given a series of tests to prove their potential.

According to Bandit, if Conner completed his apprenticeship, he would be asked to become a member. All he had to do was decline. Then, he could leave to finish his trek, with coin and supplies in hand. If he was not successful, . . . Conner did not want to consider leaving the city without food, supplies, extra clothes, or coin. He hated to admit it, but he needed this to work. The plan was simple. And given Conner's current streak of luck, that was not a good thing.

With each passing minute, Bandit grew progressively more restless, which did little to bolster his own confidence. Unable to remain silent any longer, he leaned close to Bandit. "What is wrong? Does it normally take this long?"

Before Bandit could reply, a large hooded man appeared, then signaled for them to follow. Bandit and Conner left the two burly men behind and proceeded down a long, narrow corridor with a low arching ceiling that forced Conner to bend. At the other end, he stepped through an archway into pitch-blackness. A circle of glowing eyes scrutinized him.

A voice at the far end of the circle announced, "You have been accepted as an apprentice into the guild. What say you?"

As he had rehearsed, Conner responded, attempting to sound assertive. "I am ready for my tests." Moments passed, the circle of glowing eyes on him.

"Silence speaks of the guild's acceptance. From this time forward, you will be called Vault. You will be given three tests to demonstrate your skills and spirit. Let the Scribe of the Guild so make the mark."

The circle of glowing eyes floated to the far side of the chamber and winked out; that is, all but one pair that continued to stare for several moments. The imposing eyes glided closer. "Leave us, Bandit."

Bandit paused, then leaning close to Conner, whispered, "I'll be waitin' in the antechamber."

"Now!" raged the voice with glowing eyes.

Bandit vanished back through the archway.

Conner gritted his teeth and fought against shifting into a defensive stance. He could feel the eyes inspecting, weighing, measuring every aspect of him, noting his features, storing away each of his many flaws. Hunger and lack of sleep, along with bruises and aching muscles, made him edgy. He already did not like this man, so he struggled to maintain a calm expression.

"It seems you have made a name for yourself with your ability to climb walls." The eyes floated to his left, still appraising him. "But you should know it will take a lot more than a simple skill to be accepted as a member of this guild. The tests you will be given will be hard and risky, purposely so. Before each test, you will be instructed in how to invoke a new spell critical to the success of the mission. Each test you complete, you will get paid. If you cannot cast the spell by your next assignment, you will be released. If you fail any of the tests, you will be released. Then you can deal with the city guard on your own. Is this clear?"

"Yes, guildmaster." Conner stated in a submissive voice, attempting to mask his growing irritation.

Pirate continued undaunted. "Excellent. You will be afforded bedding in a room near this chamber, away from any entrances to the city above. Morning and evening meals will be delivered, but don't get used to being served. It will end when the hornet's nest you stirred above dies away. Until you are called to receive your first assignment, I suggest you rest. It appears you need it." He paused long enough to complete his walk around Conner, the physical examination done. Conner could sense Pirate's scornful expression as he faced him. "I do not know what is going on between you and Bandit. But just so there is no misunderstanding, do not assume for a moment you can break our agreement without there being . . . consequences . . . for either of you. You will not be given a second chance." The glowing eyes gazed at the man Conner sensed approaching from behind. "Hench will escort you out."

Conner let the massive hand on his shoulder direct him back through the archway and toward the antechamber where Bandit hopefully waited. He could feel his blood beginning to boil. He was angry at Bandit for having gotten him into this. He was angry at Pirate for being such a pompous, demeaning ass. He was angry at himself for being so stupid that he'd let his principles force him down the path to this situation. But most of all, he was angry at the very Cosmos for leaving him without coin, food, or supplies to complete his trek, forcing him to take such desperate measures. He wanted to step out into the night, shake his fist at the sky, and scream his frustration for the injustice of it all. What could the Cosmos possibly want from him?

Pirate watched the Eastlander vanish down the corridor. Something was going on between him and Bandit; he would bet his next job's profits on it. He considered questioning Bandit again, but the boy could be stubborn even when put to the interrogation. He would watch them closely. And if he did not like what he saw? He ran fingers absently over a human skull, tracing the jagged edge of a fissure the width of an Anarchic war ax running diagonally across the crown. He lifted Chipper and slipped the contented ferret inside his shirt, the edges of his lips twisting upward. He was sure the city guard would pay well to have them returned, all tied up with pretty bows like a Freedom Day present.

The Final Test

For several days, the nagging in the back of Conner's head was growing ever more relentless. The cramped quarters provided by the guildmaster were stifling and confining. Sleep came in fits. He was reaching a point of desperation, ready to take on nearly any risk to be done with his promise to Bandit. So when he suggested to Pirate doing three tests in three nights, the guildmaster thought him insane. But even the haughty Pirate had to concede some credit when Vault completed his first two heists without complications. That should have been Conner's warning that something would go dreadfully awry with his third and last burglary.

The information bought from the guild's informants appeared reliable about their target. So the planning for the final heist went as the previous two. Vault, Bandit, and Stick were to retrieve a magical scroll with unknown powers from a magus traveling through the region to the southern Realm of Elvenstein. The trio had only one night to appropriate the scroll. Vault was to scale the backside of the elegant inn where the magus had acquired a room, giving his two accomplices access via a knotted rope. Then, Bandit was to break into the magus's sitting room, where the scroll was hidden, all while Vault stood guard over the magus in his sleeping chamber and Stick guarded the getaway route below. It all sounded a little too easy for Conner's liking, but he had no grounds to argue with the more experienced guildsmen who had devised the plan.

It was while Conner peered through the thick glass window that he first sensed a trap. Risking detection, he recited the Night Vision spell he had been taught. *"Ora energi anakafanos."* Immediately, he knew the form in the bed was nothing living. He turned to signal an alarm, but Bandit had already disappeared through a window into the adjacent sitting room. Conner whispered an oath. Just as he signaled Stick, a series of muffled yells broke out through the open window.

Conner's feet would not move fast enough as he danced lightly across the loose tile roof behind the two rooms. By the time he reached the window Bandit had entered, Stick had disappeared over the rooftop's edge as if the building were going up in flames. Inside, a nearly comic scene was playing out. Two city guardsmen, one tall and thin, the other short and stubby, were stumbling about in the dark, cramped space, knocking over furnishings while attempting to grab Bandit, who danced around, between, and under them with amazing agility. But the guardsmen were already beginning to coordinate their actions. It would be only moments before one of them had the boy. And with all the racket they were making, the entire city guard was about to descend upon them.

Having reached the same conclusion, Bandit flashed Conner a knowing smile and tossed a long wooden tube in his direction just as the two guardsmen sandwiched him into a vise grip. Without thinking, Conner slipped the tube over his shoulder and dove through the window, kicking a short sword from the thin guardsman's hand, followed by a long, right hook. He was as surprised as the guardsman when the wooden statuette that had somehow made its way into his hand laid the guardsman out cold.

He rounded on the stubby guardsman, prepared to repeat the same maneuver, when Bandit took the initiative to knee the man in the groin. Stubby's eyes widened, and Bandit twisted free from the loosened grip. Conner was back through the window in a heartbeat, confident his resourceful mate was close behind.

Conner grabbed the rope dangling over the edge of the roof. But when he glanced back, the stubby guardsman was climbing through the window behind Bandit, thick hands nearly snaring the boy once more. He signaled Bandit to start down the rope and squared off before the guardsman, who had pulled up, unsheathing his short sword. The man's intense focus made it clear he would not be surprised again.

Conner counted the seconds Bandit would need to complete his escape, watching the guardsman step cautiously closer. Then, with a flick of his wrist, he hurled the statuette. The guardsman, surprisingly quick for his size, leaped to the side. But this gave Conner the opportunity he needed to grip the rope and heave his body over the edge of the roof. His hands moved with speed, finding each knot as he descended. Above, Stubby hacked tenaciously on the rope until, at last, it severed. Conner plummeted the last ten paces, landing hard on the street and twisting his ankle on a loose cobblestone.

From the roof above, the blast of Stubby's whistle broke the midnight calm, a harbinger of Conner's inevitable arrest. He gripped his useless ankle, pressing his back against the inn's wall. And there he sat, each piercing shrill of the whistle sucking more resolve from him, until only futile despair and shame remained. He hoped word of his deeds did not reach the ears of his parents. This was no longer a story he wanted to tell Pattria or Pauli. Like being caught in quicksand, all his efforts to get out of trouble had only pulled him in deeper.

He sat lost in despair until hands gripped his shoulder, tugging him to his feet. He was confused. Had the city guard arrived so quickly? How long had he been there? He was even more confused when he heard a familiar voice whisper desperately in his ear. "Are you tryin' to get yourself caught after all that effort to be gettin' free? Snap out of it and let's be movin'."

Light from the windows of Cravenrock's narrow alleyways often plays tricks on the eyes, so the half dozen haggard city guardsmen rousted from their beds never noticed the two shadows in the niche of an old building they ran past. In a few moments, the company disappeared to the west, where guardsmen's whistles shrilled in the moonless night.

The shadows did not move as the clamor of more heavy-booted feet grew louder from the east. A dozen more guardsmen, swords drawn, trailed swiftly after the first. The city guard was on full alert.

The shorter shadow pointed to the other's foot. "How's the ankle?" he whispered.

Conner shifted to test the foot, then flinched at the spasm of pain. "I can't run on it. If we are seen, I will draw the guards' attention so you can get away. There is no need in us both getting caught . . ." The tall shadow thought about how strange that sounded before adding, "Again."

Bandit's voice whispered back with the sharp edge of stubbornness, "I'm not goin' to be leavin' you. You saved my life back there. Besides, we aren't goin' to be gettin' caught, so that discussion isn't worth havin'." Bandit glanced down the quiet alley where the two groups of guardsmen had disappeared. "Especially now. So lean on me, and let's be gettin' out of this deathtrap before the guard's grip be tightenin' around our throats."

Conner nodded agreement, too distracted by the pain in his ankle to suggest a better plan. He adjusted the long, hollow tube strapped across his back. Slipping his arm over Bandit's bony shoulder, Conner checked the alley both ways before giving the ankle a full test.

The shadows hobbled away from the building. Bandit did his best to take Conner's offered weight as they gradually wove eastward to the nearest entrance to the undercity.

Pending News

Veressa had hardly slept, having spent most of the warm predawn hours wearing out a pair of slippers on her bedchamber balcony while tugging at her long blond hair. Slowly, she removed the residual effects of the braids she had worn through the night. Her mother would have been horrified to discover Veressa braided her hair before bed. But that was not what occupied her thoughts. She paused to reread the parchment she had received the previous evening. The letter was from her assigned protector, Master Ranger Annabelle Loris, away the past two fortnights on a royal assignment to deliver a regiment of new Archer recruits to Striker's Keep near the eastern Borderlands. Annabelle would be arriving at Graystone shortly after dawn.

Veressa could hardly stem her anticipation. Being shackled to the castle without her protector was the worst possible torture she could imagine, even exceeding being forced to wear Gareth Nantree's horrific dresses. She scanned the northern horizon as she leaned farther over the balcony railing, pushing more of the castle past her peripheral vision. But the vast open space did little to improve her sulky mood. With the near-full face of Erebus in the west, even the brightest stars were winking out of existence.

Veressa reflected on her many hunting adventures with Annabelle, the master Ranger appointed by the king to protect her since she was five. At an early age, Veressa had been incessant in her demands for Annabelle to teach her the fighting styles of the Rangers Order, to the point that Annabelle relented. The queen would never have approved, the Rangers Council even less, so each lesson had to be secretly and meticulously planned, leaving Veressa in a perpetual cycle between excitement and frustration. She had taken to her Ranger training as easily as an eaglet to the skies, consuming each lesson, impatiently asking three questions for each of Annabelle's detailed instructions. And Annabelle had taken each question in gentle stride, attempting to calm the hasty princess. Which was why Veressa had given the woman the prestigious role of being the older sister she never had, no matter how much Annabelle disapproved of the awarded title.

It had been Annabelle's comment at the end of her last lesson that had kept Veressa in a state of anxious anticipation. Veressa had successfully scored perfect hits on two dozen randomly placed targets on the Graystone range with a quiver of arrows, a belt of throwing knives, and her sleeves stuffed with chucking stars, all while dancing through the whirling wooden blades of six practice poles. For added effect, she had deftly leaped over a blade as her last steel-pointed star flashed from her hand, sinking deep into the head of her final straw target. Shifting into a tight roll, she had come up a pace in front of her mentor, arms crossed, a victorious smile on her face.

Annabelle had eyed her pupil's empty quiver and belt, the Grenetian longbow slung over her shoulder, properly positioned for easy access. "Hmpphh!" Annabelle countered. "You could have missed that last target with your grandstanding maneuver, Veressa. If that combat had been real, the target would not have just stood there admiring your marvelous fighting prowess. You do not take your training seriously enough."

But this time Annabelle's expression had not matched her words. Veressa was too astute to miss the telltale signs of admiration in her protector's eyes and voice. The verbal admonishments had no effect on her stance or her smug smile. She waited.

Annabelle had rolled her eyes in frustration. "Cosmos help me properly train this child!" the Ranger exclaimed in mock frustration. Then she exhaled hard, and what remained of her somber guard crumbled. "Yes, Veressa, that was extremely well done. It seems you have mastered Ranger basics. Your training is now complete."

"*What?* Complete?" Her confident stance dissipated as she reeled at the Ranger's statement. "Annabelle, you can't stop training me. I haven't come this far to stop. I want to continue my training!" Each sentence came in a heated rush.

"Veressa," Annabelle responded soothingly, her strong hands gripping the princess's shoulders as she peered deep into the girl's blue eyes. "I thought I had been clear on this. The Orderman's Code is quite specific in this matter. Only those accepted into the Rangers Order can receive advanced training. I was already putting us both at risk by training you on the basic styles intended only for certain guildsmen." This did nothing to quail Veressa's anxiety. "What you ask of me is beyond reason. My hands are tied. I am order-bound to our laws, just as I am bound by the laws of Realm and gravity. I cannot teach you my order's advanced style any more than I can teach you to fly." Annabelle had let her hands slip from Veressa's shoulders, making it clear she wanted no further discussion on this subject.

Veressa had been crestfallen. She had always thought advancing to the next stage was a matter of preparation. If she could prove to Annabelle she possessed the qualities of a true Ranger, then she had the right to be trained. Sadness gave way to anger, which bolstered her resolve. She resumed her stubborn stance before her mentor. She was the future queen of Griffinrock. Senseless order laws were not going to stop her from getting what she most desired.

Annabelle had seen that stance all too often in eleven years as Veressa's protector. This was not a contest of wills she wanted to lose, though history did not bolster much success. "Why do you feel the need to take your training further?" Her question had been a veiled statement meant to remind Veressa that royalty did not need to be trained in the ways of any order. The Harmonic crowns maintained pacts with the orders in good standing to provide the necessary protection for the royal families and close relatives. She would also have a champion before she was given the crown.

"As long as I can recall, I have wanted the life of a Ranger. You, Annabelle, of all people, know I was born for this . . . as you know I possess the abilities. While my head knows I will never be given that chance"—she swallowed hard as she searched Annabelle's eyes—"nor allowed to braid my hair in the ranks of a Ranger, my spirit is that of a Ranger. My heart knows no borders nor laws limiting Cosmic justice. Do not ask me to give in to my head. Someday I will do so. Someday I will assume my obligations, but my heart is not ready to be caged. Not today."

Annabelle had been on the verge of tears as she listened. With a relenting sigh, she responded. "All right, Veressa. But there is only one way we can proceed with your training. I must leave in a few days on an assignment. While I am away, I will send word to the Rangers Council, explaining what I have done, requesting you be allowed to continue with your training. If, and only if, they give me their approval"—she emphasized this part to leave no doubt of her meaning—"I will begin training you in the advanced Ranger skills. Until I have their approval, your training is complete.

"But, Veressa," she continued, "do not let your hopes run wild. You have not yet bonded. I know of no such request to have ever been approved in the history of the order." Annabelle stepped back and bowed slightly. "I am proud of you, Highness. It has been my honor to be your preceptor." Turning with a smile, she stepped past the pair of royal guardsmen waiting anxiously at the entrance for the princess.

It was the last time Veressa had seen Annabelle—nearly two fortnights ago.

The tip of Hemera breaking over the Royal Forest brought Veressa back with a start. How long had she been daydreaming? Again, she read the cryptic letter.

I have an answer from the Council regarding the matter of our latest discussion. Meet me at dawn. —A

Turning quickly, she skipped across her room, leaving both Hemera's morning light and her anxious thoughts on the balcony. She was in such a rush that she completely startled the royal guardsman at his usual post outside her door.

"Good morning to you, Highness," Ballett said formally. Noting the simple dark green Rangers cloak, clothing obviously not designed for princesses lounging in their bedchambers, his eyes widening at the sight. "I am sorry, Highness, but I cannot let you leave." He uttered hesitantly, diverting his eyes from her piercing gaze.

Veressa donned her best regal posture, squaring her shoulders, arms folded firmly under her breasts. She scrutinized the guardsman in the way that made most men wilt. "Just how do you plan on stopping me?"

"Please, Highness. The king gave me specific orders this time to guard your chambers. I—"

"I see," she interrupted him impatiently. "Did he tell you to guard my bedchambers or to guard me?"

"What do you mean, Highness?" Ballett shook in armor that would not protect him from this assault.

"Well, if my father told you to guard my chambers, then you shouldn't care if I go." She leaned forward, prepared to step through the doorway.

"It wouldn't make much sense for me to stand guard over an empty chamber, Highness." The words came in an anxious cascade of syllables.

"Then it seems your orders were to guard me. If that is the case, we don't need to stay here. So, come along with me and do what the king instructed you to do." Her left foot was through the doorway.

Ballett was torn between blocking her exit and attempting to reason with the queen's only daughter. "Please, Highness, I don't think that is what the king meant."

Veressa paused for dramatic effect. "You don't think? Surely, you're not implying the princess is wrong in her logic?" Ballett's unsightly gaping mouth made him look like a walleyed fish. "My dear man, the king gave you specific orders, but you don't know what they were?"

The guardsman found new legs with her question. He collected himself before her. "Highness, you are trying to get me in trouble. I have a wife and two little girls at home I must feed. I will be released from service if I anger the king yet again."

Ten years as a royal guardsman assigned to protect the princess had done little to teach Ballett that begging did nothing to slow Veressa when she was locked onto something. Twice in the past year alone, she had risked the poor man's position by circumventing all his physical and mental efforts to control her. Though his best efforts were seldom a challenge, she found him charming. His heart was always in the right place. "Oh, Ballett"—she giggled gleefully as she reached out and touched his arm—"you know I would never let that happen to you. Who would father find to replace you?"

While the man seemed more relaxed, this did little to relieve him of his stress. "My deepest apologies for telling you this, Highness, but you don't have anything to say about who is accepted or released from the royal guard. That is the king's own business."

Veressa's smile broadened. She wagged a hooked finger under his nose, peering at him sidelong. "Then, Ballett, you don't understand the true relationship between a young woman and her father. It is a lesson I plan to instruct you on before your darling little girls wrap you around *their* fingers!" Her expression turned ominous as she continued. "Now, are you coming with me, or do I need to use one of the dozen remaining tricks I have to escape your clutches?"

Ballett rubbed at the back of his neck to relieve the persistent tension that plagued him around the princess. "I don't know how you do that, Highness. I think sometimes I would be better off with a different assignment."

Stepping through the doorway, a lighthearted chortle escaping Veressa's lips from her expected victory. "Ballett, you would miss the challenge of my determined ways." With a royal gesture, she added, "Besides, I plan to make you captain of the royal guard when I become queen."

"Oh, no!" He shook violently at the threat. "You wouldn't do that, would you?"

Veressa laughed. She started down the long, empty hall, pulling the green hood forward to hide her smile. Ballett failed to see the humor in the predicaments he always found himself in around her, but he assumed the proper position one step behind and to the left of the princess as etiquette dictated.

Indictment

Conner lay back on the blanket-covered straw that formed his bed, hands clasped behind his head. Lifting his leg, he gingerly rotated the ankle. At least the pain and swelling had subsided. He found some small solace in having not done more damage. He was counting unhatched chicks, but given his current situation, it would have plenty of time to heal.

Since the botched heist two days before, Conner and Bandit had been forced to stay in the sleeping room they shared to await some decision by the guild. They were not prisoners. But the guild was in crisis and the city above was alight with activity to find those responsible for the theft. The moonless night had kept the two guardsmen from getting a good look at them, but it was not a challenge even for the city guard to link the sketchy features of the thieves to the earlier events of the scaled wall and the two that had escaped the stockade. It was too risky for the two to leave the undercity.

The guard was in such an uproar, Conner was beginning to wonder if he was ever going to get out of the city unhindered. Too bad the guild had not spent as much time deliberating his last heist's plans as they were in dealing with its unfortunate aftermath. *A well-tilled field in spring saves the well-toiled farmer in summer,* his father was fond of saying.

It occurred to Conner that the guild might be considering how to make him a scapegoat, maybe even by throwing him to the wolves above to appease the city guard's lust for retribution. But several guildsmen had visited, hoods pulled forward to hide their features, telling him how they admired his conduct and giving him reassurances that all would be set right in quick order.

At least the time locked away permitted Conner and Bandit to get better acquainted. Bandit appeared interested enough to know about Conner's life on an Eastland farm. And though talking about home and family made him homesick, he found comfort in sharing his experiences with someone whose company he enjoyed. But Bandit was not so engaging when the plow was turned. The boy seldom offered more than what he had told Conner while they were in the stockade. Weary of turning conversations into interrogations, Conner finally gave up and sat in silence.

It was not long, however, before he was tired of being alone with only his thoughts to occupy his mind. Unable to take the silence any longer, he asked, "What is your real name, Bandit?"

Bandit glanced up from the hole he was attempting to bore through the floorboards with his eyes, weighing Conner with an intense stare. Conner had an odd feeling the boy was looking at him for the first time. "I don't be rememberin' much before the guild, Conner, so I don't be rememberin' what it was. I guess my real name died with my parents. Besides, I go by Bandit."

Conner was pondering Bandit's answer when a tall figure in the usual drab gray guild cloak appeared at the door. "We have been called to a conclave of the guild. You two are to accompany me." The figure walked away, making it clear the statement was not open for discussion.

This time, Conner's head was not covered, a possible foretelling of Pirate's decision. Within a few minutes, he was led through the familiar antechamber and corridor. As before, a circle of twenty cloaked figures lined the walls of the chamber. However, this time, the octagonal room was lit by two torches. A figure near a stone sarcophagus pointed at the floor near the entrance. The two stepped to the designated spot.

"Has the Scribe of the Guild sealed the room for the conclave?" Pirate asked.

The thief who had shown Conner where to stand responded, "All are present. All is as it—" The woman's voice choked off in surprise.

Movement at the entrance across from Conner drew everyone's startled attention. The two torches flickered, and a figure in a pitch-black cloak silently floated into the chamber. Without pause, it moved stealthily to the middle, the outline of its cloak shimmering like smoke in the torchlight. The black form examined the frozen gray figures, their hooded heads bowed, hands clasped before them. Conner decided it best to mimic them, even though he wore no cloak. Even intensely studying the floor in front of his feet, Conner could sense the eyes beneath the black hood pass over him, then pause. Conner's eyes watered, and he fought to keep them open. His body quaked violently, though he did not understand why he should fear the cloaked figure so.

It was an eternity before the figure asserted in a low, raspy voice, "For nearly five hundred years, those of the Assassins Order have been the guardians of the Thieves Guild, guiding and helping those unfortunate enough to be born into poverty and cruelty to make for themselves meaningful lives. I have given this clan everything you need to carve out a reasonable living on those who would otherwise quite happily prey upon you."

Conner could feel the black-robed figure moving about the chamber, could feel it float by. An Anarchic Assassin! Conner's stomach lurched. His head reeled at the thought and he shrank back.

"In return, we ask only for your fealty, to follow a few basic rules we have set before you, something any protective parent would expect from the children they have been bound to nurture." There was a sound, like the rustling of dry leaves on an autumn breeze. "But what should the parent do when there is an ungrateful child in their midst? What should be done when there is one who willfully disrespects the parent, who disregards the safety of its siblings, all for personal gain?"

A long silence hung about them. A morbid fascination gripped Conner's imagination, so he glanced up. The black figure loomed before Pirate, who cringed fiercely. Then the form blurred like thick, ebony smoke. Within a heartbeat, it crossed the length of the chamber, coalescing on the other side. The Assassin's ringed hand clutched the neck of a particularly bulky thief, whom it lifted easily into the air. The thief clawed at the black figure's wrist, feet jerking wildly in a failed attempt to pull away. The gray hood fell back, revealing face filled with such horror that Conner was compelled to do what the man seemed incapable of: to cry out in frantic terror. Other cloaked figures did as well, some falling to their knees, whimpering uncontrollably.

The black figure seemed completely unaffected by the grotesque efforts of the large man to break free, his focus instead on judging each guild member's reaction. "Here is the snitch who caused the heist of the magus's scroll to be nearly thwarted. It seems Hook felt it was not in his best interest to share the profits with yet another guild member. Maybe Hook has a point. Maybe there is one too many members." Hook's movements were becoming more exaggerated as he struggled for air.

A short, thin sword appeared in the Assassin's right hand, orange torchlight flickering off the highly polished blade. Carefully placing the tip of the blade under Hook's chin, the black figure pushed the blade upward, piercing first the thief's lower pallet and tongue, then his upper pallet. Hook stiffened, legs convulsing violently, dull eyes rolling back. Red foam escaped his gurgling mouth. None of this affected the Assassin as he pushed the thin blade into Hook's brain, stopping only when the silver tip reappeared from the crown of his skull.

The Assassin continued to hold Hook high in the air until the twitching ceased. The slow rattle of the dying man rose above the groans and wails of his comrades. The Assassin removed the blade and dumped the lifeless body in the middle of the chamber. The bloodied sword vanished. Without another word, the Assassin floated from the chamber.

Lacerus was quite satisfied with how his demonstration had gone. It was all he could do to keep from humming a favorite tune as he walked spryly from the Thieves Guild chamber, the members still inside quivering in pure horror. He especially enjoyed the effects of the Fear spell, something he had added to the drama only at the last minute. While it seldom had an effect on a seasoned orderman, it could turn a grown man into a whimpering mass of blubber for several hours. He had had the good fortune to use that spell on several occasions that would have otherwise required he fight his way to freedom. Why exert energy when there was so much pleasure in the fine art of Assassin finesse?

From all indications, Hook had not acted alone, but this did not bother Lacerus. He did not have time or will to root out any accomplices. Besides, Hook had been the leader, and that problem was no longer a concern. He was confident his little display would force the other participants of Hook's sedition to reconsider before going against his instructions again, or those of the guild.

In the adjacent antechamber, he retrieved his falcon bond from a perch she had taken before the show. He tried to calm her, stroking her ruffled feathers lightly with each measured step. "Easy, Carnia," he soothed. Sadly, she had never gotten used to his true profession.

A Ranger's Lesson

Before the Ranger could offer the necessary curtsy, Veressa crushed Annabelle in a hug, enthusiasm bubbling over with complete abandon. "I am so glad you are back. I have truly missed your company."

After so many years together, the two had long since established an unspoken rapport. Annabelle had been yeoman raised. And though being of an order had elevated her in status to just below nobility, she refused to forget Veressa's place as royalty. Rules, especially those of social etiquette, had a purpose. To break a rule once only meant it became easier to do so again, then again, until rules had no meaning. That was the road to Anarchic life. For this reason, she kept a formal line with Veressa that she had never crossed in eleven years, no matter if there was a connection that transcended the rules of Harmonic society. The love and trust between them was as strong as if they were sisters. Words were not needed; both knew it to be as true as the sky was wide.

"Highness, it is good to see you again as well," Annabelle replied with a welcoming smile. Though they were alone, she was relieved to hold the girl at arms' length to get a better look. Two fortnights away had given Annabelle a new appreciation of the girl too quickly becoming a woman. She had always been pretty, but there was now a radiant look about her. Piercing blue eyes set on a sculptured face of light complexion would melt any impassioned heart. But if her eyes did not catch a man's attention, her smile and disarming laugh would. Blond hair covering much of her shoulders framed the sides of her face, accenting the color in her cheeks and the line of her jaw.

Annabelle admired her pupil until she noted Veressa reading her like a book. The Ranger let the veil descend once more. The smile vanished as she searched for words to redirect them to the business at hand. "At least you have not broken any bones while I was away. That in itself is nothing short of a miracle of the Cosmos."

This truly delighted Veressa, who waved the crumpled parchment in Annabelle's face. "Sooo?" she purred with anticipation.

Glaring back, Annabelle plucked the letter from the princess's hand. "I thought you would know better than to leave our correspondence lying about, Veressa. If this had fallen into another's hands, you would have been brought before the queen and I put to the inquisition to extract the details of its meaning." Queen Izadora could be unrelenting if she discovered important information was being withheld from her, especially if it concerned her only daughter.

"The letter hasn't left my person since yesterday when it arrived," Veressa quipped, undeterred. "So, what did the council say?" The girl gripped Annabelle's hands tight with hers, crushing the letter more; her eyes sparkled with expected delight.

Some thought Veressa selfish and willful. But the few who knew the girl as Annabelle did knew her to be caring and open to sound reason, if one was persistent. True, the girl had a way that infuriated all who opposed her. She could strip a nobleman bare faster than a starving vulture could strip a carcass, or send the Royal Chamberlain Nantree from the room fuming with her verbal appraisal of his latest dress design. No, her confidence and determination were born out of gifts from both her parents, gifts that granted them many sleepless nights, but would also ensure the girl's place as a noble and worthy queen. Nine times in ten, the girl got her way either through her mother's tenacious spirit or her father's unmatched cunning. The other one in ten was through pure luck of the Cosmos. It was Cosmic luck that was with her this time.

After Annabelle had sent a message to the Rangers Council that she had been secretly training Veressa on basic skills and was requesting approval to continue with advanced training, the council had responded not with an answer, but with a harsh rebuke, threatening to reassign Annabelle to Dreadcreek, the Rangers' hold in the farthest northeastern region of the Narwales fiefdom and close to the Borderlands. Annabelle had nearly given up hope of receiving an answer when, after more than a fortnight of silence, she received a second message from the Rangers Order's Sovereign Lady Kyles herself approving Annabelle's request. This had been a shock. However, Lady Kyles also made it quite clear no one else was to know of this training. Further, the Rangers Council would deny any awareness of Annabelle's actions if the queen found out. In truth, the council's decision was political; it had nothing to do with Veressa's interests or demands. Something more was afoot, and that left Annabelle on edge. But with nothing more to hold her back, she would proceed with Veressa's training.

Annabelle reflected on how best to break the news to a girl so overly self-confident. With pursed lips, she folded her arms in front of her, scrutinizing the girl in the Rangers cloak. "Isn't it a little presumptuous of you to think you know the council's answer?"

Veressa's smile vanished until the ends of Annabelle's lips turned up slightly. The princess grabbed Annabelle's folded arms and shook the woman excitedly. "I knew they would approve my training. They had no choice in this matter. You know it," she added smugly.

Annabelle glared back, trying to bring some control to the situation. "Neither the Council of Rangers, nor her Lady Kyles, are so easily swayed, even by the demands of a future monarch of the three Harmonic Realms. It is as likely they want you indebted—a debt they will most certainly ask to be repaid at the least appropriate time. As much as you may think otherwise, a good lesson from this is to never underestimate the motives of the Rangers Council, or the council of any order, for that matter."

"Then that is a problem I will deal with when it arrives." Veressa beamed. "So, can we start my training?"

Annabelle sighed at the girl's perpetual impatience. "Unfortunately, I am exhausted from my travels, so we must keep this lesson short. But we can cover enough to quench your thirst." She locked eyes with her pupil before continuing. "But first, let me make this clear. What you are about to learn have been secrets of the Rangers Order for forty generations. You must not, under any circumstances, describe this to anyone. You are as order-bound as any other orderman. Do you understand?"

Veressa smiled at Annabelle alluding to her as a member of the order. "Yes, of course."

"There are no exceptions. Not even for a princess."

Veressa puffed out her lips. "I said I understood."

"Good. Let us begin by covering what you know a little about, but have not yet put together. This will serve to show you where we will be going with your training." Annabelle squatted and drew a four-pointed star in the dirt with her short knife. At the left point of the star, she drew a ring. At the opposite point, she drew three horizontal wavy lines. At the top, she drew three vertical wavy lines; then at the bottom, a solid point.

Veressa blinked at Annabelle, having expected something more profound from her preceptor. The ring symbol Annabelle had drawn on the left was the ancient Modeic symbol for the Fire elemental. The three horizontal wavy lines on the right were the ancient symbol for the Water elemental, Fire's repelling force. The three vertical wavy lines at the top represented the symbol for the Air elemental. And the solid point at the bottom was the symbol for the Earth elemental, Air's repelling force. Combined with the star, the drawing was the Modeic symbol of the Cosmos, something that could be drawn by any child in the Harmonic Realms by the age of six. Some, such as those in the Paladins Order, held to the ancient Modeic belief of using the symbols in their writings to refer to the Cosmos, believing that even uttering the word *Cosmos* was improper.

Annabelle ignored the girl's disgruntled expression as she continued. Next to the symbol of Fire, she drew a square, the symbol for magical combat. Next to the symbol for Air at the top, she drew two vertical lines, the symbol for missile combat. Continuing around the star, she drew two horizontal lines, the symbol for hand-to-hand combat, next to the Modeic symbol for Water. Finally, she drew a diamond, the symbol for clerical combat, next to Earth's symbol.

Veressa knew there were four elementals and four basic forms of combat, but she had never made the connection between them. She studied the symbols more closely, her eyes widening as the implications became clear.

Annabelle drove the point of her knife into the dirt next to the symbols of Air and missile combat. "Your basic training focused on the use of missile weapons: bows, crossbows, throwing knives, stars, and such. But as you know, these are not the sole weapons of a Ranger. Missile weapons are also used by those of the Warriors and Mystics Orders. So what distinguishes the fighting styles of a Ranger from these other two?"

Veressa pondered their differences. "The fighting style of a Warrior is in combining hand-to-hand combat with missile weapons; Mystics use magical missile weapons—bolts of lightning, fireballs, and ground tremors, allowing the Mystic to fight from a distance."

"Good. So how is a Ranger's fighting style different?"

The connections to Air came to Veressa as she studied the dirt drawing, tying Warriors to the symbol for Water and Mystics to the symbol for Fire, leaving only one elemental—Earth. Veressa squatted next to Annabelle, excitement building. Her finger traced along the wavy lines of Air. "A Ranger combines missile weapons with those of the cleric."

Annabelle studied her pupil's face. "In a way, yes. But what are the weapons of the cleric?"

Veressa had known a few true clerics. Most disavowed the use of violence and weapons, as had the Modei, but she did recall one jolly friar who believed in the heavy hand of the Cosmos . . . and a touch of the fermented brew. She smiled as she fondly recalled him. "They are of Earth—a wooden staff, for example."

"They are so much more, Veressa. A master cleric understands the significance of the Physical, as well as the other planes of existence. Her mastery is spiritual, as she works to perceive how all things are connected. This is where clerics draw their true power, not in weapons such as those of sword or arrow." She touched the bow strapped to Veressa's back for emphasis. "Through this understanding, a cleric communes with the spirits of all that live in the Physical plane, plant and animal. With practice, the cleric can see, even manipulate, that which is beyond. Master clerics have a myriad of spells at their disposal—spells of protection, restoration, command, and divination. These are a cleric's greatest weapons."

Veressa examined the solid point at her feet again. "But other orders possess clerical powers."

"More precisely, other orders use the Earth elemental," Annabelle corrected, and drew a diagonal line with her finger from left to bottom point, connecting the symbol of magical weapons to that of clerical. "Here are the Shamans, those who seek the connection between magical and clerical powers." She drew another diagonal line from right to bottom, connecting symbols of hand-to-hand and clerical. "Here are the Paladins, those who are defenders of the pure, though they may resort to the force of the sword in that defense." Then she drew a line straight downward from her knife to the clerical symbol. "Rangers are the only ones who draw upon the clerical power of the Earth elemental in combination with that of Air. This line"—Annabelle stuck her finger on the line she had just drawn—"is where you will learn the advanced skills of the Rangers."

"Now I know why there are six orders . . . as well as six shadow orders." Veressa's smile of excitement reminded Annabelle of when, as a small child, the girl waited in anticipation of her first riding lesson.

"Yes, but let us not get ahead of ourselves, Veressa. I should warn you, many would-be Rangers in the past thousand years possessed a natural talent to use missile weapons—as you do—but failed to integrate that talent with the clerical skills. They never even reached the rank of watcher within the Rangers Order." She removed her knife from the dirt. "Those who could manipulate Fire or Water went on to become Mystics or Warriors; those who could not became Archers or other specialists in guilds dedicated to projectile weaponry. That is the fate of those not possessing the true spirit of the Ranger. Now it is time to see if you have that spirit."

Veressa rose as her protector stepped closer, unsure what was next.

Annabelle touched her index finger to Veressa's forehead and whispered an incantation, "*Prosopo Koinota Afypsychi.*"

A cascading shower of sparkling flashes erupted across Veressa's vision. "What—" she started, but her mouth, tongue, and vocal cords refused to work. Instead, a croaking sound escaped her lips. Her head rang like a bell struck repeatedly. All her senses were raw and off balance, screaming for her attention. She could feel control slipping away, her body following her head as it pitched to the side.

Annabelle steadied her with a firm grip, but Veressa's muscles only shook in response.

Veressa could hear Annabelle's voice speaking soothingly. "Wait, Veressa. The disorientation will pass in a moment." Her protector actually sounded . . . pleased. There was a long pause. "You don't feel so much like a princess now, do you?"

Veressa took a shuddered breath as she tried to laugh. Annabelle's arms felt comforting around her, so any shock she was experiencing shifted to keen interest. Images danced before her on a patterned quilt extending to the horizon in every direction. She tested her ability to stand.

Annabelle's arms relaxed as Veressa steadied. "Better. Tell me what you see."

Veressa focused her thoughts as she had been taught in her basic skills. She searched for the appropriate words to describe what was there. "The objects on the range around us are outlined in a dull glow of fine sparks, like those on an Illuminary's display."

"Good. The glow is a manifestation of each object's life force in the Physical plane. What else do you see?"

There was more, but Veressa struggled for words. One part of her consciousness was moving, yet another part still. The contradiction was confusing. She recalled her first experience cantering recklessly through Griffinrock's Royal Forest, dodging leafy branches as the massive trees and grass-patched dirt moved swiftly beneath her feet. "It feels like I am riding on a patterned landscape."

"Yes, that is a good way to describe the Harmonic Weave. This is where all Harmonic beings reside in the Mental plane. I want you to take a moment to get used to the feeling. The Harmonic Weave is your safety net when you travel to the Mental plane. Consider it your mind's home. This is very important, Veressa. While in training, you are to never leave the Weave unless I am with you. Do you understand?"

Veressa noticed the intense pattern of colors across the landscape fabric shifting as the Weave floated past. Everywhere around these shifting patterns spun hazy columns of bright rainbows. The Weave rippled and twitched in response to the cylinders, as if the eddies were ripping energy from the very Weave itself. They reminded her of dust demons, those funnels of air appearing on the dry plains out of nothing, sucking dirt and grass upward into their columns, giving them their shape and name. She knew what these were—destructive forces of energy created by all Anarchic life. And she recoiled in disgust. They were the very source of a child's nightmares, of constant distress within the Harmonic Realms. *Dust demon* was a good name, one she would use to remember what they were. Repulsed, she watched them feed off the Harmonic Weave. Yes, that was why she must never leave the Weave. Unable to speak, she nodded to her preceptor.

Annabelle was unaffected by her reaction. "You have taken your first journey into Harmonic Sight, Veressa. I say 'journey,' but in reality nothing has moved. Your consciousness will shift into the Mental planes each time you take Harmonic Sight, but it is important to know that some part of you is always there, just as part of you is here. What shifts is purely your awareness, your focus. It is from the Mental plane that you will learn to manipulate, combine, and control elementals."

Veressa nodded as she listened, untying the knots that gripped her stomach.

Annabelle continued. "In time, you will learn how to take Harmonic Sight. With practice, you will do so with hardly a thought."

"Okay, but you could have warned me what you were about to do."

Annabelle smiled. "I am sorry if I frightened you. But there is no way to prepare a student for what they will experience with Sight—or for the possibility that nothing happens. So it is customary among all the orders for a student's first journey to be brought on by the preceptor."

"And if nothing had happened?"

"If you did not possess enough ability to control the Earth and Air elementals, nothing would have happened when I touched you. Your training would have been over." Annabelle breathed deep. "That is enough for one day. I want you to become aware of your breathing. Bring your focus back to your body."

Veressa did as she was told, but there was something different, something . . . wrong. She slipped again, her muscles refusing to respond. She flashed Annabelle a perplexed look.

Annabelle smiled reassuringly. "You may feel a bit disoriented. This is normal for someone new to Sight. It will pass."

Veressa wanted to believe Annabelle, but the ground began to quake beneath her. Her spine was ice, her nerves raw. She held her arms out, wanting to laugh as they quivered. It was not the ground that was shaking, but her legs. There was a high-pitched squeal. In slow motion, Annabelle grabbed her around the chest. Why was she hugging her? Annabelle never hugged.

Annabelle was wearing a look of surprise, not joy. She had never seen that look on the Master Ranger before. No, it did not fit her fine features at all. Annabelle was saying something, but the squeal was back, drowning out whatever Annabelle was saying. Veressa forced her mouth shut, astonished and embarrassed, and the noise was gone.

How had she fallen to the ground? Well, that was not important. She looked into Ballett's concerned face. What was important was the unseemliness of being seen this way with dirty hands and smudged cheeks. She heard Annabelle's voice as if receding down a long, hollow corridor. She had to listen closely to hear the fading sound. There it was.

"Veressa? Veressa, can you hear me? You will be okay. You are feeling the Calling. The sensation will pass shortly."

But she was too far away to reply.

Bandit's Choice

Conner had heard of Anarchic Assassins. He had, on many occasions, sat around campfires at night with Pauli and others, laughing at the same ghastly stories that had frightened him as a child. But some part of him had always believed Assassins were phantasms of Harmonic lore. Such men could not walk the same green fields of Gaia he worked with his hands. They were the very mythical embodiment of Anarchy, that which those of the Harmonic Realms utterly detested. No, not a myth anymore. They were as real as the fear knotting his gut. He paced his room, trying to get a grip on the terror sucking at his marrow, making his legs tremble and his heart pound like a smithy's hammer. He had to keep moving or he would freeze from sheer fright.

Death he had seen before. He had taken life hunting with his dad or fishing with Pauli; but there had been purpose to those deaths. This was different. What he had witnessed in the burial tomb was something beyond any nightmare his subconscious could ever conjure. He had stood in terror as an Assassin murdered Hook with a cold, premeditated efficiency that made his mind reel.

But something else nagged Conner. He tried to calm his nerves so he could think it through. Something about the Assassin's hand as he gripped Hook's convulsing body. No, not his hand, but the ring on his finger. He closed his eyes, recalling the details—a black stone with deep blue speckles embedded in a polished gold ring. Conner was certainly not of the Jewelers or Enchanters Guilds, but he was sure the ring was rare. That bothered him. He had, since arriving in

Cravenrock, seen that ring before, or another like it. He would have remembered encountering the Assassin before, or would he? Conner shivered at the thought. If there were two such rings in Cravenrock? That meant the Assassin was connected to someone else in the city. In either case, a lot more was going on in Cravenrock than he cared to know.

Assassins in the very heart of Griffinrock, in Cravenrock, in the Thieves Guild, in the very chamber he had just been in! He needed to get as much distance as possible from a guild that could harbor such a creature.

Over and over, he tried to think of ways to escape the city, but nothing came to him. The underground chamber he used for his sleeping room had become his prison.

Bandit's eyes tracked Conner's motion back and forth across the chamber. The Eastlander mumbled to himself, eyes constantly darting to the north. He once recalled seeing an animal pace that way. A trapper had come through Cravenrock several years back, heading west with a huge brown cat he had captured in the eastern region of Narwales. Feigning concern for citizens' safety, the city guards had turned the trapper away from the gates when he refused to pay a bribe. So the trapper was forced to camp outside the city walls. That night, Bandit slipped through the gates unseen to observe the noble beast pace the length of a cage too small for both its frame and its stature. He especially remembered the wild, haunted eyes reflecting the trapper's campfire as the animal scanned the open plains it would never roam again.

Conner had that same caged stare about him, pacing since they had returned from the guild conclave several hours before. Apparently watching the Assassin dispatch Hook had loosened a few of Conner's hinges. Such a gruesome event was certainly not meant for anyone even slightly squeamish, though Bandit thought the Assassin had been a bit melodramatic with his effects. He could think of no one more deserving than Hook to make a point. But Conner was an Eastland farmer. Surely he had seen death before. Unable to stand the pacing, Bandit broke the silence. "I'm glad your ankle do be feelin' better."

"What?" Conner looked at him, blinking as if Bandit had just appeared in the room. "Oh, my ankle," he mumbled absently. He tested the foot, suddenly recalling he had injured it. "Yes, it is much better." Then the Eastlander resumed his pacing, Bandit once more invisible.

Bandit sighed and let his head fall back against the wall. He thought about trying to sleep, but such relief would not come easy with the Eastlander's incessant strides. Something about the vacant stare and sullen expression, the way Conner carried himself, reminded him of a boy who once lived in Cravenrock, someone before he had been called Bandit. How could a wild cat, an Eastland farmer, and a lost boy be connected?

He recalled the flood of emotions, frozen in helpless horror, watching the last of his parents' death throes. He remembered how he'd stood in the rain for hours, gazing at their bodies in awkward poses, their dark blood mixing with rainwater, pooling at the end of a dirty alley. Empty, staring eyes accused him. *Where were you, son, when we needed you? Why did you not help us?* He squeezed his eyes closed. He had been pathetic, weak, and foolish, just as when the woman trapper left him. He had become vulnerable, laying his hopes at the feet of those who could not deliver. These were the circumstances the Cosmos had handed him. Well, he refused to end up like his parents—nameless, unclaimed corpses buried under a grassy patch of dirt on the Narwalen Plains. He did not want to experience such pain again in this life. So he had dealt with it, accepted it, to steel himself from weaknesses that would claim his soul and leave him helpless. He stole from marks, not real people with families and homes. He justified his actions by constantly reminding himself that those he used and robbed were better off than he. It was his way to balance out what the Cosmos failed to provide.

He thought of Hook, another nameless unclaimed corpse that would appear at the end of some alley tomorrow. He examined his hands in the candlelight, hands that had only known thieving. Was he any different? If he died tomorrow, would he be any less of what he'd sworn he would not become?

Bandit could feel something at work within him, fraying at the fringe of his consciousness. Someone was beating at his fortress. The walls cracked and he looked at Conner with new eyes. For once, he saw the Eastlander, not the mark. He saw how he had used the Eastlander, as he had used everyone who stepped into his life, for personal gain, and the walls cracked again. But Conner was different. He was here pacing in physical and mental anguish because he had stuck to his promise to help Bandit, no matter the personal risk or cost. Another crack appeared. In only a few days, Conner had saved Bandit's life several times, never once asking for anything in return. The walls cracked hard. He had overheard guildsmen speak of Vault with admiration for the night of his nearly thwarted test, taking on two guardsmen to save Bandit while Stick vanished into the night. Odd that Bandit hadn't realized how much he too revered Conner. Yet another crack formed in the walls. And if this man died tomorrow, nameless and unclaimed? No, Conner or Vault, the name did not matter; he would be remembered for his actions. No matter where this Eastlander went, he would leave behind a wake of change. *Life is not about how you die, but about how you choose to live,* the trapper used to tell him. And the walls of Bandit's fortress crumbled.

Bandit rose from the rubble of his prior self. He marked the hour to be nearly midnight. There was time, but they would have to go swiftly. Unfortunately, since their nearly disastrous heist of the magus's scroll, the city magistrate had ordered a full lockdown until the thieves could be apprehended. Everyone leaving the city was thoroughly searched. Conner could not leave Cravenrock that way. "Is it well enough to be climbin' the city wall again?"

Conner blinked as if Bandit had just shaken him awake. "What?"

Bandit pointed. "Is your ankle well enough to be climbin' the city wall?"

"No, it's not," Conner responded with a frustrated sigh, running fingers through long, bedraggled hair. This time, instead of resuming his pacing, he stood lost in thought, absently pinching his lower lip between thumb and forefinger. Then Conner renewed his interest in Bandit's question. "I've seen that look before. What are you thinking?"

Bandit answered the Eastlander with his usual knowing smile and wink. "I think it be time you be goin' on your way, don't you?"

Conner shrugged back. "I've thought all that through, Bandit. We know the southern gates are closely guarded, and my foot is not in any condition to climb the city wall. I have no choice but to—"

"Who ever said there be just *two* ways out of the city?" Bandit interjected, then waited until understanding seeped into Conner's clouded mind. "Give me five coins. I can get a week's rations of food for that, enough to get you safely away." Impatient, he snatched the purse from Conner's hands as the Eastlander fumbled with the strings. Bandit reflected on the ironic familiarity of the situation. How the world had shifted beneath Bandit's feet the past few days. He showed Conner the five coins he had removed, then they disappeared in an impressive flash of nimble fingers before he dropped the purse back in Conner's palm. "Do be gatherin' up all your belongings and be ready to be goin' by the time I return. And do be quick about it. We'll be needin' to hurry."

Bandit's questioning about his ankle drew Conner from his brooding. Why had Bandit waited so long to mention another way out of the city? He pushed the thought away to consider later. The boy was formulating another fantastic plan, to be sure. But the chance to be free from the city was all he needed.

The intense pull at the back of his mind had shifted from a constant dull tingle two days ago to a painful throb, so Conner packed the gear he had acquired the last few days: a backpack, a bedroll, an extra pair of leather shoes, a pair of pants, two shirts, a light stitched jacket, knife, salve for injuries, a tin cup, and flint. Even with these purchases, he had more coins than when he'd arrived in Cravenrock. Bandit had suggested Conner pilfer the clothing to save coins for emergencies, but Conner refused. His thieving days were over. Bandit had only shrugged, letting the suggestion drop.

By the time Conner was tying the inside pocket stuffed tight with clothing, Bandit reappeared, handing him a deerskin flask of water and a bulging sack of food. Despite Bandit's persistent demands to get on the way, Conner moved the food to his backpack, shifting the heavier items to evenly distribute the weight. As he worked, he asked softly to hide his concern. "Why don't you come with me? I could use your help."

Bandit threw up his arms to ward off the vexatious suggestion. "No. I've never been out of Cravenrock, Conner. I don't be knowin' anything about the world out there, so I would more likely be slowin' you down and gettin' you caught than be helpin'. Besides, you be needin' time to make good your escape. I'll keep the guild thinkin' you are here as long as I can."

"Pirate will find out you helped me. You'll be in more trouble with the guildmaster than when we were in the stockade." Conner gritted his teeth at the thought of what the egomaniac—or worse, an Assassin—might do to Bandit.

Bandit waved away the concern. "I have spent a lot of time convincin' that imbecile he can work any information out of me that he be wantin'. I be knowin' how to work his game. In the end, he'll be completely convinced I had nothin' to do with your escape. With no hard evidence, the guild won't be takin' any action against me."

Conner studied the boy while pulling the straps of the pack over his shoulders, looking for any signs the boy might be lying, then shook his head. What was he thinking? This was Bandit. If his lies were seeds, he could grow enough crops to feed the city. Finally, desperation won out. He would have to trust that Bandit would be fine. The leather straps secured around his chest, he nodded gratefully. "Okay, I'm ready."

Bandit led Conner swiftly through a labyrinth of corridors and tunnels. Judging by the pull in Conner's head, they were moving northward, not southward toward the gate. Shortly, Bandit stopped by a ladder and, signaling for quiet, ascended. Conner followed through a hole in an abandoned building's flooring. After pushing a large crate over the hole, Bandit trotted to a door and down a narrow street continuing northward. Conner moved doggedly on the boy's heels.

Within a few minutes, the north side of the dark city wall loomed overhead, blocking out much of the starry night sky and the massive mountain range farther on. While Bandit was searching for something on the ground, Conner surveyed the area. This region of the city was void of buildings, which was odd considering the southern section was so crowded. He wondered if it had anything to do with this side being closer to the Borderlands. Maybe people felt less secure here.

Bandit's voice swept that thought away. "Here it is," Bandit whispered, lifting the end of a thick rope buried in the dirt. "Help me lift this."

Following Bandit's lead, Conner gripped the rope and yanked up hard. The dirt pulled away to reveal a hinged, wooden door covered with cloth, dirt, and a patch of hardy grass.

Bandit leaned close to Conner's ear and pointed at the hole that had materialized under the door. "This passageway be for smugglin' ..." the boy whispered, searching for how best to explain its presence, "supplies into the city. At the base of this ladder, you'll be findin' torches and flint to light your way. Take the old tunnel north under the city wall. On the other end, you'll be comin' to another ladder leadin' to a hatch west of the northeast tower. Be sure to be coverin' it back up before you leave. And do be quiet, or you'll be wakin' the guards in the tower." Bandit winked slyly.

Conner regarded Bandit in the dim light. He did not want to think about what kinds of supplies needed to be smuggled into a city. Besides, he could sense Bandit's anxiety growing.

"You should go, Conner. I hope you be findin' your bond soon."

Or was it that the boy was uncomfortable saying good-bye? He decided to leave any remaining words unspoken. But as Conner squatted to crawl down into the narrow passageway, Bandit gripped his shoulder. Conner glanced back.

"Kriston Heldcrest," Bandit whispered.

Conner blinked, not sure what he meant.

Bandit released his grip. "My name is Kriston Heldcrest."

Conner placed his hand firmly on Kriston's thin shoulder, a custom he had learned to be the Narwalen sign for friendship. "It has been my honor to know you, Kriston Heldcrest. May the Cosmos light your path." Turning with a smile, he disappeared down the dark passage.

Bandit . . . no, Kriston hesitated for a moment, staring at the hole that had taken his only friend. Dropping the hatch back in place, he kicked dirt over the rope and along the seams of the hatch. He was no longer a nameless person. A peace flowed through him. At least someone would remember him with admiration. Taking a moment to appreciate his handiwork, he disappeared into the night.

A Hasty Departure

Annabelle slammed the bedchamber door to keep prying ears out. Guardsmen had a knack for spreading stories like dry leaves in an autumn windstorm. Pressing her back hard against the door, she folded her arms in front of her, sealing herself in with the source of her constant distress. Every muscle in her body was taut with displeasure. "I can't believe you are seriously considering this!"

Veressa was wearing the same Rangers clothes she had worn the previous day when they had met on the range. "Why not? This is not some crazy idea I just came up with, Annabelle." She paused to give the Ranger a scathing look, daring the woman to remind her of her many crazy ideas. The Ranger closed her mouth with a snap, and Veressa went back to stuffing her saddlebags. "Like most people, I have thought about this day for years. This is *my* trek, Annabelle; *my* Calling, *my* time to discover *my* place in the Cosmos." With each *my*, Veressa thrust a handful of supplies into her leather bags until the seams were ready to rupture. "I will not be put on public exhibition for others to watch. You can't seriously expect me to go on my trek dragging an entourage of royal guardsmen around my ankles, can you?" The image of Ballett standing over her as she lay on the ground overcome with the Calling made her cheeks hot.

Annabelle considered her experience bonding with Peron. She regarded the male brown falcon perched on the back of a chair near the chamber balcony. She had found the bird high in a willow tree two days out from her parents' home, but what an adventure those two days had been. She thought about what it would have been like if she'd had people along critiquing her every move. Yes, a trek was a very private matter between a human, a bond, and the Cosmos. If she'd had to do it publicly, she might as well have been riding naked through the streets of Graystone Castle. Her face flushed at the thought.

But that was different. Her family had been yeomen. How could Veressa seriously entertain the idea of going on her trek without more protection than what one Ranger could provide? "I would expect you knew your place in the Cosmos, child." The last word escaped her lips before she could stop it. She berated herself for not thinking before she spoke. Well, the girl was acting like a child.

Veressa faced her accuser, cheeks even redder than before. "We have been through all of this, so I am not going to restate what we both know. Now, are you coming with me, or am I going alone?" Annabelle might have been Veressa's protector, but the princess had no qualms playing the royalty card when it suited her intentions.

Annabelle sighed. Or the someday-I-will-be-queen-and-my-adventuring-days-will-be-over trump card. Would the girl use that well-worn excuse until the day of her coronation? Maybe the girl was impulsive. Or maybe it was her emotional reaction to the Calling. In either case, this was a new level of obstinate even for the princess. Annabelle was running out of options to maintain control of the situation. She lifted her chin as she said, "I could go tell the king what you are about. That would put a decisive end to this discussion."

Veressa flashed a sly smile. "You are bluffing, Annabelle. I have made up my mind, and nothing short of shackling me to my bed will keep me in this castle, even when my father knows. You cannot stand over me night and day to keep me here. The only thing your action would do is ensure I go on my trek without you, *alone*." She slung the heavy saddlebags on her shoulder, showering her preceptor with an impatient stare. "Go grab your supplies and let's be on our way. I have a lot yet to learn."

Annabelle nodded at words she could not refute. Still, her eyes drifted to Veressa's bed. The thick wood bedposts with lavished engravings and gold trim were certainly strong enough to keep an impetuous girl shackled in her bedchamber. She shook her head. No, she was not that desperate—at least, not yet.

Release of the Hounds

Lacerus paced across his underground chamber, hands clasped behind his back, aggressively rubbing the ring on his finger to ease his growing agitation. He sneered at the entryway through which Pirate had vanished. It had taken every bit of constraint not to end the guildmaster's life right there. Something would have to be done, but that required weighing the time he spent cleaning up the man's blunders against the time to train a replacement. Managing the Cravenrock Thieves Guild was taking more effort than he'd ever thought possible. He had too many other pressing issues for that to continue.

So Vault had disappeared. If Lacerus had not been so annoyed, he would have laughed at the irony of the name Pirate had chosen for the boy. He ground his teeth, considering the sketchy information he had to work with. Pirate could not state definitively whether the boy was a spy. At least Lacerus had gotten a close look at the boy. His appearance had not left much of an impression. And noting Vault's reaction when Lacerus dispatched Hook? The boy seemed truly shaken to his foundation.

A tall, well-built man with a large nose and wavy brown hair appeared at the door, shaking Lacerus from his introspection. Morgas Terranus wore the summer clothes of a seasoned Alpslander, but the longsword he carried between his shoulder blades spoke of something much more. He was not only a master huntsman and tracker; he had been trained by those of the Barbarians and Black Knights Orders across the Borderlands. Lacerus noted the man's serious but questioning expression as he bowed respectfully to his master. Lacerus could guess what the man was thinking, though Morgas would never ask. Morgas was wondering why Lacerus was giving someone with his extraordinary talents such an insignificant task. The truth was Lacerus did not appreciate loose ends, and this could be a big one. But he would not give his man details that would only raise more questions. As many times before, Morgas would dispatch this assignment with the efficiency Lacerus had come to admire.

Morgas began. "With but a few coins, I inquired with the city guardsmen at the gate about whether it was possible the thief they are looking for could have slipped past. Everything going through the gate is inspected. No guardsman would have accepted a bribe to let the Eastlander pass unchallenged. Such an offense would be an act of treason and, under Harmonic High Law, punishable by death. He did not escape that way. He must have scaled the city walls."

Lacerus pursed his lips. "No, I don't think so. His ankle would not have healed enough to handle the strain of such a climb. That leaves only one way out of the city."

Morgas expounded with a pride that revealed he had pursued that line of thinking. "I personally checked the passage, my liege. The hatch was covered. If he had taken that route, there would have been signs. Besides, it is not likely he knew of its existence."

Lacerus's eyebrows furrowed under the black hood. "Then, Morgas, it seems our Eastland friend acquired the assistance of someone who did know." He pondered what actions to take as he soothed his falcon bond. Maybe he would dispatch Pirate after all, but that delicious thought was a distraction. "Pick your best trackers and go after the boy. Return the prize to me personally, Morgas, alive *and* unharmed."

His man vanished through the entrance without a sound.

Alone, Lacerus absently rubbed the onyx stone on his ringed forefinger. He could yet turn this to his advantage, though his options were thinning. There could be a perfectly reasonable explanation for

Vault's abrupt departure. From what he had learned about how the Eastlander had completed the guild's tests, he showed true promise. Further, Hook's purpose in causing the scroll heist's mishap eliminated any concerns he had about the boy's talents. Most in the guild's clan actually admired the boy. Lacerus's gut told him that the Eastlander was indeed a gemstone in the rough. But he could leave nothing to chance. This time, he would use more direct means to extract the information he needed. Lacerus still had time to turn Vault into a highly polished gem of great value.

Part IV

The force for bonding is irresistible. The Physically bound Being cannot escape the calling manifested through the trek, a communion of the spirit in search of self and the Cosmos to which it belongs. Thus, the Being must remain mindful on the path to see the lessons of truth the Cosmos offers along the way, lessons uniquely designed for that Being's growth. The discoveries made by the mindful transform what is into what should be.

—The Modei Book of Water (Third Book)

Onto the Dragon's Back

The first rays of Hemera gave Conner an opportunity to measure how far he had run. The Dragon's Back Mountains loomed ominously ahead. Tall snowcapped crests outlined the northern horizon, a stark contrast to the heat blanketing the midsummer plains. He had never seen mountains before, so he was humbled by their size. And it was into that great expanse that his Calling compelled him.

Hemera was already warming the right side of his face and drying heavy dew from his deerskin leggings. But the impending heat was not the only reason he was pushing to reach the base of the mountains. He drank deep from his flask, surveying the plains he had crossed as he considered his situation. He might be naive, but he was no fool. Until he knew otherwise, he would assume Pirate, or worse the Assassin, would dispatch someone to bring him back once they discovered he was no longer in Cravenrock. He could only pray to the Cosmos that Bandit had bought him enough time to lose any would-be trackers in the mountains. Conner owed the boy dearly. Someday, he would repay him.

He slung the flask strap over his shoulder, giving him easy access to water while he ran. Then turning north, he ignored the slight twinge of pain in his ankle and let the Calling direct his feet. The wide open plains were a relief from the cramped quarters of the Cravenrock undercity. Despite all his woes, he could not help but smile, and he focused on that happiness to lighten the many steps he would take that day.

Days of neglecting the Calling had left Conner with an intense urgency. He drank sparingly without ever breaking stride. On through the rising heat, rolling plains turned to grassy hills. By mid-morning, he reached the foothills. Cresting his third hill, he spotted a well-worn footpath winding north toward the closest mountain. Unable to divine a reason why he should not take it, he removed his sweat-soaked shirt and angled toward the trail.

Even at the base of the mountain, he did not slow, forcing his tired legs to carry him on up the rocky incline. He kept his eyes fixed on the path at his feet, afraid looking farther along the steep climb would break his waning spirit. Halfway to the top, Conner's footing failed him. He went down hard, scraping his palms on the trail's rocky surface. For several minutes, he lay there, muscles trembling in protest at the energy it took even to breathe.

His rhythm broken, Conner took the moment to examine the food Bandit—no, Kriston—had purchased with his five coins. Six of the packages were travel rations, a blend of beans, rice, salt, and various meats and fruits for flavor, all cooked, compressed, and dried into tight solid blocks. Each block contained all the nutrients needed for a day of hard travel. He opened one of the packages and cut off a large hunk with his knife. A deep whiff of the tantalizing smell and he sank his teeth into the chunk. After a few seconds of exaggerated chewing, his mouth completely devoid of spit, he was forced to wash the bite down with water. He chewed on a more manageable second bite while examining the rest of his food supplies, which included two packages of dried fruit, a jar of berry jam, several rolled strips of unleavened bread, and a sizable amount of fine beef jerky. Conner marveled at the exquisite sight, then laughed, wondering if Kriston's "friend" had any notion he had parted ways with so many delicacies. He decided it best to eat the travel rations when he could, forage for food as time permitted, and hold the remaining items for special occasions.

Feeling his spirit return, Conner repacked the food, donned his damp shirt, and slipped the backpack over his shoulders. He would take the next hour more slowly to work out the stiffness in his legs. Humming the lively tune of "Old Man Garland's Daughter," he stepped lightly up the trail that would take him deeper into the mountains and closer to his bond.

Morgas kept the same hard pace he had set when he and his three trackers had picked up the Eastlander's tracks near Cravenrock's northeast tower three hours before. Judging by the depression in the grass and the difference in the amount of dew around the footprints, the boy had a six-hour head start. While Morgas had successfully tracked human and animal prey with more than that, he would push the three trackers until he was certain the Eastlander could not slip free. Then they would dog their quarry at a more reasonable pace. And when Vault made a mistake, they would be there to bring him down.

Morgas raised his hand. His three shadows trotted closer to examine what had drawn his attention. He absently rubbed Valmer's forehead as his white tundra wolf bond panted, sweat dripping heavy from his tongue. The four human figures studied the footprint in silence. The heat wave blanketing the Narwalen Plains had dried the thick north plains grass prematurely, making it challenging to read the tracks. This print was the first in an hour adequate to get a good reading of their progress. From the lay of the grass around the print, the depth of the depression, the angle and roll of the foot, even the way the toes pushed off, skilled eyes could read the size and weight of their target, how fast he moved, how he carried his weight, and most important, how long the print had been there.

Five hours. Morgas rose slowly, his eyes squinting in Hemera's mid-morning rays that would show no mercy that day. He traced the trail north toward the mountains. In three hours, they had gained less than an hour on the boy. And they had miles of plains to cover in a heat no longer affecting Vault.

Unlike most of Morgas's quarries, the Eastlander was not spending time to mask his tracks. It was possible the boy believed he was not being followed, but judging by his pace, Morgas doubted that. No, the boy had considered that he might be followed. He was relying on his speed, endurance, and a head start to get him safely into the mountains, where he expected to lose them. Morgas was finding a new appreciation for this boy.

Deep blue eyes studied the condition of the two men and woman, and of their bonds. Winded, their determined stares said everything. They would follow wherever he led, carry out whatever he commanded. They had been chosen for that reason.

Johann and Carlon Narkain were brothers. In their thirties, they had spent twenty years trapping in this region of the Dragon's Back Mountains. In early spring, Morgas had been assigned by his master to courier a valuable item to Citadel Farlorde across the northern Borderlands when he came upon the brothers with a wagonload of pelts they had collected through the winter. Twenty miles from the city, brigands were attempting to relieve them of their wares and lives. Morgas came to their aid, dispatching three of the thieves before those remaining were convinced the pelts were not worth the cost. The two brothers were honorable, compelled to request servitude to Morgas as reparation for his assistance. An Alpslander, Morgas had been likewise honor-bound. He accepted a year of their service. Both were good men, though Carlon was touched with the Yearning since losing his bond several years back. This task was the opportunity he needed to test their mettle.

Pallia Aldmar was a different story. She had been raised in the same mountain village as Morgas. But when he was taken into Anarchist bondage, duty payment for his village, he had lost track of her. Then, unexpectedly, a year ago he encountered her and her timber wolf bond, Galven, walking the crowded marketplace of Cravenrock. Since then, she had accompanied him on several missions, and they had grown close. Though he had three years of bondage before he would be free, he would on that day claim Pallia as his wife, and she would claim Morgas as her husband. Then they would return to their village to raise many strong Alpslanders.

He smiled, which confused the brothers since they had gleaned the same bad news from the footprint. For them, this was a job. For Morgas, as Pallia understood, this was sport. And it had been a long time since a quarry had challenged him both mentally and physically.

The footprint forgotten, Morgas picked up the chase once more, long brown hair whipping off his neck. He did not look back. Falling behind was not an option. He would press them harder than before, test them beyond their physical limits. He fed off the excitement of the hunt, driving the rhythm of his legs. He could only hope his faith in the boy's abilities was not misplaced. He had been disappointed so many times before.

On through the rest of the morning Conner ran, stopping occasionally to refill his flask at the many cold streams, or to stretch cramps from his legs. Several times he had thought the trail veered too sharp left or right from the direction of his Calling. Fearing the trail might lead in the wrong direction, he chose to take a more direct route up or down the mountain slope. But each time, he found himself battling through thick underbrush or steep rocky terrain, only to end up back on the trail. After that, Conner stayed on the trail that wove like a brush snake, leading him deeper into the mountains.

By late afternoon, he was heading west, walking along the thin ridge of a long mountain peak. The air was light and crisp, cool on his damp skin, the cloudless sky a brilliant shade of azure. Occasionally he passed rocky crevices and thick wooded patches of trees containing chunks of snow from the previous winter's storms. He stopped more frequently to take in the scenic landscape that fell away to either side of the trail, his body long past its breaking point. Once he reached the place where the long peak trail started a slow descent down the western side of the mountain, Conner took one last look at the majestic scene behind. To the far right of the trail on to the northeast horizon stretched the eastern region of the Dragon's Back Mountains. Some of those mountains, snowcapped even in the dead of summer, dwarfed the one he crossed. They made him feel small in a way he had never known on a farm. He could only imagine how cold the mountains got in winter. Left and south, past the smaller mountains and rolling hills, the Narwalen Plains shimmered in the midsummer heat. His eyes traced the sections of the trail he had taken visible from this height, measuring how far he had come in just one day. That was when he caught sight of movement along the southern edge of a mountain he had traversed earlier.

Wildlife was bountiful in the mountains, so he was about to dismiss it as a female bear and her cubs or a small herd of elk he had heard roamed the region, but something about the apparitions forced him to take a harder look. Even at this distance, he could tell they were human. But there was something more. They were taking the slope with a pace that made his run seem like an afternoon stroll with Pauli. Men did not run that hard unless they were being chased . . . or were chasing something. A chill ran through him, the kind he got when he and Pauli were moments from sinking hip deep into trouble.

Four figures, maybe more. The forms disappeared behind a patch of thick trees blocking further view of the trail. He froze, struggling to recall how long it had been since he'd taken that slope. Three hours at best, possibly less. Well, Kriston had kept them briefly at bay.

His heart began to race, pains and aches forgotten. He swallowed hard, fighting to control the fear knotting his stomach. Three hours of light remained, so he attacked the long, steep stretch of trail with new energy in an effort to match the speed of the pursuers at his heels.

Valmer panted contently, his black eyes closed. The white wolf enjoyed Morgas's hand on his forehead even more than the cooler air along the mountain peak. Like Valmer, Morgas felt alive up here. He grew weary of the petty selfishness and backbiting among the weak Narwalen people, and no place brought out such qualities better than Cravenrock. He was mountain born, raised by a rugged people with a history and legend stretching back longer than the Seven Realms. There was a toughness about him, a hardness in the eyes and confidence in his stride that guaranteed him personal space, even in the most crowded city streets. His father had often told him, *You are an Alpslander, Morgas. You have mountain granite for feet and mountain snow for blood.* So each time he made his way back into the mountains, he found his true feet and blood. His eyes wandered to the northeast, where the snowcapped peaks outlined the darkening sky, toward the place he called home.

Reluctantly, he pushed the distracting thoughts away and considered Vault's behavior that day. Morgas had hoped for a better challenge, but his initial assessment of the boy had been wrong. While he was clearly strong and agile, Vault had no mountain experience. Judging from his tracks, the boy was weary, and weary men make mistakes. That would be his failing. The boy had been foolish enough to attempt bypassing the mountain switchbacks in favor of a direct path, and now the Eastlander had taken to a more leisurely stride, losing valuable time.

Squatting at the end of the long mountain peak trail, Morgas turned his gaze west, down the steep descent of the trail barely visible in the long shadows of the thick evergreens. The boy had stopped here, probably to take in the scenery. He studied the next heel print—here, Vault's pace had changed drastically. He had taken the west side of the mountain like he was afire. Morgas glanced back, where the trail ran along the southern edge of the mountain to the east. So the boy had seen them. No matter.

Morgas examined the condition of the trackers. They had been stretched to their limits, and still the boy had several hours on them. They would continue to the bottom of the mountain. There, they would set up camp and get an early start to snare their young quarry. By his calculations, Vault would be bound and heading back to Lacerus by noon the next day. Luckily, given the boy knew he was being hunted, stealth was no longer a concern. Morgas could finally enjoy a bath and a hot meal in front of a fire to stave off the night's cool mountain air.

Sheer will kept Conner's feet moving up the incline. But as darkness set in, he faced a new demon. Thick clouds rolling in from the west at dusk obscured the full face of Erebus, which would have offered enough light to continue. He wanted to make the summit of the mountain before stopping, but the vision of unwittingly stepping off the edge of a cliff forced him to reconsider. He would either have to stop for the night or risk casting a Night Vision spell to press on. His Thieves Guild mentor had mentioned that others capable of manipulating Earth could sense a clerical spell, but he had no clue what the range was or if those dogging him were capable of such detection. Taking a deep breath, he whispered the words he had been taught. "*Ora energi anakafanos.*" The edges of trees, grass, and trail flared to life. Eyes aglow from the spell, he trudged on another hour.

When the effects of the spell wore off, he stopped to make camp. Not knowing anything about nocturnal wildlife in the mountains, he selected a large oak for his bed. He might not be at home on the rocky mountainside, but he was definitely at home in a tree. During many hunting trips, his father had taught him how to turn a tree branch into a reasonably safe and comfortable place to sleep. After several failed attempts to negotiate the oak's lower branches on exhausted legs, he took a series of progressively larger boulders leading to another branch and leaped into the tree's welcoming arms. After a little effort, he was settled in, his back pressed against the massive trunk, backpack and food secured.

The night was cold. Even with additional clothing pulled over his legs, he shivered. He forced his thoughts from all his physical pains, and soon he was thinking of home. He thought of his warm soft bed, the smell of his mother's cooking, and evenings at the dinner table discussing the events of the day. He wondered what had occupied the Stonefields at dinner that night. No doubt, it was his sisters' progress in schooling. He hated to admit it, but he even missed Miyra and Sayra. Ten days since he had stepped through the iron gate, his parents would soon begin to worry.

His eyes turned north, though he could not see his hand in front of his face. The Calling was tugging harder, demanding his attention. Somehow he knew his bond was close. Maybe tomorrow he would find it. But he had no energy for excitement. His light jacket pulled tight over his shoulders, Conner forced his eyes closed. He just wanted to be heading home, back to a normal life.

Sleep came in fits. Some part of him worried he would oversleep, to wake with a band of seasoned trackers under the oak, poking him with long sticks and mocking his feeble efforts to get away. In his dream, the faces of the trackers morphed into those of the angry city guardsmen shaking their fists while he teetered on Cravenrock Keep's wall. Just like on the wall, he fell backward, his fingers gripping clumsily at the edge of sanity. And he fell into the nightmarish arms of his subconscious, where he spent the night with snarling, hungry bears biting at his ankles. On through his dreamscape he ran, his deer eyes white with fright.

It had been a long time since Morgas had dried his wet, naked body in front of a mountain fire. But the contrast between immersing aching muscles into the snow-fed stream and heating them beside a fire brought them back to life. The four had eaten heartily from their rations, expecting to hunt live game after they snared their quarry. While he had pushed his comrades past their limits, the warmth of the fire, full bellies, and aimless talk kept complaints to a minimum. Even Valmer's spirits were lifted. And the two wolves slipped into the night for a late night hunt.

The evening wore on and talk dwindled with the embers of the fire. The cool night air and sounds of mountain life descended upon the camp. When the wolves returned, Morgas assigned the brothers to share evening watch; Pallia and he would take the morning shift. Nothing more was needed to be said, so he bid the brothers good night and slid under the thin covers behind Pallia. Reaching over her waist, he rubbed Galven's thick timber wolf fur, pressed against her chest and stomach. Valmer took his customary place against Morgas's back, and the camp slipped quietly into the bosom of the mountain night.

The Serf Who Would Be King

King Jonath of Griffinrock pursed his lips and slapped the letter against his thigh in frustration. Beggar, the king's spotted owl bond, had sensed his growing tension while he read the finely etched lettering and decided to watch the growing storm from a safer distance. Feathers ruffled, she stared down at the tall man outside the entrance of the royal bedchamber. Round, black eyes on a flat tan-and-white face reflected the flickering evening torchlight, giving the owl the appearance of a jester, though there was nothing comical about the moment. Next to the king, the royal messenger was a statue; her white-gloved hands holding an empty, intricately etched silver tray.

Jonath held the end of the letter to a nearby torch. He considered the implications of Ranger Loris's letter as it blackened. Turning, he extended the remains of the parchment over the tray until it was nothing more than ash and dripping sealing wax. So far, the only conclusions he had drawn from the unfortunate news was that Veressa would be the death of him.

So the girl had gone on her trek without a company of the royal guard. He knew better than to blame the Ranger; he should have seen this event coming. No, he was certain Annabelle had tried to stop the girl. But the princess had too much of her mother in her. It was a full-time job to keep from getting crushed between the queen's unyielding determination and the princess's gritty independence, leaving little time or energy to clean up after either.

He regarded the messenger for the first time while she waited patiently for the king's command. He noted the finely sculpted features of the girl's face, the precisely combed shoulder-length blond hair pinned behind her ears. The elegant blue surcoat with red trim and gold buttons, one of Chamberlain Nantree's designs, accentuated her fine features. She was about Veressa's age. But while the girl's features could have easily passed her off as Veressa's sister, their stance and demeanor were as night and day. If he commanded this girl to ride to Kallzwall Castle nearly two hundred miles to the northeast tonight with a letter, she would have hesitated only long enough to change into riding clothes. Why did the Cosmos not give him a daughter like this?

He sighed. "Thank you, Claris. You may go." The messenger curtsied with a slight smile and disappeared quietly down the long narrow hall with the silver tray of ash.

Jonath examined the royal bedchamber door looming before him while Beggar gazed down from her perch with her perpetual frown. The two royal guardsmen standing diligently at either side would offer no protection against what awaited beyond. He struggled to call forth the same confidence that had made him Griffinrock's Champion of the Realm. Resolutely, he pushed the gold inlaid handle down. The thick door swung open, groaning as if to mock his mood.

Queen Izadora was so busy perfecting the position of her hair and clothes that she hardly noticed her husband standing nearby. She looked inquisitively at him through the mirror. "You are going to have to hurry if you are to be ready in time for evening meal, Jonath. And don't give me any excuses about how you forgot my sister would be arriving tonight for tomorrow's Midsummer festivities. I am sure she will be exhausted and no doubt wanting to retire early."

He asserted to her reflection, "Why, my dear queen, how could I possibly forget such an important evening as one spent with the royal family?"

Izadora's hands stopped midway through straightening a particularly stubborn crease at her waist. He should have responded like dragon's breath in midwinter, blowing an icy chill down her back. Instead, his voice was the warmth of a summer breeze carrying the scent of honeysuckle and roses. The thought of having a congenial dinner with both her husband and her sister, the Duchess Mariette of Kallzwall, was a delusion she had abandoned years ago. Such formalities were a requirement of a royal family, so she persisted in keeping their tempers in check. But putting the two in the same room was comparable to setting a box of Illuminaries on fire, then waiting around until they went off. You could never tell when the explosion would occur, only that it was inevitable.

She scrutinized her husband. Jonath was a tall, well-built man with soft facial features, a sharp contrast to the combat skills that had made him her champion. His wavy black hair he wore combed back and shoulder length. The slight graying at his temples, which he affectionately referred to as "Veressa's Mark," gave him a distinguished, commanding look. And the steel-gray eyes that looked into her . . . She turned to examine her dress in the mirror before she got lost in them again. "All right, Jonath, what is it?"

He replied calmly, "Why is it that every time I try to reach out to Mariette, you think I am up to something sinister? I have always wanted an affable relationship with the duchess, as I did with your parents before they died. But you know your sister—and her husband—could never look past my roots to see me as your champion—or your husband."

Izadora gazed at the man in the mirror who had championed her heart shortly after he had won the honor of championing her safety. The serf who would be king, Jonath had been born to indentured servants under allegiance to Lord Terrerus Calaman, grandmaster of the Warriors Order and landed knight within Griffinrock's Warstag fiefdom. At the age of eleven, Jonath surprised and impressed Terrerus so much with his ability to control Air elemental that the knight fostered the boy as his page. For the next five years, Jonath traveled with Terrerus to every order tournament in the Harmonic Realms, watching, absorbing, and learning the skills of the competitors, secretively practicing the art of missile combat. After Jonath bonded with Beggar, Terrerus conferred upon him rights to petition for entry into the Mystics Order, where he rose swiftly through the ranks. After several difficult assignments along the Borderlands, he was selected to be the Champion Advocate for the Mystics Order. Ultimately, Jonath won the champion's competition in a hard-fought battle following the reclamation of Izadora's mother.

He stepped closer, then absently tugged at another crease along the back of the queen's waistline. "Tomorrow is Midsummer, my love. It is a time-honored Warstag tradition with the start of a new year to renew and strengthen our relationships with those who are close. I, at least, am willing to give the relationship another chance."

But something was troubling him; she could hear the tension in his voice, see it in his stance. It had taken years to learn how to get past Jonath's impassive expression to find his real feelings. She glanced up at Beggar, who had taken her usual perch near the balcony, noting the owl's anxious expression. Her eyes furrowed at the man. "Are you going to tell me what is really bothering you, or do I have to rip it from your tongue?"

Jonath hesitated, considering how best to say what was troubling him. "Veressa is gone, Iza. She left this morning with Annabelle . . . *alone* . . . on her trek."

Well, nothing like the out-with-it approach. It was so like Jonath to skip any finesse. Would he ever learn? Izadora fidgeted until she was ready to explode. "How can you just stand there when our daughter, our *only* daughter, is out there somewhere away from the castle with no protection?"

"Annabelle is with her, so I see no reason to get excited—" He stopped mid-sentence, wishing he could retrieve those words.

And well he should! *"Annabelle?* That Ranger can't control our daughter, and you know it. Half the time, I think she helps get Veressa into trouble. Frankly, since we're on that subject, I don't know why you didn't replace her as Veressa's protector years ago." Izadora's finger wagged under his nose. "There is something afoot between those two. They have too many secrets between them."

"And you didn't have any secrets with your protector?" He waited long enough for her finger to stop wagging. "Veressa has no sibling to confide in, Iza." Jonath looked suddenly pained. Izadora knew what he was thinking—he was the reason they did not have more children. So she was thankful when he charged ahead. "Annabelle is as close to a sister as Veressa ever had, an *older* sister. Veressa would have hated us both if I had replaced her. Besides, any anger you feel toward Annabelle is misplaced."

Izadora turned her gaze from the steel-gray eyes. "You are right, of course. That girl has too much of her father's crafty way and acute intellect. They will get her in trouble someday."

Jonath's hardy laugh drew her scathing gaze before he coughed to clear away the residual smile stuck to his face.

Izadora continued, wanting to get to the point, afraid of what her husband had decided. "I assume you sent companies of royal guard to find and continue with her on her trek, as we three agreed." It was clearly not a question.

Jonath held up his hands in his defense. "Iza, it is quite possible that having thirty or forty jumpy royal guardsmen to draw attention to our daughter could be more of a risk to her ..." After further consideration, he concluded what was more likely: "And to everyone else around her."

Jonath's response told her everything. This time she did explode. "I can't believe you are doing this! That is the future queen of Griffinrock, the *only* future queen," she noted for the second time, "riding through the wilderness with nothing more than a Ranger to keep her safe. Jonath, if something were to happen to that girl, you would never forgive yourself. Now call out the guard and send them after her."

Jonath stiffened. She had never seen him look so . . . formal. And he responded with the same stiffness. "Is this what my queen demands?"

For once, Izadora was stunned, no words forming on her tongue.

The icy dragon's breath she had expected earlier was now palpable. "On the night we wed, when we shared the royal bedchamber, do you recall what you told me?"

Izadora recalled that night as if it were yesterday, not twenty years before. And all the anger was sucked from her. It was the night she would cherish for a lifetime. "Of course I do." The serf who would be king had knelt before her in this very chamber before their first embrace. Her hand in his, he pledged his heart and life to her. He promised his undying love. But more, he promised to obey her every wish. The love in his gray eyes had deeply moved her; her eyes filled with tears. But it was the serf who made that promise. She had gripped his hands tight in hers, then lifted him up until he stood tall before her, until she was forced to turn her gaze skyward, to be lost in the eyes she wanted to see each dawn. She told him she did not need a servant to share her bed, but a husband who would command respect as king, one who would willingly share the responsibilities of ruling their Realm. That night, the serf became king.

Izadora stepped closer, staring up into those same eyes, as she had that first night. A faint smile parted her lips. Her fingers lightly ran down the fire-ruby amulet hanging from his neck, signifying his position and authority as Griffinrock's Champion of the Realm. Such symbols of rank were meaningless in this room. Her eyes never left his. "I believe and trust in you, my husband, for neither your heart nor head have ever failed me. You do what you believe is true."

Then, slapping his chest firmly with her palm so he knew she was still upset, she turned back to the mirror. "Why are you standing there, Jonath? It won't help your cause of getting into the duchess's good graces if you show up for dinner late."

Cosmic Luck

Just as the eastern sky began to lighten, Conner woke with a jolt, nearly tumbling from the branch he had worked so hard to get into. *Sleep* was not the word he would have used to describe what he had done, since most of the night had been filled with ghoulish dreams. So he had spent the early morning hours weighing his few options.

His ankle was throbbing again; his body would not sustain the pace he had kept the day before. He would have to change his tactic, relying on whatever cunning he could muster to keep from being captured. That meant breaking from the trail that continued west, letting the Calling direct his feet. Well, this was a good place to start.

After shaking stiffness from his legs, he packed his gear in the growing light, chewing on a thick chunk of ration while examining his leafy oak bed. One long, thick branch jutted to the north. After a quick test with his weight, he leaped to a tall boulder several paces away. With a fist of pebbles to scatter about, he stepped over a series of boulders, zigzagging up what remained of the mountain slope. From the summit, he descended the northern side the same way.

Where possible, he used trees to traverse long spans between boulders. He never moved in the same direction for more than ten minutes at a time, randomly adjusting his course but letting the Calling continue to draw him northward. Several times he was forced to alter his path, but when he did, he stepped lightly over gravel and sand, covering his tracks with a branch he had cut from a tree. On the occasions he was lucky enough to find a stream, he would take it for a mile or more, sometimes to his left, sometimes to his right, keeping his feet in the icy water as long as possible. On through the morning, Conner moved at the fastest pace he could muster, using whatever tricks he could contrive to hide his tracks along the way.

He was so focused on his feet and eliminating tracks behind that he forgot to pay attention to the northern skyline. Cresting a small, rocky cliff, Conner discovered he was standing at the foot of a behemoth of a mountain. The long, jagged snowy edges of the giant ran east to west for nearly his entire field of vision. It was so tall the tree line ended halfway up the steep slope, with snow covering the upper rocky section. He considered backtracking. But with Hemera nearing its zenith, he eliminated that idea as too risky. If his attempts to lose the trackers failed, he would be heading straight into their arms. He was here now. He would just have to do the best he could.

Conner thought he could discern a trail running from the mountain's base up to the western end, so he forged ahead and down the cliff's slope, choosing a northwesterly direction. But as he neared the mountain base, he saw the trail was actually a line of boulders that had rolled or slid from the summit. There was no possible way to negotiate that route.

Desperation more than anything drove Conner to continue west along the base in hopes of finding a foothold to climb his way out of this current trap. It was near the western base that he stumbled upon the mouth of a cave and decided a closer inspection was needed. He squeezed past a number of boulders covering the entrance. Cool air wafted lightly across his face. If the cave offered him a way through the mountain, there was still a chance he could escape. One last nervous glance back toward the cliff he had crossed and he turned his attention to the hollowed mountain and stepped cautiously inside.

The ability to read signs left by a quarry is not what separates the excellent tracker from a good one. It is instead the ability to learn quickly about the quarry, to get into its head, understand how it thinks and reacts, then predict how it will behave with changing situations and environment. Morgas had been in good spirits when they broke camp, but his mood shifted when they came upon the tree Vault had used for the night and discovered the boy had bolted from the trail. The rhythm of the group was thrown off. And they lost valuable time before they discerned his new tactic.

The boy was not bad at his new approach; in fact, Morgas welcomed the challenge of the boy's newfound spunk. He was even forced to occasionally use Valmer's nose to find the way. But soon, Morgas had discerned the boy's new pattern, one driven by pure exhaustion. Vault consistently chose to traverse larger, rougher rocks because they were safer to cross on tired legs. He only used trees with low horizontal branches easy to grip and swing from with weary arms. And he was careless in leaving slight impressions in the rocky stream beds.

By late morning, as expected, the boy's exhaustion had forced him to make his mistake. A mountain-green townsman would have seen the giant mountain to the north for the snare that it was. Still, Morgas was learning not to underestimate the boy's ability. He advanced on the short cliff more deliberately, checking for where the boy might have doubled back, leading them into an empty trap. But standing at the crest of the cliff near the rocky snowcapped beast ahead, Morgas knew he had the boy.

He skipped down the northern slope, eyes greedily scanning the length of the mountain's base, but when his initial scan produced nothing living, he pulled up hard. He scanned along the base again, but again found no movement. Had the boy doubled back after all? He silently questioned the others with a glance. Each offered only a shrugged response.

It was Valmer that signaled the boy had gone west along the base of the mountain.

Morgas grinned, relishing the boy's array of surprises.

✦

A hundred paces into the cavern, everything was pitch-black. Once again, Conner invoked Night Vision in frustration. After further consideration, with the chance there could be large, hungry animals nearby, he added a Stealth spell. *"Ora eftos kryptoichos."*

The size of the cavern was stunning. Conner had not traversed a quarter of the distance, and the walls to either side were at least as far away as he had come. The ceiling two paces above his head was as smooth and level as the floor. The air here was fresh and dry rather than stale and damp like that in Cravenrock's undercity. Not wanting to dither, he followed the light breeze deeper into the cavern.

Along the back wall, a portion of the rough surface had broken away near the cavern floor. On hands and knees, he worked vigorously to clear loose rubble at the opening. It took several minutes for him to enlarge the gap enough for his thin body to fit through. He had no clue what awaited on the other side, but it no longer mattered. He tied the shoulder straps of his backpack to his ankle and attacked the hole.

After several paces, he exited into a long, straight tunnel running left and right as far as his vision allowed. The tunnel floor was flat and made of the same rock as the cavern. But unlike the cavern, here the walls and ceiling had been crudely cut away. Down the middle of the floor ran two iron rods about a pace apart, while overhead, makeshift arches constructed from rough-hewn logs sagged from the weight of the ceiling. The scene bolstered little confidence that the whole thing would not come crashing down on his head if he sneezed. He wasted no time donning his backpack once again and sprinted upwind to the right, taking care to stay between the two rods.

A half dozen times Conner had to slow to carefully traverse piles of rotted logs and rock where the ceiling and walls had given way, heightening his concern that he had made a mistake taking this route. If his Night Vision spell dissolved before he reached the end of the tunnel, he would be trapped inside, stumbling about in the dark until he could invoke the spell again.

After half an hour, Conner emerged into the back of another cavern, smaller than the first. On the far side, fresh, warm air flowed through a large gaping hole, caressing his clammy cheeks. He inhaled deeply. The soft rustle of leaves on a summer breeze was music for his liberation. He had found a way through the mountain. The sudden release of the stress made his eyes well with joy. Hardly able to refrain from skipping, he eagerly began moving toward the entrance, skirting a large boulder that filled the middle of the cavern.

Hemera was nearly overhead when Valmer led the trackers to a large cavern. Finally, they had their quarry. Morgas reached back over his shoulder, pulling the longsword from the scabbard strapped to his back. Adjusting his grip, he turned to the brothers. "Pallia and I will go after the boy. Stay here in case he slips past us." Turning to Pallia, who also held her longsword, he nodded his readiness.

In mountain battle stance, the two stepped into the cavern and fanned out wide, signaling their bonds to find the path their quarry had taken. Mountain raised, the two knew how to use all their senses. Auditory, touch, and olfactory perceptions heightened as vision faded. Though Morgas could not see the sword he held steady before him, he could sense the size of the cavern, as well as the location of Pallia and their bonds. It took but a few moments to realize their quarry had exited through a small gap feeding the cavern with fresh air. Morgas snarled at the crawlway. He could not believe the boy's continued good fortune.

Dropping pack and scabbard, he followed Valmer through the tight space, with Pallia ushering Galven into the gap behind them. After exiting into an abandoned mineshaft, Valmer picked up the quarry's scent and led the way to the right. Down the long shaft, he caught a faint glow of light. Morgas snarled again, then followed quickly, Pallia and Galven on his heels. He began to wonder whether the boy was as green as he'd thought. Could he have known the cavern was here, and planned to use it to help make good his escape? Morgas doubted it, but he was starting to think this elusive Vault possessed the golden luck of the Cosmos.

Departure

Veressa twisted in her saddle and scanned the late morning horizon to the west. By Annabelle's calculations, it was the fifth time she'd done so since they broke camp, beginning their second day east out of Graystone. And the girl wore the same resentful expression she'd assumed when she learned that Annabelle had left a letter for the king.

"If the king had sent a company of royal guardsmen after us, we would be hip deep in them by now," Annabelle stated.

Veressa only responded with a harsh look. But a moment later, the girl visibly relaxed.

Annabelle urged her horse forward, deciding it safe to ride a bit closer. "As much as I cherish being your preceptor, I do have responsibilities as your protector. Besides, you put me in a tenuous situation yesterday."

The expression on Veressa's face beneath the Rangers hood softened.

Now that Annabelle was getting through, she added, "Did you consider that informing your father what we are doing may work in your favor?"

"No," the princess responded quietly. For the first time in a day, Veressa smiled at her mentor. After several minutes, she continued. "I know you have my best interest at heart, Annabelle. I should trust you."

Annabelle bit her lip, though it did little to stop an irritable grunt from escaping. She wanted to add that maybe the princess should then occasionally listen to her suggestions, but she refrained. Since she was making some progress, she directed the conversation to a subject she knew would draw some interest. "Now that you have had two days to think about what we discussed on the range, do you have any questions?" Learning to manipulate elemental forces was a journey of self-exploration, not of rote knowledge. A preceptor's job was to illuminate the student's path, to offer guidance through the experiences gained. So she waited.

"Several things are confusing about what you drew." Veressa was fully on Annabelle's lesson on the practice range.

Annabelle could see the girl was struggling with how to put her thoughts to words, so she paused to savor the beauty of the Dragon's Back Mountains to the north. Peron dipped and fluttered in the sky, joyous in his element. A moment later, Veressa's voice brought her back.

"It would seem that the integration of opposing elementals would be impossible. How does a Ranger mix the Earth and Air elementals when they repel each other?"

"That is an excellent question, Veressa. But you should not think of combining elementals like mixing ingredients to make stew. Elementals are given their name because they cannot be mixed. It might serve you better to think of your task as using your will to link them together, drawing from two sources to do something greater than what can be achieved with either alone. I do not want to suggest that the task of a Ranger, or a Sorcerer for that matter, who must link the Water and Fire elementals, is as easy as the other orders. You will find the more you draw upon Earth and Air, the more they will want to pull you asunder. A Ranger's power does not come so much from how much Air and Earth you can draw, but from the strength of the Ranger's will to keep the elementals close. Once you have some experience drawing upon the two elementals simultaneously, you will understand. But you are not ready for that yet." She paused to give Veressa a chance to collect her thoughts before asking, "What else?"

Veressa's second question came much easier. "I know enough about the six orders to see that they do not, as social groups, reflect the elementals they wield. For example, Mystics work with Air and Fire, the two dynamic elementals. Yet, as an order, they live by egalitarian rules, always seeking mutual agreement through logic and discourse. On the other hand, Paladins, who use Water and Earth, the two stable elementals, have been known to be quite capricious as the spiritual caretakers of Harmonic life. And the Shamans seem to be the most fluid with Fire and Earth, but are really the most unstructured gaggle of nonconformists I have ever known, while those of the Warriors Order avoid conflict at any cost—"

Annabelle's laugh caught Veressa completely off guard.

"Did I say something wrong?" she asked, confused.

With a delighted smile, Annabelle answered with a song in her voice. "I do believe you have your father's perceptiveness, Veressa. No, you hit the target dead center. If you can say one thing about the orders, it is that we are all different."

"Okay, but is there a reason for this? What purpose does it serve to adopt such styles?"

"Harmonics, Veressa. It serves the Harmonics." She struggled to find a better way to describe it. "Being Harmonic means living in balance with life. Nine hundred years ago, under the signing of the Armistice of the Orders, the six restructured orders realized they needed a framework that would bring equilibrium to the lives of those who wielded the very essence of the Physical plane. I'm afraid I can't put it any more simply."

Annabelle pulled her horse to a stop, then decided to say more. But her voice had lost its song. "Anarchists are not so compelled. In fact, for them, being Anarchic means living out of balance. That is why the shadow orders assume different structures than the orders from whence they were born. Barbarians, unlike their Warrior cousins, are held together by powerful clan leaders and embrace conflict completely, while the Necromancers, the shadow Shamans, are rigid, rules-driven, authoritative, and steeped in tradition. In a way, I suppose all of this is a holistic form of balance between the six orders and their shadows. In either case, the structures of the orders fit the specific needs of the ordermen and that which they serve."

The two rode in silence for a while, each lost in contemplation amid the scenic landscape.

Veressa broke the silence when she pointed at a tuft of dry, brown grass. "Sageweed. It can be dried and smoked with tobac to soothe a troubled spirit, but if crushed and sprinkled on an open wound, it will keep the wound from healing." She pointed with her other hand at a taller, round bush. "Tanglebrush. Arrowheads dipped into crushed spring berries slow your enemy, while the seeds can be used to extend energy."

Annabelle nodded at Veressa's observation. "Balance, it seems, is everywhere." Nudging her mare forward again, she asked, "And where would I find redwing butterflies?"

Veressa looked perplexed for a moment, then mumbled a few words while gesturing the Detect Plant Earth spell with her hands. "*Ora pheto anakavios.*" Then pointing behind Annabelle to the left, she responded smugly, "On the other side of that rock is a patch of red star thistle. I would start by looking there, since it is the redwing's favorite food."

Annabelle, despite her desire to do so, did not waste her energy with a smile. Veressa's was plenty big for both of them.

Chamber of the Oracles

King Jonath clenched his hands into fists behind his back as he paced the entrance of Graystone's central keep. Hemera's late morning rays streamed through the open windows high above, bringing out the gold inlaid flecks of the Cosmic Star embedded in the polished marble floor. Beggar reflected her bond's impatience with bristled feathers and a constant frown while watching him from a window above. The entire castle was in pandemonium. Servants, guards, yeomen, guildsmen, even noble lords and ladies worked to keep up with the queen's flurry of last-minute demands to perfect the plans for the night's festivities. But neither the list of tasks his dear wife had assigned nor the constant bustle of harried people giving him wide berth held the king's attention.

Jonath had received an urgent request from the College of Mystics to meet with him, and though he had only arrived at the meeting place moments before, the waiting already gnawed at him. The *entire* college of thirteen doyens, the ruling body of the Mystics Order—all here in Graystone! Whatever had brought the entire college to Graystone, he could most certainly rule out that it was a desire to attend Griffinrock's Festival of Midsummer's Night. Occasionally, several doyens might travel together. As many as five or six had been known to attend a royal coronation or the signing of a treaty between the monarchs of the three Harmonic Realms. But he had never heard of the entire college leaving Chateau of Brionne in the southern Realm of Elvenstein, for *any* reason. All thirteen, of course, were good friends. He had tutored under or with most of them during his thirty-three years within the Mystics Order. Many had been involved in selecting him as the order's champion advocate.

A familiar voice at his back broke his anxious reverie. "My most sincere apologies for not arriving sooner, Majesty, but it does seem the entire castle is in such turmoil I had difficulties negotiating my arrival on time."

A smile filled Jonath's face before he turned to face the shortest man he had ever known, who became suddenly shorter as he bowed deeply to the king. Jonath did not seem to care or notice the show of respect. Instead, he reached down and gripped the shoulders of his dear old friend. "Dane Norterry!"

Of noble birth, Dane had entered the Mystics Order at the same time as Jonath. Many of the other Mystic pupils played cruel pranks on Dane because of his size. But it was the proud stature of the boy that had drawn Jonath's attention. No matter how cruel the other pupils could be, Dane never responded in kind or in retribution. Jonath, who was similarly harassed because of his previous social status, befriended him. It was not long before the two became inseparable. Both possessed exceptional raw talent in manipulating the Air and Fire elementals, so with patience and perseverance, they rapidly advanced to the rank of sage. The privileges afforded them by their newfound rank included the ability to command those who before had abused them—which was more than adequate recompense.

But the years had left their mark on Dane. Though his eyes were as sharp and clear as they had always been, he was nearly bald, having exchanged a thick crown of dark, curly hair in his youth for thick graying eyebrows, beard, and mustache. What hair remained, low on his scalp and over his ears, was thinning, and it hung in curls long past his shoulders. He wore the blood-red gown of a grandmaster Mystic, with a braided golden rope tied tight around his thin waist. A wide gold and red brocade sash decorated his narrow chest from right shoulder to left hip, and down his back hung a matching blood-red cloak trimmed in thick gold braid. But what drew Jonath's attention was the large medallion around his neck, the Modeic symbols of missile and magical combat in billowing clouds etched within a raised circle of gold. Jonath's smile widened. "So you are Keeper of the Order."

Dane only nodded slightly with a smile in response, then faced the keep's arching entrance, signaling that they should be on their way.

Jonath and Dane stepped out into the bright late morning, slowing only long enough for a detail of royal guard to form in front and behind. Jonath whispered into Dane's ear as they wove through the crowded castle streets toward the eastern gates. "I don't understand the reason for the secrecy, Dane. Why can't you explain what is happening? You know the queen is in a tizzy preparing for tonight's festivities. If even one Illuminary goes off at the wrong moment, a single note is missed by the royal troupe of musicians, or a guest is seated at the wrong table, I will pay dearly." In truth, while Izadora was quite particular about the Realm's festivals, especially in celebration of Midsummer's Night, these worries paled in comparison to the queen's concern for Veressa's safety since her departure the previous morning.

"I truly am sorry for the inconvenience, Majesty. If I thought it possible to describe what you need to see, I would surely do so."

The king bit at his impatience. "And it is something that must be seen before noon today, you say?"

Dane offered Jonath a reassuring smile. "I promise you, Majesty, once you grasp the truth of the matter, you will understand its import and the reason for such secrecy."

Jonath considered this in silence while the two, along with their guard escort, stepped through the massive castle gates and into the city of Graystone that surrounded the castle. The royal castle of Graystone had been built on a massive rock island jutting out of the middle of the River Tresdan. Not only was the site central to the Realm's fiefdoms, but for nearly twelve hundred years, the natural rocky banks of the island and the wide river had provided excellent protection. As the city began to expand between castle walls and island banks, it was decreed that all structures in and around the island must be constructed from the same light gray marble quarried along the edge of the Dragon's Back Mountains twenty miles to the north. Hewn blocks of various sizes were floated on large rafts downstream to Graystone, where they were strengthened with clerical spells of command, giving the castle and the surrounding city their name. Many sonnets and verses had been put to pen by poets and bards sitting on nearby hillsides, inspired by Hemera's brilliant reflection off the castle walls.

The company moved north, proceeding along a wide and busy cobblestone street. As with all his infrequent trips into the city, the king waved in response to those who paused long enough to bow and curtsy before hurrying on. But his thoughts were on the events ahead. To send the Mystics' Keeper of the Order as a messenger was definitely the way to raise his interest. Since further questioning would not yield any useful information from his dear but determined friend, Jonath used the time to catch up on Dane's life over the past ten years.

So enjoyable was the lighthearted discussion that it seemed only moments before the entourage came to a halt in front of a large octagonal building more than thirty paces high. The lower half of the building was made from the same gray marble as all others, but what set Graystone's Temple of the Mystics apart as being truly unique was its upper section. The walls were made completely from a series of eight massive stained glass windows chronicling the early days of the Mystics Order. A golden dome roof and statue above completed the prominent building.

The royal guardsmen assumed positions outside the large temple doors while the two Mystics stepped through. It had been a long time since Jonath the Mystic had been inside the temple, so he paused to admire the stained glass glowing in Hemera's midday rays. The first depicted magicians, enchanters, mathematicians, astronomers, and other artisans coming together twelve hundred years ago to create the first mystic guilds. It was followed by one showing the creation of the first mystic orders a millennium ago to advance the basic skills of manipulating Fire. The next showed the first mystics' exploration, one hundred years later, binding Air and Fire elementals together. In the next glass was an intense battle scene from the War of the Orders between the twenty-three orders and the Armies of the Seven Realms. The next was taken twenty years later with the remaining grandmasters of the mystic orders signing the Armistice of the Orders, ending the bloodiest war in Cronoan history. The union of several orders into the modern Mystics Order one year later was shown in the next; an image of the first thirteen doyens elected to the College of the Mystics Order to follow. And lastly, a stained glass of the newly reconstructed and shining Chateau of Brionne, designed to help usher in a millennium of peace that lasted but twenty years. Nearly seven hundred years later, mankind still grasped for true and total peace. Jonath shook his head sadly at the scenes, not sure if his sorrow was for the fools so long ago who believed peace would someday be upon them or for the fools today who believed it still possible. A survivor of more Anarchist skirmishes than he dared count, he had no compassion for the first and no patience for the second.

At last, he came out of his contemplation and gazed about. Except for a few Mystic Pupils and their preceptors, the large temple was empty. Dane waited a few paces away. From his expression, Jonath could see he was worried he would not get the king to the college by the appointed time. Jonath followed him briskly to the center of the temple, where a steep metal stairwell descended into the polished granite floor. Thinking the college was below in the practice arena, Jonath had taken several steps down before Dane's hand on his shoulder gave him pause. Jonath looked questioningly up into the little man's eyes.

Dane replied softly, "We must *ascend* from this point, Majesty."

Jonath's eyes followed Dane's to the ceiling above, where a large room hung suspended from the domed roof. The Chamber of the Oracles was a secret room where the order's mysterious oracles supposedly divined their understanding of future events, using mathematics, physics, astronomy, astrology, philosophy, psychology, alchemy, and probably a dozen other sciences Jonath could not even name. No one was permitted there except the oracles and members of the college. Even his standing as king of Griffinrock, Champion of the Realm, and grandmaster Mystic did not give him privilege to enter the room.

Dane studied the king's puzzled expression with amusement, quite satisfied he had gotten the reaction he wanted. *"Aetha eftos anypzorizo,"* he chanted a spell of levitation. With hands clasped in front of him and eyes studying the ceiling above, he floated upward.

Jonath repeated Dane's incantation. *"Aetha eftos anypzorizo,"* forming a thin sheet of Air under his feet. Pushing gently away, he followed the Keeper of the Order to the domed ceiling above. He found Dane hovering in front of a large mirror.

Dane placed his palm to the mirror and recited an incantation, *"Heter energi tikoporeia."* First the surface of the mirror shimmered, then rippled like waves on the water. Giving the king another smile, he disappeared through the liquid door.

Jonath drifted closer, the surface once more solid. He tentatively ran his palm down the cold polished surface, then glanced down past his dangling feet to the granite floor thirty paces below. It was ingenious. Anyone but a grandmaster Mystic attempting to simultaneously hold a sheet of Air at this distance and transform the door would find themselves nothing more than a puddle of blood and cloth below. Jonath called forth the Fire and Air elementals, spoke the incantation to melt the door, and stepped through his rippling reflection.

The Chamber of the Oracles was much larger than it appeared from below, with the arching gold dome roof as its ceiling. Around the circular walls were the Mystics Order Doyens, seven women and six men dressed in blood-red robes identical to Dane's except for the thick white brocade stitch trim. The doyens were so absorbed with a large metallic device filling most of the middle of the room that they were unaware Dane and Jonath had arrived. At the far end, half a dozen more Mystics, wearing the white robes reserved for the oracles, were huddled studying a thin rod protruding from the floor under a skylight. Occasionally, several of the oracles would become quite animated about the rod's placement over a sheet of parchment. This would result in a flurry of pushing, shoving, and arguing until the entire gathering would, once more, sink into quiet contemplation.

Jonath stepped next to Dane to get a closer look at the contraption holding the doyens' interest with such intensity. The metal device, placed precisely in the middle of the room, reminded him of a huge spider lying on its back. The body of the metallic beast contained a tangle of gears and wheels reminiscent of the oracles' Great Clock of Brionne, a mechanical chronometer of incredible precision installed in the Mystics' chateau tower. From the spider's body, seven metal legs with springs fanned upward in different direction. From each leg sprouted several thin metal limbs extending up to more than a pace above the floor. And on the ends of these thirty or so metal limbs were balls, all in a wide range of sizes and colors.

"My Lords and Ladies, King Jonath of Griffinrock," Dane announced above another argument erupting among the oracles. The room fell silent, a few startled by their arrival. In a moment, the room burst into motion and noise as the doyens stepped around the device and greeted Jonath with smiles and wrist clasps, offering their appreciation for his arrival on such short notice.

After all the formalities had been dispensed with, Lady Mille de Noray took advantage of a lull in the noise among the oracles to call the assembly to order. "Lords and Ladies, with Jonath's arrival, I believe we should begin. If the oracles' calculations are correct, there is not much time remaining. Sir Giles, you may start."

A tall, thin oracle in the middle of the group of white cloaks bowed deeply to Lady Noray, then to Jonath. "Thank you, Lady Noray, and to you, King Jonath. Because our time is limited, I will try to be brief, and for King Jonath's benefit, summarize what the rest of you already know." He stepped forward and gestured at the spider before him. "This is a replica of the heavenly planets and moons eternally trapped by our star, Hemera. The device was constructed by the oracles six hundred years ago, led by a brilliant oracle named Orterus Montovia. Its precision challenges our current understanding. Since the time of its construction, only twice have the oracles had to make adjustments to—"

One of the white-robed oracles to Giles's left elbowed him in the ribs. "Get along with it, man!"

Giles stared intensely at the oracle. Clearing his throat, he continued. "But that is another story. Three months ago, we observed a rather interesting arrangement of the planets in our celestial model. If you will step closer, I will show you what I mean. Yes, please mind not to bump anything." He waved vigorously for everyone to come closer, but did not wait before pointing at a small, bluish ball. "This represents our planet, Gaia, our astrological reference point. Now, if you will notice, if we draw a straight line from Hemera to Gaia, then extend the line straight on, we see that the line intersects with Pontos on the other side. We know this, of course, because for the last several nights, we have been witnessing the shadow of Gaia tracking its path across Pontos's surface." Giles pointed to where Gaia's shadow had been seen on Pontos. "If we draw another line perpendicular through Gaia, running right to left"—he ran his finger from the pale blue ball to the large brownish-red ball—"we see Aether and Ourea are similarly aligned to create a perfect cross."

It struck Jonath where this discussion was likely going. He let out a sharp, short laugh.

Giles looked questioningly at the king.

Jonath balked. "Sir Giles, you cannot be suggesting what I think. It is pure coincidence these three planets and Hemera, which by chance happen to be named after the four elemental Beings, are aligned to form the points of the Cosmic Star around our Gaia."

Giles bowed humbly to Jonath, yet he countered with a touch of irritation in his voice. "I must apologize, Majesty, but we, the Oracles of the Mystics, are not in the business of making suggestions. 'The mere Mystic seeks to know what is; it takes an Oracle to find what is yet to come,'" he recited the age-old proverb with fervor. "My experience says there are no coincidences. The heavenly bodies are named as they are for a reason—Hemera for the Fire Djinn, Aether for Air, Pontos for Water, and Ourea for Earth. These, along with the other bodies"—Giles waved his arm to include all the colored balls—"are here to offer us insights into the greater Cosmic drama, if we understand how to interpret them."

He paused only long enough to take a breath. "The oracles have spent a millennium studying and relating the motion of these bodies to events on Gaia with great accuracy. I can say with certainty that never in New Cronoa's history has this alignment—this Cosmic balance—been near as precise as at this very hour. And that does not even consider that, at this very moment, on the other side of Gaia, our moon Erebus, the shadow, the keeper of the Anarchic"—Giles pointed to the small gray ball near Gaia—"is in full eclipse. Nor does it consider that the heavenly body Eros, the Harmonic lover, is precisely eclipsed by the only body that could dwarf it—Hemera herself. No, all of this is anything but coincidental. Sometime in the next thirty minutes or so, the celestial alignment will be complete. In that moment, for that one Cosmic heartbeat, the Cosmos will be suspended in precise balance."

Before Giles could continue with his monologue, Lady Noray interrupted, "What does this mean exactly? What will happen? Will the skies light on fire, the ground shake until the mountains crumble, or the lakes turn to dust?"

Giles bowed deeply again before continuing. "We can only ordain the significance of the moment, my Lady, not divine its meaning."

Tension flared among the doyens. Several animated discussions broke out until a middle-aged woman oracle near Giles stepped forward and shouted over the chatter. "Lady Noray, if I may? I believe I can illuminate Sir Giles's comment in a way that will explain our limitations in exacting the effects of this Cosmic balance."

Lady Noray replied impatiently, "Madam Gildamare, yes, if you please."

Offering a deep bow, Gildamare continued. "Thank you, my Lady. We humans, and our animal colleagues who share Gaia, go through our lives day by day believing we are in complete control of the choices we make. On the individual scale, this is generally the case. So if this is true, how does the Cosmos enact its great plan to which we the oracles subscribe? The answer to this question can be found in three Cosmic laws. First, we know our decisions, and thereby our actions, are influenced by the heavenly bodies that create forces upon our psyches, often in very subtle ways. During Erebus's full face, crowds exhibit more Anarchic behavior and become mobs, while wars are most likely when Pontos appears on the horizon. Second, we are influenced by the bonds we share with the animals. These two are generally accepted as fact. But there is a third component the Cosmos employs to guarantee success of its plan.

"We all have heard stories of several people simultaneously and independently creating a unique thought or important idea. We also know cases in which two or three people arrived at the same place and time, each capable of solving a perplexing and challenging problem that appeared suddenly. Each of us can give specific examples of times when we were faced with a life-changing situation or we lacked the capacity to do something important, and out of nowhere, a preceptor arrived to guide us. All this suggests that the Cosmos uses probability and redundancy. That is to say, when something important must be done, the Cosmos creates multiple opportunities and uses the other laws of the heavenly bodies and bonds to ensure that one of those possibilities becomes realized.

"This leads me to the point Sir Giles was making. We believe a significant event is about to occur, one that will, at first blush, be as subtle as a falling leaf, but will most certainly set in motion a cascading series of effects that will ripple through the Harmonic Weave for the next several hundred years . . . if not longer."

Gildamare raised her voice to be heard over the growing murmur among the doyens. "But what happens when the forces of the heavenly bodies are so perfectly set in balance that their effects are nullified? The laws normally guiding our path on the macro scale ceases to apply. We believe the Cosmos has created a singularity, a single possibility, which will take effect since its other laws will not be working. Further, we believe whomever the Cosmos selected for this singularity was most assuredly directed to the place of this event, but, once there, will act completely on their own volition. To summarize all of what we have said, when this moment arrives, the Cosmos will be at the mercy of that singularity. That is why we cannot divine what will happen."

The doyens stood in silence. Finally, Lady Noray asked, "Is there a way to at least know when and where this event will occur?"

Giles held up his ink-smudged finger in triumph. "Ah! We can indeed! If everyone will gather back here, I will show you how." The entire gathering encircled the tall man next to the rod protruding from the floor.

"With some rudimentary mathematics at our disposal, we narrowed the location of the event to the eastern region of Griffinrock. That is the reason for requesting King Jonath's attendance in this matter." He nodded courteously to the king before proceeding. "Since the event will occur precisely when Hemera is aligned with Gaia and Pontos, we know the star will be exactly at the event location's zenith, where no shadow will be cast. At that same precise moment, here in Graystone, there will be a shadow. By scaling the distance to Hemera, we can use our inverted map of Griffinrock here"—Giles pointed at the parchment on the floor—"with the rod positioned in Graystone to find the event's locus. Once the bodies on the model have reached their precise alignment, we will hear an audible click of the gears. The shadow of the tip of the rod will pinpoint the location."

As if on cue, a loud mechanical clang reverberated from the metal spider. Giles bent and marked a spot on the map. "It seems the event is taking place at this very moment, approximately fifty miles north of Cravenrock, within the Dragon's Back Mountains."

So immersed were they in their pensive thoughts and discussions about how best to proceed that no one noticed one of the doyens, Lord Tenarian Andermann, slipping away from the group, his hand hidden beneath his robes clutching a large, flat amulet with black onyx stone.

Night of the Necromancers

Breanen Sagamore stared out the chamber window high in the Academy of Thanatos. Her long, straight hair, silver and thin from age, hid the amulet hanging from a thick chain about her narrow neck. Absently, she rubbed the amulet's black onyx stone with a withered hand. Tired eyes scanned the landscape below.

The view offered no solace from the hours spent staring at the four walls of the dark room. There was nothing scenic about what she beheld. The thick green forest that had once surrounded the majestic fortress and Academy of Thanatos was gone, except for the gnarled, petrified trunks and branches of trees ravaged by the Necromancers who had tried in vain to hold back the mighty army of the Seven Realms over nine hundred years ago. The grounds around the fortress walls had been so utterly seared from powerful Fire-Earth spells and summonings that flora still refused to grow. But when the Necromancers broke from the Shamans Order at the start of the Great War six hundred years ago, they rebuilt the fortress of Thanatos and its Academy exactly as their Supreme Lord Shazarack had designed it. The horrendous scene outside was a constant reminder to those calling Thanatos home of the prejudices and offenses committed by those incapable of appreciating the important work they performed.

But all that was about to change.

She closed her eyes and licked parched lips, her mind wandering. Hemera had crossed its zenith here in the northern Anarchic Lands, so the long-awaited moment was upon them. The countless years did little to ease her impatience. Too much time had been put into these plans to not feel anxiety boiling up through her frail mortal frame. And though she had been waiting for a message from Tenarian, she inhaled sharply as she sensed her Brother's consciousness. Her eyes opened wide with Tenarian's news. Turning, Breanen examined the hollow, expectant faces of the Lords and Ladies of the Night standing about like cadaverous phantoms in midday shadows.

They marveled at her clairvoyance. But why should she care if they clung to heathen hocus-pocus? Some things were not meant for mortal minds, no matter how deeply they hungered for the knowledge of the Cosmos. Feigning respect, she bowed slightly to them. "It is as I said. The balance has arrived."

In his flowing dark purple robes, Galan Martesian, Sovereign Prince of the Necromancers, responded with a smile void of feeling. "Your services in this matter are deeply acknowledged, Breanen." To the Lords and Ladies in the chamber, he continued. "The time is with us, my friends. The Night of the Necromancers will return when we have rebuilt Shazarack's mighty army and reclaimed what was his. Give the command. Tonight we begin the summonings with the corpses we have at our ready."

Breanen's thoughts drifted, her hand vanishing beneath the silver hair draped across her chest. She found the cool touch of the blue-specked onyx comforting. Even with all the time here, it never ceased to amaze her how predictably simpleminded they were in their endless pursuit of power and wealth. She watched Galan depart for their bedchamber to get the rest he would need for the night's arduous work. Convince a powerful mortal you held the key to rule the world and he would gratefully follow you into the torrential depths of the Anarchic planes.

It was several minutes before Breanen realized she was alone, staring at the tainted land below. She started down the dark hallway leading to the bedchamber where Galan lay sleeping. She was growing tired of this drab place. Someday she would enjoy the unending sweetness of physical pleasures. But much work remained before obtaining that reward.

Anthem

For a hundred millennia, the harsh Antaric Sea winds beat cold waves across the northern edge of the volcanic island, only to receive heated white foam churned against molten rocks for its efforts. Still, the wind whipped hissing steam, ash, and sulfur on rising jets of air a hundred paces up the formidable craggy cliffs, serving to cool the drafty caverns that honeycombed the massive island.

It is possible a human adequately schooled in volcanic structures would have noted that many of the cavern openings potting the island walls were too smooth and evenly spaced to be a natural effect of the island's active volcano. But no human had ever reached this island. The decomposing bones of ships and their occupants served as a constant reminder to passing vessels to steer clear of the towering sea spider's treacherous shallow reefs webbing outward. A human would surely have marveled at the intelligent makers' cavern design. Skillfully carved conduits relieved deep volcanic pressure by venting lava to fissures lining the base of the island, leaving the upper regions untouched by liquid rock since the architects' arrival nearly a millennium before. But no human had ever laid eyes upon this refuge.

The caverns teemed with life unsympathetic to the misfortunes of the ship-bearing creatures caught in the island's web. Deep pockets, pooled with a mix of nutrient ash and heated rainwater, served as dens for the recently hatched, while keepers maintained diligent watch until first molting. Molted youths frolicked in endless games through deep nursery tunnels guarded closely by young adults. Along the southern rocky ledges, adolescents tested their bravery and maturing leathery wings through thick, swirling steam in a dangerous dance of tag. The more adventurous adolescents flew south, letting the strong Antaric winds carry them on to the mountainous mainland shores eighty miles away to dine on more exotic foods.

It was a particularly warm midday when the four remaining Ancients of the Cloudbender family were stirred by the Cosmic shift. Milky blue eyes peered hesitantly through narrow slits before horned black heads lifted from the cavern floor. In unison, the four rose on ancient legs and engaged massive muscles that should have long since atrophied. Sharp claws, long from lack of use, clicked metallically on the cavern floor as the mighty beasts lumbered to the nearest sky-bound shafts. Then, digging deep into the shaft walls, the four behemoths climbed upward into daylight they had not felt in decades. Rocks rumbled and cracked under the straining weight. Aged scales broke away from the bulky bodies, descending down the long shafts like ebony summer rain.

Driven by powerful Cosmic forces, the four iridescent forms walked the volcano's upper crater. Assembling reverently around the sacred totem constructed long before their arrival, they began a ceremony performed only once before in their family's history. Impulses dormant since their summoning sprang forth. Under the brilliance of a cloudless blue sky, they rocked back on bulking heels and unfurled black wings larger than the sails of the greatest frigates. Filling their lungs to the point of pain and beyond, they began to sway rhythmically and sing the epochal verses of their family's anthem.

The caverns were carved precisely to match the resonating vibrations of the Ancients' chords. The entire island structure responded sonically. Decomposing ships nearby trembled; some succumbed to natural forces, shuddering, cracking in agony, and disappearing below rising waves whipped up by the vibrations crossing the island.

With the first low rumbling chord, life within the island ceased its hectic bustle. Those who had lived to know the early verses closed their eyes, and with heads arching to the cavern ceilings, joined in the anthem that honored the works and deeds of those who had come before. The voices of the Ancients wove the intricate patterns of shifting harmonics, with each succeeding age joining in, guiding the anthem in the long procession through the generations. They sang in praise of the Shaman God who brought them into the world, they sang in joy for their release into the world and to the den they built to raise their family, they sang with pride for bonds they once had forged with humans, and they sang in honor of those who died keeping a promise that was never meant to be made.

And when at last the anthem reached its final verse, and all but the hatchlings joined in to achieve the full height of the crescendo, Hemera neared its zenith. In that moment, as if unwilling to relent without giving a last call of warning, the island quivered one last time, and the sea sent out one last wave, and the air blew one last gust upon the sea winds. Then there was silence.

Bonding

All Conner could think about was getting out from under the oppressive weight of the mountain, feeling the fresh breeze on his face, letting the midday rays warm his skin. But his eyes kept drifting to the black rock in the middle of the cavern. Light reflecting off its surface shimmered in waves. Halfway to the entrance, his step faltered. Well, he was heading in that general direction. Surely a closer look could not hurt.

Three paces from the rock, it occurred to Conner that the black surface did not look like any type of rock he was familiar with. At two paces, he noticed the side of the rock was undulating. Conner mentally ran through the short list of large mountain creatures he knew of, but nothing fit. Fascinated by the odd shape, and with his Stealth spell invoked, he was not concerned that he might awaken the slumbering beast. One pace away, he could make out a shifting blue iridescence to the creature's skin. He moved yet closer. No, not skin. The surface was made of . . . scales.

Captivated by the iridescent blue flowing across the scales, Conner reached out slowly so as not to disturb the creature. Fingertips slid gently across the rough surface, igniting faint cobalt sparks that tingled up his arm. And in that moment, the world around him seemed to shudder.

Part V

The Cosmos knew its unfolding and was moved with great love. And through the vessel of its love, all Beings received two gifts so that each could avow its part in the great drama that unfolds. The first gift was the Cosmos's very spirit, the essence of its energy, so all Beings could feel the persistent will to live. And the second was discernment, so all Beings would feel the illusion of their separateness, their aloneness, from their Creator. Thus it is that Beings are forever caught in the Cosmic drama of life, to wisely use their first gift to shed consciousness of their second, just as a snake sheds a skin it has outgrown. So it is that all return to the One, but only if we take care not to be the skin that sheds the snake.

—The Modei Book of Water (Third Book)

A Simple Misunderstanding

Skye-Anyar-Bello Cloudbender sighed contently in his sleep. Muscles rippled as he stretched his legs across his bed of dream gold. Nothing felt as wondrously soothing as gold infused with a dragon's essence. In his dream, three mature females appeared about him, crouched and prancing in the classic display of affection and admiration. Well, maybe *one* thing was better. Sharp talons dug deep into the mound of shiny metal; blue eyes rolled up under double eyelids in sleep-filled rapture.

The feeling was so delightful that the shock of being awakened dwarfed even the realization that the gold and females were nothing but sleep phantoms. Five days and nights enjoying the warm solitude of the cave to reach that altered state of blissful consciousness dragons craved, only to be so rudely aroused. Rage filled his emotional vessel that had so recently been overflowing with contentment. Whatever had pulled him from his dream sleep would soon realize its mistake. Sensing a presence in the cave, his horned black head swiveled around on a long, slender neck to take a look at his antagonist—and his lunch.

He had never seen a human, but he had heard enough dragonsong to know the quite unimpressive two-legged stick standing a tongue's length away could be nothing else. A few dragons had tried eating humans, and the one thing they all agreed on was that the meal was dreadfully unsatisfying. In fact, in dragon tongue, *dragork* was the name given to a crazed dragon; it meant "two-human-eater." The meager amount of meat on its bones and a putrid smell that made his empty stomach lurch could only appeal to a demented dragon. That

Skye-Anyar-Bello Cloudbender would not even get the satisfaction of quenching his hunger only fueled his annoyance.

There was still a chance to return to that blissful sleep state. Giving the scrawny human a good look at the source of its annihilation seemed the perfect place to start. He held the paralyzed human's gaze with icy blue eyes while his body flowed like black water. He rose on two powerful legs, chest expanding forward. Black wings fanned wide and his head arched toward the ceiling to complete the awesome display. He fancied his carriage must be truly awe-inspiring to such a lowly, small creature.

Skye-Anyar-Bello Cloudbender's lightning strike was certainly no less impressive. His right leg slashed forward, sharp talons arcing downward at the creature's thin chest. The dragon peered down with delight to watch the human's entrails spill out across the cavern floor. But vindication turned to astonishment when the nimble little beast dove to the left, coming up in a ready crouch.

Blue eyes glowed like lightning bolts. Nostrils flared. He snorted incredulously at the deft little critter. In an incredible feat of quickness, he whipped his spiny tail to send the human careening into the cavern wall. Instead, the human gracefully leaped over his tail, going into another roll and coming up behind a boulder. Unable to bring his tail in for a backstroke, Skye-Anyar-Bello Cloudbender roared.

This was quite enough. With wings unfurled, he propelled his head forward and down. Searing fire streamed from his gaping mouth, exploding across the boulder until the rocky surface glowed red and molten rock dripped to the cavern floor. But the spry creature just stepped from behind the boulder, flicking away steaming chunks of rock from his shoulder.

The dragon studied the human with newfound respect. No animal should have survived that inferno. That is, unless the creature was enchanted. A cold-blooded tremor ran down his spine. Of course, he had heard of dragoncatchers, humans who could enslave dragons to their will. But dragoncatchers were night fantasies to keep amphitheres from straying from the den. Skye-Anyar-Bello Cloudbender took a measured step back.

Conner studied the monster with respect. No animal should have been able to create such a blast of heat. That is, unless the creature was enchanted. A chill ran down his spine. Of course, he had heard of dragons, creatures that could kill a man with a single stroke. But, dragons came from fables invented to entertain children. Conner took a measured step back.

At least the black beast had stopped trying to kill him for the moment. It occurred to Conner that he should, as his dad liked to say, make hay while Hemera shined. Quick as a twitch, he spun about and sprinted for the cavern entrance as fast as his legs could churn.

Morgas smiled at the sounds drifting down the long mining shaft. It seemed Vault's luck had run out. Whatever animal the boy had encountered, he hoped it would entertain the Eastlander long enough for their imminent arrival. Sensing victory, he picked up the pace, feet dancing lightly down the middle of the dark shaft.

Just as the spritely creature started for the cave entrance, Skye-Anyar-Bello Cloudbender caught the sound of more two-legged creatures approaching through one of the narrow shafts behind. "Of course," he snorted. "I am a fool!" This imp was only a diversion while its comrades slipped in unaware. And the enchanted human was rushing to block his only way to freedom. He could almost feel dragoncatcher jaws biting into his loins. He flinched at the vision. Intense anger turned into an intense will to live. And as anything lucky enough to survive an encounter with a dragon knew, nothing was more alarming than an alarmed dragon.

Gone was his desire for the blissful state; dreams of gold and females faded like morning mist. Wings pumped frantically to get his lethargic body moving. Survival instincts drove the pounding beat of his wings . . . and his back slammed hard into the low ceiling. The entire cave trembled in response. Rocks rained down. Off balance, he tilted and swung wildly to the left . . . and his shoulder found the cave wall. Pebbles danced across the floor as the cave shook from the beating. He twisted to get away from the wall pinning his wing, and his forehead cracked into the ceiling. He groaned from the force of the impact. The ceiling groaned back.

Skye-Anyar-Bello Cloudbender scrambled in a mimic run to beat the scrawny human to the entrance, sharp talons unable to catch on the smooth cavern floor. Finally, his wings found the air to lift him, taking him directly along the human's path. That would give him one last opportunity to appease his wounded pride. Talons shot forward; his tail whipped upward. He would end the miserable creature's existence.

Blasts of dust from the monster's pounding wings swirled around Conner, stinging his eyes. He staggered through the haze toward the entrance. But the sound of the creature behind convinced him it was more prudent to get out of the way. Sensing that the monster was nearly on his back, he took another diving shoulder roll to the right. A black tail whizzed past, hammering the mouth of the entrance hard as the winged shadow of destruction glided through the thick, swirling clouds of dust and on into the daylight beyond. Rocks shook under his feet, disrupting his roll. Unable to steady his footing, Conner's shoulder struck the wall with a crunching thud, and he disappeared beneath a shower of gravel and dirt.

The distant rumble of thunder made the ground and air quake. Morgas and Pallia hesitated, trying to make sense of the sounds. With the second clap, pebbles and dust rained down on them. With the third, Pallia yanked Morgas hard to the right as a section of the wall collapsed where he had been standing. Galven yelped, then let out a frightened whimper.

Morgas coughed, his free hand covering his nose and eyes from the blinding dust. "We have to get through this shaft before it becomes our tomb!" he growled audibly in a grimace.

Pallia and Galven took the lead, Morgas stumbling behind with Valmer pressing on his heels.

Conner dug his way out from beneath the rubble, trying to find solid footing, coughing up dust and spitting grit from his cotton mouth. Everything was a light gray blur. He reached for the wall to steady his wobbling legs, but a spasm of pain shot up his shoulder and neck. His ears rang with the sound of a tornado growing steadily louder. He staggered forward, waving his arm to keep from running into a wall. Then the ground began to rumble again, only this time it did not stop. The entire mountain was coming down around him.

He weaved and bobbed toward what he hoped was the remains of the entrance, his feet working to find footing over the shifting rocks littering the cavern floor. Dust filled his lungs and he gagged. Rocks of every size pummeled his body. One hit him hard on the right side of his head and he staggered from the blow. Arms over his head, Conner ran in desperation, no longer caring if he was moving in the right direction.

Then everything was still.

Cautiously, he lowered his arms. For the first time in what seemed like eons, Hemera's rays warmed his face. He blinked several times in surprise, not sure if he was crying from the dust or the relief of being alive. His head throbbed like an Anarchic war drum. Gingerly running fingertips along the growing lump on the side of his scalp, a memory flashed across his mind. He and a much younger Pauli were playing Queen's Defender and Anarchic spy. Pauli, always the Defender, had cornered the evil spy in the Cloverdale shed, where a great battle with wooden swords ensued. But Pauli always insisted the Defender be victorious. On that fateful adventure, Conner had failed to duck one of Pauli's zealous swings, receiving a solid crack to the skull for his mistake.

Through spinning eyes, Conner examined the red, sticky goo coating his fingers. He would have laughed at the familiarity of the memory, but he was unconscious before his body struck the ground.

What Remains

From the rumbling sounds at the far end of the mining shaft, Morgas knew what they would find. Well, almost. Pressing up close behind Pallia, he surveyed the wreckage over her shoulder. Their wolf bonds proceeded into the dust-filled cavern to sniff out their quarry's path, unaware their efforts would be in vain. The entire entrance, along with the left half of the cavern, had been buried by an avalanche of rock and dirt. But that was not what surprised Morgas and his mate the most. Instead of total darkness, what remained of the man-made mining hall was bathed in a deep blue pulsating light.

"What do you make of it?" Pallia asked breathlessly, their quarry momentarily forgotten.

"I don't know. I've never seen anything like this." He stepped cautiously around her and proceeded left along the wall. Taking his cue, Pallia fanned right. Morgas had seen at least twenty such abandoned mining halls. Ore and gem miners common to this area would carve a circular cavity into the side of the mountain, then extend a series of mining shafts, like fingers on an open hand, in hopes of striking a solid vein. If the initial search produced nothing of significance, the mine was abandoned. His first thought was that they had stumbled upon a mine containing some magical form of rock, but he dismissed that idea. He had never heard of a glowing magical ore. Besides, this hall had been abandoned for centuries.

Having passed two more mining shaft fingers to his left, he came to where the rubble began, forcing him to turn right. He followed the edge of destruction to where the wolves waited patiently, near the center of the hall where the pulsating blue glow was brightest.

Judging by Valmer's reaction, Vault had come to this spot. Morgas bent and hefted a fist-sized glowing rock. Something familiar about the glow nagged at his memory, something he should have known.

Immersed deep in thought, he was unaware of Pallia standing beside him. She pointed into the rubble, where the entrance had been. "Do you think he was buried under there?"

He smiled at his mate's puzzled expression. "Somehow I doubt it. No, our friend has had the Cosmos's luck since we started this journey. I wouldn't be surprised if he was even involved in causing all this." He gestured with his arm, then went back to examining the rock in his hand. He was coming to appreciate Lacerus's keen interest in the boy.

Remembering the sounds they had heard before entering, Morgas nodded at the devastation. "There was something else in this hall when he arrived. Whatever it was, it was the cause of this destruction." He stuffed the pulsating rock into his backpack. "Let's get back to Johann and Carlon. I must consider what to do next."

Pallia's expression turned from puzzled to perplexed at his cryptic words. She thought the next step was obvious, but Morgas would never waste time stating the obvious. They had been together long enough for her to trust his decisions in such matters, so she silently nodded her acceptance before retracing their steps.

Several sections of the mining shaft had not fared well during the avalanche, so it was hours before the two arrived exhausted at the entrance of the southern cavern where Johann and Carlon waited.

"Well met, my liege. We feared the worst," Johann exhaled. The brothers had felt the avalanche even at this distance, and had been worried the couple and their bonds lost. He glanced over Morgas's shoulder, but when their quarry did not appear behind him, the smile faded. "So our work is not yet complete."

Morgas inhaled fresh air. "We cannot assume the boy died in the avalanche. It is more likely that he escaped through to the north. You are to circumvent this mountain and check for tracks. If you find any sign of him, you are to capture him and bring him back to this cave." He measured their reaction. The tone in his voice told them there was more. "Pallia knows where to find the mining entrance. She is in charge. You are to follow her as you would me."

Pallia stepped in front of him; her intense stare and stance made it clear that whatever he was considering would not go unchallenged.

Morgas's expression softened. Stepping close, he pressed his right cheek to hers, his right palm lightly to her left temple. The brothers quietly stepped away to give them privacy. Even then, he whispered, "I need you to do this for me, my mate. I must report to Lacerus. What we witnessed cannot wait until we have the boy. I will return to you as soon as possible."

He would not have put her in charge if he did not trust her abilities. Further, Lacerus would not have taken audience with anyone but Morgas. And a written message would not suffice. She pressed even closer, emulating his gesture of affection with her palm. "It will be as you wish, my mate. May the paths of our forefathers guide your step." She stepped away, holding his gaze for a moment, then, turning to Galven, checked her bond for injuries.

Morgas found the brothers nearby. "There is something about this boy. He is not the country bumpkin he seems, so keep your wits around him." Unable to put into words anything more specific, he hoped either his gut was wrong or his warning was adequate to protect them. The brothers deliberated with Morgas about the fastest route out of the mountains, but the urgency of his message kept the discourse terse.

Looking back, Morgas held eye contact with Pallia. He hoped he had the energy to make the trip to Cravenrock at the speed he would need to maintain. At least the shortcut Johann had offered would trim several hours from the run. He disappeared over the southern ridge.

Valmer paused at the top long enough to take one last look at Galven; then he too was gone.

Midsummer's Night Visitors

Once Conner was certain his bouts with queasiness were subsiding, he gingerly raised his throbbing head, then sat up. Heaving on an empty stomach would only worsen his misery, so he would take it slow. That gave him time to inspect his surroundings.

As suspected, the tunnel had discharged him along the north side of the mountain's western base. Farther to the north, a narrow, overgrown wagon trail ran precariously along the side of the mountain. West of the road, a steep, forested drop-off descended to a stream thirty paces below, while a rocky incline jutted nearly vertically to the east, ending in the snowy summit high above. Along the upper slope, a few scruffy trees and bushes eked out a meager existence, roots clinging tenaciously to mountainside crevices. Conner surveyed the devastation behind him. If he had not passed through there, he would have denied a cavern ever existed. He was thankful he was able to get free before it collapsed.

Hemera was already sinking beyond the mountains. Conner estimated he had been unconscious for about five hours. Given the darkening sky, Conner could not depend on remaining safe where he was; he rose on wobbly legs. Thinking made his head hurt, so he let the road do the thinking for him. It had to lead somewhere. Slinging his pack over his shoulder, he focused on putting one foot in front of the other and staggered north.

He had no idea how long he walked, his body working involuntarily through the scrub brush and saplings reclaiming the old, winding road. But stumbling over roots and bushes in the dark brought him out of his sleep walk. The road had settled into a hollow splitting two mountains, with a rocky stream nearby. He collected an armload of branches. After negotiating a number of large boulders to reach the riverbed, he sank his naked body into the fast-moving waters and methodically washed away all the mud and dried blood. The cold stream breathed new life into his exhausted body and relieved some of the throbbing in his head as well. Refreshed, Conner started a small fire halfway to the road.

After changing clothes, he wrapped his last clean shirt around his head and pulled it tight to get some relief from the throbbing. Not shackled and on his way back to Cravenrock easily qualified as a "special occasion," so he rummaged through his backpack until he found the packages of dried fruit, jelly, strips of jerky, and rolled bread. He ate voraciously while a chunk of ration soaked in his tin cup with water over his fire.

His belly finally full, Conner leaned against a boulder, finding some paltry satisfaction that he had not only successfully evaded his pursuers another day, but survived an encounter with a mighty mountain beast. The warmth of the fire and sounds of nature evaporated all his worries as he considered what to do in the morning. His foot tapped in rhythm with the crickets and the stream as he hummed the ancient Narwalen melody "When I Come A-Courtin'."

Suddenly, he stopped humming, his eyes bulging wide. He rocked forward and looked around. Something was ... wrong. Conner struggled for understanding. He rummaged through his mind, but it was not there any longer. Apprehension flooded over him, this time not for who was behind, but for what was no longer ahead. He rose with a stiff groan. But no matter how hard he tried, he could no longer sense the Calling. He began to pace about, trying to think of what Karlana Landcraft might have mentioned that would explain this condition. After some time, the only explanation he could contrive was that it was due to his head wound, still pounding with every motion of his body.

He was tired; that was it. Conner nodded to himself as if that would convince him. He threw a few more branches on the fire, and in the flickering glow, packed his belongings, as if being prepared for the morning would make it all better. Stuffing his pack behind his lower spine for support, he rested his head against the boulder and drifted off. But he did not sleep long.

An unnatural breeze and the sounds of movement pulled him from a dream of fishing with Pauli while telling outlandish tales. He cautiously lifted his head and waited. His patience was rewarded by another sound, closer. He leaned forward and gripped the end of a thick branch protruding from the fire. Something was out there watching him. At least he thought so. Standing, he held the burning bough out, then declared with as much confidence and force as he could muster. "I know you're out there. Go away." Conner hoped his voice conveyed enough authority to scare whatever was there.

Two glowing sea-blue orbs appeared over a hearty azalea near the edge of the firelight.

Conner's nerve evaporated. He gripped the log tighter. "I don't want to fight you," he stated. Thinking that might be taken as a sign of weakness, he continued, more for his own benefit than to what crouched behind the bush. "I don't know why you came back, but I don't have any food. So go away."

A deep voice floated back from the bush. "I don't think I would like human food."

Conner hesitated. Did "human food" refer to what humans ate or …? Wait. The beast spoke? The forgotten log he held sagged in coordination with his jaw. He thumbed through every possible explanation for what he had heard, but just two possibilities stuck out—either someone was hiding in the bushes in the middle of the night attempting to frighten a boy in the desolate wilderness, or Conner's head wound was worse than he thought.

While Conner debated the first possibility, the glowing orbs floated around the bush, and the scaly, black beast he had encountered in the cave stepped into the firelight. He sensed its growing impatience as it came forward. "Besides, I ate already." It smacked its lips contently, glowing eyes squinting. Its head slipped closer on a snakelike neck.

Conner nearly tripped over his pack behind him, unaware he had stepped back. He gripped the log in both hands, and the burning end shot up between them.

The monster jerked its head back in surprise.

This bolstered Conner's confidence, though he knew that the log offered no real security against the fire-breathing beast. "Then what do you want from me?"

The beast stared back, astonished by the question. "At the moment, conversation will suffice."

Conner had no desire to spend any more time with the monster, no matter how lonely it was. After all, the beast had tried to kill him. "I don't have anything to say to you."

"I can understand your anger, human. I apologize for the incident in the cave." The beast lowered its body before Conner, nearly touching its chest to the ground. "But you did surprise me." It paused before adding, "And that was before I knew."

Conner was more fascinated by how the beast was speaking than by what it was saying. Maybe it was the flickering firelight giving an illusion that its mouth moved, and his malfunctioning brain was filling in the rest. Its words seeped through to his consciousness. *Knew?* Knew what? "I am not one to hold grudges, but I really do need to sleep. And I'm quite certain I won't get a wink with you about."

The beast snorted.

Conner could sense it was offended by what he said, but that was no more his problem than the creature's feelings of loneliness. "Maybe you should find some of your own kind."

It stepped closer. "I do not think you understand."

Conner whipped the burning log back and forth before him.

The creature's eyes followed the flaming end with interest, but clearly without concern of being harmed.

Conner raised his voice to draw its attention. "What I understand is that you should not even be talking. So either I am asleep or my injuries are worse than I thought." Anger brewing, he stepped forward, taking yet another threatening swing with the log.

The black monster retreated and grunted its annoyance.

The reaction renewed Conner's confidence. Maybe it was expecting a response to its apology. "If it matters, I forgive you for your actions back in the cave." He waited, but that did not get the expected response. Maybe the creature was slow. A more direct approach was needed. "Now please, just go away." Conner drove his fear for the beast out of his mind. Heaping the burning branch on the fire, he strolled to where he had been sleeping and gave his best imitation at looking nonchalant, careful not to bang his head against the rock as he sat, eyes never leaving the beast. He forced his eyes shut, pretending to fall asleep, but intently listening for any alarming noises. Minutes flowed by. Unable to stand the tension any longer, he opened his eyes to rebuke the beast one more time, but it was gone.

"What do you make of that?" Johann puzzled to the Alpslander woman next to him.

Pallia shrugged, not able to find any words that would assist them in knowing what was going on below.

Since Pallia had no comment, Johann continued. "I have heard tell the Eastlander folk have strange customs, but I didn't believe them until now." After pausing, he added, "This is Midsummer's Night. Maybe it's some peculiar ritual to the Cosmos."

The two stood along the edge of an old road leading north away from the collapsed cave Vault had used for his escape. Farther on down into a hollow and through a sparse patch of trees, they could make out the orange glow of a fire. Near the fire, they could see someone swinging a burning branch back and forth, as if *trying* to draw their attention.

"It doesn't matter what he is doing. It is clear he believes he is no longer being tracked." She studied the trapper in the full glow of Erebus. "Get Carlon. I see no reason to waste time setting up camp here when there is a perfectly fine fire down below."

Johann grinned. Nodding at her command, he left to find his younger brother.

Pallia pondered Morgas's words of caution. However, it was hard to watch Vault flail about with his branch and not think he was anything but a country bumpkin.

For the second time that night, Conner awoke to strange sounds. This time, the firelight was glowing brighter than when he had fallen asleep. He sat up stiffly to the sight of three figures huddled about his fire. Newly added logs popped and crackled on the glowing embers.

A woman about thirty stared over the fire at him as if she had just noticed his presence. "I hope you don't mind us taking advantage of your fire. We have been traveling a long way." She gave him a faint smile that did not convince him she was happy.

Maybe it was natural among mountain people to share campfires. "No, not at all. Help yourself," he mumbled groggily with a wave, feigning politeness and giving her a similar smile before adjusted the cloth hanging over his eye.

The three sat around the campfire in silence as they ate ravenously. The woman moved like a seasoned fighter, the sword strapped to her back a sure giveaway. The two men, however, carried no visible weapons, dressed instead like freeman trappers common near Cravenrock. Still, Conner could have cut the tension with a knife.

The woman finally broke the long silence. "I am Pallia, and that"— she pointed to the large wolf studying him intensely—"is Galven. This is Johann and Carlon Narkain." The two men nodded as if noticing him for the first time. Appearing for its introduction, a white ferret poked its head from Johann's vest, pink eyes inspecting the new human. Pallia jabbed a thumb at the new arrival. "And, of course, Goose." The ferret squeaked in response to its name.

Silence fell over the camp. Finally, Pallia asked, "And you are . . .?"

He responded instinctively. "Conner Stonefield," then bit his lip. Too late. He noted the expression on Carlon's face, the clue he needed to puzzle together what he already feared. Conner dropped his head and sighed. "I suppose you know me as Vault."

This seemed to please the woman. She nodded. "You are a hard person to catch up with."

Conner sighed again, this time in resignation. Well, at least there were no more pretenses. He preferred it that way. He studied the woman in return. "Where is your other comrade?" He got a partial answer from Carlon's surprised look. So there was someone else. "I hope he was not injured in the avalanche," he probed.

"No, he's fine," Johann responded with a smile.

Pallia rewarded him with a scathing look. Johann looked away.

Well, it was clear who was in charge. But given the feel of newness in their relationships, maybe the missing man was the true leader, which begged a vital question. Where was he?

Yet again, Pallia studied the boy with admiration, certain he was no rube. Within a few minutes, he had extracted more information about the small troop than she would have willingly given before his safe return. But that was not her concern. The lad was well past exhaustion and sporting a nasty head wound. An injured, weary captive would slow them down. "You should get some sleep, Conner. We will start back to Cravenrock with first rays. If I have your promise you will not try to escape, I will not be forced to tie you up. Do I have your promise?"

The boy grinned wryly. "I hate when people ask me to make a promise I can't keep."

It was not at all the answer Pallia expected. "Very well. Carlon, please take care of our guest." She tossed the younger brother several long leather strips, then departed to scan the perimeter and place dead branches at strategic points to alarm them of anything coming into the camp. The boy was alone, but with his luck, she was not going to leave anything to chance.

His ankles and wrists tightly bound by the leather strips, Conner adjusted his weight against the boulder. He had never been a gambler, but for the first time, he'd seen no reason not to take a chance. And it paid off. An unbound prisoner would have been watched closely throughout the night, promise or no. But one secured hand and foot? Well, that was a different situation.

Strategically positioning his head, he closed his eyes to slits, watching the three trackers prepare the camp with a weariness Conner felt throughout his own body. Pallia assigned Carlon to take first watch, so the man reluctantly shuffled off toward the road. Before long, the other two forms were breathing rhythmically, with the large, gray wolf stretched out before Pallia.

The several days Conner had spent locked up in Cravenrock's undercity with Kriston had left the two with little to do, so the young thief had shown Conner how to tie, and more importantly untie, various types of knots. According to Kriston, the simple trapper's knot was used by trappers to hang drying pelts on long strings. It was also the type Carlon had used on him. Watching the forms for any sign of movement, he pushed his elbows together. The straps loosened. He worked at the dangling knot for several minutes before it fell away. *Easy as growing weeds,* he thought, fighting back a triumphant smile.

A successful getaway was going to require using a few of the clerical spells he had been taught, so this was a good time to test a theory. After working blood back into his fingers, he whispered the Stealth spell, "*Ora eftos kryptoichos*," then waited to see if he had been detected. He was pleased to discover there were no clerics among his captors. His eyes on Carlon by the road, Conner pulled his feet toward him, releasing the knot but leaving the straps dangling about his ankles.

This was where his escape plan got fuzzy. Slipping away into the dark would not work. Worse, if he failed, he would not get a second chance. To stay awake and work through his anxiety, he practiced tying various knots in the leather strap that moments before had bound his wrists. Kriston, the little kleptomaniac, would surely have had a plan by then. The Stealth spell would not last long, so he would need to act soon. What he needed was a distraction to allow him a chance to slip away.

As if on cue, a large branch snapped near the riverbank farther north. Galven caught the sound too and leaped up, crouching, large, white fangs flickering in the firelight. Pallia was up a moment later with her large sword in hand.

When the other sleeping form did not move, Pallia kicked it hard, hissing in frustration. "Get up. We may have company."

Johann flailed in his blanket for a moment, disoriented by the rude awakening, then stumbled from his roll in alarm. He pulled a large knife from his waistband, his head swiveling side to side in an effort to locate the unseen enemy. Another branch snapped, louder and closer. Carlon noticed Pallia's alarm and started back, but she signaled him to stay by the road. Sword at the ready, Galven at her side, and a groggy Johann on her heels, Pallia cautiously pressed north.

While all three's attention was on whatever was making noise, Conner incanted the ancient words to the Cloak spell, "*Ora eftos apokryptofanos*." Snatching up his backpack, he disappeared over the boulder heading south, running like a man possessed.

He decided staying along the riverbank was less risky than taking to the road above. He danced nimbly between boulders and over wet rocks glistening in Erebus's full light. Occasionally, he tripped on a rock or stumbled into the stream. His palms soon were bruised and bloody. But he kept his legs churning.

Conner came to a shallow, rocky section of the stream and crossed to the other side, hoping to bewilder his pursuers, though his heart held no illusion such tactics would work for long. His head began to throb again, pounding with each beat of his racing heart. Still, on he ran.

Carlon was so enthralled with what his comrades heard that he failed to notice their captive vanish into the night. When he did glance back toward the campfire, he blinked, then sprinted to where the only remaining traces of Vault were the strips of leather he had used to bind the boy. He may be slow of wit, but he knew well that Morgas would hold him personally responsible for Vault's escape. The drama playing out on the other side of the fire forgotten, Carlon leaped upon the boulder. The moonlit traces of the boy's footprints along the rocky riverbed were all he needed to take up the chase. Carlon never glanced back.

Galven growled irritably, sensing Pallia's frustration, then licked his muzzle, for once unsure what to do. He waited for his bond's dark form to decide.

Following the sounds to the north had produced nothing, raising concerns that they were meant as a distraction. Pallia and Johann returned to find the camp deserted. Pallia snatched up the leather straps she had given Carlon to bind Conner, noting the dozen various knots running the length of the cord. So the boy was toying with them, mocking the group's attempts to return him to the Assassin. Worse, he might have gathered enough information about his pursuers to keep them at bay. When they caught him next time, she would personally hobble his hands and feet together until he was back in the Assassin's charge.

Johann ran to the road, then headed south in hopes of keeping Conner to the stream.

Pallia signaled to Galven. Tracing Conner and Carlon's tracks through the riverbed, they took up the hunt once more.

The sounds of footsteps behind had been growing steadily louder for half an hour, but Conner refused to yield. Though his head throbbed with each step, fear kept his legs moving. But soon, he realized even fear would not be enough. If he could no longer count on outrunning his pursuer, then he would stand and fight. And he would need to make his stand before his energy was completely sapped.

Staggering to a halt, Conner reached down and hefted a long branch. It would have to do. Winded and worn, he turned and drove one end of the stick into the loose dirt, his feet spread wide as a statement of defiance.

This time, he would not be taken so easily. The realization of it all ending here, so far from home before he had been bonded, filled him with pangs of sadness. Erebus was nearly overhead, casting eerie shadows about him. Still, he waited, footsteps nearing.

By the time Carlon appeared between two large trees, he was prepared for whatever the Cosmos had planned. Carlon pulled up hard, his surprise expression visible in the shadowy light.

Cautiously, the man drew a knife and came in slow. Conner waited, eyes measuring each stealthy step, looking for an opening. Two paces away, Conner moved, putting all his reserves into the only strike he would get. Holding the staff near one end, he whipped it over his head as he spun about. Extending his arm, he fired the weapon at the man. Conner thought, having surprised Carlon several times already, such a strategy would not work. So when it did, Conner was more shocked than Carlon. The tip of the makeshift staff struck Carlon's extended hand, sending his blade careening into the night. Unfortunately, Conner had aimed for Carlon's head. The stick continued on its course, whirling out of Conner's weak grip and striking the man on the shoulder.

Carlon staggered from the force of the impact. But the astonished look on Carlon's face vanished, eyes narrowing with rage. Shaking his knife hand, Carlon snatched up Conner's weapon. In a fashion similar to Conner, he tested its weight and stepped forward. Only Carlon began to spin the stick expertly in his hands.

Carlon had never been so humiliated. He was fully prepared to take the blame for letting the boy escape, but Vault's surprise attack was an affront to his decency. Besides, the knife had been a gift from his deceased father. He wanted nothing more than to break the stick over the boy's bandaged head.

It was only the thought of further humiliation in telling Morgas he had disobeyed his master's command to return Vault alive that stayed his actions. But he would need to subdue the boy until the others arrived. He stepped forward, picking Vault's forehead to be his target—just enough to subjugate the feisty lad.

He moved closer, deftly turning the long stick in his hands. Spinning on his heels, he brought the stick up and over his head in a controlled arc for the measured strike to properly restrain the boy. But as the stick shot forward, his vision went black. The makeshift staff struck something hard and snapped. Before he could react, something the size of a tree trunk hit him in the chest. The force of the blow lifted him off his feet. Moonlit trees rushed past. He fought to breathe, but his lungs refused to work. It did not matter. Carlon struck a tree with a resounding crack. A fog took him as he slumped forward, arms and legs splayed awkwardly.

❖

Conner had given his most valiant effort, but he was no fighter. If he had one millistone of energy remaining, he would have used it to kick himself for not letting Pauli give him a few lessons on combat. But Conner had always contended that Eastland farmers did not need to learn such skills. He had been sorely mistaken. Hopeless and helpless, eyes closed, he waited for the stroke that never came.

Something heavy hit him in the chest, sending him reeling backward. Then there was a sickening, bone-crushing sound. He rolled to his stomach, panic taking him. He tried to stand, but he was struck again from behind. He staggered from the shock.

To Conner's utter amazement, he was lifted from the ground with a single jerk. Moonlit trees and bushes about him receded as he rose higher. He tried to scream, but his chest was clutched in a lumberjack's vise. He struggled for air, pulling at the clamp about his chest, no longer caring that he could see more and more of the mountainous landscape below. It was fate that the blackness of unconsciousness claimed him.

Festival of Midsummer's Night

Jonath waited patiently near the royal balcony as he marked the moments leading to midnight. It had been a taxing and at times stressful day, but with only the finale of this year's Festival of Midsummer's Night remaining, he began to relax and take in the magnificent sights around him.

Poets and balladeers had been known to travel to Graystone Castle from all corners of the Harmonic Realms, even the unclaimed outlands beyond, just to gaze upon the castle's beauty under the full moon of Erebus. But on this particularly calm, starlit night, Erebus seemed to reach down and touch Graystone Castle's three towers. A flag fluttered from each tower in recognition of the three Harmonic Realms—Griffinrock's bright red griffin rearing on lion's legs with wings spread wide before a sky of azure blue, Elvenstein's majestic white unicorn with long flowing mane and tail upon the summit of a grassy hill, and Grenetia's black pegasus flying over a summer-green forest and crystal blue lake.

To Jonath's left, Tyresus and Beggar waited anxiously on perches. His eyes darted to where seven of the thirteen Mystic Doyens, along with the Keeper of the Mystics Order, Dane Norterry, had gathered in their blood-red robes, quietly admiring the evening's festivities. Behind the doyens, the Mystic Oracles in their pure white robes huddled around an ancient text Sir Giles held before him. Oblivious to the surrounding celebrations, the oracles gesticulated in animated discussion. Their appearance was disconcerting; they seemed as disoriented and uncertain as Jonath felt. The light touch of a hand drew him from his troubled reflection.

The king gazed at the woman pressed against his side and returned her warm, reassuring smile. A rainbow of colors danced along the finely cut jewels in her crown, accentuating the sparkle in her eyes. His heart skipped a beat. He did not want to be awakened from this dream.

But the queen's words shattered the enchantment. Without altering her loving expression, she spoke for the first time since leaving the royal banquet hall. "I am still upset with you, Jonath. So do not flash those beautiful gray eyes my way and think you can make up with me so quickly."

Jonath's smile faded. He had been pleased that Dane had chosen to stay for the night, and not only because it was a perfect excuse to stay clear of Duchess Mariette's incessant references to the king's heritage. The king had placed Dane's banquet chair near his own, and as the wine flowed through the evening, the two began to recount fond moments from their time together as Mystic pupils. Each story they told brought a raucous response from those around, forcing those farther away to lean or move closer in hopes of catching the next tale, their expectant looks goading the two all the more. By the time Dane told of the night he'd levitated Jonath's bed into an old oak tree outside their dorms, the two had half the hall's attention.

But the queen had grown annoyed by her king and champion's unseemly display. Izadora honored him with her most disapproving glare, while her sister, Mariette, sat at her side looking aghast at the man's unabashed and all-too-expected behavior. Aware of their disapproval, Jonath had attempted to stem the Keeper's inebriated tongue with several coughs and glances, but finally was forced to resort to a hard kick under the table to the red-robed figure's shin. The king felt a pang of guilt observing Dane later walking with a noticeable limp. Still, the evening had been the perfect remedy for his mood, if not for Izadora's temper.

"I am sorry, my queen," he apologized sincerely.

But before he could continue, Izadora entwined her arm in his, never taking her eyes from the royal balcony. "We will discuss this later." She patted his arm reassuringly, making it clear he could expect more.

But Jonath held no concerns. The trials they had faced together with the royal family over her choice of a serf-born king had proven their bond of trust was stronger than anything that could be wedged between them. He placed his hand on hers. Moments before the stroke of midnight, the matriarch of Griffinrock and her husband stepped forward to the castle balcony fifteen paces above the castle grounds.

He had shared many Festivals of Midsummer's Night with his queen, yet each year, he was left breathless. Moonlight shimmered off the River Tresdan flowing southward around the castle's island while the magically enchanted castle stones glowed a muted silver, turning Graystone into a towering beacon for the last-minute travelers arriving for the festival's final event. Throughout the castle grounds below and on into the city across the River Tresdan, a vast sea of people in colorful clothing and costumes ebbed and flowed in a tide of dancing and singing. Since Hemera's setting, freemen had celebrated next to noblemen and bonded serfs next to guildsmen, while minstrels, troupers, jugglers, troubadours, and every other style of artisan offered their talents to rejoice in another year of Harmonic life. Tomorrow, they would return to their normal lives, beginning a new year by preparing for the changes coming with the cooler season. But here at the Festival of Midsummer's Night, for this one night each year, social status was discarded.

Several below noticed the royal couple's appearance on the balcony, signaling the final moments of the year. Shouts rose from the Royal Gardens of Graystone. "Queen Izadora! Long live the queen!" Blissful faces gazed skyward to glimpse their matriarch, and they too joined in the chorus until it morphed into an exalted chant echoing throughout the castle grounds. "Queen Izadora! Long live the queen!"

For several moments, the queen stood admiring her subjects below, for she loved the people of Griffinrock as greatly as they loved her. She nodded lightly toward the red-cloaked doyens. Mystic Lady Noray incanted the Air spell Voice, then nodded back to the queen.

When Izadora spoke, every person throughout the castle and city could hear her as if she stood next to them. "To the good people of Griffinrock, to those visiting from our sibling Realms of Elvenstein and Grenetia, and to the Outlands beyond, I bid you serenity and goodness." She spread her arms wide, waiting for the accolades to subside. "Every Midsummer's Night since the signing of the Treaty of Alignment ending the Anarchic War five hundred and fifty years ago, the matriarchs of Griffinrock have spoken those words of goodwill for all who are guided by the ways of the Harmonics. But this night, more than any before, I am deeply moved and humbled by the generosity, kindness, and love of the people of our fair Realms. It is my privilege, as with my ancestral mothers before, to inaugurate the five-hundred-and-fifty-first year of prosperity into existence. I am honored to serve as Griffinrock's queen. You are truly a great people. Long live the people of the Harmonic Realms! Peace be with the Harmonic Realms!"

Izadora raised her arms toward the star-filled sky, a signal to the three Shaman Dons standing inconspicuously to her left. Caped in the flowing earthy brown robes of the Board of Shamans, the grandmasters pushed up their sleeves and began to incant. Jonath could sense the powerful pull of Fire as the dons drew deep from the elemental wells. He knew they pulled equally from Earth, though as a Mystic he could not perceive it. The moments slipped by while the three figures continued to gesture in perfect synchrony. Below, the shouts of anticipation reverberated off the castle's magical stones in a growing crescendo of excitement. The very air on the balcony began to crackle with life. The stones beneath them trembled.

In unison, the three dons threw their arms wide, eyes cast skyward, and the night lit up with cascading images in brilliant colors.

Using the sky dome like a painter's cloth, the Shamans created breathtaking portraits—radiant flowers in tall grass on rolling meadows, snowcapped mountains painted under a deep blue sky, rugged coastlines with mist rising from massive waves that beat against the rocky shore, and ever-changing dunes of desert sands sparkling like polished emeralds in Hemera's light. Jonath was captivated by the shifting kaleidoscope. On and on, the stream of sky paintings flowed, each image exploding to life with a series of loud hissing pops, high-pitched whines, and booming sizzles, only to have their colors run and blend like too much watercolor splashed on a dry leather canvas. Then the mix of dull browns and drab purples faded from existence in time for the next painting to be born.

As quickly as it had started, so the show came to an abrupt end. The painful stillness of the night assaulted Jonath's eyes and ears. Ten thousand people were transfixed in silence, afraid moving or speaking would break the spell. Finally, applause erupted throughout the castle and city, and once more, the streets were flooded with the sounds of music, song, and laughter.

Izadora's forearm around his, the two waited in silent contemplation, absorbing the joyous celebration of the new year about them. Jonath thought how the Shamans' show was life in a microcosm: life's moments, no matter how beautiful and precious, are as painfully fleeting as the images in the starry sky. The best that can be done is to admire each moment then let it go, and have faith that the Cosmos will offer a different beauty in the next.

He pressed his palm to the top of his queen's warm hand. The troubling events in the Chamber of the Oracles that morning had intruded on his serenity. What could be made of a Cosmic balance of force? He was certain the Mystic doyens and Oracles had not told him everything. The Harmonic Realms were celebrating the start of a new year, but the shift also marked something much greater that they knew nothing about. He regarded the surging mass of people below.

What would be these good people's future when prophecy no longer could be foretold?

Jonath considered telling his queen about the morning, but the little he understood would only exasperate her, especially with their daughter on her trek. He looked on as she waved at the people below. No, he would rather admire the beauty of the moment. Troubling discussions could wait until he acquired more information. His queen had plenty on her mind.

When Cold Logic Prevails

Indignant, Skye-Anyar-Bello Cloudbender faced the human with whom he had spent the early morning hours arguing over something that was as obvious as the marvel of his iridescent scales. In triumphant display, he unfurled his wings with the first rays of Hemera breaking over the mountain crest to the east. Then puffing out his chest and stretching his neck skyward, he rose up on his two bulky legs. "Then what do you think I am?" his voice boomed at the small creature before him.

The human made an indiscernible gesture. "Maybe you're a large bat. I have heard bats grow to be quite large in the mountains. Since I have not seen one here, that is a possibility."

Skye-Anyar-Bello twitched his tail irritably, snapping a pine sapling at its trunk. "Bats don't grow near this large, they don't have scales, and they surely can't breathe fire." He rocked forward, thrusting his face close to the human's for added emphasis. "Have you ever heard of a talking bat?"

The human adjusted the cloth wrapped about its head. "Okay, I concede you are not a figment of my imagination."

"Well, that is a breakthrough," the dragon interrupted victoriously.

"But how do I know you are really talking to me?" The human continued undaunted. "I got hit pretty hard on the head yesterday. I know a farmer who fell off his wagon and spent the rest of his life trying to convince everyone spirits from another plane spoke to him." The human studied the display in front of him. "Besides, aren't dragons supposed to have *four* legs?"

He snorted at the human's ignorance. "I am a wyvern."

This did not seem to impress the human, who responded, "Okay." It sat blinking, clearly expecting something further.

The dragon stared back. "Are you a guivre?" he asked irritably.

"I don't know what a guivre is, but I think I would recognize a dragon if I saw one," the human shot back with a touch of his own annoyance.

Skye-Anyar-Bello sighed wearily from trying to break through the human's irrational logic. The creature was like an amphithere chasing its tail. He decided a different tack was needed. "A dragon once said, 'Once you have eliminated all impossibilities, and only one possibility remains, then that must be the truth, no matter how incredible it seems.' So why is it so hard to accept that I am a dragon?"

The human scrunched up its face. "Are you sure a dragon said that?" It paused, then added while waving its arms, "Oh, never mind." It exhaled loudly. "Look, the logic is really very simple. If you were a dragon, then you would be the first dragon seen within the Harmonic Realms since the Anarchic War. That leaves the obvious question. Where have all the dragons been for the past twenty generations, through all the troubles and conflicts we have had since? No." The human shook its head emphatically. "If there ever were dragons, the kind the ancient ballads describe, they wouldn't have let things get to the current state of affairs. They would have been here all this time." It hesitated, then added, "Maybe even bonding with humans, to protect the lands from Anarchic invasions."

The human stood and kicked at the rock it had previously occupied. "Oh, what am I talking about? Those are fables to give children false hope, pitiful offerings of sanity in a world gone mad. Maybe there were dragons long ago. I don't know. But not any longer. If there ever were any, they died out with the Anarchic War."

Skye-Anyar-Bello listened to the human's depressing words. Could humans truly have forgotten so much so quickly? True, the small creatures did not live as long as dragons, but the Ancients spoke fondly of humans with songs and legends to teach their young. Was this one crazy, or was it indicative of what humans had become— selfish and irrational? He pushed down the growing concern that he had bonded with a human version of a dragork.

Skye continued, more softly this time. "We did not die out. When your War of Breaking ended, the Cosmos no longer needed our bondings, so we returned to our homelands." He settled his body on the small patch of grass the two had taken to mark off the time since before dawn. Then he folded his wings against his body to give him needed warmth from the cool mountain air. "Maybe you should know I am as surprised by our bonding as you seem to be."

The human stumbled backward as if the dragon had struck him, waving its arms wildly between them. "Bonding?" it repeated incredulously. "No, that is not possible. I have trekked here to find a small, friendly animal to take as my bond." It pointed south. "I have a fiancé back there. And I am starting my apprenticeship training under Master Cleaverbrook. I can't be spending the rest of my life with"—it jerked his arms at the dragon—"a fire-breathing bat thingy."

Not sure what a *fiancé* or a *Master Cleaverbrook* was, Skye-Anyar-Bello opened his mouth to continue his attempts to soothe the distressed spirit, but the human flew on with hardly a pause.

"And don't try to convince me we are communicating through some mental telepathy." The scrawny creature leaned forward and pointed at the cloth wrapped around its head, tilted from all its wild gesticulations. "I know enough about bonds to know that doesn't happen."

The fact the two could even hold this argument was enough to convince Skye-Anyar-Bello they were bonded. There was no other possible explanation. He leaned forward in mock imitation of the human, eyes narrowing. "How do you know we are not bonded? Can you sense the Calling any longer?"

The human blinked. "No." It faltered, then found a new rising column of air. "But it will come back once the throbbing in my head goes away. And that won't happen with you chatting my ears off." He bounded on, unaffected by the dragon's logic. "If I"—he waved his arm between the two of them—"were bonded to a dragon as you suggest, then that would make me Dragonbonded. Well, I am merely an Eastland farmer, not some high-minded nobleman or defender of Harmonic truth. I don't even know how to fight. So you see? There are holes all through your theory."

Skye-Anyar-Bello snort-sniffed at the humor coming from the animated creature. He leaned even closer to the human. "*Dragonbonded*? Bonding with a dragon does not make you Dragonbonded." The dragon was losing patience. Maybe it was time to put this argument to rest. A definitive demonstration of their bonding was clearly needed.

Without warning, the dragon's head bolted forward, teeth snapping shut where the human's head had been. His wings fanned open, sails catching a strong gust to give him balance while his head followed the creature in its roll. Teeth flashed and snapped, an attack that should have severed the human's legs from its body. His wings beat down hard. Lifting and spinning in a single motion, the dragon whipped his tail around and down in a fluid arc. The earth shook from the impact, spraying dirt and dry leaves into the air.

Completing another roll, the human rounded on him and screamed. "What are you doing? Are you crazy? Stop it!"

The dragon's eyes flared a vivid blue. "Demonstrating we are bonded!" he snapped back. "You say you are not a fighter, yet I cannot harm you with my most formidable attacks. And still I easily bested your three seasoned captors." Skye-Anyar-Bello rocked back smugly, certain the human could not resist this logic.

Instead, the human gestured at his head angrily. "And who was it that caused the rock to drop on my head?"

The dragon blinked, unable to find a good explanation for that.

The human's head bobbed. "Uh-huh! Well, I've had enough. Either you are legitimately insane or I am for imagining all this. I'm heading north to find some peace and serenity until my head stops pounding. I just need to think straight enough to get my bearings again. Then I am heading home with my bond to live a quiet, tranquil life." The human snatched up his pack and, without even a good-bye, stormed away.

Skye-Anyar-Bello watched the rude human's back recede into the trees. He could feel emotions he had never sensed before. He was reminded of a few hunts when he could not finish the kill swiftly, leaving his wounded prey cornered. His new bond had that same look in its eyes.

Without hesitation, the dragon winged westerly up the mountain slope, then dipped, taking a route parallel to the human. Recalling the dragonsong verses his father had added about the Dragonbonded, he did not remember any trouble *he* had to work out with *his* bond.

Conner walked briskly north, well, except for stopping occasionally to kick whatever would not bruise his foot. He was going mad. The trauma of Cravenrock had been too much. That was it. Coupled with lack of sleep, too long alone in the wilderness, a body long past its physical limits, and a nasty crack to the skull—it was beyond any human's ability to handle. It brought a whole new meaning to the term "bat crazy." He laughed out loud. "See? Crazy!" he yelled at a tree.

Besides, when had he become so cynical? No, that he knew. It was when he realized that Assassins were not only in childhood nightmares and campfire stories. He kicked at a finger-thin oak, which retaliated with a slap to his face.

Conner glanced about, struggling with how to let his anger go. Pauli once told him, *No trouble is ever so big you can't walk away.* Conner was no longer sure. He gazed south through the wake of his destruction. The clearing was hidden through the trees, yet he could sense that the creature was no longer there. His eyes darted westward at the thought of the black beast. Doubt was seeping into his bones.

What if he was bonded to a dragon? He desperately wanted to cling to *any* other possibility, but he was no longer sure he could. Was it any more insane to accept an impossible reality over one he knew to be false?

He continued walking north, letting the rhythm of his stride mark his thoughts, struggling to find flaws in the black creature's logic. But he could concoct no more rationalizations. Conner shuffled to a stop, staring at nothing specific. Then, leaning his forearm and bandaged head against the nearest tree, he whispered as if casting a spell to waken from a dream. "Why me?"

The Aradorm

On their third day out of Graystone, still tracking northeast along the southern edge of the Dragon's Back Mountains, Veressa and Annabelle arrived at an immense river. Fed most of the year by melting snowcaps and frequent spring rains, the Aradorm ran swiftly south from deep in the majestic central mountains. Spanning fifty paces at the base of the mountain range, the river wove southward through the middle of the Narwalen Plains into the thick, lush Stonewell Forests more than two hundred miles to the south. The river was the lifeblood for half of Griffinrock's people.

The two riders had traveled hard for most of the afternoon to reach the river before sunset, occasionally dismounting and jogging alongside their horses to keep their mounts from overheating in the dry air. By the time they reached the edge of the raging torrent, Hemera was dipping near the mountain peaks at their backs. For the third time in the past hour, Veressa scanned the horizon to the west as Hemera vanished behind an encroaching line of dark clouds.

Annabelle also turned her gaze behind them. "It will be a bad storm," she stated with confidence. The Ranger dismounted her sorrel mare, Karra, with a renewed sense of purpose. "We will ford the river before we make camp. The river will be swollen by morning, and we'd be forced to travel south to Bell's Ferry."

The Calling was becoming more urgent with each day for Veressa. The thought of traveling forty miles out of the way was all she needed to find the energy to make the crossing. She dismounted her gray gelding, Toran, and began preparing.

Each rider had a watertight skin large enough to hold their food and one set of clothes. Once packed and sealed, the skins were strapped securely to the only place that might remain dry—above their horses' withers. Annabelle checked Veressa's knots and buckles, then nodded approvingly.

Mounting Karra again with a pat on her neck, the Ranger proceeded to the river's edge, guiding her seasoned mare into the swift waters while Peron dipped and fluttered nervously overhead. The mare's first tentative step into the river brought a snort as she sank halfway to her knees. But with soothing words and gentle nudges from her rider's heels, Karra stepped into the current.

Veressa followed. At first, Toran ignored his rider's urgings, refusing to pass the rocky shore. But once he realized Karra was leaving him behind, he reluctantly forged ahead. Moments later, Veressa understood the horses' hesitation. The water was ice cold. The frigid water soaked through Veressa's warm Ranger leggings and up her calves and she gasped, feet and ankles already numb. Something struck her knee and she watched a chunk of ice spin past.

Nearing the middle of the river, Karra's back sank below the water and Annabelle slipped from the mare's back to give her horse the buoyancy to swim the deep river. Karra curled her lip and snorted to keep icy water from her nostrils.

A moment later, Toran's barrel sank, forcing the princess to follow Annabelle's lead. The shift from hot to cold forced all air from Veressa's lungs. She tightened her grip on Toran's mane, letting him pull her toward the safety of the far shore. She closed her eyes, giving over completely to her steed.

Toran's hooves found river bedrock once more. Veressa slipped her numbing thigh over his back. Finally, the winded horse stepped from the river, but Veressa continued to cling tight to her mount. Energy sucked from her, she found the gentle rock of his panting body soothing. The air was cool against her wet clothes. Veressa shivered against Toran's warmth as she slipped in and out of consciousness.

Annabelle's firm grip upon the princess's shoulder broke her trance. "Veressa, you need to climb down and change clothing quickly. And we must wick the horses or they may come down sick." The Ranger made sure the princess's feet found solid ground before releasing her.

Veressa opened her eyes and was greeted with her preceptor's caring face. She beamed back weakly, then gave the Ranger a soggy hug of gratitude. Annabelle did not approve, but she would have to live with it.

Lightning flashed along the dark western sky, followed by reports of rolling thunder echoing through the mountains to the north. Each rumble marked a shorter delay from the flashes of light. A chill wind had picked up, stirring sparks from the modest fire the Ranger had built to dry their clothes and inject some warmth into their bodies. Veressa pulled her knees tight to her chest and drank from the hot tea cradled between her palms. She leaned toward the fire, charmed by the orange sparks dancing and spinning upward, fleeing into the starry eastern sky, drawn to the only semblance of serenity in a landscape going wild. Still, it was a welcome distraction from the constant tugging from the east. Anticipating whatever awaited the next day on the plains, she had never felt so alive or content.

At the edge of the fire's glow, the horses nodded and nickered, ears pulled back as the wind gusted through the creaking oak branches overhead. Annabelle went to check on them for the third time since dinner, then returned just as the first drops of rain began to fall. The preceptor squatted and studied the smile on the princess's face. "Yes, it has been a good day, Veressa. I am pleased with your progress in Ranger skills. You showed true fortitude crossing the Aradorm. But it is time to retire. Put out the fire. Let's get some sleep." Without another word, she snagged the dry clothes from the tent line and disappeared into her tent.

Veressa focused on the fire, watching the flames within the glowing logs lick skyward. Slowly, she drew on Air elemental and sucked the air from around the flames. "*Aetha energi pnigofotia*," she spoke softly. The fire snuffed out, casting the camp into darkness. The last sparks followed their brethren into the night sky and were gone. Rain growing steadily heavier, Toran nickered his uneasiness. "You'll be fine, Toran," she reassured him, then slipped into her tent. The sounds of wind and large droplets pelting her tent, she pulled her blanket tight around her. Sleep came swiftly.

Veressa crouched next to the stag's fresh track. Fingers trembled with exhilaration, lightly tracing the broken oval. He was close, moving fast, and knew he was being followed. She took up the chase once more, eyes adjusting to the darkness of a cloud-shrouded Erebus. She sprinted without sound over fallen trees and protruding rocks on legs meant for the hunt, never winded, closing in on her meal. She danced effortlessly between two trees, the rush of wind in her ears, and caught the wild motion of the stag bounding ahead. Each powerful stride, she gained on her prey, until she could feel the heat from his trembling body. She sprang at the bobbing white tail. Her claws dug deep into its flanks. The stag's hind end buckled from the impact of her weight. The momentum of the two forms at full speed carried predator and prey careening into the thick undergrowth with a thunderous crash. She gripped the stag as they rolled, feeling the slap of brush across her face, the snapping of dried branches under their combined weight. The full bulk of the stag bore down on her as they tumbled. Veressa roared.

Veressa's arms flailing against her collapsed tent. And the tent fought back. Wind pushed at her back while raindrops battered her arms and head. The night sky flickered bright, turning her soggy tent a brilliant brown. Thunder and the sharp sound of wood cracking and splintering was her only warning before something heavy crushed her to the ground. The residual vision of the dream stag crashing down on her confused her and she panicked. She cut at the side of the tent with a knife that had somehow made its way into her palm. Struggling through the gaping hole, she swam through a sea of branches and wet leaves. Rain pelted her face.

Something grabbed her from behind. She spun on the apparition. But the cold, hard slap of a hand across her cheek stunned her. The next bright flash of lightning brought the image of a drenched Annabelle gripping her shoulders. Before anything sensible could form, the Ranger shoved Veressa hard into her own tent and quickly followed.

The tents they used for the trek were small and lightweight, comfortably fitted for one person with supplies. They were not designed for two. Peron squawked his indignation at the uninvited guest, but then moved to the side when it was clear the girl was not going to leave.

The princess shivered uncontrollably. Mistaking the girl's shakes as chills, Annabelle hugged her close to give her warmth. Veressa found comfort in the welcoming arms and, releasing the fear she held bottled up, she wept.

The Ranger understood and hugged her tighter.

Hope's Surrender

Throughout the morning following his liberation from the three trackers, Conner ambled, stopping frequently to eat and rest, or more accurately, to contemplate his situation. He had taken a southerly direction until he stumbled upon another narrow trail going east-west. Still not feeling the pull of the Calling, even though his head had stopped throbbing, he walked west, sensing he was moving closer to the black beast that had aided in his escape. By early afternoon, he was resigned to the fact that he had bonded with the creature, though he remained skeptical it was a dragon. Whatever it was, the two needed to work out what to do next about the situation.

He tried to imagine going back to Creeg's Point with the winged creature in tow, but whatever stories he concocted, the only reasonable effect he envisioned was one of town folk running, screaming in total panic at their approach. The image of the beast pulling his dad's plow, effortlessly digging deep furrows while Conner scrambled behind to keep up, brought out a sharp chuckle. But others sucked the humor from him—studying under Master Cleaverbrook while the bored and curious creature ripped the guildmaster's apothecary apart, an angry farmer demanding retribution for a cow the beast could not resist eating, and the creature accidentally burning down the Stonefield barn because it had an allergy to hay. Conner was so deep in thought that he nearly ran headlong into the creature balled up in the middle of the trail. He pulled to a stop.

The creature raised its head to study him. "So, have you come to your senses, or are you back to argue some more?" Conner could sense its annoyance, but it smacked its mouth anyway, showing two full sets of gleaming white teeth.

"Any arguing we do is clearly at my peril," he shot back at the black wall.

The creature only grunted in response, blue eyes measuring him.

Conner sighed, but took a formidable stance with arms crossed. "Yes, I accept that we are bonded. There is no other reasonable explanation. But that leaves us with a very perplexing situation. Since I don't have any idea what it means to be bonded to a creature such as you, I am at a loss for what to do next. So what exactly do you suggest?"

The creature rose and stretched legs and wings as though it had all the time in the world to consider the question. "We find a cave."

Conner blinked. "We what?"

"Find a cave." The long, snakelike neck swiveled, its nose pointing to the northwest. "There is a storm approaching. It will be upon us tonight. I would prefer to stay dry if possible."

Conner craned his head over the beast's back, making out a line of dark clouds above the mountain ridges to the west. He responded skeptically, "I have been walking all day. I haven't seen a cave or cavern. How do you suggest we find one big enough to keep both of us dry while making sure you don't crush me against the wall?"

The creature closed its eyes and snorted several times. Conner sensed amusement from the creature. "Let me start again. You should at least know the name of the creature that might crush you against a cavern wall." It lowered its chest to the trail, wings spread wide. "I am Skye-Anyar-Bello of the family Cloudbender."

Conner tried to repeat back. "Skye An . . . Anyor . . ." But Conner stopped when he sensed a flash of the beast's irritation.

"Skye-Anyar-Bello of the family Cloudbender," it repeated.

Not ready to try handling the name again or the beast's annoyance, he diverted the discussion. "That is quite a name. I am Conner Stonefield." Assuming the beast's gesture had been a bow,

Conner afforded the beast his best imitation at one, though as a freeman Eastlander, it felt awkward. However, the attempt appeased the creature.

"With homage, I greet you, Conner of the family Stonefield. May your days add honorable verses to your humansong." It declared in a singsong voice.

"Please, call me Conner. And I will call you Skye," Conner suggested quickly.

"That is not my name," appealing to Conner's good senses with an emphatic wag of its head. "I am Skye-Anyar-Bello."

"Are we going to argue over everything we talk about?"

Skye blinked.

"Because if we are, this is going to be a very long evening."

Conner's stance seemed to have convinced Skye it was best to return to Conner's question. "We look for mountain's breath, Conner of the fam ... Conner." Noting Conner staring blankly, Skye continued. "All living things breathe."

Conner laughed. "Mountains aren't alive," he stated, and waited for the punch line to the joke.

"Are all humans as sure as you about things they do not understand?" Skye grumbled back. It sniffed a yellow flower growing by the side of the trail. "How do you know this flower is alive?"

Conner answered as if to a child. "It grows. It responds to light and dark, cold and heat. Therefore, it is alive." He was confused about where this was going.

Skye pressed on. "So then, if a mountain also responded, let us say, from being dug open with the sharp picks you humans seem to enjoy using? Would you say it is alive?"

"But mountains don't respond to such things. They are inert. They are neither alive nor dead."

Skye sighed. "A human's life is on a scale that prevents you from seeing these things, so you believe they cannot be so. The mountains come from somewhere; one day, they will return. In the time between, they are infused with Earth, giving them their unique breath of life. The Ancients in my family have seen such wonders." Rolling thunder echoed through the rocky canyon. "Consciousness is not limited to those who think or feel like you. One day, we will discuss this more. But for now, trust that I can find a cavern. I shall return shortly." Skye kicked up hard. Several strong beats of his leathery wings sent him off to the east.

Mouth agape, Conner stared until the creature was a small, black dot. Grumbling about what he had done to deserve being bonded to such an annoying, egocentric beast, he pulled off his pack and leaned against a warm rock. He tried to understand what Skye had been talking about, but realized it was useless thinking about such nonsense. Instead, for the third time that day, he napped.

That night, Conner sat drenched and shivering from collecting enough branches to build a small fire in the cave Skye had found. After his fifth flint stick burned out with no more success than the first four, he sat back in resignation, trying unsuccessfully to ignore the soaked shirt wrapped about his head. He looked at the iridescent black creature nearby who had been watching him with intense curiosity. Skye had not spoken for several minutes, which was a miracle in itself. The beast possessed an endless supply of questions about humans and their lives, consuming the entire afternoon while they traveled to the cave Skye had found.

What is the purpose of living in wooden boxes? Why do humans spend so much time growing food when there is so much available? How do people eat? Who are the human Ancients and where do they live? Can you sing me a humansong? Why do humans kill other humans? What is a fiancé? How do humans raise their young?

Conner did not mind Skye's inquisitiveness. In fact, the constant questions kept him from thinking about the treacherous trail getting to the cave while he attempted to educate the creature on human Harmonic life. But describing and occasionally defending ideas he had taken for granted his whole life had taxed him. He was mentally exhausted.

Skye's focus on understanding Conner's life was so intent that he was not willing to turn the plow. However, Conner was able to extract some fragments about Skye's life. During the creature's inquisition about marriage, for example, he discovered Skye was an adolescent male, too young to form a coupling. He also uncovered his species did not marry, though they did have long-term monogamous relationships based on individual needs. He was perplexed when Skye mentioned age was not a part of such arrangements, though experience did influence how a couple might relate. Skye used the example that a young male, feeling the need for a teacher or sexual mentor, might mate with a much older and more experienced female who felt the need to nurture or be wanted, until the couple's needs had been fulfilled.

It was all very strange.

Unexpectedly, Skye's body started to heave. The beast's long neck protruded forward. His eyes disappeared behind double slits while his mouth opened wide in a gesture reminiscent of a cat coughing up a hairball. Just then, the beast expelled a searing fireball. The wood Conner had stacked in the middle of their cave burst into flames.

The fire grew and sizzled over wet logs while Conner stared incredulously. "If you could have done that before, why did you let me go through all that work the past half hour?" He flashed bolts of lightning at the beast, then sighed, tossing the flint box by his pack.

"I thought you wanted to do it on your own," Skye stated with a touch of confusion.

Conner leaned forward, the fire melting away some of his irritability. "Well, coughing up a fireball must have been painful." He tried to suppress a sense of satisfaction at the thought.

Skye shifted into a more comfortable position. "Not painful, but I needed to control the flow. If I had used more Fire, you would have been left with ash instead of flames."

The two sat quietly in the flickering light while the storm raged outside. Conner could not quite believe his circumstance. Here he sat huddled in a cave calmly chatting with a fire-breathing, scaly, winged creature that had tried to kill him . . . twice. This situation would take time to get used to. He stared out of the cave as lightning coursed through black clouds and rain continued to fall in buckets. He missed home. All he wanted was to be in his house, sleeping in his warm, dry bed and eating his mother's fine cooking. The ration he was chewing became all the blander, and he had to force the chunk down.

Conner realized he was sulking, so he broke the long silence. "Where do dragons come from?" Skye's surprise seared through Conner's mind. Well, he had used the word and he was not going to take it back. *Dragon.* The wait was deafening.

Skye shifted his bulk. "Our first dragonsong tells of a very powerful Shaman God named Shazarack, who created the four families of dragons. But this god made the Ancients his playthings and kept them locked away. One day, the Ancients grew restless and broke from their prison. Each family flew in a different direction. Finding suitable lairs for the females' eggs, they began new dragonsongs."

The story had all the trimmings of mythology, but some essence of truth probably resided in the fable. "And the other three families? What happened to them?"

Skye answered softly, "Our verses of the days of the Dragonbonded tell of a time when the humans' order held members with bonds from all four families. But I cannot say what happened in the time since."

Silence descended upon the cave. Sounds of thunder, rain, and popping logs filled the void. Conner was caught wondering how the emotions of his bond flowed, mixed, and influenced his will. He could sense his resistance weakening. But with the growing acceptance that Skye was a dragon came a flood of sadness and fear that chewed at his spirit. He would decide what to do tomorrow, knowing that giving his thoughts free rein would keep him from needed sleep. Shifting to a more comfortable position, he barely caught Skye's soft voice in the dreamy distance, nearly drowned out by a boom of thunder.

"I am glad you are not a dragork."

Conner grunted in his semi-dream state. He would try to remember to ask Skye what a dragork was in the morning.

Unwelcome News

Lacerus gently stroked his distressed falcon bond. Still, Carnia flinched at the Assassin's apprehension, which grew steadily by the minute. He had received an urgent message from Morgas, just back in Cravenrock, requesting an immediate audience. But the message had said nothing about Vault. That was surely a harbinger of unwelcome news. He sighed in resignation and lowered his hand. His failed efforts to ease his bond's tension were no help to either of them. Why had he been afflicted with such a creature, one so repulsed by his lifestyle? He glared into her eyes with cold indifference. She killed, sometimes even tormenting her prey before dispatching it with an efficiency even he admired. Were they really so different?

Lacerus sensed the heat and vibration of someone approaching, though there were no sounds. He turned as Morgas appeared at his door, Valmer by his side. He waited a moment, staring behind his man. But the absence of a bound and blindfolded Eastlander on his tracker's heels told all. Still, Morgas would not have returned alone without good reason. And judging by his expression, the Alpslander had a lot to say. "Yes?" he asked with the sharpness of a skinning knife.

Morgas spoke quickly, recounting the time his group had spent tracking Vault. Lacerus's smile, hidden in the dark shadow of his black hood, grew as Morgas described with frustration how Vault had thwarted their attempts to apprehend him. When the Alpslander detailed the events of the cavern and the avalanche nearly ending

Morgas's and Pallia's life, the Assassin chuckled heartily, stifling his man's tale mid-sentence.

The silence stretched on, Morgas unsure how to interpret his liege's reaction. No doubt the Alpslander wondered whether Lacerus would allow him to take another breath. Lacerus and his bond were not so different after all.

Finally, the Assassin broke the tension. "I am merely impressed with the boy's ability, Morgas." But failure could not go unpunished. He paused for added effect, then buried the figurative knife into his proud man's heart. "However, I had thought you would have been up for the challenge an Eastlander youth had to offer. It seems I dreadfully overestimated your talents." He feigned indifference, knowing his rebuke wounded more than any pain an Assassin's dagger could inflict.

Morgas winced at his liege's assessment.

In truth, Lacerus was more impressed with the Eastlander's skills than he was angry with Morgas's failures. His man's personal and direct tutelage under the best Barbarian and Black Knight instructors should have been more than adequate to deal with any normal situation. That meant the boy was anything but normal. Sensing there was more, "Go on."

Morgas continued, describing the man-made cavern they had chased Vault into and how it had been laid to near-total waste before they reached the boy. Lacerus tensed visibly, his breathing shallow as he listened to the man recount the strange blue light he had seen pulsating from the cavern's walls and floor. Morgas placed the pulsating rock on his table, and Lacerus gasped.

The Assassin was so entranced by the glowing stone that he nearly failed to catch the Alpslander's final comment. "I do not know the meaning, my liege, but it is clearly significant in some way. I thought you should know immediately. There are ballads my ancestors sang describing caves that could be seen at night pulsing a deep blue such as this." Morgas shrugged, lowering his eyes, then shook his head.

"But all I can recall is that such lights were meant as a warning to stay clear."

Lacerus was transfixed, watching the stone's heartbeat pulse. Sensing Morgas's apprehension, he shook free from ancient memories. "You did right bringing this to me." Without thinking, he reached for the rock with his left hand. When the rock touched his ring, a blazing flash of brilliant blue sprang from the onyx stone, casting shifting shadows about the dark room. In the sudden blaze, Lacerus noted Morgas's astonished gaze, arms raised to block the blinding azure glow. Then, just as quickly, the room was cast into darkness.

Lacerus snarled at his folly, but it was too late. Morgas had seen. It was yet another matter for later resolution. The thought of what he might have to do with Morgas once the boy was successfully returned disappointed him. He had grown attached to the man. However, at least for now, Morgas would not wag his tongue in front of the wrong ears. Besides, how many would understand the rock's significance?

Urgency to have Vault in his grasp drove the Assassin to conclude the conversation. "How long before you return?"

Morgas stared back into the glowing eyes hidden deep within the black cloak. Both understood the Alpslander's life hung in the balance of the deeds he would accomplish in the days to come. He spoke with certainty of the work ahead. "I need but an hour to replenish my supplies, my liege. I wish to make the mountains again before dawn."

Lacerus nodded his approval, giving Morgas a smile parents reserved for their obedient children assuring them of rewards to come. He carefully hefted the glowing rock as he weighed his options. Again, plans would need adjustment. "Good. Take care not to damage my young treasure, Morgas. I sense its value has increased a hundredfold."

"I will return with the boy," came the reassuring reply.

Lacerus was left alone to reflect on the pulsating rock, unaware of his falcon bond's cries of stress.

✦

Pallia stood shivering at the mouth of the large cavern, while Johann worked unnoticed trying to start a meager fire with the damp wood they had gathered. They had been drenched to the bone before they reached the cavern, hampered by the unconscious Carlon's weight on the makeshift stretcher the two lugged between them. *How things can change in but a single day,* she mused, but her concerns grew as the steady drizzle whipped into a hard, wind-driven rain. Her eyes never veered from the southern ridge, even during the infrequent moments when lightning bolts were not exposing the rocky terrain.

The flickering glow of a fire marked Johann's success. She turned reluctantly from the storm. Worrying about Morgas would not change anything. Johann was already removing his soggy clothes, any semblance of modesty the trapper once had dissolved with his need for warmth. Goose appeared, her wet fur glistening in the firelight. And Carlon, drenched and strapped to the stretcher, laid motionless next to the fire, his breathing slow and shallow.

For the first time in her life, Pallia felt disheartened, a combination of exhaustion, hunger, unsuccessful attempts to retain their quarry, and weather that refused to cooperate. But what tore at her heart most was the shame of what she would have to tell Morgas. She had failed him. How could she ever look into his eyes again? She hung her head in disgrace.

A cold wind blew into the cavern, bringing rain that pelted her back. She shivered again, but not from the cold. Forcing her feet to move, she went to the other side of the fire and rummaged through her pack to remove the few pieces of clothing at the bottom that were not completely soaked. After dressing, she assisted Johann in removing Carlon's clothes. They left the unconscious man near the fire covered in the only dry item Johann had—his sleeping blanket.

As she had done through most of their journey back to the cave, Pallia tried to piece together the events following Conner's escape from camp. She did not want to believe that the sounds she and Johann had heard were merely a distraction, but with the leather straps Conner had left as a gift, laden with knots, it was hard to see it differently.

Following Carlon's trail along the stream had been easy enough. They could not have been more than five minutes behind. But the tracks ended when they came upon the dark, moonlit grove west of the stream where Carlon and Vault had fought. Johann and Pallia made several spiraling loops around the battleground, calling Carlon's name, before she found the other brother slumped against a tree with several broken ribs and a displaced shoulder. He had remained unconscious since.

She inspected the younger man, his face pale and gaunt, even in the orange fire glow. Without weapons, and against someone of Carlon's skill, those injuries indicated an attacker with a keen mastery of fighting skills. Pallia had trouble believing that Conner, at his age, was capable of such elemental control. The Assassin would have warned them if he possessed such powers. No, someone other than Conner, someone very powerful, had attacked Carlon.

Searching through the morning hours had not produced Conner's tracks, heightening the confusion. The boy could not have grown wings and flown away. But with no tracks to follow, and a growing concern for Carlon's health, the two had chosen to rendezvous with Morgas as discussed.

"Morgas," she whispered. Just saying his name stole the chill away. The man was truly her light on a crisp winter's morn. And for the first time since she had left home two years ago in search of her love, she pined for her mountain village. It did not take the village prophet to feel a storm growing across the landscape, one that would dwarf the one that now gripping the mountains, one that would devour all those unfortunate enough to be in its path. She wanted to return home with her mate, braid her hair with summer mountain orchids as all her friends had long since done, and raise many strong children with mountain granite for feet and mountain snow in their veins. Maybe these last few days would convince Morgas it was time.

A soft groan near the fire drew Pallia from her daydream. Johann bent over his brother. The younger man sluggishly raised his arm, weakly clasping hands with his brother. Carlon rasped something and the two leaned closer.

"What was that, brother?" Johann asked, his ear pressed to Carlon's lips.

The younger man took a deep breath, grimacing at the pain. "I said, did you find father's knife?"

Johann glanced up at Pallia, relief washing concern from his eyes. "He is going to be fine."

Morgas gathered the supplies he would need for his return. Thunder rumbled in the northwest while flashes of lightning arced across the otherwise serene night sky. He would have to travel through the storm. Nothing about the last two days had been rewarding. No, there were a few things, he corrected, relishing the image of Pallia and Galven as he had left them at the southern base of the mountain.

The thought brought a new urgency to his actions. Morgas had left his mate and friends to deal with the boy, or whatever he was, without him. Anger flashed. His liege knew a lot more than he cared to offer. And given his apparent need to return Vault unharmed, there were secrets the Assassin would not willingly share at any cost, even if that included risking the lives of those in his group. Next to him, the white tundra wolf growled, teeth bared at the sense of Morgas's flash of anger.

Morgas patted Valmer reassuringly. "No worries, my dear friend. We're not going to let anything happen to those most important to us."

Part VI

Only through the giving of ourselves to others do we discover that the true gift is the opportunity a Being offers another to share oneself. In this, are not all rewarded?

—*The Modei Book of Air (Second Book)*

After the Storm

The high-pitched warble of a meadowlark pulled Veressa from restless dreams that had kept her on the edge of sleep. Even the extra room after Annabelle and Peron had vacated the tent had not helped. But the sounds and smells of rations cooking over a crackling fire brought a warm smile to the princess's face. She stumbled from the tent and was greeted by Hemera rising slowly above remnants of the storm along Narwales's horizon. For the first morning since leaving Graystone, the air was cool and light on her skin. She knuckled her lower back to work at kinks she hoped were not permanent.

"I bet you wouldn't have minded being tied to your bed now," came a somber voice from behind.

"My bed never sounded so inviting," Veressa mused as she turned to find a very haggard Annabelle overseeing the morning fire. But her smile evaporated, eyes sweeping across the scene about her. "Oh no," she exhaled.

Annabelle was pouring hot, thick liquid into two tin bowls. "Yes, it seems the Cosmos's luck was not with us last night."

Veressa looked glumly at her tent, shredded into long strips of canvas. The storm's strong winds had finished off any parts the huge oak branch and her knife had not destroyed. Next to her tent, Annabelle had meticulously laid out the few supplies not blown away or soaked by the storm. Limbs, twigs, and leaves littered the campsite in muddy devastation. A quick scan of the terrain prompted her to exclaim, "The horses too? Now what are we going to do?"

"There is nothing we can do at the moment, except thank the Cosmos that you were not crushed beneath the tree." Annabelle offered the princess a weak smile and a cup of steaming brew. "It is never wise to make decisions on an empty stomach, so come eat before we discuss what is next."

Veressa noticed Annabelle's bandaged hand as she took the cup. "You are injured."

"Yes, someone got a bit zealous with a knife last night."

Veressa's mouth fell open. Gripping the Ranger's wrist, she slipped the bloody cloth from her preceptor's hand to examine the deep gash across her palm. "I did that? Annabelle, I am sorry. A strange dream frightened me. My head was not clear . . ."

The Ranger ushered the princess to a rock near the warm fire. "It was as much my fault for not being more attentive." She had no anger in her voice as she wrapped her hand again. "Now, no more until we have eaten."

They ate in silence, watching life return to the grasslands. A small flock of barn swallows swooped and fluttered over the open plains to the east, feasting on insects that were looking for drier summer grass. Peron squawked at the dizzying display of bright blue wings, but he had eaten and was content on his makeshift perch near Annabelle. To the west, the swift Aradorm had swollen to twice its normal size. Veressa finished her morning ration, appreciating the spectacle of life before her despite their recent setbacks.

Their hunger satisfied, the two discussed their options. Based on their tracks, the horses had fled the storm at a dead run, southbound along the river. Karra was smart and would surely cross the river at the first opportunity, then head straight for Graystone. She was a good horse, but devotion to her rider did not supersede the draw of a good meal in a dry stall. Toran was generally obedient, as long as there was a bit in his mouth. A typical male, however, he was quite content to keep the mare's hindquarters in his vision. He would follow her to the castle without so much as a grumble about their speed.

This left the two women with a dilemma. Chasing after the horses on foot made no sense, since the two steeds would be at the castle gates by the morrow's evening. Yet continuing the trek as they were meant the king would become extremely worried when the horses arrived without riders. Then he would, without question, dispatch runners to find the two. Veressa would end up in the predicament she had worked so hard to stay out of—escorted by a legion of royal guardsmen for the rest of their journey.

Only one option remained.

Annabelle stood and stretched as if all had been decided and there were things to do. "Salvage what supplies you can, but leave your saddle and anything burdensome. Pennington Point is more than twenty miles southeast. I want to reach it long before dusk. *Aetha energi pnigofotia*," the Ranger snuffed out the fire and began sorting her supplies, tossing more than half of the items under the oak branch covering Veressa's tent.

Veressa sat confused. "But isn't Clovendale near Bell's Ferry closer?"

The preceptor studied the girl for a moment. "Pennington Point is the midpoint between Kallzwall Castle and Cravenrock Keep. Using the station is the only way to ensure we will get a message to the king before our horses arrive home. Knowing your mother, if our horses get to Graystone before the message, we will be surrounded by every Defender she can muster within two hundred miles." The Ranger went to the river to refill their flasks, leaving the princess to consider her words. By the time she returned, Veressa was adjusting her lighter pack on her back, a renewed sense of urgency in her eyes.

Annabelle smiled, quite pleased with having discovered a way to motivate the girl.

A New Direction

The first late morning rays of Hemera broke over the eastern rocky mountain crest. Conner sat studying Skye curled in a black ball on the other side of his fire's ashy remains. Given their first encounter, he imagined it nearly impossible to sneak away from the sleeping dragon. But his impatience to get a start won out over any attempts to be polite. Eyeing the beast as it twitched and snorted, he reached for his backpack. He was so engrossed trying to be quiet that he forgot he had placed his tin cup and utensils on the pack the night before. The cavern walls resounded with the loud crash of supplies. Conner cringed as the cup rattled across the rocky floor, coming to rest against the dragon's foot.

Skye's leg twitched. Then, with a long groaning exhale, the dragon listed to his side, coming to rest with legs and tail extended. He concluded the lethargic maneuver with a loud snort, the deep rhythm of sleep returning.

Conner stared incredulously at the motionless black creature. "Of course! I get a dragon that sleeps through anything," he exclaimed to the cavern ceiling, then stormed out the entrance. He wove his way across the rocky terrain to a clear, fast-moving creek. Following the water upstream, he came to a small waterfall where he bathed, changed into clean clothes, and scrubbed his dirty garments on smooth rocks from the riverbed. Before leaving, he checked his head wound and was encouraged to note that the knot was smaller.

He returned to find Skye in the same position. Remembering how the beast had responded the first time he woke him from a deep sleep, he thought it best to let Skye wake on his own. He got comfortable near the entrance and watched the dragon snore contently as he considered his course of action.

After nearly another hour, the dragon stretched and yawned several times. Blue eyes appeared through double eyelids. Lifting his head, he studied the human. "What is it, Conner?" he asked.

Conner jumped at the question. He had forgotten Skye could sense his emotions. He would have to work harder at hiding his feelings. Not sure how to broach the discussion the two needed to have, he decided to dive straight in. He cautiously eyed the black creature. "We have to find a way to break our bond."

He could sense Skye's reaction, a cascade of emotions—confusion, uncertainty, even remorse. But it was the dragon's verbal response that helped Conner recognize the source of those feelings. "You are angry about my demonstration yesterday or about the fight in the cave the day before. I should not have done those things, but you should know I would never purposely harm you."

Conner smiled. It was difficult not to like the beast. "I know that, Skye. This has nothing to do with anything you have said or done."

Skye blinked sleep from his double eyelids. "Then what is it?"

Conner sensed more emotions—disappointment, distress. The reasons were as clear to Conner as the morning after a storm, but Skye obviously saw their bonding differently. He just needed to explain his reasoning in a way the creature would understand. "Since leaving home a fortnight ago, I have felt like a kernel of corn in a field of hungry crows. I have discovered things about the world that should not be. I have seen things that should not exist. I have witnessed murder and have seen, even shamefully partaken in, the ugliest sides of being human. I do not like what these experiences have done to me."

He began to pace to give him mental fortitude as he pressed on. "The world is too big, too . . . complex . . . for me, Skye." He wanted to say *too scary* but doubted the dragon would have understood. "The

Realms have done quite fine without me for thirteen hundred years. They will do fine for another fifty or so. I need to go home, back to that quiet, simple corner of the world I can't live without."

The more he talked, the more he could sense growing agitation in the dragon. So he tried to redirect his words. "I don't think you want to live out your existence on an Eastland farm or in a small town while I practice my Apothecary arts and raise a family."

"I cannot say what I will want until that moment arrives. And you cannot run from what the Cosmos has given you because you do not find it convenient. It has been my experience that life will seek you out, no matter where you try to hide. All you can do is choose how to deal with what is given." The dragon's annoyance was palpable.

Conner considered his decisions since leaving home. He could not recall having a choice in anything that had happened.

Skye continued when he was certain Conner had nothing more to add. "Of course, you must do what you think is right."

Feeling Skye's gloominess, Conner's frustration churned into anger at his inability to get through to the creature. "I don't know what is right, Skye. I don't even know if it is possible to break this bond. Or if so, what that means for the rest of my life. All I know is I cannot live like this," gesturing at the dank cave they had slept in. "We have to find another way."

He paused before attempting to explain the wild idea he had contrived while watching the dragon sleep. Then taking a deep breath, Conner plunged in. "Last night, you said dragons were created by a great Shaman. I was thinking . . ."

"I said a Shaman God," Skye corrected.

"Yes, well, there are great Shamans still living today, Skye. I know of one such person, at least by reputation, among those of the Griffinrock Realm. He is my preceptor's teacher and guide for the Apothecaries Guild, apparently a great physician of both humans and animals, and the greatest authority on herbology. His name is Grimmley Rollingsworth."

Skye grunted doubtfully. "You think this Shaman has the power it takes to break our bond?"

"I don't know. But if he doesn't, maybe he can tell us who does. In either case, it seems worth spending the time to find out. I won't put the plow away until I have dug every furrow. When I have done that, *then* we can decide what to do."

Skye gazed at the mountains outside. "Then you must find this great Shaman and see if he can help you."

"Yes." Conner had been unsure what reaction he would get, but this was not what he had expected. "I was thinking of heading south out of the mountains, and finding someone I know who can give us directions to this Shaman. Then I will return here for you. We can travel to his home together."

"Of course," Skye responded, his eyes never leaving the cave entrance.

Conner struggled to think of something to add while packing his supplies, but nothing came that would help explain his decision. He was grateful when he had the weight of his pack adjusted on his back. The silence had been painful. He stepped to the cave entrance, and without looking back, mumbled, "I will return as quickly as possible." He headed down the slope to pick up the trail they had taken to reach the cave.

Skye-Anyar-Bello Cloudbender was unsure what to make of the recent shift in his relationship with Conner the family Stonefield. According to dragonsongs, bonding with a human was a gift from the Cosmos, each link established for a unique purpose. It was unconscionable to even consider breaking such a link. It was for this that he had gone out of his way to seek some agreement, even giving on ground dragons did not naturally give. And last night, he had believed he was making progress.

He lay gazing out of the cave, considering the human's reactions that morning, and began to see that the human was right. Conner was not made for such a bonding. He would not force the human into a situation against his will, nor would he be the one the human blamed for the consequences of their bonding. He would rather not be bonded at all than to be bonded to a human who did not value such a connection. As the morning wore on, the dragon became convinced that he wanted nothing more to do with the selfish creature.

Pennington Point

The Anarchic War, also known as the Great War by those of the orders and the War of Breaking by the Anarchists, was not only sparked by growing contention within and among the six orders. For centuries, the orders had maintained a reasonable balance of power among the seven monarchies and the multitude of fiefdoms within each realm. With orders powerful enough to sway the outcome of a dispute, nobility vied for support with bribes of land and coin. And the crowns were well rewarded for their efforts. Town folk and freemen received valuable assistance from the orders in defense of their communities, and the orders were revered for their deeds, though ordermen seldom acted without personal or political gain.

Those in the guilds relied on the arcane skills and close guidance of their parent orders to sustain their membership and provide goods and services vital for the health of the Realms. So when the Anarchic War broke out, the orders fragmented, their focus turning inward. The guilds suffered the worst. An entire social class nearly vanished. Sorcerers no longer trained those of the Scribes and Jewelers guilds. Warriors forgot their Blacksmiths, Architects, and Brickmasons guildsmen. Clergymen and Monks were abandoned by the Paladins. Horsemen and Fletchers were left by the Rangers. Mystics deserted the Astrologers, Engineers, and Glassblowers guilds. Even the enigmatic Shamans ignored the pleas for help from those in the Physicians and Apothecaries guilds. With the collapse of the guilds, prosperity turned to poverty. Chaos ensued, feeding the flames of war that ravaged the Realms like an autumn brushfire. The Anarchic War consumed everything.

After the Treaty of Alignment was signed, the Harmonic orders struggled to return to their prior ways, including the reclamation of what remained of the guilds. Pennington Point was at the center of the Griffinrock Realm, a well-protected, thriving community in the western Narwalen Plains near the River Aradorm. So it was here the six orders chose as the birthplace and center for their guilds' revival. As Griffinrock returned to the old ways, communities prospered once again; the city became Griffinrock's hub for forging new guild alliances.

Long caravans of supplies arrived nearly every day from all over Griffinrock and beyond, lumbering through a maze of dirt streets and alleyways dissecting the city into guild regions. Pelts, captured animals, uncut gems, and raw ores came from Pennington Point's sister city, Cravenrock, to the northeast. Marble, granite, and other stones arrived from Loren Canyon along with crops raised by freemen farmers in the Eastlands. And stocks of oak, evergreen, and maple trees along with rare and important herbs and plants were hauled from the green Stonewell Forests from the Realm of Elvenstein far to the south. All converged here, where guildsmen and their overworked apprentices put skills to the test, creating the diverse and extraordinary goods sold at Pennington Point's massive guild auction grounds.

It was on one of the city's primary arteries that two cloaked Rangers stood in Hemera's late afternoon rays under a sign reading *The Physicians Guild*. A caravan rumbled sluggishly along the street, churning puddles into thick soup while draft horses fought against the earth sucking at massive hooves and the thin wheels of wagons laden with supplies.

The taller figure flexed a bandaged hand and gave the other Ranger a tired but content smile while they waited. "For once, I am glad I listened to your suggestion, *Caralynn*. In a day, my hand will be good as new."

The second Ranger cringed at the first's use of her name. The two had spent a great deal of time that morning, when they were not arguing, putting detailed touches on their story. Further, Annabelle had made Veressa repeat the entire litany of specifics several times before setting foot in Pennington Point. No further reminders were needed. After the two had picked their way across the street behind the caravan's last wagon, Veressa asked hopefully, "Does that mean you will listen to my other suggestions as well?"

Annabelle did not respond until she had successfully negotiated the muddy street and was under a large, brightly painted sign of a pewter mug and the words *Dorry's Alehouse*. "With our message on its way to Graystone, our top priority is to not draw any undue attention to ourselves until we have safely acquired our supplies and are on our way in the morning. That includes behaving as two traveling ordermen would." She worked at cleaning mud from her shoes and glanced up at the sign. Her eyes were bloodshot; her cheeks red from the sun. "That is why we are going to enjoy a few hours in conversation while we consume a hot meal and drink some fine local ale. Then we will retire to our night chambers. The inn we chose will do, but I'm afraid you will have to forego a hot bubble bath a few days longer."

Veressa gazed forlornly at the sign, then sighed before trailing the older Ranger through the tavern's creaky wooden door. Maybe not all aspects of a Ranger's life were so wonderful.

The haggard bartender and owner of Dorry's Alehouse glared at the heavy, middle-aged freeman fighter across the bar. "You haven't paid your dues from yesterday, Bargo," he hissed, unable to hide his frustration. A black raven eyed the fighter from a perch behind. "No more ale until your tab is settled."

Bargo Steerman leaned closer and met Dorry with his own scathing stare. The left side of his unkempt face twitched, a sign the freeman was growing irritable. He barked with his usual gruff voice. "Just give me two mugs without causing a ruckus, Dorry. I got something in the works to fill me purse. Yer will get paid soon enough."

The strong smell of skunk assailed Dorry's nostrils. He involuntarily pulled away, giving the ex-Defender a foreboding look. A statement like this from Bargo meant there would be trouble soon. But such things were not his concern, as long as he was paid. Besides, he knew better than to push his luck too far with the unstable man. A few had grievously mistaken his tick for a wink, only to later find Bargo's blade between their ribs. It was common knowledge Bargo had been washed out of the Queen's Defenders for offenses no one in the community cared to know. Yet everyone acquainted with the man was sure he got off with leniency. Dorry nodded, then dropped two full pewter mugs in front of him. "Pay up soon." He bolstered enough courage to meet the fighter in the eye, and was rewarded by another tick—or maybe that time it was a wink.

Bargo turned triumphantly with trophies in large, callused hands. He surveyed the noisy room with an experienced eye before walking back to his round table, a pronounced swagger in his bulky frame accentuating the sway of the battle-ax dangling loose at his waist. He studied the thin, dark-skinned man in bright blue Sorcerer robes across the table and plopped into the chair he had vacated moments before. He offered the man a toothy grin, shoving one of the mugs at him. A small mouse near the thin man's hand squeaked and disappeared up the Sorcerer's sleeve.

Bargo's cold hazel eyes darted to the two female Rangers on the other side of the tavern. "So, what did yer find out?" He did not wait or take the time to offer the customary toast to his companion before drinking deep from his mug.

Lest Targameer frowned at Bargo's expected impoliteness, then took a measured sip of the cool brew before speaking over the tavern noise. "They arrived several hours ago, and went immediately to the Defenders station, where they sent an urgent message." The thin man's eyes continuously scanned the tavern. Obviously, he was not accustomed to intrigue.

Bargo's smile broadened. He leaned forward expectantly. "And?" His left eye involuntarily twitched at the man.

Lest cleared his throat, though it was no longer parched. "It cost me three coins to determine the recipient of that message, Bargo. Don't expect me to give it to you—"

"If me gut is right on this, Lest, yer will be more than adequately repaid for yer troubles. What did yer find out?"

Lest lowered his voice, though Bargo's foul smell ensured no one would willingly stray within earshot of the two. "The message was sent directly to King Jonath himself," he muttered over the ruckus of inebriated patrons and bonds.

Bargo sat back in his chair, beaming triumphantly at the news. "I knew it!" Realizing he had nearly shouted, he rocked forward again. "I have never seen the older one before, but the younger one . . ." He shook his head to jog his failing memory. "I know that one from somewhere. She is someone important, no doubt from *rich* nobility." He took another satisfying gulp from his mug. It was taking the edginess from his mind. He winked at Lest to let him know what he was thinking, but failed to catch that it nearly unhinged the thin man.

Finally, Bargo leaned even closer. "We just need a little surprise party and I can take out the older one before she knows what struck her. The young one won't even be enough for yer to handle," he jabbed.

Lest was offended. "My binding spell will have the apprentice tied in a bow quick as a sneeze, so she will be no bother. And I can handle the Ranger. She is nothing—"

Bargo's face twitched again. He pulled in close and growled. "Yer pseudo-Sorcerer mumbo jumbo might work on these simple town folk to put a few coins in yer purse, but yer are no more than a charlatan. If these folks discovered yer were pretending to be an orderman, they'd have yer hide drying on city hall by first rays. And yer pretty parlor tricks wouldn't stop them."

The long silence was all Bargo needed to be sure both knew who was top dog in this partnership. Satisfied, he nodded with pursed lips. "I want yer to go acquire the services of a few locals to help out in case the little one gets too rowdy, and yer can't find the right spell to tame the lass. I will find out where they're staying so as to pick an appropriate spot to throw our little reception." He leaned back, their conversation complete.

After Lest departed, Bargo drummed thick fingers nervously on the table. This was the break he had been waiting for. Nobility were all alike, denying him a reasonable living, tossing him like an unwanted dog into the street. He had been an officer in the Queen's Defenders. Well, he had suffered long enough. It was time for them to pay their dues. And they would pay dearly.

Testing the weight of his departed colleague's mug, he washed the remaining contents down his throat. A little luck of the Cosmos, the right backdrop for a party, a little time to acquire a hefty ransom, and he would be living the life he had been meant to have. He studied the exquisite features of the young Ranger from the corner of his eye. And just maybe he could partake in some pleasures he had nearly forgotten existed.

Homage to Mountain and Sky

Morgas listened intently to Pallia as she recounted the events of the previous two days. He sensed her pain as she spoke of finding Carlon nearly dead after the Eastlander's escape, felt her frustration and shame at losing any hope of finding the boy's tracks after the storm, and bore her sorrow with their struggles reaching the cave. After she had concluded, he placed his forefinger under her chin, forcing her to look into his exhausted eyes. "There is no reason for your shame. You did everything you could." He glanced at Johann sitting in the late afternoon rays of Hemera chatting with Carlon, still strapped to the makeshift stretcher. "All of you did. I could not have done more myself. I am glad you are safe."

Pallia's eyes hardened at his words. "Maybe you could not have done more, but it is also possible we could have kept this Conner Stonefield captive if your *liege* had been more forthright in what he knows of this boy."

Morgas considered his encounter with Lacerus the previous evening and started to pull away. He did not think he could bear to hear her say what tore at his own heart.

But she gripped his shoulders and held his stare. "I do not think you see what I see, Morgas. Lacerus would willingly sacrifice your life, my life, even the lives of all you hold close"—she gestured at the brothers—"just for a slim chance to get what he desires. This Assassin, like all your Anarchist orderman masters who exploit our people, uses your very strength to bind you to his will. He manipulates you by wielding your mountain pride for his personal gain."

Morgas closed his eyes, unable to speak against her words. He had been taken from his village chieftain father at the age of twelve. Consigned to serve the Anarchists ever since, he had been conditioned to do as commanded, trained to conform to their every wish and demand without question. His whole life had been with that one thought. What meaning would he find in the past twenty years if he tossed all that away?

Pallia's voice softened, though her hands were steel on his shoulders. "I cannot imagine what you endured in those years away from our home, Morgas. But I also know this Assassin does not understand the true ways of the Alpslander, the source of our strength, or the meaning of our pride. No whip or cage could break that connection. We are an old and rugged people who have survived the hardships of a millennium in these mountains. We will endure them long after the Harmonic Realms and Anarchic Lands have crumbled."

Finally, he responded. "I know what you wish of me, Pallia, but you are asking me to dishonor myself and my family. I am an indentured servant to Lacerus."

"You are only speaking the words the Anarchists have taught you to say, not the words etched into your bones, Morgas," she shot back with growing impatience at his stubbornness. "I am asking you to honor yourself and your family. There is no dishonor in breaking a pact that does not respect the bloodbond."

Morgas breathed deep to consider her words. When a pact was entered, the two parties began by recognizing each other as equal. Even if it was an agreement for one to be indentured to another, as with the Narkain brothers, the servant held some element of power. The master was as much indentured to the servant for protection, shelter, or food as the servant to the master. This was the bloodbond, an acceptance of mutual kinship. It was the essential basis for all relationships between mountain people.

Pallia confided reverently, "It is time for you to find new honor, Morgas, by taking the reins of leadership your father always wanted for you." Her voice changed inflection, lovingly. "It is time for you to respect and honor me in the Ceremony of the Pledging, and to take me into your home so that we can add to the numbers of our mountain village."

She continued, speaking words he had not heard since he was a child. "We are mountain people, born with mountain granite for feet and mountain snow for blood. Just as the long, harsh winter snows harden our resolve, so the spring nourishes our lives and ways with the snow's melting." She waited.

Morgas's mouth opened and long forgotten words flooded from his lips. "The mountains contain the bedrock of our strength, the sky our hopes and dreams." He smiled lovingly at Pallia. Together they finished the ancient saying. "May we always remember to walk our path in homage to both."

For the first time in many years, true peace descended upon Morgas, and he released burdens he had endured for far too long. One of four youths taken from his village that day, he had been too young to comprehend the pact his father had made with the Anarchists in payment for saving his village from destruction. He recalled an image of his mother crying while he was bound and tied behind a horse, his father's lips quivering on an otherwise stoic face as he was dragged away. He had forgotten those and many other images of his home before he was taken. Fragments of his past slowly returned. And the Anarchic shackles slipped from his heart.

Morgas knew Lacerus. Domination was the only power the Assassin understood. No matter the cost, once he discovered Morgas had broken his pact, his liege would make him an example for others who might also consider defying an Assassin's authority. Let the Anarchists come. This time, he would stand next to his woman. Together they would let their longswords ring until the mountain streams ran dark with Anarchic blood and the canyons were filled with

Anarchic bones. He placed his right palm to Pallia's cheek, then touched his forehead to hers in a sign of affection. "Let us go home."

After several minutes, Morgas moved past Valmer stretched out and panting next to Galven. The two wolves had spent the time since their reunion playing and nipping at each other's legs. He came to stand over Carlon, examining the younger brother's weak smile, then turned to Johann to speak the customary words. "I declare with an open heart and eyes, brothers of Narkain, that you have paid your debt. We walk in balance now. May your steps go light upon the mountains."

He started to leave, but Johann's reply held him fast. "We would stay with you, if you have need of two trappers." Morgas understood the plainsman's meaning. Johann knew what the Alpslander was planning. He might someday be in need of men who could fight.

Morgas sniffed the light summer breeze cooled by the snowcaps above. Changes were coming. With the browning of the leaves, there would be war. Johann's resolute stare and Goose's gaze with understanding eyes were all he needed. "Pallia and I return home with first light. We would be honored if you chose to travel with us. Carlon will be well tended, and you can stay as long as you desire."

This pleased the brothers.

That night, the troop would discuss the plans for the coming day. A strong fire would be needed. The mountain extended its dark, shadowy reach across the peaks to the east, so Morgas went in search of dry wood. But thoughts of Conner Stonefield invaded his serenity. The boy had shown him choices he did not know he possessed, ones that changed the path he and Pallia walked. The mystery about the boy was tangible, too many unanswered questions to simply let go. Lacerus would not relent until the boy was in his grip. Morgas made his way back to the cave the boy had led them to, shrugging off the uneasiness. Tonight, he would burn more than the logs weighing him down.

An Offer Too Good Often Is

Hemera's setting rays were hot on Conner's face as he stepped from a field of well-tilled peas onto the dirt road leading into the city. He had stopped frequently on the way south to take rests and to ask for directions from traveling yeomen and serfs tilling farm fields, so the journey had taken longer than anticipated. And though the city was not what he expected, he was relieved to be among people to whom he could relate. He pinned back his sweat-soaked hair and washed mud from his leggings and shoes with the last of his water.

For a quarter mile, he passed row after row of single-story thatched-roof homes, all exactly the same, separated by stone walls running along both sides of the road. As he walked, he nodded to the many exhausted merchants and guildsmen with frowning faces making their way out of the city and disappearing with bonds through equally spaced wrought-iron gates. By the time he reached the edge of Pennington Point, the street was nearly void of people.

Ahead, wooden buildings three and four stories tall ran along both sides of the muddy street. His initial thought was that these were similar to the ones in Creeg's Point, but closer examination proved him wrong. Here, each building was a single shop or store stuffed with supplies reaching to the rafters far above while work benches and equipment stretched fifty paces or more to the back. Black iron bars covered spacious windows across much of the lower face of the buildings. And small white signs attached to the doors simply warned: *Closed*.

The only sense of friendliness Conner got from the buildings came from uniquely shaped cloth banners dangling from posts high above the doors. The banners were brightly painted in different colors and contained guild crests along with their names in large, flamboyant script—*Hostlers, Carpenters, Thatchers, Blacksmiths, Tailors, Armorers, Hawkers,* and *Metallurgers.* The only thing the banners had in common was the emblem of the Warriors Order painted at the bottom of each—a water droplet under two crossed swords.

Conner crossed another side street to the right and picked up his pace until he came to a light-green banner cut into the shape of a cinnamon leaf with the painted image of a thyme plant over the script *Apothecaries* and the small emblem of the Shamans Order. He stepped to the door, relieved to not find the usual Closed sign. He entered and gently pushed the door closed.

A middle-aged man with gold-rimmed glasses dressed in an oversized brown apron, the only guildsman about, was intently tapping a brown powder from a stone mortar onto a scale. An opossum hanging by its tail from a rod nearby silently studied the intruder. "We're about to close for the night, so please come back tomorrow," the guildsman mumbled without looking up.

Conner waited by the door until the guildsman had set the mortar down, then cleared his throat. "I apologize deeply for bothering you, sir, but I am looking for Student Jess Tandoor. I understand he is assigned here."

The man studied the Eastlander suspiciously with furrowed brows over glasses, not sure what to make of the boy's disheveled appearance. "And who is looking for Student Tandoor?"

"My name is Conner Stonefield from Creeg's Point. I am to be Apothecary Guildmaster Merich Cleaverbrook's new apprentice."

The man beamed suddenly and, dropping his pestle into the mortar, stepped forward to get a better appraisal of the mud-clad youth. "Ah, yes! Apprentice Stonefield." After rubbing his fingers across his apron, he slapped Conner's shoulder repeatedly with one hand while vigorously pumping the boy's arm with his other.

Conner glowed at the sound of the name.

"Master Cleaverbrook was here recently and told us his intentions. From what I hear, you are quite a smart lad. He has high hopes for you and thinks you better than even Student Tandoor." The guildsman bit his lip, aware he had said more than intended. Then he continued, giving Conner a wink and smile. "But maybe I should not be telling you this. I am Adept Barclay Anclar, assigned to guide young Tandoor to his next level."

An apothecary's life had to be lonely, for an hour passed before Conner extracted enough information from the talkative adept to be confident he could locate Jess Tandoor. By the time Conner exited, the adept chatting about a potion he hoped would cure hiccups, the sky was dark. The town crier had filled and lit the street lamps.

On his way to the place Jess frequented for evening meals, Conner happened upon a grocer's shop still open, where he succumbed to purchasing the supplies he would need for the journey back. Conner was so engrossed counting his remaining coins that he bumped into a lanky, dark-skinned Sorcerer stepping swiftly up the street.

"Say, be attentive where you are, boy!" The orderman snapped gruffly at the Eastlander's rudeness. But when the man noticed that Conner had been counting his coins, his thin face shifted into a reassuring smile. "Now, what was I thinking?" The Sorcerer recanted his words with a wave of his hand before Conner could reply. "Say, don't mind me, boy. I have had a busy day, and have hard work ahead before I can head home for a delicious, hot meal and well deserved rest." A thin gold chain dangling through three rings in his left ear swung as he gazed skyward while patting his narrow stomach for effect.

Conner decided it best to apologize. "It was my fault, sir. I should have been watching where I was stepping. Please accept my—"

"Well, what a polite, young man you are." The Sorcerer interrupted in a hurry. "It is seldom these days that I meet such a well-raised lad." He shook his head sadly, then stuck a bony finger into the air as if he had developed a thought. "Say, it looks as if you are in need of some coin, and judging by your looks, you most assuredly could use a hot meal and rest. I bet you are a strong lad. How would you like to earn, say, ten coins for a few hours of work?"

Conner forgot about apologizing. Despite the bad vibrations he sensed coming from the orderman, he could deal with such problems for that kind of money. But his experiences in Cravenrock had taught him to be cautious. "What does this work entail?"

The Sorcerer glanced up the street, then stepped into the shadow of the lamp nearby, ushering Conner close, though no one else was about. Conner cautiously stepped near. The orderman suddenly seemed incapable of speaking above a whisper. "Well, boy, I can't give you any of the details, you understand—at least, not yet. It does involve the most minimal amount of risk on your part, but nothing I am sure you can't handle."

The word *risk* was all Conner needed to know the offer was too good to be real. Minimal or otherwise, he had taken on enough risk of late to last the rest of his life. Hastily, he replied. "I am sorry, sir, but I am on my way to see a friend. Maybe if I am in Pennington Point again soon, I can look you up for some work."

The orderman stiffened with a huff, his warm smile gone. "Why didn't you say that earlier and save me from the trouble of wasting my time?" Without another word, he stepped past Conner and turned up a side alley. In a moment, he was gone.

Conner stared down the dark street, the city's feelings of familiarity vanishing with the odd Sorcerer.

Dorry's Alehouse

Discovering the most likely place to find his old friend, Jess Tandoor, had required an incredible amount of fortitude on Conner's part. He had waded patiently through Adept Anclar's long-winded story about how acquiring living space in Pennington Point involved complex negotiations between the six orders all competing over limited quarters. He had no idea Apothecaries could be so talkative. Like other new guildsmen, Jess had been forced to obtain temporary arrangements at a nearby inn until permanent quarters were available. Conner gazed up at the bright-colored sign of a pewter mug and the words *Dorry's Alehouse*. According to the adept, it was here Jess often ate his evening meals. It was time to see if the time had been worth the price.

Pushing through the hinged doors and scanning the crowded tavern brought a relieved smile to Conner. Weaving carefully through the room bustling with people and their bonds, he came to a small table in the back where a young man with long blond hair sat intently studying a book and making cursive notes on yellow parchment. A tiger-striped feline sat next to him, intently watching the wispy end of his quill pen.

"So you still have to write down everything to remember what you're studying?"

Jess looked up, puzzled by the interruption; then the pen fell from his hand. "Most of us can't remember everything we see and hear," the man quipped. He rose, grasping Conner's outstretched hand with ink-stained fingers. A smile overlaid his otherwise tired expression. "My, but it is good to see a familiar face, and so far from home." He waved at a vacant chair at the table and gave Conner a slight but teasing bow. "Sit, *Apprentice Stonefield*. Let me buy you dinner. It is the least I can do for someone who just lightened my weary day."

Conner disguised his smile with a smirk and returned the teasing bow. "Then I accept your offer, *Student Tandoor*, for I do believe you buying me dinner will lighten my weary day as well." By the time he was seated, a young woman with delicate features on a porcelain complexion appeared next to the table, her arm casually draped over Jess's shoulder as she examined the new arrival. A large crow with glassy, ebony eyes perched on her shoulder.

Jess hooked his arm around the woman's waist and waved at his new companion with his other. "Tara, this is my dear friend Conner Stonefield, arriving just tonight from the Eastlands. I would be most grateful if you would treat us each to a bowl of your mother's delicious stew and your father's finest ale."

Tara, quite comfortable with Jess's arm around her, curtseyed to Conner. Her cheeks reddened. "I will personally ensure that the ale arrives as cold as the stew does hot, dear Conner." She moved lithely away, though her eyes stayed on Conner's until she was out of view.

Jess closed the forgotten book and pushed it to the side, watching Tara slip through the bustling tavern. "She is truly a wondrous lass," he sighed.

"As I recall, you thought that about all the lasses in Linkenton Point." Conner was rewarded with a hurt look that made him laugh. Formerly from Linkenton Point, fifteen miles east of Creeg's Point, Jess was the only son of a Cartwright guildsman who made wagons and carts for many Eastland farmers and townsmen. Jess's suave style, handsome face, and lavish guildsman way of life made most of the young ladies' heads turn, much to the chagrin of their protective parents. At sixteen, Jess's father sent him to live for the summer with his aunt in Creeg's Point. By fall, when he received his Calling, even that quiet community was unsafe from Jess's charm.

Conner was in the midst of teasing Jess over whether he would be asked to leave Pennington Point before he had his living arrangements settled when Tara returned with a tray of cool mugs, steaming bowls of thick stew, hot bread, and melted garlic butter. The smell of freshly cooked vegetables, Grenetian spices, and black pepper captured all of Conner's attention. For the moment, the two ate in silent ecstasy.

Annabelle shook her head sadly at her comrade across the corner table while Peron watched with disinterest from above. There was no doubt that the desire for a Ranger's life webbed deep into the princess's spirit. She possessed a natural elemental talent the preceptor had never seen, even in a watcher. And the girl's passion to learn and live the ways of the order was as unbreakable as the Warder's Stone. But a Ranger was more than all these things. The true strength of a Ranger was measured by fortitude of character and willingness to cooperate with others, things Veressa's life of royalty had failed to bestow upon her. But mostly, a Ranger needed to be able to drink a mug of ale without becoming hopelessly intoxicated. Her lips tilted upward. Unfortunately, the Cosmos had seen to it that the girl lacked this quality as well.

Annabelle leaned forward so she would not have to shout above the tavern noise. "Don't you think you've had enough to drink, *Caralynn*?" She emphasized the name again to remind the princess they were not supposed to draw attention.

Veressa broke from a raucous chorus of "Whose Pants Am I Wearing" and shot her preceptor a strange look. "You thaid we should act like two traveling orde'men." She eyed the half-empty mug with a confused look. "Bethides, thith is my firtht mug. No need to be unhappy because I am thtarting to enjoy mythelf. Thtop being my protective older thister for once and relacth." She waved at her preceptor as if shooing away a pesky insect. Something struck Veressa as funny, but when she leaned forward, she wore a serious expression.

CALL OF THE DRAGONBONDED

"You're just cranky becauth mom alwayth loved me more than you." This set the princess into a guffaw, nearly doubling over with tears rolling down her cheeks. Luckily, her laughter ended before the last howling words of the song.

Annabelle's cheeks burned at the princess's last comment, but she was not going to let the girl dig under her skin, especially here and now. The Ranger gingerly removed the mug from Veressa's hand. "I am going to enjoy watching you deal with the headache you will have in the morning." But before she could continue, someone started singing the Narwalen ballad "Riders of the Order." The man's melodic tenor floated through the tavern. A somber hush fell over the crowd. Soon, others joined in the ballad, and it grew into a crescendo marking its final words.

In the time of the breaking
And war ruled the lands,
Elvenstein's Darmascus did fall.
So a pact in the making
Was sealed by the hands
Of the mysterious ones heeding our call.

Hail to beasts whose bonds you did find,
Hail to the castles that hid your ways,
Though your secrets died with the last of your kind
You won our freedom for all days.

Take care as you sail
Into the morning sun,
Turning our teal skies to black.
We'll always prevail
If we remember the ones
Who rode on dragons' back.

Hail to the winds that carried you away
Hail to the mountains that now stand alone,
For bringing us peace, but in our dismay
Will not see you safely back home.

Heroes of the Order,
Heralds of old,
Just where did your days so wing?
A battle o'er the border
As omens foretold.
It is for you we now sing.

So let's raise our mug in good spirit,
Let's raise our glass in good cheer,
And drink to the intrepid spirits
For those the dragons held dear.

As if everyone had practiced the act a hundred times, each lifted their mug or glass high, then drank deep from each. Knowing it undignified for Annabelle to stop her, Veressa reached across the table and, with a smug expression, stole back her ale. Tilting her head in imitation of the best Moorestone friar, the princess gulped the entire remains, then wiped foam from smiling lips with the back of her hand.

Yes. I am going to enjoy watching her deal with this tomorrow, Annabelle thought as the noise and chaos returned to the tavern.

Bargo's eye twitched with growing impatience. A few people shifted in response to give him even more space. He stared at the door with a dark expression, ignoring the songs and ruckus while drumming fingers on the table noticeably void of drink. *What is that imbecile doing? Can't he even handle a simple instruction?* He leaned forward and glanced at the two Rangers under eyebrows that hid another tick. The two would be leaving soon, and he wanted to be fully prepared to throw them a reception party before they departed.

Just as the insufferable crowd finished their rendition of "Riders of the Order," the door swung open and the lanky Sorcerer stepped through. The charlatan glanced about nervously as he edged through a crowd of standing patrons. Giving the big man at the table a winning smile, he took the other chair no one else had the fortitude to secure.

It was all Bargo could do not to reach across and snap the thin man's neck. He fought back another tick with a snarl. Lest's smile evaporated. "Did yer do what I asked?"

The pretend Sorcerer continued to scan those about them. He leaned closer, his mouse bond occasionally peeking timidly from under his bright blue robes. "I found three capable young men quite willing to do whatever is necessary." Reading Bargo's thoughts, he elaborated, "With discretion. They wait up the street for your orders."

Bargo got up with a nimbleness contradicting his size and inebriation. Thumbing his ax, he said, "Then let's be on our way. I want our prize properly packaged and stowed before anyone is the wiser." He stepped past Lest with zeal for the work afoot. The swiftly parting sea of people and bonds afforded Bargo the space he needed to swagger his way to the tavern door.

The two Eastlanders began the lengthy task of getting caught up on two years of busy life whenever their mouths were not filled with bites of chunky, hot stew and buttered bread dipped in gravy. For the first time since receiving the Calling, Conner laughed and joked until tears ran down his cheeks. Tara visited their table often for no other excuse than to ensure everything was fine and to give Conner a pleasant smile, earning them scowls from those at nearby tables who felt neglected. Neither man cared, for the world had stopped revolving for a few precious hours. Conner took in the breath of life—connecting with a dear, trusted friend.

Jess asked about Conner's family, and Conner laughed at the guildsman's blushing response when he mentioned that Miyra, now fourteen, still asked about him. Jess quickly diverted the discussion to Master Cleaverbrook while ignoring Conner's teasing, going into some detail about their preceptor's teaching style. "He won't tell you anything until you ask, Conner, unless it is to hide vital information in the middle of what you think is simple, unimportant talk. So keep your wits about you at all times." He shook his head at the memory. "And he won't proceed to the next phase of your training until you have every minuscule fact he's given you accessible at a moment's notice."

This was the opportunity Conner had been waiting for. "Jess, I need to find a certain Shaman. I am hoping you can help me."

Jess noticed the shift in the younger man's demeanor, piquing his interest. "Who would that be?"

"His name is Grandmaster Grimmley Rollingsworth."

Jess whistled in amazement. "Conner, Grandmaster Shaman Rollingsworth isn't *any* certain Shaman, you know. He may be the most brilliant Shaman in several generations." He leaned forward to tell Conner a little-known secret. "I heard he rejected a position on the Shamans council," he whispered, eyes wide. "No one has ever turned down becoming a Don, but apparently *he* did." He glanced about the nearby tables to be sure no one had overheard. "Who would be crazy enough to anger the Board of Dons by turning down such a position?"

Conner felt pangs of uncertainty about his plan.

Jess leaned even closer, his shirt nearly in his bowl of cooling stew. "I met him once, you know." He sat back and nodded as if what he had seen was proof of the old Shaman's dementia, then wiped at the gravy spot on his shirt. "I had to go with Master Cleaverbrook to get some very rare and expensive herbs for the cow sickness that struck a year back. Rollingsworth *gave* the herbs to the guildmaster. And judging by the small cottage he lives in, the Shaman could have used the money to fix it up. To be honest, I don't think I would willingly go within a mile of the old man."

"Well, I'm not sure I have a choice. At least I won't be alone." He hesitated, not wanting to say so much he would need an hour to explain, but neither did he want Jess to be unnecessarily suspicious. "So how do I find him?"

The student shook his head. "You always were a bit crazy, Conner, but if that is your wish," he continued with resignation. "His cottage is in a valley between some hills twenty miles west of Kallzwall Castle, halfway between the mountains to the north and the Queen's Highway to the south. If you find a large series of groves containing every type of tree in the known world, you'll find his cottage in its midst. Just take care. The old Shaman treats those trees like they were his children."

A hush through the tavern drew the two from their discussion, a tenor voice singing the ballad "Riders of the Order." The words were clear and in perfect pitch. Conner stiffened. Others joined in, until the entire tavern was a chorus of voices in anthem to the legends. He cringed at the words and slumped in his chair. It was as if the crowd was heaping each weighted line of the song upon his shoulders, denouncing him for his plans, crushing him with their honored lament for the old order, until he could hardly breathe.

Conner jerked his head toward the crowd in the middle of the tavern, peering through the mugs raised in silent honor to the Dragonbonded. People and bonds milled about everywhere. He wiped at beads of sweat burning his eyes, then blinked away the sting in hopes of catching sight of the singer. Instead, his eyes fell upon the thin Sorcerer he had encountered earlier in the street. He jerked back around and slumped farther forward, hoping the man had not seen him.

"Are you all right, Conner? You look like you've seen a phantom."

"I'm fine. I'm just not used to the strong Narwalen ale." He hefted his mug to his worried friend and took a sip with a wink.

Jess relaxed at the false gesture. "I swear I think you spent too much time around Pauli. I would be half crazy if I had to deal with his continuous string of antics. How is that wily would-be fighter, anyway?"

Conner was grateful for the change of subject and began to impart a few of the many recent sordid stories about Pauli, pausing to let Jess finish a hearty laugh or wipe tears from his eyes. As he talked, he watched the Sorcerer approach a lone, burly fighter on the opposite side of the room. While the two men chatted, the fighter kept glancing toward a dark corner where two Rangers sat drinking and looking like they wanted to be left alone.

He considered the Sorcerer's invitation. Surely the men did not intend on mugging ordermen. That was pure foolhardiness, even if one was well beyond being a bit tipsy. Then he recalled how the Thieves Guild in Cravenrock had obtained the location of the magical scroll he had stolen. What if the two Rangers were couriers? A little muscle could be worth the cost for what the Sorcerer had called minimal risk.

Conner shook the thought away. He did not like the Sorcerer, and was certain he would like the burly man with him even less. Whatever the two men were planning, it was surely unsavory. But that was no reason to get involved. The two Rangers could handle themselves.

A few of Jess's words drew his attention. "You were always there to drag Pauli feet first out of the fire." Jess winked slyly at Conner. "No doubt, that oversize fox has dug himself into all kinds of chicken-coop mischief since you have been away." The student swallowed a chunk of stew as he contemplated the words forming in his head, then wagged his spoon toward Conner. "You know, Conner, while you clearly have the aptitude for being a great Apothecary, I think it was your saintly demeanor and honesty that tipped the scales for Cleaverbrook to bring you into the guild. I swear that man has a standard . . ."

Conner's cheeks burned. He feigned attention with an intense nod. What would Cleaverbrook say if he learned of Conner's misdeeds in Cravenrock? He stifled a shudder at the thought. Out of the corner of his eye, he saw the fighter stand and clear a hasty path to the door.

Conner's thoughts began to race. Was it pure coincidence that someone had chosen to sing "Riders of the Order" right then? Was it an accident that the same orderman he'd run into five streets from here showed up in this very same tavern at that very moment? And what of Jess's reference to his moral character? Conner shook his head. Was he exhausted and seeking meaning in purely random events, or was he being given an opportunity to atone for Cravenrock? *No, in the final outcome, it doesn't matter which*, he thought determinedly. He was in control of his destiny.

He settled and sensed a force nudging him, shaping his reactions. Somewhere in that churning haze of feelings, Conner sensed there was something he could use to guide him. So he rambled through the halls of his mind, tracking Skye's emotional scent, until he came upon what could only be described as a capped conduit. He touched it with his thoughts and the cap broke free. Stars danced across his vision; daggers stabbed the insides of his eyes. Everything tilted with the intense rush of profound feelings. He struggled to control it, or at least direct it, but it fought back with its own purpose. And he succumbed.

He became aware that Jess had stopped talking. Conner stared down at his friend with half-vacant eyes. "Jess, would you please get a message to my parents to let them know I am fine? I will be returning home, but I have something very important to do first."

"Of course, Conner. Consider it done. But where . . .?"

Conner raised his palms. "There is something I need to take care of. I will explain everything the next time we meet, but for now, good-bye my friend. I thank you for a delightful evening." On his way to the door, Conner winked and smiled at Tara, making the girl's cheeks flush. Without looking back, he slipped out. On legs no longer aching, he started up the street, dogging the two men who had left the alehouse moments before.

Wallis Arkman glanced up at the young Eastlander moving toward the door. The lad was so focused on the pretty lass at the bar that he failed to notice the man's beaming smile. Not that he was much to notice; the man possessed no particularly distinct features other than a hawkish nose and a melodic tenor voice. The two yeomen he had struck up a conversation with at his table were deliberating their accounts of a freeman farmer who had recently climbed Cravenrock's wall. But while both claimed to have witnessed the event, the two seldom agreed on any specific point. Of course, Wallis had been there himself. After all, someone needed to point the bumbling city guardsmen toward the lad called Bandit. Neither story came close to the truth.

His work for the night concluded, the man pushed away the mug he had been nursing for the past hour and rose. Tipping his broad-brimmed hat politely to the pair still arguing, he announced with an odd accent. "It seems it is well past my time for sleep, so I wish the Cosmos bestow safe travels and a fulfilling life to you both." Undaunted by the fact neither noticed his departure, he stepped into the cool evening air. He paused to lightly stroke the soft fur of his gray squirrel bond while regarding the Eastlander trailing two men into the darkness. It was not like him to feel smug, but then again, it was hard not to feel an element of pride, especially when his handiwork altered the Weave. The balance of force was shifting, but not all his labors were for naught. That was the core difference, he knew, between his deeds and those of the mischievous Kindred. Laws like Cosmic discernment, free will, and cause-and-effect could be weakened, or bent, but they could never be broken. Turning the opposite direction, he stepped spryly up the street alone, spinning a short wooden cane between his fingers and whistling an ancient tune.

In A Bind

Annabelle stretched a body that had sat too long in a wooden seat and was rewarded with an inquisitive look from Veressa. Slowly this time, she repeated, "Yes, Caralynn, it is time we found our beds." She wanted to get started early in the morning purchasing supplies and horses so that they were out of town before the streets became a beehive of activity. The fewer people who saw the two, the less likely it was that the princess would be recognized. Of course, no harm letting the girl enjoy herself for a few hours. But Annabelle would need her strength to deal with the effects of the princess's drinking.

Staying in the shadows, she led the way to the door, steering clear of a red-tailed hawk agitated from having to share a perch with a golden eagle above their drunk bonds' table. Once outside, she pulled her dark green hood forward and started up the street toward their inn, occasionally keeping Veressa from running into buildings or tripping over the wooden boardwalk.

It did not take much mental effort to know that an endless list of things could go wrong with whatever Conner might devise as a plan; but he found some solace in one aspect of what he was doing. While in the Thieves Guild, he had learned Sorcerers and fighters were not likely to detect Earth spells. He followed the two men to a dark side street and paused in the shadow of a building. After making certain no one else was about, he cast the three spells he knew—Night Vision, Stealth, and Cloak, then waited. Confident the spells had not drawn attention, he moved forward again, a flowing shadow from the flicker in a distant street lamp. Soon, Conner picked up the sounds of whispering voices ahead.

Through his Night Vision, he could see the clear outline of the thin Sorcerer and the bulging frame of the fighter standing before three more men. He crept closer, sticking to the shadows of shadows. Still, he could not discern enough of the conversation to know what they were planning. Turning around, he discovered that the siding of the building he was pressed against was made of horizontal wooden slats. In less than a minute, he was atop an awning that extended out over where the men had congregated.

"Yer to leave the older Ranger for me to deal with," the fighter whispered with a snarl at the men. "Once she is down, and only after she is down, are yer to subdue the other one. Under no circumstances is the girl to be harmed. She's worthless dead. Is that clear?"

The three young men glanced at each other to muster some courage. They nodded their understanding, then dispersed into the shadows of the street beyond.

Conner had no choice but to wait with the faint traces of skunk rising from below.

Annabelle studied the princess, relieved enough to relax her grip on the girl's shoulders. Fresh air and a brisk walk were reviving Veressa's dulled senses. "Feeling better?" But the faint flashes of three Earth spells from the dark street ahead distracted her from Veressa's mumbled response. Ranger instincts took hold. Her pace slowed, body tense. Senses sharpened as she scanned the empty street for any signs of a trap.

Minutes passed and still nothing happened. Annabelle shook her head. Too much time near the Borderlands or being the princess's protector had made her paranoid. Maybe some guildsman was working late in practice with an apprentice. The spells were clearly not powerful enough to be of any real concern to a master Ranger. She was about to berate herself when three young townsmen appeared out of the darkness in front of them.

The one in the middle stated in a wispy, nervous voice, "Excuse me, but we have been walking these dark streets for over an hour. It seems we have lost our way. Could you please direct us to the Whispering Inn?"

Annabelle released her grip on Veressa, hands disappearing up her cloak sleeves where she lightly gripped two knives. The three spells she had sensed before had made her wary. "I am sorry, young man, but we are Rangers and obviously not from this city, as you well should know. So if you would please step aside, we will be on our way. We do not want any trouble, but if you take a step closer, I will hurt you."

From their reaction, her response was not what they expected. Even with her warning, the men stood their ground; their tense, uncertain stance signaled something more was afoot. Annabelle caught the slight shift in the middle man's eyes over her shoulder, the sinister twitch of his lip, and a faint shadow of movement from behind. She spun and crouched, her blades flashing in the distant lamplight, but already she knew she had reacted too late.

Conner was forced to reassess his initial impression of the Rangers when the burly fighter slipped stealthily up behind the taller one, both hands in a death grip on his large ax. He wanted to shout, but knew he could not warn the Rangers in time. Or worse, he would be rewarded with a knife in his chest. The angle was not right, but with no time to concoct a better plan or even take better aim, he leaped from the awning. Some part of him wondered with wry wit if he should have taken the Sorcerer's offer for the job with "minimal risk."

The luck of the Cosmos made up for Conner's bad aim. The burly fighter stepped right under his descending body. Conner kicked out hard, his feet striking the man solidly between the shoulder blades. Though merely half the fighter's weight, the force of the unexpected impact propelled the big man forward. The fighter waved his ax before him in a futile attempt to regain his balance and blundered headlong into the Ranger, his momentum driving her two sharp blades deep into his chest. His left eye twitched as the side of his ax struck the Ranger on the temple. And the two went down hard into the mud. Neither moved.

Meanwhile, Conner's body recoiled from the kick. Unable to keep his feet under him, his shoulders and back struck the ground, stealing the air from his lungs. He tried to inhale, wanting to scream a warning, but his chest refused to cooperate. Pain coursed down his spine, so he rolled to his side with an urgent need to breathe and came face to face with a skunk. The creature's horrific, mournful cry tore at Conner's heart. Then it flashed a fluffy striped tail his way and sprayed Conner squarely in the chest before scurrying down a dark alleyway.

As Veressa's head cleared, she realized she wanted nothing more than a good night's sleep in a dry bed. So when three young townsmen appeared out of the dark to thwart her progress, she developed a terrible itch of irritation. Before she could rebuke them, Annabelle let go of her and she went down on hands and knees into the thick mud. *Oh no! Not again! A princess should not be seen like this.* The thought struck her as amusing until a big man fell next to her, splashing mud across her face and down the side of her cloak. She rose with slow deliberation, blood boiling. Muck dripped from her chin. That was when some unfortunate soul grabbed her from behind.

Conner took a breath, then wished he had not. His eyes stung; his nostrils screamed at the smell. Dizzy, staggering forward, he surveyed the scene about him. He could make out the lifeless body of the fighter in the mud and the dark green-cloaked figure buried beneath. Conner groaned at his failure to save the older Ranger.

By then, the Sorcerer had finally mustered enough courage to step from the shadows, moving toward the three townsmen standing bewildered with their leader dead at their feet. "You there," he screamed at the flatfooted men. The orderman would be taking charge in a moment, so Conner reacted. Gagging and unable to see clearly, he grabbed the younger Ranger's arm. He was not prepared when she spun about and slapped him hard across the cheek.

Conner rocked backward from the blow. He met the Ranger with his own intense glare. "So that is what I get for trying to save you? Fine! Stay here and fight if that is what you want. Just don't complain when you find yourself shackled to a slaver's block by morning." In indignation, he staggered down a dark street and away from the fight.

A glance over her shoulder at two townsmen holding a cloth sack was all Veressa needed to know she was not in a safe place. Unable to locate Annabelle, she felt alone and vulnerable in the middle of the street.

The Sorcerer who had appeared from the shadows shouted, "Don't stand there! Grab her!"

That was all the coaching she needed. Adrenaline wiped away whatever was left of her inebriation, and she chased off after the shadowy Eastlander with eyes glowing gray from a Night Vision spell.

Conner caught the sound of footsteps from behind, then a female voice calling out, "You there! Wait!" She should have waved a lantern at her ambushers and saved everyone the time of a chase. He melded into the shadow of a building and waited. When the Ranger ran past, he snagged her arm.

She jumped with a start.

"Down here," he whispered and redirected his feet along a new route that led them down a narrow alley.

"I wish you would stop doing that," she whispered, working to keep her feet behind the shifting human shadow.

Conner bit his tongue so as not to comment on her lack of gratitude, then dithered when he noted that the alley opened out into another wide street. He started again toward another alley on the opposite side, but the Ranger's hand held him in place.

"Wait! Where is the Ranger I was with? Isn't she with you?"

He faced the girl, not sure how best to break the news, especially here in a dark alley with a gang of thugs about. "No. Your comrade went down back there with the fighter."

The Ranger caught a full whiff of Conner and nearly gagged. Instinctively, she shoved him hard in the chest, forcing him out into the street. Realizing she had touched him, she rubbed her palm vigorously over her cloak. "I have to go back. She could be hurt. I can't run off—"

"That would be insane!" Conner interrupted, slipping back into the alley's shadow. "Those men want you or something you possess. They don't care about her. If she is alive, it is only because they haven't caught you yet. Once they have you bound, she becomes expendable. The best way to keep her alive is to not get captured."

"Oh." The Ranger exhaled hard, holding the back of her hand to her nose. Her eyes watered. "So where do you think you are taking me?"

The Ranger's question struck Conner as odd. Even he knew enough about High Law to know the Ranger's best chance to get free of this skirmish was to take the grievance directly to the high court. He wanted to get moving, but her interrogation was delaying them. He impatiently studied the quiet street ahead. "I remember passing the High Chancellor's regional court earlier. I think I can find it again."

"No!" the Ranger exclaimed. Under Conner's disapproving glare, she lowered her voice. "I . . . I mean we . . . I mean I cannot go there," she sputtered.

Conner was confused by her reaction.

The Ranger lifted her chin into the air. Speaking with a regal voice to end their discussion, she commanded, "Take me back to Annabelle."

Conner threw his hands up to ward off the thought of going back into that pack of mad dogs. "Oh no! I'm just an Eastland farmer trying to come to aid someone I *thought* was in need. So if you are foolish enough to think you can handle a master Sorcerer and his three assistants, help yourself." He gestured back up the murky alley.

"First, I'm insane? And now, I'm foolish?" She fumed. "Fine! Stay here. To be honest, I don't need you getting in my way." The Ranger turned and disappeared into the night.

Leaning his aching shoulders against the corner of the building, Conner dropped his head back with a sigh, trying to ignore the reek wafting from his chest. But that paled in comparison to the spasm of pain in his neck that was as much figurative as it was literal.

Veressa stepped cautiously into the street near the big fighter's body. Dull, vacant eyes glared up into the Cosmos. "Annabelle!" She risked a harsh whisper, then held her breath as she scanned about anxiously. Shadowy street phantoms danced with her imagination. But no response came. The street light was inadequate to discern which way Annabelle had gone, forcing her to reconsider her decision to return.

"How nice of you to come back, little one." The Sorcerer and his three men stepped from the shadows. "I'll try to be gentle to repay you for saving us all the time and trouble of running you down." Veressa stiffened; the Sorcerer had already begun an incantation.

You called the young Ranger insane and foolish. Well, just look at you now. Conner rebuked himself. But the jabs at his stupidity did not slow his feet. He ran swiftly through the alleyways, turning this way and then that, hoping luck or memory would guide each direction. He was not sure if he had either on his side until he sprinted down a narrow alleyway and nearly ran headlong into the Ranger standing in the middle of the open street. He was about to admonish her for being so blatant when he heard the Sorcerer's incantation. "*Hetos eftos pagiprosopo.*" Just as the Sorcerer finished the binding spell, Conner leaped in front of the Ranger and wrapped his arms around her.

A blast of hot air tugged at his back. He held the Ranger tighter, protecting her as the inferno whipped into a whirling frenzy. Just as quickly as it had begun, it ended. He opened his eyes, staring straight into the deep blue eyes of the Ranger. For a single heartbeat, a tranquil silence gripped him. And then the heartbeat was gone. An explosion of dazzling lights spiraled outward, the sounds of a hundred crackling Illuminaries reverberating off the buildings. Then, once again, all was still.

Reluctantly, Conner worked to release his grip, though his muscles were slow to respond. His arms tingled with the energy he sensed flowing between him and the Ranger as if they had been bound together. The Ranger apprentice did not fight him, or make any further remarks about his intense odor; she only stared back questioningly. The moments became more awkward and his cheeks flushed. Slowly, he pulled away and turned his attention on the destruction about them. The forms of the Sorcerer and his men lay sprawled on the ground near a building, blown back by the force of the spell's explosive backfire. The body of the fighter at their feet had been scorched beyond recognition. And all around them, the muddy street was dry and hard like fired clay. A slow-moving form at the corner of a nearby alley drew their attention.

"Annabelle!" the young Ranger exclaimed in relief and ran up the street, hugging her companion. In the light of his fading spell, Conner could see Annabelle awkwardly return the hug.

The Ranger Apprentice

Six hours north of Pennington Point, the three stumbled along in silence. Attempts on Conner's part to strike up a cordial conversation with the two Rangers during the long night had resulted in nothing of value, other than learning their names. That was hardly worth the grief he had received from the Ranger apprentice for all his troubles. To be sure, he was just an Eastlander, but did they have to treat him like a serf? Risking his life for them should have at least been worth a minute of civility.

The silence had left him with time to ponder what he had, quite literally, jumped into. He studied the two green-cloaked figures, who maintained a safe distance upwind. Little he had gleaned about them made much sense, unless everything he knew about ordermen was wrong. He pondered the contradicting facts as Hemera broke across the horizon.

First, judging by her braids, Caralynn was a Ranger apprentice without a bond, which was an extreme rarity. Second, Caralynn treated Annabelle, a very young master Ranger, more like a hireling than a preceptor. Maybe Rangers had strange customs in training their apprentices, but judging by the way the two interacted, Caralynn was used to getting her way, especially with Annabelle. Third, an orderman attacking another was a serious crime against the Canons of the Orders, punishable by order banishment or death. But whenever Conner probed into why the two had refused to take the grievance directly to the High Chancellor of the region, electing instead to flee the city on foot, all he got was silence. Finally, the Rangers couriered no valuable merchandise. No. It was the apprentice the gang had wanted, unharmed. Caralynn was the key to this riddle. Well, he did enjoy a good mystery.

Conner examined the outline of Caralynn's features against the morning light. He had heard of merchants in the uncivilized outlands who marketed young women as slaves or concubines. Someone with her looks would surely bring a handsome price. But the dead fighter had taken the gamble and lost. And neither the fighter nor his hapless Sorcerer accomplice had seemed the type to risk their lives all for the coins a young woman would fetch on a slaver's auction block, beautiful or otherwise.

That left two possibilities. He remembered the night in the Palaver Room, when Estora Elflander told of Karlana Landcraft. Karlana was twelve when she was taken in by the Sorcerers Order because of her extraordinary abilities. Maybe this Caralynn had such powers. But considering how she'd conducted herself last night . . . He shook his head. No, if he was a betting man, he would put all his money on the other possibility—the girl was the pampered daughter of a rich and powerful nobleman. Either there was a reward for returning a runaway or her coddling parents would pay a sizeable ransom to her kidnappers. It was the only scenario that fit all the facts.

The side of Annabelle's head ached, but she was not about to complain over something she deserved. She should have sensed the fighter coming at her. For the third time since leaving Graystone, Annabelle had failed the princess. The throbbing pain was her reminder of what happened when she did not stay alert.

Hemera was breaking over the plains. A few scattered clouds along the eastern horizon reflected the orange glow as the star evaporated the morning dew, breathing warm colors of life back into the plains. Plans never went off without some kind of trouble, so times like these brought her back to what was important—to remain calm and reflective, and enjoy life's beauty when offered. Annabelle never needed plans to experience the wonderful rise of Hemera.

In Hemera's first rays, Annabelle examined the Eastlander at her side. Tall and lanky, with long hair, there might have been someone handsome under all the mud and skunk odor. But there was something more—he looked familiar. Years along the Borderlands had taught her to put every face to memory. At last, when she had placed his features, she decided to extract some information about the lad. "I believe Creeg's Point is in the opposite direction."

Conner jumped as if pricked with a knife, then glanced sidelong at the Ranger with penetrating eyes. Frowning in concentration, he replied with a hint of suspicion, "I don't recall that we've met. I think I would remember a Ranger."

Annabelle scanned the tall mountain peaks looming ahead. Peron was a streak in the sky. *A cockatrice won't give up her eggs if she knows you want them.* No need to show too much interest, lest he became too guarded. She let the silence linger, noticing Veressa's interest as well. "I nearly shot you and a rather large Eastlander out of a tree in a wooded area along Brighom Road a fortnight back. That was you, wasn't it?" She noted a slight lurch in his otherwise graceful stride. A smile touched her lips.

"I guess it's good for all of us you didn't. Otherwise, there's no telling where your *apprentice* would be now."

Annabelle grimaced at his obvious skepticism, then noted that the boy had detected her reaction.

"And you would be waking up, if you were lucky enough not to get your throat cut, without purse, pack, or pupil." The lad scanned the southern horizon as if expecting someone to be chasing them. "I seriously don't know why I risked my neck to pull you two out of such a situation."

Through the boy's tongue lashing, Annabelle could see Veressa growing hotter, until it was more than the princess could take.

Veressa rounded on him. "We would have been fine without your help. Everything was under control. And if you haven't noticed, you are speaking to a master Ranger as if she were a *commoner*, so watch yourself!"

"Enough!" Annabelle shouted at them both. The throbbing in her head would not take another outburst between her renegade companions, accusing each other of every aspect of the previous night's calamity. Besides, Veressa's heated interjections were preventing Annabelle from digging out what the Eastlander had discovered about Veressa's true identity. She would not make the mistake of considering herself paranoid again. She had to consider the possibility that he was part of some elaborate façade working in concert with the thugs they had left behind. How else had he known of their attack? And why would an Eastlander think there was a need to come to the aid of ordermen? She had also witnessed how he had protected Veressa by reversing the Sorcerer's spell. And there was the matter of his glowing eyes. Where had this freeman learned to use a spell reserved for Rangers and their guildsmen?

Seeing the situation building for another heated round of arguing, Annabelle stepped in decisively. "Do you always speak your mind so openly?"

"I do when there is injustice, whether perpetrated by thugs or by an ungrateful harpy!" He shot a glaring look over Annabelle's shoulder.

"A *what*?" Veressa's voice went up an octave. She dropped her backpack. "All right, that's it. If I had my bow, I'd end this right here."

The boy responded with a laugh, which developed an edge of hysteria.

"Look!" He pointed a finger in the princess's direction with a taste of anger. "In the past fortnight, I have been chased, mauled, beat up, arrested, stuck with a sword, shot at, and spelled. And for three days, I have endured the constant harassment of a"—he gestured vigorously in the air—"a *thing* wanting nothing more than to eat me for lunch. So threats from an insolent apprentice do not exactly frighten me."

Veressa stepped toward the boy, taking an ominous stance. "Oh, frightening you is the furthest thing from my mind."

Annabelle considered telling Conner that a prudent and wise man would be concerned about his well-being around this particular "apprentice." Noting the determined look on Veressa's face, however, she bit back the words. It was too late to offer him fair warning. Besides, maybe it was time this conflict came to a more conclusive end.

Veressa took the opening.

The girl shifted her feet and came at him, raising her arm in an awkward attempt of an attack. Conner fell for the ploy. Committed to blocking her unbalanced assault, the girl spun in a circle, shifting to a crouching position before him. Caught off guard by her speed, Conner pushed his other arm forward to block her changing attack. He could only look on as her moves played out in a single fluid motion.

Completing her spin, she reached up, gripped his wrist hard, and twisted his hand downward, wrenching his elbow up. The pain took him off balance. Planting her left foot in front of his, she drove her shoulder into his stomach and twisted her left hip up with a quick snap. His light body was lifted from the ground. Reaching a horizontal position over her back, her legs uncoiled, forcing Conner's hips and legs to follow the upward motion of his spine. A hard yank on his wrist sent his body in full rotation. Head, shoulders, buttocks, and legs slammed into the ground simultaneously, stealing any air left in his lungs.

Deftly, Veressa released his wrist and walked away, snatching her pack as she passed Annabelle. She never looked to see if her preceptor followed.

The Ranger hesitated, stepped to the boy's side, and bent next to him. "For what it's worth, I thank you for your assistance last night, Conner Stonefield." She smiled kindly as he gasped his first breath.

Veressa was out of range, yet still she whispered. "Caralynn does too, though she would never say so." She gently patted his cheek, then trotted off after Veressa.

When Annabelle caught up, Veressa spoke without looking to measure her preceptor's reaction, not wanting to give the Eastlander any impressions she might be looking his way. "If he is from Creeg's Point, what is he doing out here alone?"

Annabelle was surprised the princess wanted to continue the conversation. "I would have thought it obvious considering his age."

Veressa grunted. "Well, I feel sorry for whatever unfortunate creature has to share its life with him."

It was several minutes before Conner could sit up. He painfully gulped air strong with the odor of skunk. Every muscle in his body ached and his headache had returned. He squinted toward the two silhouettes shrinking against the backdrop of the bright star. "Sure," he breathed, rubbing stiffness from his neck. "Well met."

Entangled

An hour after parting company with the Eastlander, the silence was still palpable. But Annabelle continued to hold her tongue. It was best to let the princess work off her anger at her own pace.

Finally, Veressa broke the silence, still boiling. "A *harpy*! He called me an ungrateful harpy!" Annabelle did not reply. Finally, with a softer voice, she asked, "I'm not ungrateful, am I?" She stared at her preceptor. Veressa respected Annabelle because the Ranger never held back if something needed to be said.

The teachable moment is lost on the sleeping unless a teacher is there to awaken the student, her own preceptor used to say. So Annabelle deflected the conversation in a different direction. "Why don't you admit why you're *really* angry?"

Veressa turned away. It was often her response when she did not want to discuss anything that required a hard look at herself. "Whatever do you mean? It's quite obvious why I'm angry."

"Of course it is. But you're not saying it." She waited for her statement to have full effect, a tactic she had picked up from observing the queen interacting with the girl. "You're not angry because he interfered in our business. You're angry because for once, a man has actually caught you in a situation requiring his assistance. You're not even angry at *him*, Veressa. You're angry at yourself and at your own vulnerabilities." She was not done, but it was best to feed the girl in small bites.

After a minute, she proceeded, this time delicately. "But even that is not all of it. I have seen you hold your own in a room full of noblemen and ordermen, then systematically dismember them to a man with eyes and tongue. But back there, for the first time, a man stood toe-to-toe with you, and you were helpless to do anything about it. So you used the argument as an excuse to physically attack him. You had to prove you were superior—and not to him, because he didn't care either way. What's unfortunate is he really *did* come to our rescue, and you treated him like . . . well, like a *commoner*." Annabelle threw the princess's word back at her. There were times she disliked being the girl's preceptor, but Veressa needed one if she was to become a truly great queen.

Veressa gazed skyward to hide tears of embarrassment. She watched Peron dip and flutter carefree in the morning sky. Annabelle's arrow had struck true. But Veressa could not chance her preceptor noticing there was more. The Eastlander had sheltered her from the Sorcerer's attack and something had happened that shook her very core. She had lashed out in confusion and fear. Even now, she could feel the deep pulsating currents she shared with Conner. She could *feel* him climbing up a narrow trail carving its way deep into the mountains. She inhaled to hide the tension surging through her. At least there was some solace knowing he would never discover her true identity.

Newfound Urgency

After finding the trail that would take him back to Skye, Conner stopped near the summit of the first mountain. Hemera had burned away the remnants of cool morning air on the plains, so he was glad to be back in the highlands. Though the Rangers were lost among the green summer grass toward the eastern horizon, he could sense Caralynn. He shook his head at the stupidity of such a thought. *All this time alone with that beast is making you nuts, Conner.* He scoffed at himself for entertaining such foolishness. Coming upon a thin stream, Conner removed shirt and pants infused with the smell of rotten eggs and sulfur, tossed them down a ravine, then bathed before donning his last set of clean clothing. At least he had gotten the information he had sought—the location of the grandmaster Shaman Rollingsworth. Pushing away the infectious image of Caralynn's blue eyes, he took the trail with a weariness greater than any he had known.

Hemera was nearly overhead before Conner arrived back at the cavern. He expected to find his bond asleep, but instead the dragon lay stretched atop a large boulder above the entrance, his black body and wings molded against the warm rock. "Aren't you up a bit early today?" Conner asked, but was disappointed when the facetious question was lost on the creature.

"I considered flying south to meet you, but you did say you would return here," Skye responded formally. He made no attempt to move from the boulder.

Conner rummaged through his pack and dug out a ration and two apples. He would need to eat quickly, so he bit ravenously into an apple. "That's okay. I passed a trail leading west just south of here. We will need to make our way to the southwest. But I'd rather you not create widespread hysteria across Griffinrock, so we'll stick to the mountains as long as possible."

Skye did not bother to lift his head. "So you discovered where this great Shaman lives?"

The dragon's apathetic demeanor was grating on Conner's nerves already, but Conner also sensed a strong undercurrent of excitement. He studied his bond with interest. "Yes. If we leave soon, we could arrive there the day after tomorrow."

Skye lifted his head and squinted at his bond. "What is that smell, Conner of Stonefield? How long has it been since you bathed?"

Conner's irritation deepened at the dragon's formality given what they had endured the previous day. He looked innocently at the dragon. "What? Bouquet-of-skunk? Why it's the latest craze among us humans."

Thankfully, this silenced further questions from the dragon, who was probably happy not to know any details about the strange human custom. Conner finished his meal in blissful silence.

Conner jabbed a long stick at the burning embers of his meager fire, sending glowing sparks high into the black sky where a million stars winked at him. The waning face of Erebus was rising over the eastern mountains, casting the rocky landscape into deep grays. The gentle sounds of tree frogs and crickets filled the cool night air, while the noise of water rushing over river rocks below echoed up the gorge. He was well past exhaustion from hiking all day, and his stomach was full. Still, restlessness kept needed sleep at bay. "Do you miss your family, Skye?"

Two glowing eyes coalesced in the darkness near him. It was the first time Conner had asked a question about the dragon's heritage. "Cloudbenders are social dragons, Conner, more so than the other three families." His gaze went to the northwest. "So yes, I miss my kind."

After a moment, Skye added, "But we do not have families as your kind. We are not attached to the need to see only those in close lineage as family. Our entire Cloudbender community is our family. Each member participates in sustaining communal life. One day I may have such responsibilities."

"But your name reflects your paternal lineage," Conner noted with confusion.

"Yes, and every dragon knows every other's entire line going back to the Ancients. There is great honor in recognizing birthright, Conner." Skye snort-sniffed a deep chuckle. "We live a long time, so we have short lines. My father's father, Bello Cloudbender, was an Ancient."

"Was," Conner repeated aloud. Conner expected to sense sadness through their link, but instead felt pleasure. Skye was happy Conner wanted to know about him. In some strange way, Conner was honoring the dragon with his questions.

"There were eight ancient Cloudbenders made by the Shaman creator. Only four still breathe."

Conner remembered a name Skye had once used to call him. "What is a guivre?"

The dragon snorted his pleasure at the question. "They are dragon hatchlings that live in the nursery of ash and mud. Once guivre grow wings, they become amphitheres." Skye twitched as if from some distressing memory of his youth. "They are troublesome little nymphs requiring constant supervision by the Keepers. Those surviving their first molting become wyverns like me."

Conner considered mentioning that Skye was once one of those "troublesome little nymphs." Too much like Pauli, the dragon surely paved a route to Trouble Lane. He realized he was humming the tune to "Riders of the Order." "What do you know of the Dragonbonded?"

Skye examined the stars overhead before speaking. "There is not much in our dragonsong about our bonding with humans. Little more is known about the Cloudbenders that bonded with humans. They spent very little time with the family after bonding. Our songs say this is because humans cannot survive in our den, though I have my doubts about that."

The dragon's comment sounded suspiciously like stories Conner had heard about Dragonbonded, aloof and secret, disconnected from human society, wanting little to do with others' affairs. Conner continued jabbing at the fire while calling forth what little he had heard about the legends. He wished he had paid more attention to the old tales.

The dragon continued. "During your War of Breaking, the humans of the other orders feared the Dragonbonded as much as the common people revered them. They must have possessed truly amazing powers, for the Dragonbonded were few compared to the number of ordermen. And yet they brought about the end of your war."

Conner recited the words he had heard many times about the secretive order. "'And yet with all their power, none possessed the will or desire to rule the lands.'" He lay back on his bedroll. "You said bonding with a dragon did not make one a Dragonbonded."

"So what does?" The dragon completed Conner's thought. "I believe the Dragonbonded had to complete a test before they were accepted into their order. Those who failed were sent away, exiled, I think you would say. But I do not know what the test involved or why one was needed, Conner."

His incessant questioning was not going to quench his restlessness, so Conner let the night sounds tug at him, and he began to drift in and out of sleep. He imagined being one of those mysterious black-dressed Dragonbonded, six hundred years ago, respected by noblemen and serfs alike. He envisioned standing atop a white castle tower, waving the blood and ink flag of the Order of the Dragonbonded. At his side was the beautiful Ranger Caralynn with her bright blue eyes looking up at him in adoration while a mass of people cheered him from below.

The soft snores of the dragon and the warmth of the crackling fire lulled Conner deeper into sleep and he drifted into a nightmarish landscape. The sound of a great warhorse rose from behind, hooves pounding the charred and dried road. Conner glanced over his shoulder. In the distance, the Assassin rode like dark lightning on a magnificent ebony steed, his black cloak flapping in the sharp wind. From beneath his hood, the Assassin's eyes seared into Conner, seeing through his pathetic attempts to hide the panic rising in his bones. As in Cravenrock's undercity, Conner's knees went slack at the sight. Bent in terror, he shook and sobbed. He wanted to flee before the Assassin.

Skye watched with piercing blue eyes as Conner fumbled with the saddle strapped to the dragon's back, fearless of the approaching black death. The dragon laughed at the boy's comical attempts to climb into the black leather saddle, too large for Conner's puny frame. Below, the crowd had stopped cheering him. He gazed down into the blank faces of the Cravenrock city folk. Their passive stares became the knotted and contorted jeers of the Cravenrock city guardsmen. They pelted him with their accusations. Some laughed at his antics as he tried to ride the dragon; some shook their fists, asking where he had been all these years; others screamed at him, calling him a charlatan who should be hung for his crimes.

He felt frail and weak. His cockiness from that day on Cravenrock's wall was gone, along with the confidence he'd had when he faced the Sorcerer in the dark street of Pennington Point. A feeble part of him fought back, grabbing for something solid, and he found Caralynn's arm. But the Ranger apprentice turned with the same accusatory expression and slapped him hard across the face.

Conner bolted awake, nearly shouting aloud before realizing he had been dreaming. Except for the crackling embers of his dying fire casting eerie shadows across the small clearing, all was still. Huddled near the fire, he could hear Skye's deep breathing nearby, accentuated by occasional twitches, snorts, and grunts. The residual trauma of his nightmare echoed through his mind, cleansing away any remnants of doubt he might have had. *I am bonded to a dragon.* Conner repeated the words over and over like a mantra until its significance chilled his very soul, stealing away his spirit. For in the vacuum of its place sprang forth something new—a self-loathing for having the audacity to imagine being Dragonbonded. And with the humiliation of his limitations came a newfound sense of urgency to find this Grandmaster Shaman Rollingsworth as soon as possible so that he could return home to the life he always meant to lead.

Epilogue – The Kindred

"I have news that could force us to reconsider our plans yet again,"

Lacerus thought to the ethereal spirits assembled in the Psychic plane. He had summoned this gathering of the nine Kindred, whose clandestine membership included a representative from each of the Anarchic orders—and a few from the orders within the Harmonic Realms.

"It is too late to stop what has begun, Brother." Breanen's waving form lashed back. Even here, the wife of the Sovereign Prince of the Necromancers assumed the shape of an old woman wearing dark Necromancer robes. "We have begun building our necro-army. Our minions gather more cadavers to fill the ranks. Those in our order work even into the dawn hours when our energy ebbs so that we may complete our task on time. What news do you bring that would force us to alter our course?"

"I have evidence that a bonded dragon is among the Harmonics."

Several of the Brothers wailed in agitation.

"Enough!" the Brother named Jarvus of the Warlocks Order commanded. "What is this evidence?"

Lacerus continued. "I possess a rock imbued with dragonfire. Further, my man described finding a cave filled with the pulsating rock at the very apex of the event predicted by the Oracles of the Mystics."

There was a long pause. The weaker Brothers grew restless in the silence.

Jarvus asserted, "We have no choice but to proceed as planned. Citadel Farlorde is the closest Anarchic fortress to the apex. Groegan, we will see that you are given a small force of Barbarians to take across the Borderlands to hunt down this dragon and his human bond. Those of us in the Anarchic Lands will make up whatever story is necessary to gain the support of the Anarchic order councils."

Tenarian's form added, "Find strength, Brothers." The doyen of the Harmonics' Mystics Order paused until the lesser forms settled. "None remember the old human-dragon bonds. Even more, their abhorrence to heed their ancestors' failings will be their unraveling. If we can reach the dragon first, it is possible to turn this revelation in our favor. This may indeed be a blessing from the Cosmos rather than an ill wind in our sails."

Nothing more to debate, the forms dissolved away.

Lacerus sat in the dark chamber deep under Cravenrock recovering from the Travel. The rock on his desk bathed his solitary chamber in pulsing spectral shadows. Nearly forgotten memories drifted across his consciousness, memories of a time called many names—the Great War, the Anarchic War, the War of Breaking. Warrior Heroes in long-pitched battles until they were awash in their brothers' blood. Grotesque screams of men, horses, and bonds lit up like candlewicks under Sorcerer spells or ripped asunder by Shaman undead. Great castles pummeled with spells forged by teams of Mystics until the bulwarks crumbled, burying their defenders beneath the rubble, while hordes of Rangers flooded over the debris to take out their bloodlust on the unlucky survivors. And holy Cardinals of the Paladins Order turning on their brethren, shouting crazed proclamations of blasphemers and heathens among their Holy ranks, then burning half of their own at the stake. Oh, wondrous and glorious memories indeed.

Sensing dawn was nigh, Lacerus placed the glowing rock in a box behind his desk. And with sudden spryness in his step, he began the journey that would take him to his chambers high in Cravenrock Keep above, where he would resume his arduous duties as Marcantos's preceptor Blake Friarwood once more.

Carnia hesitated only a moment before winging silently behind.

- THE END –

BOOK 2: ORDER OF THE DRAGONBONDED

Being bonded to a peevish adolescent wyvern can be pretty irritating, and Conner Stonefield wants nothing more than to ditch his dragon and get back to his simple life. But he soon discovers that the dragon may be the only one on his side. While human and dragon struggle to find common ground, word reaches both the Harmonic and Anarchic orders of the first human-dragon bonding in over five hundred years, and an urgent race to find the pair begins.

Meanwhile, Princess Veressa finds her bond, but her connection with the animal is stronger than she could have imagined. And the future that's revealed to her in a vision veers far from the path she is expected to take. When tragedy strikes, Veressa is faced with a host of new responsibilities, and she must find the courage and wisdom to begin making difficult choices.

Unforeseen circumstances force Conner and Veressa to cross paths again—this time resulting in a connection that will prove anything but fleeting.

Be sure to visit the Dragonbonded website to find out more about upcoming books or to sign up for the monthly newsletter:
http://www.thedragonbonded.com

ABOUT THE AUTHOR

JD (Jim) Hart's own fantasy adventure began when, during college, *The Hobbit* was literally dropped in his lap. With the turn of that book's first page, he was forever bound to worlds of magic, dragons, and epic adventures. After many years working as a software manager, engineer, and organizational change consultant, he has decided to leave the fast-paced, high-tech world behind. His new adventure is writing imaginary tales that explore humanity's immense diversity in philosophy, and our connections to each other and to the natural world. Jim lives in North Carolina.

His debut series, **Return of the Dragonbonded**, introduces readers to the distant lands of the Harmonics and the Anarchists, home to Shamans and Necromancers, Rangers and Assassins, Warriors and Barbarians, Sorcerers and Warlocks—and, of course, those who bond with dragons.